SOPHIE RAMOS

The Woman Who Welcomes ANGELS

a novel

Jeffrey McClain Jones

The Woman Who Welcomes Angels

Copyright © 2022 by Jeffrey McClain Jones

All rights reserved. No part of this book may be reproduced in any form by any electronic or mechanical means including photocopying, recording, or information storage and retrieval, without permission in writing from the author.

John 14:12 Publications

www.jeffreymcclainjones.com

Cover art by Damonza

To Lillian, always reaching for new heights.

Distracted by a Bit of Sparkle

 Sophie allowed her eyes to land on the silvery image for no more than a second at a time. Though she tried to pay attention to the meeting, her focus flitted back to that bright spark like a moth fluttering into a porch light. And it seemed as if that angel was aware of Sophie's tactics. Wasn't it watching her watch it from the corner of its eye? Was that a slight grin at the corner of its mouth?
 Taking a deep breath, Sophie tugged against her preoccupation and hauled herself back toward what Becky was saying to Vince, Sophie's boss. It wasn't like Sophie was ever going to tell her boss's boss about the shiny friend who followed her around.
 Then Becky made eye contact. Did she catch Sophie staring at that place near her ear? That was where the silver sparkle was hovering. Was the little angel whispering in Becky's ear like in a cartoon?
 Sophie stiffened and held her breath. Then she released that lungful.
 Becky had turned her attention to the guy next to Sophie.
 Sophie hoped her boss's boss was just assuming she was obsessed with her dangly earrings. They *were* pretty cool, like tiny chandeliers. Snorting and furrowing her brow to hunker back into the topic of the meeting, Sophie could feel herself blush. Caught obsessing over earrings was only a little

better than getting caught staring at an alien being whom Becky would surely never believe was there. She was a really good person, but not at all religious in any way Sophie had noticed. Still, there was that angel.

What would Sophie be doing for the next update to the website? Her part of the new marketing effort—that was where her focus was supposed to be. That was the reason she had come into the office. Not to stare at shiny beings or dangly earrings.

This organization was trying to reach women from a wider range of ethnicities, including recent immigrants. They hoped to extend their mission, which was helping single mothers find employment. Training, networking, and job leads. A great cause. A very good thing for Sophie to work on. A cause that provided justification for getting dressed and coming into the office a couple times a week. A job that offered decent pay and benefits. And a workplace fairly free of creepy critters.

But the embarrassment at her apparent earring obsession loosened the lingering memory of the embarrassment she still felt from the previous evening.

What an exploding car crash that had turned into!

She had agreed to help some students from a local Christian college confront a dark angel that was plaguing one of their friends. Barry, the skinny theology major, was supposed to be in charge, but he repeatedly stuttered his sincere gratitude for Sophie agreeing to help. Barry's mother was part of Detta's church.

Maybe that twisted path of associations—college kids to a woman at Detta's church, to Detta and then to Sophie—should have warned Sophie away from taking on that mission. There had to be a more reliable way to find ministry partners.

Sophie noticed Becky looking at her again. Back in the meeting. The outreach director was saying something about the new pages being more dynamic and attractive than some of their current pages. Sophie nodded like she knew what Becky meant. *"Just what I was thinking."* And, really, Sophie had been thinking their site was too stark and corporate. Then Becky moved on, her eyes scanning others around the conference table.

Back to Sunday. Sophie sighed softly at recalling it. Never again. She would only work with people she knew directly. No matter how wonderful his mother thought he was, Barry was not a great partner in the kind of ministry Sophie did. And the girls working with him kept contradicting each other.

"I think we just have to believe, and faith will set her free." Nadine was pretty angelic in some ways, but she didn't seem to know much about actual spirits or spiritual warfare.

"Yeah, but we need to assert our authority." Barry refereed between the girls with textbook responses. He had a firm grasp of the basic facts.

"How do we know if we have enough authority?" Stacy was as skeptical as Nadine was naive. At least that was how Sophie saw it.

"We just have to trust that God has brought us together for this mission." Sophie kept her voice low, trying not to spook the youngsters. "Obeying the leading we're given from God is generally enough authority in a particular situation." She felt so old among those college kids. But she had been impressed that those representatives of the next generation were willing to deal with demonic oppression head-on. Barry's upbringing in the same church as Anthony probably accounted for some of that.

Betsy, the girl they were there to help, was growling deep in her throat during part of the debate. To Sophie, it wasn't clear if the growling was about natural annoyance with the amateurs in that living room. More likely it came from the green-and-black demon sitting behind Betsy and using her like she was a cute ventriloquist dummy. The beast was about twice Betsy's size.

"Barry, you have to take charge of this situation. That demon is manipulating her pretty freely now." Sophie was going with the ventriloquist explanation. She watched the demon grin like it was so clever for getting away with so much.

The skinny kid with the big ears stuttered again, which opened the floor to Stacy, the skeptic.

"How do you know? How do *we* know you're seeing something? And how do you know it's real?" She batted her long lashes, aiming her dark eyes at Sophie.

That would have been a good place to start a conversation before this session. Stacy had just sat nodding and scowling during their initial meeting. She didn't have any spiritual luggage strapped to her as far as Sophie could detect, so Sophie hadn't poked too deeply into Stacy's closed posture. Maybe the scowling girl with the perfect round Afro just had plain old disbelief, not a spirit thereof.

As Sophie hesitated over how strongly to defend herself, the two-tone demon and its ventriloquist dummy seized the stage. Betsy leaped to her feet, sending the big armchair toppling backward, a chair that probably weighed as much as she did. Then the petite sophomore sprinted for the door. She was across the room in one second flat.

Something snapped sharply when Betsy slammed through the screen door as if she had pushed through it without turning the handle. Sophie heard the demon laughing over the sound of running feet, aluminum breaking, and her ministry team gasping and screaming. Sophie was pretty sure the scream had come from Barry, which was not encouraging.

"We should go after her." Nadine was out of her chair. As decisive as her words sounded, the girlish blonde didn't advance toward the door, either waiting for someone to agree or maybe hoping someone would talk her out of it. She was even paler than she had been when the meeting started.

Sophie was about to encourage discretion when Stacy found an area of agreement with Nadine. Her face flushing from caramel to russet with a surge of adrenaline that launched her out of her chair, Stacy led the dash to the screen door. Nadine stumbled as she turned to follow. They also pushed through without having to turn the handle, the screen door latch apparently gone now.

"But ..." That was Barry's contribution.

Already standing, Sophie figured all she could do was follow the girls, who were following the other one, who was being dragged out of the house by the giant demon. How had she gotten herself into such a fiasco?

Someone was talking to Sophie. In the office meeting. Not outside that little bungalow in the suburbs.

"Uh, I'd be happy to work with an outside page designer if you want, to update the look. I could suggest someone ..."

She prayed silently that she had heard the question—at least the gist of it.

Vince nodded from the other end of the table. He didn't look freaked out, so Sophie's reply must have at least come close.

"I think we have good enough in-house resources, including one of our clients who has offered to exchange design work for job search help." Becky's response started woodenly but loosened at the end. Maybe Sophie's answer had missed part of the question.

She tried to recover. "Oh, that's great. I look forward to it." As soon as she said that, Sophie wished she'd gone with something more neutral. She wasn't even sure they had decided she would do the coding.

"Well, I like your attitude, Sophie. Go ahead and take the lead, then." Becky was looking at Sophie in a way that reminded her of her mother, though Becky was many years younger than Sophie's mother, probably.

This time Sophie smiled silently as she realized she had jumped too high without asking first what they wanted her to reach. But it seemed to have worked out okay.

She resorted again to silent prayer. This one, a prayer of humble thanks.

Debriefing with Sophie

Detta had been out to dinner with Roddy and two other couples from church when Sophie was working with those college kids. She called Sophie on Monday evening to check in. Kicking back in her recliner, she found a bit of relief for her aching back and neck.

"Oh, Detta, it was a disaster."

"What? How bad could it be?" She started to straighten the recliner but changed her mind in response to the ache running up the right side of her neck.

"How bad? Well, police. The team stomping away in tears. Young girls losing their faith. Barry dropping out of school to join a mission agency."

"What? Sophie, you're not serious?" Now she did sit up straight.

"Okay, not that last part. But there were cops involved by the end. And I know those two girls who were supposed to be helping are never gonna speak to each other again. Barry was crying when I saw him last."

"Oh my. What about the girl you were ministering to?" Detta had the phone in one hand, her elbow on the arm of the chair, the doily there slipping a bit.

"I gave her Jonathan's contact info. She needs big-time help. I don't know if she'll go after it, but she seemed to sort of trust me."

Detta adjusted that doily. "Really? Even after it all blew up?" She breathed a sigh and slowly leaned back again, pushing on the recliner arms so her feet rose almost as high as her knees.

"I think she knew I was seeing what was manipulating her. I think she could tell my gift was real. I even saw a look in her eyes, like maybe she felt sorry for me having to work with those other kids."

"They were really that bad?"

"A total mess. Barry wasn't taking charge. The two girls seemed to have some personal rivalry going on, on top of having completely different understandings of their faith. The white girl even said something to the black girl that I thought was pretty racist." Sophie huffed over the phone. "I guess it could have been worse, but I don't wanna even try to imagine an evening worse than that one."

"What were the police doing in all this?"

"Well, the girl we were working with busted out of the house and made a run for it. The two girls followed her and tried to drag her back to the house. A police car was cruising past and saw the struggle on the sidewalk just as I arrived on the scene."

"Oh no."

"Yeah. Picture me trying to sort of generically explain deliverance ministry to a hefty cop. I was trying to keep those two girls out of the back of his squad car." More huffing.

Detta leaned her head on the back of her recliner. That relieved most of the soreness in her neck. "Oh dear. I had a bad feeling about that whole meeting. I guess I should have said something."

"Yes, you should have." Sophie paused. "But I saw it too. I should have made better arrangements. I need to figure out how I can get a team together that I can trust."

"Oh, Sophie, that sends a confirmation right through my spirit. That's exactly what you need to be focusing on now. Let's pray that God will bring in the workers to stand beside you. There's gotta be some folks he's preparing for this work."

"You still feel like you should stay out of it?"

"I'm cutting back, Sophie. Me and Roderick are working on the wedding. I just feel like that's where I should focus my energy right now. The prayer group is enough for me at this stage."

"I know. I know that's right." Another pause. "I can consult with you though, right?"

"You better, or I'll get that cop to go after you again." Detta sniffed a laugh at her own joke but had to relax her neck again to calm another twinge of pain.

"Ha. Very funny." Sophie didn't sound amused.

"How did you keep those girls out of trouble, by the way?"

"Well, it probably looked more like a spat between girls than a riot or some kind of abduction. And I quietly bound a spirit of fear that was hanging on that cop. He sorta settled down when I did that. And he kept looking at me as he got back in his car. In the end, it felt like he was basically leaving the girls in my custody."

"Custody. Yeah. Spiritual custody. Maternal custody too. You're a potential mother figure for girls like that, Sophie."

"Huh. Maybe. I suppose you're right." Sophie hummed for a second. "I wonder how Hope is doing."

"Interesting you would think of her when I said something about you being a mother figure. Though maybe you're more of a big sister to Hope."

"Yeah. She is like my little sister ... who somehow ran away to California."

"You think she would come back here to help you out?"

"Hope? Come here? And leave her fish tacos and ocean breezes?"

"We have fish tacos around here, I think. Though I can't say I ever tried one. Maybe Anthony and Delilah ..." Detta paused, interrupted by a sudden feeling of folks coming home. A reunion feeling. "Sophie?"

"Yeah?"

"Are you feeling that? Like a kind of leading? Like an answer to our prayers already?"

"When you said 'Anthony and Delilah?' I did get this ... feeling. Huh."

"You sensed, like, an answer to our question?"

"I did. Especially since we were talking about Hope. Homecoming. Or like returning from a long journey. But team is the big thing in my mind right now." Sophie was breathing a bit harder. "It would be quite a miracle for Hope to agree to come back to the Midwest."

Detta shuddered as a warm sensation rose through her back and into her neck. A small pop between vertebrae loosened something. "Well, I'll be! My neck just got freed up."

"What? You were feeling sore?"

"I was. I was stiff and sore since I got up this morning. And it just went away when I felt the Spirit confirming that direction for you."

"Ha. That's cool." Sophie seemed to be tapping on something. "You think I should get together with Anthony and Delilah and also try to talk Hope into moving out here?"

"I got all kinds of confirmation in my spirit for that. And you just said it yourself."

"Yes, I guess I did. And I guess we were both hearing that ... leading." Sophie snickered. "My main angel guy is glowing like the sun over here. Wow. Okay. Not too hard to figure out what that's about. Clearly an angel is telling me to go for it."

"Did that angel just literally say, 'Go for it' to you?" Detta chuckled deep in her chest.

"Well, not in so many words. But yeah. He basically ... gave me a green light, so to speak."

Detta laughed harder, celebrating Sophie's new direction as well as the new freedom in her neck.

A Time to Build

Anthony hooked the claw of the hammer on the bent nail and cranked it free from the doorframe, knocking his hand against the coat hook inside the closet. He winced and forced himself not to swear aloud.

"You okay in there, Anty? Should I get 911 on speed dial?"

He also kept his eye roll to himself but chuckled at Delilah's 911 joke, probably loud enough for her to hear from outside the closet. She was just barely in the bedroom. She wouldn't want to be caught in there with him even if it was entirely innocent. And though there was no one there to catch them.

"Seriously, you okay? I feel bad for you wounding yourself just to prove your love for me. I'm already confident about your love, Anty."

No one in all his life had consistently called Anthony by a nickname. *Tony* had never stuck. His friends sometimes squeezed his name down to *Anth'ny*. Two syllables. But *Anty* was a thing now, between him and Delilah. The lady he loved.

"Thanks, babe. I know you love me. I was just wantin' to keep this job simple and not have to hire some other guy to climb into your closet." He was standing outside the closet now.

"Okay, so you're protecting my virtue. How heroic." She was leaning on the dresser next to the bedroom door.

He squinted at her, trying to judge how she would respond to some kissing and cuddling just now. Her big dark eyes were inviting him, not just reassuring him. He was pretty sure he was reading that right.

Dropping the hammer onto the carpet, he rubbed the back of his hand. "I got it so the trim doesn't stick out anymore, but it still needs a couple more nails to keep it from coming lose again." He stepped across the room, stopping just in front of his girlfriend.

She edged out the bedroom door, but slowly, like she wanted him to follow. "Okay. I'll keep those big boxes outta there so I won't have to push 'em past that trim anymore. That way I won't be wreckin' your work."

"Thanks, I appreciate that, hard won as it is. And I'll look for a couple straight nails." He reached for her hand when she paused in the hall outside her bedroom. Even as he suspected her of maneuvering away from the bedroom for propriety's sake, she was still inviting with those eyes. Eyes with the gravitational pull of two blackholes. Of course he would never say anything to her about black holes. It probably wouldn't sound as good outside his head as it did inside.

Just when Anthony got his hands onto both of Delilah's thin shoulders, shoulders bare in a sleeveless yellow shirt, his phone buzzed in his pocket. The timing was perfect, if his phone had an app on it to prevent intimate contact between him and his girlfriend.

"I think it's something important." Her eyes narrowed just a little. The invitation in those eyes was put on hold, perhaps.

He contemplated her full, moist lips for a second longer. "Uh, how do you know it's important?" He reached for his jeans pocket and extracted his phone. "Is that one of your ... things? Your intuitions?" His brain was still trying to find a forward gear.

"Yes." She pushed off his chest and continued toward her living room.

It was Sophie.

"Hey, girl. How ya doin'?" He sounded friendlier than he felt. Maybe that was just a hint of an attempt at making Delilah jealous. Just a little. He sniffed an embarrassed laugh at the thought.

"I'm good. How are you doing? How is Delilah?" Maybe Sophie was throwing a defensive block against his little jealousy gambit.

Not that Anthony was admitting to anything. Was he overthinking again? "She's good. I'm helping her fix her closet doorframe."

"Oh, that's handy of you. Did you break any fingers or anything yet?"

"Hey, my infamy as a handyman has been way exaggerated. You can't believe everything my mama tells you."

Sophie laughed for just a second. "Okay." Then she slowed. "I really called with a serious agenda."

"Agenda? That sounds like business."

"More like ministry. Can I meet with you two sometime this week?"

"Huh? Me and Delilah?"

"In my mind you're a team, Anthony. I want to meet with team Delilah and Anty."

Anthony had winced the time Delilah used her nickname for him in front of Sophie. He knew it would come back to bite him. But he didn't hear any irony in the way Sophie said it now. Maybe she wasn't really making fun. "Yeah, we are a team. I believe you. And we've been thinkin' about what we should be doing with that." He had followed Delilah into the living room by now.

Delilah was concentrating on him and this conversation. "She has something for us. I feel it. We should meet with her soon." She got this look on her face at times like this, like she was already visiting the future. That look reminded Anthony of the Mona Lisa. Focused on something out there, pretty serious with just a hint of a smile. Anticipation, not humor. Except for one thing. Delilah was way better looking than the Mona Lisa.

"Delilah says we should meet with you soon." He let his eyes remain on his girlfriend as he answered Sophie.

"Good. Your mama said she was getting a leading about something for us. It sounds like Delilah has heard something too." Sophie paused. "What about you, Anthony? You feelin' the women ganging up on you?"

The sensation raised by that question was like a warm embrace. Sophie in his ear, his mother not far from his thoughts, and Delilah filling his eyes with her luminous face. "I could think of a lot worse crews to be ganged up on by."

That got a laugh from Sophie and a gleaming grin from Delilah.

Angels in Focus

The first time Delilah noticed Sophie Ramos, the Hispanic girl was crumpling under a gigantic load of glory from heaven or something in a nighttime church service. Sophie had been with Anthony that night. Delilah had assumed they were a couple. But when she spent time with the two of them, they seemed more like brother and sister. Obviously the children of a mixed marriage. Or maybe it was Detta adopting Sophie that made them siblings. Delilah had never met Sophie's mother.

She adjusted the microscope a touch tighter, and the layer of dead bacteria gave way to a deeper layer of swirling creatures clearly still alive. No matter how many times she had seen what lived in tainted water, Delilah hadn't lost the fascination. And a bit of disgust. The public water system in a neighboring suburb was still recovering from flooding in the spring. Much cleaner than a month ago, their system still wasn't sufficiently microbe-free for human consumption.

Delilah scribbled some notes she would type into her laptop over lunch. She focused the microscope in and out again, the living microbes appearing and disappearing. Maybe this was like what Sophie saw. Could Sophie focus in and out, seeing and then not seeing the angels? That's how Delilah pictured it.

She was thinking about Sophie because they were invited to eat Mexican food at Sophie's apartment tonight. It was cool to think of Sophie cooking for them. Something normal. Something mere mortals did. Delilah was still pretty intimidated by Sophie's superpowers, as Anthony called them.

But, when it came to Anthony, she was grateful to Sophie. As far as Delilah was concerned, Sophie had kept Anthony away from some dangerous women who might have ensnared him. Not just women who would have kept him from dating Delilah, but ones who would have kept him from God's design for his life. She knew he was meant for more than tending a computer network. More than watching sci-fi movies. More than attaching himself to some woman who would miss his potential as a leader and minister of the gospel.

"Good news." Why she said that aloud wasn't clear, but maybe it had to do with the rising feeling of a gospel calling and the meeting with Sophie. Delilah had been watching herself and Anthony drift along lately—attending church, going out on dates, talking about getting engaged. But the bigger point of it all wasn't yet manifest, not evident in their actions. If they were going to be a forever couple, it had to be for some greater purpose. That's what her daddy had taught her.

"Help me live up to my calling to please you, Lord. Not to just live up to the memory of my daddy." She took off her lab glasses and checked to be sure she was the only one in the room. The other three lab stations were empty, as was the sink area at the other end of the laboratory. She was glad a coworker hadn't caught her praying aloud, but she didn't feel alone in the silent room. And it wasn't her daddy who was with her now.

"Thank you, Lord."

That evening when Anthony picked Delilah up at her apartment, she held on to him for a few extra seconds. She lifted silent prayers for their wisdom and their unity. Then she pulled away and smiled. "Okay, Anty. Let's go see what Miss Sophie has for us."

"An adventure, no doubt." He closed her front door behind them and waited while Delilah locked it.

"That's right. That feels exactly right when you say it."

"You know, you sound just like my mama when you say stuff like that."

Delilah took his chin between her thumb and forefinger as she paused from dropping her keys into her purse. "I count that as a supreme compliment, baby."

He chuckled as if he'd meant the comparison as a personal admission more than the compliment it felt like to Delilah.

When Anthony parked his quiet electric car on the street in front of Sophie's building, he seemed preoccupied with studying the street signs. That gave Delilah a chance to study him. His slow movements and dogged preoccupation betrayed his tiredness at the end of the workday. She was feeling it too.

"Lord, give us the energy to have a good evening with Sophie and clarity to hear your direction." That prayer foamed out of her spontaneously, like an activating chemical poured into a beaker.

Anthony looked at her for a moment with his hand on the car door. "You feelin' tired from work too?"

"Sure. But I'm excited about this meeting. Something good will come from it. I just know it."

His eyes tightened a little. Maybe not a wince. Maybe he was just thinking about something. Delilah didn't know everything that had happened between him and Sophie. Was there still something between them? Something …

Anthony scowled at her. "What are you thinking about?"

"Huh. My mama told me to never ask a man that."

"Ha. My mama asks that kinda thing all the time, especially if she gets one of her feelings about something wrong." He pulled the handle on his door.

"You got a feeling?"

He nodded. "Like a little cloud just settled down right onto your head."

"Well, now you're sounding more like your mama than I do."

He snickered. "I guess that's unavoidable." They bumped shoulders next to the car.

"No. I think you have some of the same gifting as her. I don't think it's just DNA."

"Is that your scientific observation?"

She shrugged one shoulder and started an eye roll. Then they laughed together. She wasn't one hundred percent sure they were laughing about the same thing.

Finally upstairs after Sophie buzzed them in, she greeted them with a lopsided grimace and a haze of smoke behind her. "Burnt the enchiladas. Really sorry."

Anthony pulled out his phone. "I know a good Mexican place that delivers pretty fast around here." He had half a smile on.

Delilah couldn't tell how serious he was. She was still stunned by the news that dinner was ruined. That news was still in the air, not just on Sophie's sad face.

"I got to talking to this new ... Well, I guess I wasn't paying attention." Sophie allowed them both into the apartment. Her hair looked recently cut. It was tinted with a bit of purplish-rose dye. Tufts of various hues were sticking out and up like she had been gripping her hair with clenched fists.

Just like Delilah's place, the walls of Sophie's apartment were all white. Three of the windows next to the eating area and living room were wide open, the white linen curtains puffing toward the three folks standing in the little entryway.

"Maybe leave this door open?" Anthony caught the front door as Sophie allowed it to swing closed.

Delilah suspected Anthony had noticed what she had—the airflow was coming in the windows, not going out. He was observant about things like that even if he wasn't a proper scientist.

Sophie just shook her head and shrugged, shuffling toward the kitchen. Exhaust fans were on high in there.

"You said you were talking to ... who?" Anthony had bunched the doormat in a way that held the front door open.

"Oh. You know." She tossed one hand over her shoulder.

Delilah followed the direction of that gesture. Somehow she knew Sophie was indicating a particular presence in the room, not just an idea in general. "Does that happen often?"

"Ruining supper?" Sophie nodded as she pivoted toward the stove.

Anthony and Delilah stood in the kitchen doorway. The enchiladas were probably edible from what Delilah could see, but they surely had a much bigger carbon buildup on the bottom than Sophie would have wanted.

Delilah diverted her attention from the carbon content of the food. "If you're busy talking to angels, can't they remind you to check the oven?" She ended her question with what she hoped was a permissive smile.

"They can. They probably do. But I guess I don't always listen like I should."

"Still?" Anthony said that like he was familiar with the problem.

"I'm getting better. This is the first conflagration in months."

"Conflagration?" Anthony snorted.

Sophie wasn't laughing, even if she had been teasing herself with the exaggerated description of her cooking failure.

Delilah paused over this deeper look into what it was like to be Sophie. More evidence that it was entirely possible to see and converse with angels and still be completely human about it. Even messing up once in a while. And not just messing up dinner.

You Know What This Is?

Sophie was exaggerating about how often she incinerated a meal while talking with an angel. Maybe it had only been a couple times, but doing it more than once felt stupid.

Was she inflating the size of the problem to help Anthony better appreciate Delilah's skills? They probably didn't need that kind of help anymore. Maybe it was just Sophie indulging in some false humility. Detta had been warning her about that. Her mother had too.

"So, seriously, I don't think it's dangerous. Just not so tasty." Sophie lifted the baking dish to show them.

"We could just skim the part that didn't burn." Anthony still held his phone, but he might have been kidding all along about calling out for food. "It does smell good. Your mother's recipe?"

"Of course." She turned to Delilah. "He knows that if it started with my mother's recipe, then it was probably good at one point."

"What was the conversation about, that it was so ... distracting?" Delilah was clearly more distracted by the idea of Sophie conversing with an angel than with the enchilada recipe.

"Uh, maybe I'll talk about that later. Kinda complicated, but important. Let's decide if we want to eat this first." She checked to see if Delilah was offended by this clumsy delaying tactic, but the tall woman's tight smile seemed more sympathetic than offended. Sophie couldn't imagine beautiful Delilah burning a meal, but nobody was perfect. Not even Delilah Little.

"I agree with Anthony. Let's eat the part that's edible. It still smells good." Delilah stepped up close and put a hand on Sophie's upper back.

Sophie nearly choked up. "Oh, thanks guys. You're too generous."

"You cooked us supper, and you're calling *us* generous." Anthony grabbed a sharp metal spatula from the utensil holder next to the stove.

"I was working from home today. It seemed like a no-brainer." Sophie rolled her eyes but refrained from apologizing again.

Once the smoke was all cleared, no alarms going off in her apartment or the hallway, Sophie closed the front door and said goodbye to the new angel, who had apparently just been there to deliver a particular message. An angel who believed in doors, an architectural feature most of her heavenly visitors ignored.

When she turned from the front door toward the kitchen, Anthony was standing behind her. Sophie startled and then giggled.

"Who was that?" He nodded toward the door behind her.

"Who? What? You heard me?" She wasn't even aware of talking aloud to the angel just now, but that didn't mean it didn't happen.

"I just thought I saw something go out, and you were looking right there."

"What? Really? You never told me you saw ... things."

He shrugged. "Sometimes I think I do. I kinda think the pattern is things that ... I mean, I see a hint about angels who are ... relevant to me. I can sense them around. Maybe not exactly see them."

Delilah was behind Anthony now. "Dinner is served." She said it with sufficient inflection to assure Sophie she was aware of the irony.

Sophie sniffed and shook her head. "I'm getting the feeling this is going to be a very significant night for all three of us."

"Really? Me too." The higher voice in which Delilah said that brought a much younger version of her into the apartment.

They all took turns staring at each other.

Anthony didn't break from that mutual freeze when he said, "Supper is getting cold."

"Ironic after burning it." Sophie harmonized with Anthony's stilted tone.

"We should eat it." Delilah sounded as much like a sleepwalker as the other two.

Sophie started the uncomfortable laughter that broke them out of the three-way staring contest, and she led the way to the table. Delilah had indeed finished setting things out. The half-chiladas, as Anthony dubbed them, were no longer steaming, but they probably weren't really cold.

Sophie gestured to the other two seats, which would put Anthony at the head of the oval table and Delilah across from Sophie. Sophie sat with her back to the kitchen so she could get up and get things if needed. Salads had been in place for a while. Fortunately there was no chance of burning those.

As they ate, Anthony adjusted his description of the main dish to "smoked enchiladas," which wasn't a bad assessment. Not something Sophie would ever try to reproduce, but not a bad meal.

When they finished, Sophie was already into the story about last Sunday's disaster ministry session with the college kids. "I heard from Jonathan this afternoon that the girl contacted him. I guess she wanted me to know, so she gave him permission to tell me."

"Well, that's a relief. I was really starting to worry about that girl." Delilah carried two salad bowls to the kitchen. She paused next to the counter.

"I didn't tell you who it was, did I? The girl's name?" Sophie was worried she had spilled some confidential information. She paused by the sink hoping to recall what she had said.

"Oh, no. I don't know who she is. But still, I was worried." Delilah parked her thin white sandals in front of the sink. "I have what my mama calls a sympathetic soul. I kinda pick up on what's going on with people even without meeting them, sometimes. Has to be a God thing, I think."

"Sure. Of course. I've met people who have gifts like that. It can be really valuable in a ministry time. Sometimes folks we're helping can't tell us what's going on with them when we're right in the middle of it." Sophie was reevaluating Delilah. "So you have that. Huh." She looked at Anthony. "And how long have you been detecting spirits?"

"Detecting? Oh …" He avoided eye contact. "For a while."

"How long's a while?"

"A … a longish while."

"Since before I met you?"

"Yes." His grin was a little sheepish. "Since before I met the girl who sees angels."

She remeasured Anthony as well. Sophie wasn't really surprised. She had long suspected he was hiding some gifts behind his self-deprecating jokes and his ready humility.

"You know what this is?" Delilah leaned toward Sophie, her shoulders forward, as if preparing to grab her.

"What this is?" Sophie paused to appreciate the array of angels filling the spaces between the people in the kitchen. On earlier visits with Delilah, she had noticed the womanly angel with the purple sash. Probably Delilah's main angel. And she knew the guy with the piercing eyes was Anthony's usual guardian. But there were a few she didn't recognize.

Both Delilah and Anthony were staring at Sophie. Anthony shivered visibly.

That seemed to trigger an even more dramatic shiver from Delilah. "This room is full. It's just filling up with the presence of God."

"They bring it with them." Sophie said that without even meaning to. She knew exactly what Delilah was talking about. She knew what the shivers were about.

Anthony and Delilah were checking over their shoulders and monitoring Sophie. Then Anthony shouted and clattered his plate onto the counter. "Holy—! Holy. I mean, whoa!"

Sophie started to laugh. Hysterical laughter. She was laughing at Anthony substituting one use of the word *holy* for another in a totally unhinged moment. When he blurted all that, he had been looking squarely at the angel she thought of as his main guardian.

"Are you seeing this? Do you see this? I mean, is this real?" Anthony was locked onto that guardian.

Sophie laughed harder, like a fire hydrant of relief was gushing out of her.

Delilah seemed the only one who hadn't gone nutty. Her eyes were focused like she was studying a specimen in her lab. "I'll tell you what this is. This is a team. This is a ... a crew. An alliance. God is assigning us to support you, Sophie. You need someone to support you. People you can trust. And God is calling us to help." She had a hand on Anthony's shoulder like she was prepared to prop him up if he needed.

Anthony released a hissing breath through his teeth, shuddered violently, and grabbed hold of the counter next to the sink.

Sophie stopped laughing when a pitch-black spirit flew up off Anthony's back as if it had been hiding down his shirt.

"Oh, yeah!" He shook one more time. Then he started to laugh.

Delilah wasn't laughing. She was following something in the middle distance. "That's what this is. I just know it. It's a commissioning."

Time for a Change of Venue

Her phone app insisted it was a hundred degrees outside. That was desert hot. Triple digit temps were not so common in the hills above Los Angeles. Not like in Bakersfield or deserty places like that. Hope believed her phone. At least on this one point. The furniture on her deck had become too hot to touch by one o'clock in the afternoon. She sat in her favorite chair inside her apartment, in front of her computer. That chair had developed a squeak lately. A familiar and homey sound, really.

Her phone buzzed again. She knew who it was. What she didn't know was what to do about it. It was too hot to go out and meet him somewhere, so she had that excuse. But he probably just wanted to talk. At least that's what he wanted this time. And his call would include an apology, no doubt. Well, maybe a little doubt. Gerry had been pretty unpredictable since she'd met him.

The slouchy confidence with which he'd filled a chair at the Narcotics Anonymous meeting had been familiar and oddly enticing. Maybe it was just that he was someone she could relate to. And there was the lack of visible critters accompanying him at the beginning. Only at the beginning. Well, live and learn.

If Hope told him about the tangle of dark angels she discovered when they finally went out, maybe he would leave her alone. Could she possibly come across as scarier than him? In a way, she *was* scarier than Gerry. And yet she was also scared. Scared of his history and leery about his entanglements. Something about the twining knot of spirits bound to Gerry reminded her of her ex. But Hope had no idea what that meant. What was the significance of the similarity? It wasn't like the spirits that had tried to get at her through Marcus were following her around. They couldn't, could they?

Instead of responding to Gerry, Hope checked the clock and tried to guess what Sophie would be doing at four o'clock in the Midwest. Done working? At home today even if she *was* working?

"Hope." Sophie answered the call with a level of urgency that implied she had been interrupted while plunging a flooding toilet ... perhaps.

"Uh, yeah. You okay?"

"I was just thinking about you."

"Oh, cool. What about, exactly?"

"I felt like ... Well, I wanted to talk about something. But it just felt like it was kind of urgent all of a sudden."

"Whoa." Hope was pretty sure Sophie's powers didn't include reading her mind, but at that moment, it felt as if Sophie was tapped into Hope's internal security alert about Gerry. She sorted through all that in one second. "So, what did you wanna talk about?"

"But you're the one who called me." Sophie made a little wumph sound, as if dropping herself onto her cushy couch.

"Ha. Well, yeah. That's true." Hope waited for two breaths as her main angel girl faded into sight and smiled at her. This was more than the usual friendly smile. More of a *knowing* smile. But, then, that girl knew everything. So maybe the knowing part was about letting Hope know that she knew ... or something. "I guess I'm worried that I might get myself in trouble if I stick around here much longer. I keep meeting interesting people, but they're not rock solid like you and Detta. Or Anthony and Priscilla. Like them."

"Wow. Okay, my turn." Sophie chuckled. "I was calling to see if you were up for a longish visit out here, maybe with some possibility of considering moving here for a while."

Hope swore. Then she apologized. "You sure you can't read my mind?"

"I'm pretty sure. Are you afraid of what I'd find in there?"

"Uh, yeah. My head isn't all church-lady clean."

"None of us are pure church-lady clean all the time, Hope."

"Including obsessing about a hot bad boy?"

"Including that. Especially that." Sophie laughed freely.

Hope released a relieved laugh of her own. Not just relief at Sophie's words, but relief at her own trust that Sophie was telling her the truth.

Hope's angel girl added a knowing nod, while keeping that knowing smile going.

"This guy in the NA meeting is gnawing at my head. Or my obsession over him is doing the gnawing, I guess. And part of it is that I just know he has some critters with him, but I can't always see them."

"Ah. Yeah. That makes him seem extra dangerous."

"Right. But I know my sponsor would say this is about me, not about some guy named Gerry. I mean, the issue is that I'm feeling ... vulnerable, but I'm not necessarily in danger right now."

"Sounds like good advice." Sophie paused, as if waiting for the conversation to come back to where she had originally wanted to take it.

"So, you were thinking just now that I should come out for a long visit?"

"I've been thinking and praying about that for a while. Detta and Anthony were thinking it too. But none of us knew how feasible it would be for you."

"I can work from anywhere, of course."

"What about longer term?"

"Hmm. Leave sunny Cali and move back to the snowy Midwest?"

"At least consider it. I would love to have you come back here. You could share my place at first, until you decide if you wanna stay around. Then we can figure something out."

"Something like sharing a bigger place, like you said way back when you first visited me?"

"Yeah, I remember that. It's still worth thinking about. But first, I gotta get the girl out of California, even though I know I can't get California out of the girl."

Hope sighed hard. She changed the subject without apology. "I keep trying to talk to Detta about my sex obsessions during our phone calls, but I can never seem to breach that door. Do I just talk to you about that kinda stuff?"

Sophie hummed for a second. "I suggest you try harder to break through and talk to Detta about it. I know getting everything out into the light is important with the kind of pastoring stuff Detta does with you." She did a heavy pause. "But that doesn't mean you and I can't talk about it too. I mean, it's different. I'm not looking to be, like, your pastor or mentor or anything, really. More like a big sister."

Swearing again and skipping another apology, Hope focused on not bawling over the cell phone connection. "I'm so glad to have you as my big sis. That's for sure." The intensity of the surge coming out of her chest prompted Hope to check for any aliens that might be riding on it. There was nothing she could see, but she was beginning to believe what Detta had told her—that emotions are usually stronger than spirits.

"When can you ... fly out here?" Sophie dropped her question in a way that implied she was willing to back off if she was pushing too hard.

Hope assumed that hesitation was about money. Flights were more expensive these days. "I can see about getting tickets at a good price. Fly out of Santa Anna. How flexible are you? I can play the market a bit and just come out when the first reasonable fare comes available. I'll bring my laptop. And I won't need to take much time off, whenever it is."

Sophie started with a big breath. "That's great. Of course there's no deadline, but I am feeling like it's time to sorta get my own team together for the ministry stuff." She hesitated. "Anthony and Delilah are encouraging me to get that going."

"Did something happen?" Not exactly reading her mind, Hope did feel like she understood Sophie pretty well.

"Uh, yeah. Remember I told you about helping those college kids? Well, it was a hot mess. They were the opposite of a supportive team, which was a real wake-up call."

"Anybody injured?" Hope was thinking of the exorcism session she had sat in on with a local priest. She had been amazed at how violently a person could be tormented without being totally physically destroyed. But the girl she had been helping with that time was pretty bruised up by the end of it.

"Minor scrapes. The worst scrape was with a cop, really. Hard to explain to him what was going on. Looked like a little race riot with girls from all the colors of the rainbow wrestling on the street in the dark. It probably helped that it was all women."

Hope knew Sophie wasn't telling her everything. There was a longer story awaiting a late-night discussion, she assumed. "So you think I can be part of a team, like, helping people get free?"

"Obviously." Sophie's voice was a little raspy. She sounded surprisingly tired for so early in the day. Relatively early. "I think it helps a lot to have another person present who sees like I do. I mean, I've gotten caught reacting to some beasty thing while something else is going on with another person in the room. The angels overwhelm me sometimes too, so I get, like, blinded by the light, sort of."

"Sounds like an old song title."

"Wasn't sure if you would get the reference."

"You testing me?"

"Testing to see if you're really as young as you are? You're a pretty old soul."

"Huh. I guess that comes with the territory."

"The angels we see are really old."

"Any of them ever tell you how old?"

"No. Not the good ones. The bad ones are always bragging about stuff like that." Sophie put on a creepy voice. "I am the spirit that brought Ra to the pharaohs, blah, blah, blah." Her ominous tone faded as she laughed at herself.

"Hard to know if any of it's true."

"Yeah, but Jonathan was right. What does it matter? I mean, the nasty thing's gotta leave, no matter how old it is. Jesus is way older, if that's important at all."

"Ha. I like to think of God the Father as old, but of Jesus as young and hip."

Snorting a laugh, Sophie didn't answer for a few seconds. "I think I've seen him a couple times now, but I'm not gonna argue with anyone who doubts me on that."

"No use arguing, I say."

"Uh-huh." Sophie hesitated. "So you're coming, then? You'll get a flight as soon as you can find an affordable one?"

"I will. I definitely will."

"Awesome."

Life Is Vulnerable

Detta sat on the couch. Though this seat was only about eight feet from her recliner, it felt like visiting someone else's house. At least someone else's perspective. But she sat there not for the experience of a different viewpoint. The air-conditioning fell most directly on this particular couch cushion. She had been cooking all afternoon and now cooled off while waiting for Roddy to arrive.

When did I let him talk me into calling him Roddy? Maybe she really was seeing from a new perspective. A new look at herself. But before she could answer her own question, she heard a strange sound at the front door. That the thump was at the front door was part of the strangeness. Another oddity was the low moan that came in a familiar voice.

"Detta, I think I need some help here." It was Roddy. He was on the front porch and had gotten the screen door open, but the interior door was locked, of course.

Rising to meet him at the door, Detta hoped her heart wouldn't explode out of her chest. "What's the matter?" she asked as she struggled to quickly unlock both the bolt and the knob.

When the door swung open, Roddy staggered in. His right arm hung from his shoulder like dead weight, and he leaned on the doorpost as he dragged himself into the living room. "Something's wrong." He sounded like a person just come from the dentist after a big shot of Novocain.

She grabbed both his shoulders and wrestled him into a dining room chair. For a second, the rolling chair threatened to run away from them, but she managed not to dump him onto the carpet. "Roddy, are you having a stroke?"

He shook his head like it was as loose as his dangling arm. His right leg was curved in an unnatural way under his chair, and his left leg was shaking.

Detta let his head rest on her shoulder as she bent down and pulled her phone out of her apron. She dialed 911.

Seeing Anthony arrive in the hallway, with Delilah and Sophie close behind him, sprouted new gratitude out of dry soil. And Detta wanted to get out of the chair next to the exam room to greet them, but she just couldn't get her legs to cooperate. She knew Roddy's stroke wasn't contagious, she was just exhausted from the shock and from the desperate struggle to get her man to the hospital.

"How is he?" Anthony slid into the chair next to her and wrapped a long arm around her shoulders. Delilah stood in front of them with arms folded. Sophie remained silent, fists tightened at her side.

"He's gonna live. He's gonna make it. But it's too early to tell how much damage was done." A sob lodged in her throat, but Detta refused to let it out.

Sophie spun around and landed her backside in the other chair next to Detta. She put a hand on her knee. "Time to pray for this, Detta. Time to go to battle for Roddy."

Detta started to laugh, a sort of visiting chuckle that had snuck into her gut. It didn't last. That laugh was a visitor introduced by this new-and-improved version of the girl who sees angels. Now she was the girl who talks to God and gets her prayers heard. Detta couldn't find words to answer. She just closed her eyes and squeezed Sophie's hand.

But it was Delilah who started praying first. Maybe she jumped in where she expected Sophie would hesitate. Or maybe she and Sophie both just understood that Delilah would go first.

"We come together for our brother Roderick, Lord. Your son, your servant. He's in your hands already. You're already preserving his life. And we know you want the very best for him. We're all confident that full recovery would be best for your glory. So do your work. Do what you intend to do. And show us how we can be partners with that."

Detta couldn't help recalling the skinny little girl who seemed so serious and so silent during most of the years she'd known Delilah from church. Part of her wonder over who Delilah had grown up to be was that Detta had seen it coming. Like recognizing the shoot for what it would one day grow into—the leaves, the branches, the flowers, and the fruit.

"Amen," was all Detta could say. And she just kept saying it as Anthony prayed, and Sophie, and then Delilah again.

When they all took a deep breath together, Detta found her voice. "Oh my Lord, I feel better. Thank you, Jesus. I feel so much faith that Roddy is gonna be okay. Thank you, Jesus." She let the tears flow now and wiped tissues along her cheeks as the kids all settled into seats.

Candace was the next one to arrive, walking purposefully but slowly, still recovering from her hip replacement surgery. It wasn't clear to Detta whether the polished wood look on her face was a gloss over Candace's own pain or stoic sympathy for Detta and Roddy.

"He's gonna be fine. I can just feel it, sister." Candace took Detta's hand when she stood in front of her chair. She didn't seem as tall as she used to be, even with Detta still seated, but her faith had not shrunk an inch.

A physician's assistant exited the room where they were testing Roddy and getting him ready for admission to the hospital. The man, with amber skin, black eyebrows, and dark eyes, aimed a brief scowl at the gathering outside the room. But then he hustled off without saying anything. They were probably over the capacity of the waiting area.

Sophie stood now so Anthony and Candace could comfort Detta shoulder to shoulder.

The physician, a short woman named Doctor Tan, was smiling primly when she removed her surgical mask outside the exam room. "Mr. Harper is going to be fine. He's in good spirits, though he's having a hard time speaking. We can work on that, of course, with some experienced therapists we have here on staff." She nodded confidently. "In due time. All in due time." She was probably in her fifties, but Detta sensed a wisdom beyond her years. Maybe the voice of weary experience.

"Bless you, Doctor. I know Roddy is in good hands here." Detta was spurting gratitude that she couldn't back up with anything more than her instincts and hopes.

Doctor Tan took Detta's hand and thanked her for the blessing. "Let's wait until they move him to a room before seeing him." She looked around at Detta's supporters. "Just two people at a time, I think." Then she smiled and headed down the hall, pulling her phone out of her lab coat pocket.

"Okay," Anthony spoke next. "I'll take the first shift, unless you wanna stay for a while, Mrs. Maynard. If you do, then I could come back later."

Detta noted that her son was assuming the role of the man of the family. She couldn't help smiling at that thought.

"I can stay for a bit, if you don't mind, Anthony. But none of us have to go home yet, just not go into the hospital room in a great mob." Candace's face had softened a little, perhaps at the doctor's assurances.

Looking around at the loved ones all turned toward her, Detta couldn't help making a joke. "And this is a very great mob, indeed."

They laughed together before sorting a schedule that would assure Detta was never at the hospital alone. Sophie and Delilah took Anthony's copy of her house keys and went to pick up a few things for Detta, things that hadn't crossed her mind while waiting for the ambulance.

Detta looked down at her big canvas shopping bag of hastily gathered items, thinking she could probably get rid of some of it, like the curling iron she'd included in a panic. But she would work on that later. Like the doctor said, all in due time.

Hope Is Here

On the day Roddy left the hospital with Anthony driving him and Detta, Sophie drove her old hybrid car to the airport to pick up Hope. Something about this trip reminded her of meeting Ross at the airport in Iowa over a year ago. Was it really that long ago? Less than a year, actually.

So much had happened. So much had changed. Was Sophie so different?

That she was gathering her own team for freeing the spiritually oppressed implied serious progress. Growth. A new chapter or something. Was Hope ready to be part of it? Was her faith firm enough? Were her addictions under control?

Those questions rode in the back of Sophie's mind, if not in the back of her car, like those frumpy spirits that used to follow her everywhere. With Detta, Sophie was committed to Hope, to bringing her closer to Jesus. Hope was all in, as far as Sophie could tell. But she seemed to test and reconsider her doubts more often than most Christians Sophie knew. She could understand why, but she feared that Hope's testing would keep her from being and doing everything God had for her.

When she left the highway and began to wind toward the arrivals pickup area, Sophie prayed for her young friend and for her own wisdom. That seemed a heavy lift. But seeing Hope waiting by the curb removed some of that weight.

"Yo. Can you give me a ride, lady?" Hope's blonde hair was shorter than Sophie had ever seen it. The short bob revealed a half dozen piercings in each ear. Hope slid her soft-sided luggage off her shoulder and let it dangle an inch above the gum-spotted pavement.

Sophie laughed only briefly, hitting the unlock button as she shouted out the window, "Get in before someone hears you." The humor of Hope's greeting had vanished quickly as Sophie recalled that college girl she'd tried to help. An innocent offer of a ride had once turned into all kinds of darkness when Betsy was a kid.

"How are ya?" Hope looked a little uncertain when she bent to look in the passenger window before opening the front door. She wore no makeup, as usual, but maybe she had a bit more sun-kissed color of her own.

"I'm great. I was just remembering someone who got … well …" Sophie reconsidered. "No. I'm great."

"Ah." Hope nodded and glanced away. She got into the seat and closed the door, avoiding Sophie's eyes.

"Never mind me. I'm still reeling from that ministry mess a couple weeks ago. The girl was abducted when she was young. Got into a car with a stranger, enticed by some means or another."

Hope swore. "Sorry. Insensitive of me. I gotta watch my mouth." She hesitated. "Sorry for the swearing too. Another bad habit."

"Right. I understand. Yeah. I'm just as likely as you are, and almost as likely as Anthony, to make an inappropriate joke. Working on that. Seems like you find out how serious life can be for folks when you agree to help 'em out with their … stuff."

"Have you done any of that since that thing that fell apart?" Hope was wearing at least two tank tops, one bright green and one bright blue. The combination electrified her blue eyes.

"We—me and Anthony—were part of a group working with an old man at his church the other day. Turned out to be mostly about emotional trauma. The spirits were almost, like, spectators at the point when we met him. They didn't really have access to this guy in a controlling way. He has a strong faith. Just needed to clean up some things left from pain and resentment way back."

"But I bet it was helpful for you to be there to see what was and wasn't going on." Hope rested her elbow on the open window.

"I'm sure it was. It kept the assistant pastor from sticking with her assumption that the guy just needed deliverance from some spirits."

"How hard was it to convince this pastor lady?"

"Well, she's a youngish pastor, just a few years older than me and Anthony. She and Anthony have known each other forever. Anthony convinced her to listen to me. He, of course, has my back." She snorted. "I mean, the real point was to help the man get healed. But it felt good to have Anthony, like, declaring authoritatively that I knew what I was doing."

"Nice. He's such a great guy." Hope's eyes followed a motorcycle that roared past, dodging between lanes of highway traffic. "Big ugly thing on that bike with that dude."

"Looked like the Wicked Witch of the West to me." Sophie only focused there after Hope called attention to that clinger.

"You think he's driving so fast to try to get away from her?"

"Lord, have mercy on that guy. Get him the help he needs." Sophie would rather pray than just observe and speculate. Part of this new chapter for her. She shrugged in answer to Hope, which helped cover a shiver that ran up her spine.

Hope was staring at her.

"Are you seeing something now?"

"What makes you ask?"

"I've suspected I have one of those assignment things like I saw following Ross last year."

"Huh. Kinda blurry, but there is something there."

Sophie just stopped herself from swearing. Time to clean up her language too. Good time to start, with Hope listening. "Just tell it to get lost for me, will ya?" She checked with Hope to see how she would respond to this spontaneous request.

"Blurry dude, you get lost now, in the name of Jesus. I'm tellin' you for real. I got these angels that are gonna torture you like ... heck if you don't leave Sophie alone." When she said that, two very stern angels materialized in the space between her and Hope. They showed up as small enough to fit into the cabin of the car but were still intimidating.

Like a magnetic pull that suddenly let go, Sophie sensed the departure of the spirit that had been following her. She regripped the steering wheel and forced the car to stay in her lane. It felt like the departing spirit took a shot at something in the car before it left.

"I claim the protection of Jesus on this car." Sophie covered that part just in case.

"Amen and amen." Hope said it like she was quoting someone. It made Sophie think of how much time Hope was spending talking to Detta.

The car steadied, and the back seat felt unoccupied. She noted now that she had been recalling the spirits that used to ride in her back seat. And thinking about Ross and his assignment. No coincidences in all that. "Thanks, Hope. We're an awesome team."

"And not just us. Anthony and Detta too."

"Yeah. I think of Detta as, like, home base. Along with my mother. But they're not gonna be in on the ministry team, as the plan goes."

"Well, you get to plan it. You're the captain of this here A-team." Hope tried a ghoulish voice. "And I am the one who taught Ra how to dance like an Egyptian." She bent her wrists at right angles, her pointy nose just about fitting the photos the pharaohs left on their ancient social media walls.

Sophie stared at Hope longer than she probably should have while driving. "Dang, girl. You *are* an old soul."

Nighttime Visitor

Hope lay on Sophie's couch. It was super soft. Embracing her through the fresh yellow sheets. Those fresh sheets were pale gray in the light from the street. She had pushed the top sheet off. The breeze from the window had died while she dozed. She closed her eyes to get back to sleep but flapped them back open at a hissing sound. A human hissing sound. She had heard people hissing. Seriously hissing only since she started helping folks with their demon problems.

"No. Go. Get outta here!" That shout came from Sophie's bedroom.

Swinging her legs and sitting up all in one move, Hope had to slow down while a dark wave blocked her vision. Probably just from sitting up too fast, not some kind of demon invader. Before she gathered her balance to stand up, she noted her angel girl was standing by Sophie's door with the angel Hope thought of as The Ranger. A guy right out of *Lord of the Rings*.

Her angels didn't usually say much, but not much was needed just now. Hope hustled to the bedroom door and knocked.

"Yeah." Sophie answered with a tone of regret, her voice descending from her earlier scratchy shouting. "Sorry about that."

When Hope stepped into the room, a faint glow was fading from the far corner. Though that departing thing had a glow, it gave her only dark feelings. Sophie's three angels were arrayed around the bed, the beautiful one and the big guy on opposite sides, and the warrior at the foot.

"What was that?"

Sophie blinked hard. "Just a dream."

Hope nodded to the far corner and then counted off the angels with her eyes. A total of eight in here now. "You sure?"

Apparently not so sure, Sophie did that same head count. "Huh. Did you see something?" She tilted her head back and glanced toward that corner.

"Like a blue glow, sort of. It was retreating when I came in."

"Oh. Maybe I was just *hoping* it was a dream." Sophie took a deep breath as she looked at her main guardian guy.

"Your enemies have been trying to get in, Sophie. Into your mind, into your life."

At these words from the biggest angel in the room, Sophie's mouth slowly opened.

Hope turned to stare at the big guy. She glanced at her security angel. The Ranger never said anything. Strong, silent type. Then she considered her main angel girl, trying to think of the last time she'd delivered a message like that. As soon as her thoughts turned there, that lithe, feminine angel fixed her with another one of those knowing stares. A nonverbal answer.

"Oh. I guess I haven't been listening."

Sophie looked at Hope, a furrow in her brow.

"My angel girl. She's lasering me with her eyes to explain why I haven't heard any messages like that from her lately."

"Oh. That's her over there by you? It's getting crowded in here."

Hope had figured out that she didn't see everything. And she knew Sophie was the same. She wasn't surprised that Sophie wasn't seeing the girl one as clearly as she was. It was Hope's guardian, after all.

When Sophie said that about it being crowded, the three unfamiliar angels took off, heading in the same direction as the eerie blue light.

"I guess they're going to make sure that thing stays gone."

Sophie glanced toward that corner again and spoke in a clearer voice. "Lord, send your angels to whoever is involved in this nightmare, if that's what you want."

"How does that work?" Hope was next to the bed, her knees against the mattress. Sophie's beautiful woman angel was right beside her.

"Can't say it always works. And I sure can't say how exactly it would work if it did. But I just had this idea I should do it once, and Detta said I should follow that kind of leading." She was sitting up a bit higher now, leaning her head and shoulders against the headboard. "I mean, God can say, No. Request denied, if I get it wrong."

"Your Father is glad to send blessings to whomever you choose. Even blessings that are not well received." Sophie's beautiful angel addressed both Sophie and Hope, turning from one to the other, then landing a smile on Hope.

"So I could do that too? Like, send an angel?"

"Send a blessing. God will decide how to deliver it."

"Oh. Sure, that makes sense." Hope was trying to think of more questions just so she could hear the angel answer them. "Am I ignoring my guardian angel too much?"

The woman angel looked at the more girlish angel, who was on Hope's other side. "She has messages to deliver. You should expect that. It doesn't hurt to ask."

"Like, God could always say no?"

Sophie's angel nodded deeply.

Hope turned to her guardian. "Any unread messages?"

The friendly angel smiled at her as if enjoying the joke. "You are here to watch Sophie's back in ways her other friends cannot, but she is also here to watch yours."

As with previous messages, Hope didn't feel like this was totally new information. Maybe more of a confirmation. Certainly a good reminder. A pretty authoritative reminder.

"So I'm here because of those enemies?"

"More than that." That was from Sophie, not an angel.

Hope wondered if Sophie was passing on a message she had heard from an angel, but that was probably just a distraction. The point was clear. Her assignment was pretty clear. And not a hard one to accept.

"Okay, girl. Does that mean I don't get any sleep?" She faked rubbing her eyes like a tired kid.

Sophie seemed to be checking with all five angels in the room. "We can sleep. We have a night guard."

Hope was sensing more angels arrayed around the building too. "Well, you're all welcome to the party." She glanced toward the ceiling. "But keep it down please. I need my beauty rest." She turned toward the door.

"Thanks, Hope. Thanks for running in here just now."

"Pretty brave, huh?"

"Like a mama bear guarding her cub."

"Raaarrr." Hope snorted a laugh and exited through the door.

There in the living room, she found two new angels. "For me?" She looked from the new arrivals to her angel girl.

That familiar angel answered. "For you and Sophie. And for the King."

"Oh."

Tell Me My Little Girl Isn't Crazy

Sophie was at her mother's house with Hope when she got a call from Julius, her church's senior pastor.

"Hello. What's going on?" Sophie wandered toward the back door.

"I need your help. Actually, a mother and her girl need your help to get some peace."

"Well, okay. What's happening?" She stepped out the back door onto the patio. It had rained as they ate supper. The whole backyard was wafting aromas that remained hidden in dust and leaf and flower during the dry times.

"The girl sees things. She says they're angels, but her mother is doubtful."

"Is this someone from our church?"

"No. They attend another church. I guess the mother doesn't dare tell the folks at her church what's going on with the girl. She thinks they'll accuse her of witchcraft or something."

Sophie expected he was exaggerating, making a sort of joke. Though maybe the joke had originated with that mother. But Sophie was following a current into memories of her own childhood, with priests and doctors telling her mother she was crazy, if not possessed.

"Sophie? Can you help us?"

"I will. I have to. This is what I do. And now it feels personal."

"Oh. That gave me a chill. I ... Well, yes. I can see how this would be familiar territory for you." Julius knew her history. She had spoken with him often in the past year, including preparations for ministering to several folks caught in spiritual snags and traps.

"Can I bring my friend Hope with me? She sees too. I think this will be helpful to her. And she can definitely help that girl."

"Oh, sure. I'll trust your judgment on all that."

When they ended the conversation, Sophie stayed on the patio, watching a patch of the last sunlight break through a glowing rip in the cloud cover. "I'll take this assignment, Father. And I'll look for some healing for myself in the middle of it, okay?"

Her female angel appeared in front of her, smiling as if excited by a piece of news she wasn't yet permitted to tell. Anticipation was written all over her. It fed Sophie's expectations enough to overwhelm her doubts.

"Who was that?" Back in the kitchen, Hope was closing the dishwasher, a towel draped over her bare shoulder. She wore a light pink sun top with spaghetti straps, probably the most feminine thing Sophie had ever seen her wear. Was that to make Sophie's mother more comfortable? Not exactly dressing up.

"My pastor, Julius. Though don't call him Pastor Julius."

"Huh. Okay."

"He needs your help again?" Sophie's mother was right next to Hope now.

"He needs *our* help." She raised her eyebrows at Hope.
"He said that?"
"I told him I needed you there. He didn't argue at all."
"What is it?" The way her mother leaned into the question hinted at some anxiety.
"A little girl." Sophie slipped a pair of unused measuring cups into the drawer as she spoke. "She sees things, but people at her church don't believe her. Or her mother thinks they wouldn't. I'm not sure exactly, but clearly the mother has her own doubts."
"The girl sees angels and things?" Sophie's mother took a plate out of Sophie's hand and slipped it into the dishwasher. The last of the dirty dishes.
"We'll see. Hope and I will see."
Mrs. Ramos looked at Hope for a second, as if just noticing something tattooed on her face. Words that needed an explanation. "This happened to you too, Hope?"
Sophie couldn't recall everything she had told her mother about Hope's childhood, but maybe her mother would ask even if she knew, to get Hope's perspective directly. Their guest had been pretty quiet all evening.
Hope nodded. She seemed to be studying Sophie's mom. She glanced at Sophie and then back at something just past Sophie's *madre*. "I bet that was hard with Sophie. Finding people to believe her. People willing to believe you."
Surprised at how Hope had turned the question around, Sophie focused on the space around her mother. As if rising from the kitchen sink, a small crowd hovered behind her mom. Spirits. Witnesses. Not a cloud. Not the good kind of witnesses. Accusing witnesses.

Her mother squinted just slightly at Hope, then tightened her mouth and eyes.

"I command this crowd of accusers to flee here right now in Jesus's name. Get off my mother and stay away." Sophie stepped toward the little chorus of interlopers and pointed at them.

"Yep." Hope added her agreement with one syllable.

Sophie's madre lowered her head, seemed to hold her breath. Then she wriggled her shoulders the way she did when her neck was tired from work. "Gracias, Señor. Thank you, God." She closed her eyes for a moment, then met Sophie's gaze.

"You were still carrying some of that weight. The accusations about what happened when I was little."

Hope took a big breath. "I kinda think you were, like, allowing it somehow, maybe." Her voice coasted just above a whisper, as if she was prepared to say she hadn't spoken at all.

But Sophie was with her, feeling the truth in what Hope said. "They must have been there all along."

"Spirits?" Sophie's mom turned to check behind her.

"I don't know. This is one of those times where I think folks would call them spirits if they were people from, like, an ancient culture. But these things sort of felt more subtle than that. Like they were ideas, memories, feelings. Some sort of echo of stuff that happened to you. To us." Sophie shrugged. She wasn't trying to start one of those speculative conversations she had with Detta or Julius or Anthony. She was just trying to erase that startled look in her mother's eyes. And erase some guilt of her own over not seeing those accusers before.

"They were pretty small and not very attached to you." Hope was helping with that guilt erasing. "So it kinda wasn't that big of a deal, I would guess." She looked at Sophie as if for confirmation.

Sophie didn't answer aloud. She just nodded and slid her arms around her mother. In that embrace, Sophie could sense a change. Something removed from between them. It was like no longer having a heavy necklace trapped between their breast bones. Or perhaps some less decorative type of chain.

Let Me Tell You What I See

They met in one of the kids' rooms at the church building. Sophie and Hope laughed at each other with their knees halfway up to their chins. They were sitting in little pastel plastic chairs. When Julius entered the room with a woman and child, Sophie seriously needed Hope to help her climb up off that low perch.

"Oh, I guess I'm too big for these chairs." Sophie arched her back a little.

"I'll get us some full-sized chairs." Julius paused before exiting. "Sophie, Hope, this is Marlene and Lily."

Lily was staring at the two strangers as if she was searching for an explanation.

At first, Sophie thought the girl was seeing the angels she and Hope brought with them. But the girl really seemed more focused on her and Hope. What had she been told about them?

"Pleased to meet you." Sophie offered the mother her hand, forcing herself to act like an adult. Not just a child too tall to sit in the little-kid chairs.

"Thank you. Thank you for agreeing to meet with us. Julius says you … you know about things like this. I … do believe … I want to believe … that …" Marlene was about the same height as Sophie. Her brunette hair was cut medium length with bangs straight across her forehead. She had the look of a startled animal standing still and hoping not to be seen by a predator.

Hope introduced herself, ignoring Marlene's truncated greeting. She stuffed her fingers into her jeans pockets after shaking hands.

When Julius returned, he held four regular-sized plastic stacking chairs. Sophie smiled toward him, pretending not to notice the strain he was putting on his skinny arms. Hope hustled to help Julius set the chairs down one at a time. Apparently Lily would do fine in a small chair.

The girl seemed to be about seven years old, maybe small for her age. Her eyes were large and active, constantly shifting to follow the movement of the adults in the room. Her eyes were the same brown as her mother's, but her hair was a mousy blonde.

Sophie was trying to watch Lily without scaring the kid. She tuned in to a glowing presence just over the girl's shoulder. As if made of living sapphire, an angel radiated rich light when Sophie focused on it. Whether she should describe the new angel as male or female paused her for a moment. Then she concluded that gender wasn't an important part of this particular spirit's identity. At least from what she could see.

When Sophie stopped examining the angel, she checked with Hope.

Hope met her eyes and nodded.

That gave Sophie an idea. "I think we can help you out, Marlene. Would you mind if we played a kind of game?" She glanced at Lily and then at Julius.

Marlene followed Sophie's bouncing gaze and perhaps agreed the way parents do when a child asks them to play with them. *Okay, if that's what you want.* "Of course. Tell me what to do."

"Why don't you and I go out of the room? Then I'll describe something I've seen in here. And Hope can stay here with Lily and describe what she's seeing."

"You prepared ...?"

"No. This idea just came to me. We didn't prepare this. I'm just confident that we both saw the same thing." It did occur to Sophie that Hope had described various spirits differently than she would have on a few occasions, but she decided she just had to trust God would sort that out in this instance.

"Uh, okay. Sure." Though the mother was answering, she did it in a questioning tone. She checked with Julius one more time before following Sophie out of the room.

Sophie just nodded once more to Hope before leading the way out the classroom door.

Hope was sitting on one of the grown-up chairs. She rested her eyes on Lily. "When I was your age, I figured out that it was best for me not to tell people what I could see sometimes."

Lily's eyes were wandering among the toys and art supplies arranged around the room. She nodded. Then she stopped and focused on Hope. "Wait. You mean—you mean you saw things that no one else could see? Was it, like, shiny people?"

"Yes. Exactly. Shiny people. And I found out I could call them angels."

Lily's eyes narrowed just briefly. Then she looked at Julius. Was she checking whether he was in on this joke?

He answered her unspoken question. "Hope is a good friend of Sophie's. They both see shiny angels. Most people don't see them even though the angels are really there. I don't see them, but I believe all kinds of things are around us even when we can't see them."

"Like the dark ones too?"

"You see dark ones too? Not just the shining ones?" Hope wasn't surprised, she just wondered why the girl hadn't mentioned those yet.

"Some of them shine dark."

Hope nodded. "I know what you mean. Well, right now I'm seeing a glowy green person just next to you. It seems to be staying close by your side."

"Not *it*, *he*."

"Okay. I wasn't sure." Hope looked more closely. "His eyes shine white, and he's about my height. He looks like he's ready to block anything that tries to get at you."

Lily squinted slightly again, taking in Hope's words, before turning to look at the green angel. Then she looked at the slender girl angel next to Hope. "When did that one get here?"

Hope only glanced at her beautiful guardian. "She's always with me, but I don't necessarily see her all the time. It might work like that for you too."

Lily locked onto Hope's angel and started to smile. "She's pretty. And I can tell she's nice."

"Yes. She's very nice. She protects me and brings me messages from God sometimes."

Sophie knocked at the door of the classroom. She turned the handle when Hope gestured a welcome with one hand.

Entering with Marlene, Sophie could sense a more buoyant atmosphere in the room. There were about a dozen angels visible now, including a couple Sophie hadn't seen before. She was familiar with Julius's usual lot as well as Hope's, of course.

Sophie addressed Lily. "Did Hope tell you what she saw?"

"Yes. And that pretty girl one just showed up too." Lily pointed to Hope's main guardian. She was apparently seeing only selectively, but that was normal even for a gifted seer like Sophie or Hope.

"Hope, tell Marlene what you see." Sophie and Hope made brief eye contact.

Hope didn't hesitate. She carefully described the green angel, obviously tuned in to the point of this exercise. Surely she was seeing a lot more than that one messenger.

As Hope detailed the medium-sized angel that stood right beside Lily now, Marlene's hand rose to her mouth. She nodded as she began to tear up, drops falling from her face as her nodding became more vigorous. Then she completely broke down and covered her face with both hands, weeping freely and trying to speak at the same time.

Lily stood from her small chair and walked across the rough little circle between the chairs. "It's okay, Mommy. You don't have to be sad. The glowing people are angels. They protect us and give us messages."

Sophie met Hope's smiling gaze. She prayed a silent prayer about Hope feeling the same cooling salve the little girl's words were spreading over her heart.

Assembling the Team

Anthony was looking for a text Delilah had sent him with a link to a restaurant she wanted to try. But before he tapped on her cute and smiley avatar, he noted other texts he had received recently. His mother was getting better at texting, almost second nature for her now. He expected he would have been getting more from her if Roddy wasn't in the picture.

There was a recent one in there from Roddy, who was recovering at home now. That guy was a gentleman with a capital G. He did a proper thank-you note in a text.

Then there were the messages from Sophie and Hope. Her California number was now recognized by his phone. They had a text group with Delilah. The four members of the team.

Shaking his head at the notion of him being part of that kind of team, he hesitated over a text from a still-unrecognized number. He hit that message.

"Anthony, great to meet you. I'm loving the church. Maybe we can hang out sometime. Will."

No abbreviations or misspellings. That was suspicious. Anthony snorted at himself for this odd thought. He tapped a couple times to connect Will's first name to that number in his contacts for future reference. Maybe they would hang out sometime. The new guy seemed bright and just nerdy enough for Anthony to relate. Although maybe nerdier about church than Anthony was.

He found the restaurant link and was perusing the menu when his mother texted.

"The bishop wants some help with a person struggling with spiritual oppression. Can you connect with him and see what your team can do for this person?"

His mama wasn't going to be in the middle of this one, just passing it along, apparently. With Roddy recovering and Mama talking about retiring from things, it was to be expected. Still, it was a big adjustment. Anthony paused over the degree to which he was taking his mother's place. That prompted a literal LOL. But he didn't text that to his mother.

"Do you have his cell number? Is that how I should contact him?"

Anthony had put his phone away and gone to his kitchen for water before the reply arrived. Maybe it took that long for his mama to figure out how to find that number and send it. He thanked his mother and decided to talk to Sophie before investigating the bishop's request. They hadn't really talked about doing ministry yet—the how and who and when of it.

In the meantime, he and Delilah could do other kinds of ministry that Sophie wouldn't need to be involved in. They were going to Roddy's house this evening to pray with his mama and someone else for the old guy's healing. Should that be part of the mission of Sophie's team in the future? Anthony was just doing this one because it was family, not because he had any kind of gift for healing people. Though maybe Delilah did. And Mama, of course.

By the time Delilah and Anthony arrived at Roddy's immaculately maintained single-story ranch house, Anthony owed Sophie a return text about their team meeting in person. She had shown no interest in the virtual meeting he proposed. Maybe in person made more sense for Sophie and Hope. Did the angels and stuff ever show up over video calls? Did he need to know the answer to that question? Maybe teammates should know that kind of thing about each other.

"Hello, young man." Roddy greeted them at the door. He still spoke out of one side of his mouth with a slur to certain words. "And pretty lady. Welcome. Thanks for coming over." He was propped between the doorknob and a knotty wooden cane.

Anthony wasn't surprised that Roddy wouldn't settle for the utilitarian metal cane they gave him at the hospital, but he was surprised to meet the old man at the door. Mama was standing behind her fiancé, smiling at the new arrivals. Past his mama was Gerty Wayans, a woman who used to be part of their church, but who had moved elsewhere. Clearly she had stayed in touch with his mama.

"Hey, everyone." He patted Roddy on the shoulder on the way to giving his mama a hug.

Delilah followed him down the greeting line.

"Mrs. Wayans. I haven't seen you in a long time."

"Oh, I was at a wedding this year at the church. I saw you there." She craned her neck upward to meet his gaze.

"Oh, yeah. I think I do remember that. Well, how are you doing?" Anthony stepped out of the way as Delilah gave Mrs. Wayans a hug.

Mrs. Wayans was probably a few years older than his mama. She was much smaller and a bit bent over, but she still moved nimbly, even if her face seemed to be collecting wrinkles by the hour. "I'm fit. And still full of faith. I was happy your mama invited me over to pray for Brother Harper."

"Roddy, please." He was still playing host even as he limped in slow motion.

Mama took Roddy's arm and walked with him to the tan leather couch opposite the picture window. Above the couch was a cityscape that looked to be about fifty years old, judging by the cars, buildings, and the clothes of the people it portrayed.

"My cousin painted that when she still lived around here." Roddy spoke more slowly since the stroke. "She's on the West Coast these days. Retired, mostly." He smiled appreciatively at the painting. "Isn't it interesting?"

Anthony nodded as he studied the colorful portrayal of a city street. A broad scene illuminated by streetlamps switching on early in the evening. The artist made the most of those lights. That was Anthony's amateur observation.

Delilah seemed equally fascinated, leaning on him and studying the painting from the middle of the room. "Did your cousin make a living from her art?" Delilah asked as she turned to follow Anthony across the room toward two big recliners in that same tan leather.

"She did. Probably still does to some extent. She's one of the heroes in our family for how she made her own way. Found a large measure of success."

"Nice of her to give you a painting." Anthony watched Mrs. Wayans lowering herself onto the couch cushion that had been left free by his mama and Roddy. She was looking at Roddy, not at the painting. The way she focused on their host reminded Anthony of Sophie. Was the old woman seeing something on Roddy?

"Actually, I paid for it. But she did give me a family discount. That was some thirty years ago." He was still sustaining that crooked smile.

"Well, that makes sense for her to sell it with her making a living from it." Delilah's response sounded generic, as if she was also paying more attention to Mrs. Wayans than the painting.

Anthony envied Sophie and Hope for their apparent mind link, but maybe he did have some of that with Delilah. He was pretty sure she was watching the same thing he was.

His mama brought the meeting to order. "Well, I know you all have other things to do, so let's get to prayin' for this old man. He needs some help with the full recovery we've been believing for."

"What old man are we here to pray for?" Roddy looked around the room with childish innocence in his eyes and a slanted smirk on his lips.

It was a funny response, but it gave Anthony a cold sensation. That fake confusion awoke a dread about his mama and her future husband getting old and losing some of their faculties. But he kept all that to himself and laughed politely at the joke.

Delilah covered for him, laughing more freely. She seemed a bit nervous around Roddy. She had little exposure to the old gent. His attendance at Anthony and Delilah's church was sparse, still loyal to his old church. Anthony hadn't heard how Roddy and his mama were planning to work that out when they got married.

Again, Anthony was drifting, but Mrs. Wayans looked like a watchdog that had spotted an intruder. She wasn't growling, however. Fortunately. Was she seeing a spirit?

Mama was looking at Mrs. Wayans now, across Roddy who still grinned gamely, perhaps in the afterglow of his latest joke. "You have something, Sister?"

"I believe I do. I believe there's a sort of gap left from the stroke. I believe we're supposed to pray for that gap to be filled. Like a brain connection. I can see it like it was etched into your head, Brother ... uh, Roddy."

Anthony was pretty sure he could see Roddy formulating a joke about something being etched on his head. At the same time, he wished he had serious insight like Mrs. Wayans for this healing process. And it occurred to him that something like what Mrs. Wayans just did would be helpful in their ministry sessions. Healing was often part of the spiritual battle. Seeing precisely what needed to be fixed was almost always key.

Gathering them all around Roddy, his mama took the lead in praying and then turned it over to Mrs. Wayans. Anthony and Delilah were standing there for support, no expectation they would lead out. Still, Anthony had no problem imagining Delilah piloting a session like this, or a mission with Sophie, for that matter.

When Mrs. Wayans prayed with her hand on Roddy's forehead, Anthony noticed Delilah wriggle next to him in perfect synch with a sensation running up his back, like a thousand tiny fingers tip-tapping every nerve.

"Whoa ha!" Roddy was apparently feeling it too. "Oh my Lord. Oh my Lord. Thank you, Lord. Thank you, Jesus." His voice seemed clearer and stronger.

Anthony's mama joined in with echoing expressions of gratitude. Those ramped in volume when Roddy stood from the couch. Not perfectly steady but not using that cane. And his smile seemed straighter now.

With that, a praise service broke out. Mrs. Wayans had a strong alto voice that drew them all in her wake as she began to sing one familiar old praise tune after another. Before long, Anthony and Delilah were on their knees with hands in the air.

Even as he sang along and soaked in the atmosphere, Anthony understood that their team would need to expand. He wanted more of this, and he knew Sophie wouldn't mind at all.

Catching his breath, him and Delilah getting off their knees, he received a message tossed from her eyes to his. Even with still lips she was speaking to him. And he knew Delilah was thinking the same thing he was about their new team with Sophie.

Having that mind link turned out to be as cool as he thought it would be.

Drawing a Crowd

Sophie had never been to Delilah's apartment before. Delilah shared a two-bedroom place with Zeezee Millar, a young woman who grew up in the same church as Delilah and Anthony. Sophie had never seen her at Detta's church. In fact, she had never seen Zeezee anywhere, as far as she knew. But she saw evidence of her existence in the apartment. For one thing, there was a room full of books.

After arriving with Hope, Sophie was checking out the place for clues about what she and her temporary roommate might look for if they got a more permanent place together. But Sophie kept her nosing about to a polite minimum.

Part of the advantage of meeting at Delilah's place was the chance to sample her cooking. She was a trailblazing amateur chef, according to Anthony. *When are you gonna marry her?* That was Sophie's internal response to his description. She kept that thought to herself, however.

It was Asian fusion short ribs tonight, with colorful stir-fried vegetables and wild rice. Even vegetarian pot stickers for an appetizer.

"I should never tell people in advance what I'm gonna cook." Sophie stood in the kitchen doorway watching Delilah pull the short ribs out of the oven.

Delilah glanced at her curiously.

Sophie snickered. "I need the option to totally ruin it and then order something else to replace it before anyone shows up."

Hope replied to Sophie's confession with deadpan seriousness. "Yeah. I would just order out to begin with. Kitchens are dangerous."

Sophie took note, given the possibility of rooming together long term. *Need to order a fire extinguisher.* She decided not to tell her phone assistant to put that on the shopping list right now.

Anthony was working on setting the table. "Are the drinking glasses up there?" He pointed to a cupboard next to the fridge.

"Yes, Anty. You can use those."

"I didn't know you had more than one set."

"Ah. Well, I still have a few things I haven't told you."

The big-eyed fright face Anthony made got a laugh from Sophie and Hope. Delilah probably didn't see his clowning but chuckled at her own little joke.

"I can hear your stomach growling." Hope was leaning on the opposite doorpost between the kitchen and the entryway. She closed one eye as if trying to see what might be possessing Sophie's belly.

"The chef is provoking me. Blame it on her." Sophie nodded toward Delilah.

Looking at their hostess, Sophie knew exactly why Anthony was attracted to her. And she knew exactly why she would never compete with women like Delilah. Too much work. Sophie didn't even aspire to be like her own mother when it came to housekeeping and beauty care. She shuddered to imagine how much time Delilah spent on her perfect curls and shiny skin.

Water glasses set on the table and filled, food on serving dishes, they all sat down in the dining area outside the kitchen. An open window nearby billowed a yellow curtain with a delicate flower pattern. That reminded Sophie of her enchilada debacle. But more compelling than the comparison between her cooking and Delilah's was a strong sensation saturating the place, a feeling of home that clearly included Hope as part of this family.

With a nod, Delilah prompted Anthony to say grace. They joined hands, and he kept it short and sweet. Sophie's growling gastro system appreciated his economy of words.

"Did your mother do international cuisines at all?" Hope just took one small rib before passing the plate.

Delilah shook her head. "No. She was pretty traditional when I was growing up. She's gotten a bit more adventuresome lately when she has time. She's still pretty busy with her work."

"I don't know what your mom *does* for work." Sophie stabbed a fried dumpling with her fork and dropped it on her plate. That was before she noticed a serving fork on the other side of that plate. She grimaced privately at the faux pas.

"She teaches at a community college now. She was a high school math teacher when I was a kid, but she got an advanced degree a few years ago and graduated to older students." Delilah's eyes drifted away from the table as she spoke of her mother.

Sophie was starting to notice how small the apartment felt just now. But the size of the place hadn't changed, of course. And it had seemed plenty big before. She pried her eyes away from the food to note a collection of glowing folk around the table. She found Hope staring at the expanding assembly as well. They were surrounded. Not a space between the dozen plus angels gathered close to the table.

"Wow. I hope there's more food in the kitchen." Hope rotated her head slowly around the array of visiting messengers.

Instead of staring at the colorful crowd, Anthony and Delilah were staring at Hope and Sophie. Delilah seemed to be holding her breath, or maybe panting in tiny puffs like some weird birthing ritual.

"Lots of angels." Sophie wasn't sure she needed to provide that commentary for Delilah, but Anthony's face was morphing through degrees of confusion toward stages of annoyance. She looked at her main guardian. "Is it okay if we just go ahead and eat?"

Hope murmured, "This isn't a fasting intervention or something?"

Sophie's guardian nodded and gestured toward the table with a pleasant look on his face. No hint of wanting to join the meal, much to everyone's relief, certainly. How much did angels eat? Sophie had often wondered about the part in the New Testament that said people sometimes hosted angels unawares.

The angel choir backed off a bit and refrained from singing altogether, but Sophie guessed the other humans in the room were rushing the meal a bit. She couldn't help anticipating something important in the meeting part of their evening. The angels had kind of given that away.

Dessert of tiny chocolate lava cakes concluded the meal. Hope had eaten small portions of meat, rice, and veggies, but she snatched two of the little cakes. Still, Sophie could see her young friend keeping an eye on the angel gang, which still seemed to be adding to its membership.

"Is this making you nervous?" Hope sounded nervous as she and Sophie wound their way through the gathered throng into the living room.

"I've never seen anything like it outside of a really intense deliverance session. At least not so many good angels."

"Yeah. I went to a party once that was this crowded with the other kind." Hope folded her bare legs under her, pretzel style, as Delilah and Anthony laughed about something in the kitchen.

"This is one of those times when I'm not sure if I envy the folks who can't see all this." Sophie waited for an unfamiliar angel to move out of the way and took a seat in a cushy chair that surprised her when it rocked. Her jumpy response started Hope laughing.

Anthony wiped his hands on the front of his jeans as he entered the room, presumably performing the final cleanup after putting dishes in the dishwasher.

As usual, Delilah was the most delightfully dressed of them all, wearing white capri slacks and a crepe-textured pink blouse that reached nearly to her knees. A white T-shirt peeked out of her loosely buttoned blouse. This was one of those moments when Sophie told herself to admire Delilah and not to envy her. Admire. Admire.

"Do we still have a capacity crowd of angels?" Delilah was setting down a tea tray. Never done being a hostess, obviously.

Sophie didn't recall either her or Hope saying capacity crowd, but it was a fitting description. "Do you sense it?"

"I sense something. It feels like when you take in a breath just before something big is supposed to happen." Delilah stood up straight now, next to the painted black coffee table.

"Does it feel weird that there are four of us here and we all pay rent on separate apartments? I mean ..." Hope blinked rapidly for a minute.

Sophie wondered if the lava cakes contained some kind of truth serum. Hope's comment felt like an intimate thought that should have kept its clothes on for a while longer.

Anthony and Delilah looked at each other. Anthony grinned. "Well, we won't be living in separate apartments for much longer."

"We?" Sophie perked up.

"We who?" Hope wasn't far behind.

He was still looking at Delilah. "We're not announcing it to everyone yet, but we thought you two should know, if we're really gonna form a serious ministry team."

"What? You're getting married?" As soon as Sophie said it, more than a dozen angels started jumping and dancing around the apartment. Others clapped and laughed.

"What the—" Hope recoiled and stared at the impromptu angel party.

"What what?" Anthony curled his eyebrows and tried to follow Hope's gaze.

Sophie laughed at the sight of the dancing angels and also at the silliness of the humans in the house. As inarticulate as they had all become, the message was still clear. Anthony and Delilah were forming a serious team of their own. And they wanted Sophie to be one of the first to know.

Down to Business

Hope suspected Sophie had never seen an angel celebration like that one. She wondered if Detta would know what to do. What it was about. Maybe all the laughing and crying the four humans did was the best response. But by the time they were ready to work on their original agenda, Hope was weary and glad to let others do the talking.

To her, it seemed like Delilah was the most natural leader in the group. It was like Sophie was the rock star, or the best player on the team. But Sophie seemed fine with letting others handle some of the arrangements or logistics or whatever. Not like a group administrator exactly, but someone with more big-picture vision, maybe.

Hope knew it was often hard to see the whole thing that was happening in the room if you focused on what the angels were doing, but she had been thinking she could obsess over that part while Sophie stepped back and did strategy. Hope could see Delilah and Sophie working together in all kinds of situations, mostly because neither one seemed like she wanted to do the other one's job. That probably applied to ministry as much as it did to hostessing.

Anthony and Delilah were getting married. Probably in the spring, they said.

"No need to butt into Mama's wedding plans." Anthony was settled on the couch, Delilah close beside him.

"Not a double wedding?" Sophie was probably teasing about that.

Delilah just shook her head, not dignifying Sophie's joke.

"So, it is good you guys told us. It feels like you're really taking this ministry seriously." Sophie turned toward Hope. "But I'm kinda curious what made *you* say that thing about it being weird that we all have our own apartments."

Hope had been holding out for not having to explain that part. "I have no idea why I said it. I was assuming I would have to apologize and maybe leave early after I did."

Delilah gave Hope a sort of three-quarters scrutiny that might have been intended to convince. She chuckled a little. "No. It feels to me like it was discernment, a kind of discernment that's not just seeing angels and demons."

"What are you saying? That I have other superpowers?"

"I think she's right. It was like a preview of what we should talk about." Sophie looked as tired as Hope felt. Maybe they wouldn't accomplish much tonight—unless they counted this Hope-evaluation session.

"Okay. So, what? Does that mean whenever I have these random thoughts crash through my head, that's really God talking to me?"

"Not if those thoughts are about fish tacos." Anthony grinned big.

"Oh, I don't know, I've heard of stranger things God has told people." Delilah was smiling at Anthony's joke, but she had no problem making a serious point out of one of his wisecracks.

"And you gotta admit, what you said about individual apartments was both totally random and totally on the point." Leaning her head back on the rocking chair, Sophie didn't seem inclined to close some kind of deal with Hope. She just let her point rest where it lay.

"Speaking of new superpowers, Delilah and I saw a woman give this really spot-on word to Roddy when he was healed of some of the stroke damage this week."

Detta had told Hope and Sophie about that healing. And she had mentioned another church lady who was a big part of it.

Delilah followed Anthony's opening. "And we both thought that kind of word of knowledge about healing would be really helpful in lots of ministry settings."

"So, do we start recruiting?" Sophie didn't seem to require convincing or explaining, though Hope felt a little lost.

"Seriously, I don't think it's so much that we should start recruiting. Just that there are some other gifts that could be helpful, and we should look out for them in people. Worship leading would be useful." Anthony looked at Delilah. "She has a great voice and can play guitar, but I'm not thinking that should be her focus in most sessions."

Sophie smiled and breathed a laugh through her nose. "You two have really been thinking about this." Her eyes sparkled with gratitude and fascination.

Delilah fidgeted in her seat. "It's a big deal for us, Sophie. It answers this huge question we've had since we started dating. It's like we always felt we were called to some kind of mission together. Something important. And it feels so right that the mission is supporting you. Working with you." She smiled a little shyly, maybe feeling vulnerable for her enthusiasm. Hope would feel bashful if she shared that freely.

"Yeah, but we're a team. Not just you supporting me. Supporting each other." Sophie sat up straighter. "And I agree—we need some other skills on this team. One thing I was thinking of was a social worker or therapist who can see things from that angle."

Anthony and Delilah did another one of those couple mirror turns. If Hope didn't like the two of them so much, that could get annoying. But her meta annoyance was interrupted by the sound of a key in the lock and the front door opening.

Somehow the shock of another person entering the room, an actual human being who required a key, seemed to revive the strangeness of Hope's comment about apartments. Five of them now. Could someone else join their team? That was the shape of the thought that held her suspended while a smallish woman with purple plastic-rimmed glasses and her hair in tight braids gently trod down the hall toward them. She had apparently taken her shoes off as soon as she entered.

They were all looking at her when she peered into the living room, perhaps on her way to that other bedroom, the one with the books.

"Zeezee." Delilah broke the mirror pose and stood from the couch. "Zeezee, come meet my friends."

Zeezee raised one small hand in a static wave as she followed the tidal draw of Delilah's invitation. "Hello, everyone. Hi, Anthony. Sorry to interrupt."

"No problem." Sophie appeared about to say something more but had apparently pocketed the words for the moment.

That was when Hope rewound to the discussion about needing other skills, including maybe a therapist or social worker. "You wouldn't happen to be a therapist, would you?"

Hope had forgotten to say hello. She would try to fix that soon. "Or a social worker?"

"Uh, yes, I am. Why do you ask?"

Everyone laughed. Except Zeezee, of course. She looked at Delilah, who was laughing the hardest.

"Sorry, girl. You just walked in at exactly the right time. Or maybe the wrong time. You can decide. We were just saying how we should probably have a therapist or social worker be part of our ministry team."

"And do you know a good worship leader?" Hope figured she would just keep up the randomness until someone told her to stop.

"Nathan is a worship leader." Zeezee was scanning the room under crouching eyebrows, either trying to figure out the joke or wondering if she had stumbled into the twilight zone.

Hope was trying to figure out if she had seen the two angels that were standing behind Zeezee before she entered the apartment. And she was getting caught up in a pretty good feeling about some guy named Nathan. She did, however, restrain herself from saying anything about that.

Tryouts for the Team

Sophie had faked socking Anthony in the shoulder when he called this a team tryout. But looking across the room at Zeezee and some guy named Will, it kinda felt like Anthony wasn't kidding.

Anthony was obviously being serious at the moment. He was seated in front of a guy named Sean, a light-skinned guy with a tight Afro who wouldn't look squarely at either Anthony or Delilah. Intimidated was the impression Sophie was getting. More than that, she was seeing a spirit with long arms pulling at Sean's shoulders from behind, as if trying to hold him back. Hold him back from what?

She looked at Hope, who sat to her right, as close to Sophie as Delilah was on the other side.

Hope raised an index finger from her folded hands, pointing covertly at Will and scrunching her eyebrows.

Sophie sent a glance toward that other strange guy in the room. Strange, as in unknown to her.

Behind her was the third guy she hadn't met before their prep session. He was an assistant pastor of a church they were sitting in. She hadn't expected the bishop himself to be there. Really, she had hoped he *wouldn't* be there. And, as she expected, Joseph, the assistant, seemed content to sit back and observe.

Her glance at Will was aimed past Zeezee, who was seated on the far side of the little semicircle the team formed in front of Sean. It was Sophie's team plus Zeezee and Will. But, compared to Will, Zeezee felt like she was already one of them.

Will was not quite as light skinned as Sean. His Afro was on the natural side, a couple of inches worth. He was probably younger than Sophie and older than Hope. But he seemed ambiguous in a lot of ways. He was here because he was a friend of Sean's, and the assistant pastor had vouched for him. Will agreed to only observe and not intervene. Still, he made Sophie a little uncomfortable.

Delilah interrupted Sophie's distraction with a direct question. "What are you seeing, Soph?"

"A spirit holding his shoulders back. It looks ... familiar. I mean, like it's related to him. Maybe a family spirit."

Hope was nodding vigorously. "Yeah. Family."

As soon as Hope spoke, Sean let out a howl that froze Sophie's blood. She paused over the apparent delay between what she said and the howl. Who knew why the disruptive spirit reacted to Hope when Sophie said the same thing? Maybe it was the one-two combination that provoked it.

Anthony commanded the family spirit to be quiet and let go of Sean. Every time Anthony said the name of Jesus, Sean winced. Will, just off to the side, was wincing too. Maybe he was just being sympathetic to his friend's apparent suffering.

Apparent suffering. Sophie was watching that spirit. It hadn't moved much. Why the howling?

Hope leaned in close. "I don't feel good about that Will guy. I don't see anything on him, but that seems wrong. He isn't being real. Or something." She gave an apologetic shrug.

Sophie caught Will watching her and Hope instead of watching the little verbal struggle between Anthony and Sean. She let that odd observation go to the back burner when Delilah took over from Anthony.

"I sense that you're holding onto a resentment about the abuse, Sean. Like you have a right to hate this person. You're going to need to let go of that right if you wanna get free." Delilah spoke those words with the kind of certainty she probably applied to her work in the lab. No surrender of resentment meant no freedom. An irrefutable equation.

Sean started speaking in an unfamiliar language.

Anthony told him to stop it.

Hope affirmed that shutdown with a vigorous nod.

Glancing over her shoulder, Sophie made eye contact with the assistant pastor. He did one of those blinks that said, I see what's going on. Go ahead and do what you know to do. At least that was how Sophie read his placid response.

She had permission to shut this down. She had authority. But she wanted Delilah and Anthony to come to the same conclusion first. Was that selfish? Not wanting to be the bad guy who was saying Sean wasn't ready for this? She sensed he wasn't really committed to freedom yet.

Delilah was explaining that very problem to the quivering guy in the hot seat right then. Sophie could tell Delilah was near the cutoff point as well.

Hope seemed distracted, like she was just done. Ready to move on.

To her left, Sophie once again caught Will watching her. He averted his eyes as soon as she looked at him. This was wrong. Something about this was wrong. She reached a hand to touch Delilah, landing her fingers exactly where one of Delilah's regular angels was touching her back.

Not even turning to look, Delilah responded to Sophie's prompt. "I think we should take a break for a bit. Let's see what we want to accomplish here tonight now that we know some of what's behind this trouble."

Delilah was probably better suited to the lead chair than Sophie because of how easily she shifted into diplomatic language like that.

A few of them took bathroom breaks. Sophie waited to call a huddle until her team members all returned, and while Sean and Will were still out of the room. "I don't feel like he's ready. I think he needs some more counseling or something. He's not very open, as far as I can tell." She looked at the others, any of whom might have a better sense of Sean's emotional state than her.

"I agree." Delilah nodded, and others joined her.

Except Zeezee. "I don't know how you normally do this, but it doesn't seem to me like time to give up yet. He may just need a break and another try at it. He clearly needs some kind of help."

Sophie quickly checked her watch. They had only been meeting for fifty-five minutes so far. She was willing to keep pushing if anyone else thought it might be worth it. It did occur to her that continuing would be valuable for some of her less experienced teammates. Which included all her teammates.

Entering the cool room in the church basement, Sean's lowered eyes and tight lips looked penitent to Sophie, though she couldn't tell exactly what he was repenting about. Had Will talked him into something? Will entered the room right behind Sean. That might be a friend's role in this situation. Encouragement to continue and to cooperate.

"Ready to start again? Sophie signaled her decision to keep going with that question directed at Sean. In reality, he also had to decide.

"Yeah. Yes. Let's try again." He mumbled the words as if through swollen lips. His eyes actually were red and swollen, but not his lips.

When she checked for Hope's reaction, the person who appeared to be the most done with this session, Sophie found her staring at Will. Hope covered her mouth and spoke. "No angels with him. You notice?"

Sophie had been checking for dark angels, but she hadn't begun to worry that Will didn't seem to bring any good ones with him either. Her next furtive glance at Will, however, revealed a white wing rising over his shoulder before fading from view.

That view of an angel, light or dark, was odd. The phenomenon of seeing shining persons that most of the world could not see was entirely odd, of course. But that particular appearance of a shining wing was uniquely strange, and its sudden disappearance stranger still. Before Sophie could check if Hope had seen it, Sean pulled her attention back.

"I don't want it. Don't touch me. I don't want to have anything to do with this. This is wrong."

"He's reliving the trauma." Zeezee had pulled her chair closer to Delilah where she could have a more direct view of Sean's face.

It certainly appeared that Sean was reliving a trauma, but that didn't fully explain the pair of spirits that were flashing in and out behind him. One was pale blue, almost white, the other dark red, almost black. They switched places, and each phased through a narrow spectrum of colors when they appeared.

"Deception," Hope whispered to Sophie.

Delilah was nodding, but not looking at Hope. She commanded the spirit of deception to shut down and stop interfering.

Sophie whispered that there were two of them, like evil twins.

The phrase evil twins seemed to raise a small smirk on Anthony's cheek. He wiped it off immediately, however.

"There's a bad link between Will and Sean. He's not here to help." Hope spoke low with her hand over her mouth again.

Sean couldn't have heard, but immediately a huge voice boomed out of him, and a giant black form overwhelmed him. "You're just kids playing games. You have no power! You have no authority!" That voice filled the room with palpable terror.

Sean was deep red now. The spirit controlling him was looming larger and larger.

Anthony was shaking.

Delilah was checking with Hope and Sophie.

"We're shutting this down. This is not what we came here for. There's some serious deception behind this whole evening. This is not what it appears to be." Sophie stood up, ready to march out of the room if necessary. She felt like she had been lured in here, and it was clearly a trap.

Hope was standing next to her. She whispered a name in Sophie's ear.

Sophie used that name, a proper name. Not a descriptive name. The specific name of the spirit.

At the revelation of its name, that huge black beast disappeared. Simply going invisible. The deception spirits remained, still flashing in and out of view.

"Do you have something you want to tell us, Sean?" Delilah was still the diplomat.

Zeezee was quivering in her chair when Sophie turned to check on her. If this was a team tryout, one of the candidates was probably getting cut. But that was something to think about later.

Sean stuttered and then just lowered his head and wrapped his arms over his chest.

"It's okay, buddy. This is stressful. It's a lot to deal with." Will rose from his chair and stepped up next to Sean. His tone would have fit a kindergarten teacher soothing a five-year-old. There was something about Will. Something missing. Something hidden. Something he wasn't telling them.

"I have to go." Zeezee had her purse and notebook in hand. She wasn't making eye contact with anyone.

"Delilah, you better go with her." Sophie raised her eyebrows at Delilah, who didn't need any convincing.

Joseph, the assistant pastor, stepped into the place abandoned by Zeezee. "Okay, well ... we'll talk and see where we wanna go from here." He was a solid guy and didn't appear to be shaken emotionally any more than he looked shakable physically.

Anthony was quietly nodding. His eyes were landing on Will and then jumping off. The calculating process apparent on his face reminded Sophie that Anthony had met Will first.

He had sort of vouched for him. Was he reconsidering that? Exactly what did he know about this guy?

She rested a hand on Anthony's shoulder for a few seconds before starting her goodbyes and thank-yous.

"We'll be in touch," Joseph said as she shook his hand.

Sophie bumped shoulders with Hope and offered a small encouraging grin. She only paused for a minute to explain to Sean that they really had to stop here. Explaining without explaining. She still didn't know exactly what had happened. And she surely didn't know what role Sean or Will played in it.

"Outta here." Hope rasped that into Sophie's ear as they beat a quick retreat.

So, What Was That?

They met in Delilah's apartment, mostly to check in with Zeezee, whom Delilah and Anthony had driven home. Sophie expected she owed the young social worker an apology. Though she also felt like someone else owed her an explanation, if not an apology.

No grand apologies were exchanged as they first settled in. The conversations were small and insignificant until they were all seated around the living room.

"I'm—" Anthony stopped when Sophie raised a hand.

"Let's pray for a while and settle down a bit before we say anything." She looked around for approval.

"Sounds like a great idea." Delilah set her mouth in a straight line, just short of a grin, then let out a large sigh through her nose.

Anthony did smile. Maybe he was recognizing his mother's influence on Sophie. Certainly Detta had significantly influenced most of the people gathered here.

Sophie started them out, and everyone joined in the group prayer with at least a sentence or two.

Hope's contribution was, "I'm glad you're in charge at times like this, God, 'cause I'm totally depending on you."

Couldn't have said it better. Sophie smiled all around the circle after saying the amen. Then she asked the key question. The obvious question. "Was it a setup?"

Hope barked her answer. "Of course it was. But by who? And why?"

"A setup?" Zeezee hadn't said much during the prayer. She was acting like a girl coming down with the flu.

"That was a very high-level spirit that interrupted us. We weren't told anything that would have implied Sean or Will were involved in occult activity. So that makes it feel like they blindsided us. Like it was probably a setup." Sophie wondered if this was time for her to apologize but waited for others to respond first.

"I wasn't sure about Will. And Sean was completely unknown to me." Anthony shook his head and twisted his lips.

"I should have said something during the interview session." Delilah gave another sigh, this one less relaxing, more frustrated. "I knew there was something off."

"Me too." Hope swallowed hard. "Can I get some water? Anyone else want some?" She stood and aimed her bare toes toward the kitchen. She shook her plastic water bottle, which hardly made a sound.

"Trip to the waterhole." Anthony stood up, lifting his black metal bottle from the coffee table.

Sophie led the laughter, which camouflaged most of Delilah's apologies about not taking care of them all.

Hope led the way to the kitchen where a water filter was attached to the tap.

While waiting in the close knot of people in the kitchen, Zeezee asked another question over the sound of the faucet. "Has anything like that ever happened to you before?" She was looking *up* at Sophie, which reinforced the little-girl impression she was giving off.

Sophie wasn't used to being the taller one. "It has happened a few times where some high-level spirit like that interrupts. But usually we have some warning that the people we're meeting with have been involved in contacting, or cooperating with, occult spirits."

"Oh." Zeezee was visibly deflated. "I was hoping you would say that sorta thing had never happened before." Her voice barely rose above a mumble.

"Sorry to interrupt. Anyone hungry? Cheese and crackers? Fruit? A veggie tray?" Delilah lingered behind in the kitchen as others from the herd began migrating back to the living room. Her wide grin was tipped to the side. An apology? Irony?

"Got any stir-fried tofu?" Hope said it in a goofy voice.

Zeezee was headed to her seat. She paused and blinked vigorously. "Are you guys really kidding around? I mean, aren't you totally freaked out? Are you ... in shock?"

Sophie guessed Zeezee was in shock, given her departure from the social-worker decorum she had maintained during their earlier meetings. A new question occurred to her as she evaluated the baffled look on Zeezee's face. "Do you believe that spirits are real, Zeezee? Did you believe it before today?" She didn't think that sounded like an accusation.

Her big eyes even bigger and her eyebrows high, Zeezee shrugged. "I guess I was thinking—before—that it was sort of up for interpretation. You know? You might call it a spirit. I might call it ... psychosis."

Delilah stuck her head out of the kitchen. "That was before. What about now?"

Shaking her head, Zeezee just stared at her roomie. No words.

"Hmm. Do you know a therapist or social worker who might be more comfortable with spiritual things like that, though?" Hope snapped the lid onto her water bottle and settled it into her lap, legs pretzeled under her again.

Sophie wasn't ready to pursue that angle yet, but she didn't feel like contradicting Hope either. Then it occurred to her that this might be another of those instincts Hope was experimenting with lately.

Zeezee nodded, her brow tight, as if trying to remember. "There was a guy. He was an intern a few years ago at the agency where I work. He told a couple wild stories about some voodoo things where he grew up in Brazil. He was serious about it. He might ..."

"He's a therapist? Does he live around here?" Sophie set her water bottle down and stretched her legs out, her feet venturing under the coffee table.

"His name is Carlos. Yeah. I think he works in a child welfare agency in the suburbs now. I'm pretty sure. I saw him at a conference this year."

"It would be nice to get another guy involved." Anthony cast his eyes around the room. He was the only man currently on the team.

"Feeling outnumbered, Anthony?"

He smiled but turned serious quickly. "Really I was feeling outgunned at the church. I don't know about outnumbered, but I don't wanna get caught off guard like that again."

Sophie took a deep breath. "One good takeaway I'm seeing is how united we are in our reaction. That makes me more confident this team can work. We're generally on the same page. And we understand each other." She surveyed her crew. "We trust each other. So I'm not discouraged about what happened."

"Yeah, but are you wondering if it was on purpose?" Anthony leaned toward Sophie, his lips puckering.

"Uh-huh. There is that. Not so encouraging." She watched Delilah carry a tray in from the kitchen. No stir-fried tofu, but grapes, cheese, and crackers. "We all interviewed Sean. I wonder if we were interviewing the wrong guy. At least the wrong guy if we wanted to check for the real agenda of that session."

"It is possible that Sean was sincere. He seemed sincere to me. He might be manipulated by Will or by someone else." Zeezee was first to collect a snack from the tray, arranging it neatly on a small plate that Delilah had included.

Sophie was glad to hear Zeezee's observation, if only to affirm that she wasn't totally traumatized. "I'll know better next time to interview anyone who's gonna be present in a session. That's where I made the mistake."

"He was hiding stuff, though, so just interviewing Will might not have prepped us for that monster showing up." Hope bobbled her head. "But I would have known better if we met him before we started. There was something not so helpful about that guy." She crunched a cracker and caught crumbs with her hand before vacuuming them with her lips.

"Yeah. I guess Joseph was convinced that Will would be helpful. Hard to tell if Sean agreed with that assessment. Will was inserted too late in the game." Anthony scratched his head and rubbed his hand over his hair, recently cropped very short. Maybe a summer thing. He looked good no matter how he wore his hair.

Sophie tried to remember photos she had seen of his father. A handsome man with sharper features than Detta. But she needed to focus on a demon ambush now and not Anthony's genetics. "It's hard to guess what the motivation was for that. Could have been a mix of things, not really aimed at messing with us. But, I gotta admit, that's my first instinct. Someone is trying to mess with us just as we get started." She sighed. "It felt like Will was studying me."

"But who would do that?" Hope said it with a note of paranoid horror. She sounded like she was pretending to be the suspenseful narrator, but Sophie guessed she was asking a real question.

Shrugging, Sophie leaned way forward and reached for some cheese to replenish her plate. "I'm not generally a conspiracy-theory girl, but when you deal with these demons enough, you realize there really is a worldwide conspiracy. So who knows what humans are taking part in this one."

"Okay. Well, I can try to contact Carlos. I think he'll get what you guys are doing. He was pretty … He was unusual." Zeezee seemed less in shock now, but still deflated.

"Weird. I think the word you're looking for, Zeezee, is weird." Hope said that with a mouthful of cheese or grapes or both.

Zeezee laughed almost silently.

Watching the Pros in Action

While they waited for word from Zeezee about her colleague, Carlos, Hope joined Sophie and Delilah at a session run by the therapist Sophie had worked with before, Jonathan Chalmers. And there was a church lady there called Sister Ellen. Hope refrained from addressing her by name to avoid having to decide if she was willing to call her Sister Ellen.

Delilah had no issues. "Pleased to meet you, Sister. I've heard so many good things about this team. I'm so glad to learn from you all."

"Well, we trust Sophie entirely. And I have a good feeling about you." Ellen held on to Delilah's hand longer than necessary for a normal handshake.

No fist bumps here. Hope and Sophie and Anthony still did fist bumps. It was a carved-in habit. But Anthony wasn't here this afternoon, a Saturday when he had to work on some network crisis for his job.

Mostly the others were here to learn. Delilah wouldn't be taking the lead seat this time. Hope was just backup for Sophie. And Sophie was in her usual role—the girl who sees angels. Or the old lady who still sees angels, as Hope liked to call her. Sophie had burned through almost half her thirties by now. What a mind bomb that was.

They were gathered to minister to a young teenage girl. Her mom sat off to one side with red eyes and nose, as if just recovering from a good cry. The only other person in the room was this really big African American guy who Sophie knew and Jonathan obviously trusted. He looked like a bouncer. His name was Raymond. No one dared call him Ray, apparently. That was Hope's impression, at least.

The location was a carpeted room with only a few institutional stacking chairs in it, plus one more comfy armchair occupied by Cindy, the young girl. This was a shared meeting room in the building where Jonathan had his counseling office. He shared the suite with a few other therapists. That set Hope wondering if she might like to see one of them on a professional basis sometime.

A small chorus line of spirits drew her out of that speculation. "What do you make of those?" She nudged Sophie and raised a hand approximately toward the half dozen or so young female-looking spirits. They were squished against each other in such a way that seemed to crowd out one and then another. Out of sight, at least.

As if she didn't see them clearly at first, Sophie paused to consider the odd collection. "I'll tell Jonathan and Ellen and see what they think."

Hope thought the ones she was seeing were spirits that should be shown the door. But they weren't the ghoulish, nasty kind. They seemed clearly linked to the girl, even related to her. That was all she was getting. Or maybe guessing. Presumably Jonathan and Ellen wouldn't just be guessing.

"What are you seeing, Sophie?" Jonathan had finished opening prayers and some introductions, then turned to Sophie as if that was next on the usual agenda.

"Well, Hope pointed out a collection of female-looking spirits that all remind me of young girls around Cindy's age. They look like they're waiting for something."

As soon as she finished speaking, the crowd of girl spirits shuffled around again like kids trying not to be seen. Or trying not to be picked by a team captain they didn't like. No wailing and screaming. No threats or fangs.

"Hope?" Jonathan surprised her by addressing her directly.

"Um, I'm thinking they don't wanna be here. But maybe it's more that they don't wanna be visible. Like someone else has pushed them forward to take the rap."

Instantly, the six or seven reluctant girl spirits scattered, and a big witchy thing with flashing eyes and a skeletal face barged in. And the game was on.

After some back and forth, Sister Ellen explained that the young girl ones were probably kept around to help Cindy not freak out and lose her mind entirely. They worked for that witchy one, who was likely working for another one. Or something like that. Hope missed some of the subtleties of what Ellen said. She was preoccupied by the feeling that the witchy spirit was lunging at her, pushing some kind of vicious energy toward her.

That was when Hope recalled her resolve to keep praying throughout the session, as a sort of experiment. Suddenly it didn't feel like just an experiment. "Okay, Jesus, this is on you. You got me into this. You can take what that thing is aiming at me." It wasn't like prayers she had heard from most people, maybe any people, but she expected Jesus understood.

"Oh, Lord. Thank you, Jesus." Meanwhile, Delilah was doing her Detta imitation.

Then Hope caught a glimpse of something. Only a glimpse. It was a man. Not an angel. But he wasn't a regular human like Hope or the other people in the room. A good guy. A really good guy. That was her impression. But who?

She edged toward the possibility that he was the person she had just been praying to. She shivered hard.

Hope really wanted to stop right there and do some interviews. Did Delilah see that guy? Did she think that guy was Jesus? That would explain her sudden switch to Detta mode. Probably it was just the usual church-lady mode for their particular church. But Hope was digressing. She took a deep breath and finally got back to praying. "Thanks for helping. And even for showing up, if that's what you just did. Go for it, is what I say, Jesus."

Sophie glanced over at Hope. She was sitting close enough that she probably heard some of those rough-draft prayers. Sophie was sitting forward in her chair like she was prepared to jump in and wrestle that wicked-witch spirit.

Hope was leaning back. Not interested in wrestling. Not this time.

When she settled down enough to pay attention to the other people in the room, Hope allowed her fascination with this team to build. Jonathan and Ellen were taking turns talking to Cindy and commanding the spirits to get lost. They were focused on that witchy one, which they just called the witchcraft spirit. More dignified than Hope's label. Not that the thing deserved any dignity. It had apparently been part of the ordeal that included physical abuse against Cindy when she was ten years old.

Watching Jonathan and Ellen practically dance a waltz together was pretty inspiring. Hope could tell that Delilah was tuned in to this too. Maybe she was picturing her and Anthony being like that. Hope was pretty sure Jonathan and Ellen weren't a couple. She seemed quite a bit older than him. And they didn't give off any couple vibes.

Delilah, on the other hand, was giving off a serious adoration vibe. But Hope wasn't worried. She would love to work with Anthony and Delilah if they could be like Jonathan and Ellen. Brother Jonathan and Sister Ellen. Maybe the reason Sophie needed her own team was so they could do it without the churchy feel. No sistering and brothering among them. Fist bumps instead.

Again, Hope remembered to keep praying. She also forced herself to keep monitoring that witchcraft spirit as it tried to twist itself inside out before tossing more of those frightened girl spirits under the bus. Even as she prayed, Hope was thinking this was what it looked like when pros did this work. And that further clarified why Sophie needed support. She needed serious people around her, people willing to focus on this ministry and do it with credibility and confidence.

The big question now was whether Hope could really be part of that. Maybe she could. Especially if they did a sort of next-generation version of what Jonathan and Ellen did. And as long as Jesus always showed up, in one way or another.

Not Your Usual Interview

Anthony sat down on the concrete planter wall that led toward the entrance of a modern building with tall glass doors and windows. His left shoe was untied.

Sophie and Delilah stopped and waited.

Hope didn't stop until she reached the revolving doors, where she must have noticed she was alone. She seemed to be watching something through the glass, though Anthony couldn't see anything from where he sat.

"What was the last part of that session? I mean, how did it end?" He was more than a little jealous of Delilah and the others after hearing them go on about seeing Jonathan and Ellen in action.

"The girl was crying with joy as far as I could tell. Totally free." Delilah watched as Hope wandered back toward them. Then she focused on Anthony again. "That was the only thing more inspiring than watching Jonathan and Ellen at work."

"Does it make you wonder if maybe we should just refer people to them instead of trying to do this ourselves?" He probably knew what they would say, but he wanted to test their reaction.

"Jonathan has a regular therapy practice. He meets with people pretty much full time. And that's the main thing he does. Ellen has grandkids she takes care of most days and Bible studies she leads. They don't have time to do more of the deliverance stuff. And it could be a burnout risk if they did." Sophie turned toward the entrance again as Anthony stood up.

"But you work with those other people who do it pretty much full time." He put a hand on Delilah's back as they walked side by side.

"The Albrights. Right. But they really have to be careful to manage burnout too. That's why they work with local people and why they bring someone like me in once in a while."

Delilah turned toward Sophie as they reached the front door. "You haven't done that with them for a while, have you?"

Sophie shook her head, pausing before pushing through the revolving door. "Been a few months."

The trip through the revolving door, all four of them in there at one point, gave Anthony the feeling of a rock band. This would be a good music video. Too bad he couldn't carry a tune or play an instrument.

"We gonna meet that musician guy, Nathan, soon?" He wondered if anyone was following that other lead for a new group member.

"Zeezee is talking to him." Delilah took Anthony's hand, the way she often did when they walked together.

"She's like our HR department now." Hope snickered, clearly not concerned about Zeezee's role.

"She's gonna be here with Carlos. Did I say that already?" Sophie seemed a little nervous, glancing around the lobby as if looking for someone.

"What do you think those are?" Hope nodded toward something Anthony couldn't see.

"I get, like, this impression that some of them have to wait down here when the people who are patients or clients or whatever go upstairs. Maybe." Sophie did half a shrug.

Anthony and Delilah looked at each other. The elevator door opened with a digital tone, and none of them said anything more about Hope and Sophie saw. If Hope accepted Sophie's speculation, she didn't need to say anything. Did she accept it? What did it mean? Anthony checked with each of the others as they rode up to the fourth floor together. He was tempted to go into full speculation mode, but that wasn't so helpful when there was real work to do. Real people to meet.

Another tone announced their arrival. The doors opened to a floor carpeted in pale beige, glass-enclosed rooms with dangling blinds behind the windows. A receptionist desk was positioned to their left.

The woman seated there greeted them in a pipy voice. "Can I help you?"

"We're here to see Carlos ..." Did Sophie not know his last name? Had she forgotten it?

Unnecessary, apparently. "Oh, yes. He's waiting in meeting room two. Magnolia. Just that way." She pointed down the hall.

"Magnolia?" Hope whispered with her face turned away from the reception desk.

"I don't think she was calling you Magnolia, Hope," Anthony joked as soon as they got past the receptionist.

"Good. I hate it when people call me that."

When they reached the room with the nameplate Magnolia next to the door, Hope raised her eyebrows and flashed her eyes as the others laughed.

"Hey, guys." Zeezee was just inside that door. "This is the place." She turned and gestured toward a guy standing behind her with caramel skin and black hair, dark eyes, and a bright smile.

"Carlos," he said, offering a fist bump.

The four visitors knew what to do with that. Hope snickered about something as she executed a double bump, but her humor ended abruptly.

Sophie was half turned toward Carlos and half toward something behind him. Then she turned fully to Hope, who replied with silent google eyes.

"What's up?" Zeezee's voice quavered. She probably had an idea about the answer to her question.

Carlos looked less well informed. "Something wrong?"

"Uh ..." Sophie was surely calculating how much to say so early in their acquaintance. But it wasn't like she had the option of saying, "Oh, nothing." Anthony could tell she and Hope weren't very good at bluffing.

"Let's have a seat." Delilah took charge, to Anthony's relief. He hoped she was following more than the nonverbal clues being billboarded by Sophie and Hope. At least Delilah was responsible enough to get them beyond the deer-in-the-headlights moment at the door.

Carlos sat on one side of the room in an armchair upholstered in brown linen.

Zeezee banged a knee on a similar chair and then managed to sit down an arm's length from Carlos.

"You guys are freaking me out a bit here, I gotta say." He spoke with a slight accent that resisted definition. British, African, Portuguese? Maybe none of the above. Carlos was a skinny guy with long fingers, one of which was propped against his temple, his thumb stretched along the line of his cheekbone.

Anthony tried to decide if the taint in the air was just the social tension between Carlos and his strange visitors. Or was there more? Was Anthony feeling whatever it was Sophie and Hope were seeing? He checked with Delilah. She had her business face on—the one she used to meet strangers, the one she held up when she wasn't entirely comfortable. She was usually comfortable when Anthony was with her.

"I'm sorry, Carlos. I don't mean to leave you hanging. So I just wanna go ahead and say what I think I'm picking up." Sophie was using an alternative voice too. Diplomatic. She was a gentle and articulate person, but not always diplomatic.

"So, Zeezee told you what we do. And it all started with my ability to see things in the spirit realm." Sophie looked around the room. "Zeezee told us you believe in spirits." She hesitated when Hope jumped up from her armchair and closed the meeting room door the rest of the way.

"Sorry." Hope grimaced her apology.

"Go ahead." Carlos nodded to Sophie.

Anthony noticed him glance over his shoulder as Sophie started explaining. Not over both shoulders, just his right.

"You sense it, don't you?" No diplomacy for Hope, thanks.

Carlos turned his head more fully now and hiked a thumb over that shoulder. "I feel it sometimes. Like there's a sort of weight behind me."

Hope swore and then apologized even louder than the curse.

"Okay, so you know. That makes it easier." Sophie only glanced at Hope for half a second. Maybe she was deciding whether she needed to add to Hope's apology. The office they were in was a child welfare agency sponsored by a coalition of evangelical churches. Appropriate language only for sure.

"What? You can get rid of it? Do you know what it is?" Carlos was gripping both arms of the chair now.

Anthony suspected the slim guy could get out of that chair pretty fast. Probably too fast for Anthony to catch him before he reached the door. But he hoped it wouldn't come to that. Well, actually he *knew* it wouldn't come to that.

"The word is death. It feels like a weight." Delilah answered instead of Sophie or Hope. But Hope's impressed pucker and nod confirmed Delilah's assessment.

"Yeah. It keeps fading in and out. It feels to me like a projection from far away—something that can just barely reach you." Sophie raised her eyebrows at Carlos and then checked Hope and Delilah. "It's like it's rooted somewhere else. Not here. Not on you." She paused. "Was there someone in your family who was into ... some kind of spiritual ... manipulation?"

"Hmm. My grandfather was into Candomblé in Brazil before he became an evangelical. And his mother was a practitioner of spirit possession when he was a boy, but I never met her. And most of my life, we didn't live near that grandfather."

"A distant connection." Sophie nodded. "Most of what we see is symbolic. The thing I'm seeing looks faded, like a distant image being projected through clouds, sort of." She paused and took a deep breath. "But it *is* big."

"Big? Like, significant?"

"Yeah. Size is symbolic too. Indicating influence and power, mostly."

"Does that mean it will be hard to get rid of? Because some people prayed for me in my mother's church in Cameroon when we lived there." He paused at what were surely a few confused looks. "We traveled all over for my father's work in mineral research." Then he seemed to lose track of what they were talking about and just stared at the door. Maybe he was doing that calculation about beating Anthony to the hallway.

"I feel like it's powerful but not deeply connected to you. I don't think it would be hard to break it off you. To send it away." Sophie glanced at Delilah.

Delilah nodded and looked at Anthony.

Anthony raised a hand but managed to not point to himself and say, "Why are you looking at me?" He knew why.

"Okay. We can do this. If you're willing, Carlos."

Carlos raised and lowered his eyebrows so many times in just a few seconds that Anthony worried he would get a cramp. Then something seemed to clear away from his face. The calm and rational guy that was now looking at Anthony was probably Carlos unencumbered. The guy he was before Hope and Sophie freaked him out. Before they outted the death spirit.

Even though Anthony sensed that something had already shifted, he wanted to make it official. "Spirit of death, I break your ties with Carlos. I break all family ties that give permission for this spirit to follow him. Permission revoked, in the name of the Lord Jesus Christ."

Out of the corner of his eye, he could see Sophie nod once. Decisively.

Hope said it aloud. "Outta here. That thing is gone."

"Yeah. I felt it. I felt it even before you spoke ... Anthony." Carlos sniffed through his nose. Almost a laugh.

Anthony didn't mind not getting credit. That would generally be the case, he expected. "Yeah. I just said the words to seal what I already felt happening."

Delilah was grinning with the sweet little smile that said how proud she was of her man. Or something to that effect.

A Lunch Break from Death

When debriefing what had just happened with Carlos—and some other introductory discussion—tapered to silence, Sophie perked up. "I think we owe you a lunch. Can you go out to eat?"

Carlos looked at the wall clock. "I was just thinking I owed *you* all a lunch. But I'd better check with my supervisor to see if she and I can meet later. I'm supposed to see her at one."

Sophie couldn't help shaking her head when Carlos left the room. "I can't think of a better introduction."

Zeezee went saucer eyed. "Really? I was just thinking how glad I was you didn't do anything like that to me."

"Is there something you wanna tell us about?" Hope was ahead of Anthony these days in the joke department. Maybe she was feeling the obligation of her youth.

Smiling shyly and rolling her eyes, Zeezee apparently recognized the usual Hope humor.

Sophie hadn't seen anything significant on Zeezee, though she had seen a couple things flash in and out during their times together. She wondered how much Hope had discerned, how much her joke had a serious frame on it.

But she didn't have time or opportunity to go there. It was time for lunch. Carlos got his boss to reschedule. Did he tell her he wanted to take the deliverance team out for lunch after they chased the spirit of death out of the conference room? She guessed probably not.

They paraded to a Mexican restaurant near Carlos's office.

"Any good Brazilian places you like?" Anthony and Delilah were walking next to Carlos as he reached for the restaurant door.

"None that I can afford on a social worker's salary. But that one downtown, Fogo, is where my dad takes me when he visits. Mexican fits my budget better." He grinned at Antony over his shoulder as they entered the air-conditioned restaurant.

"Where are your parents now?" Sophie was right behind Delilah.

"They've settled in Bolivia the past few years. My father's employer has exploratory mines there."

"He's a miner?" That didn't sound right. And Sophie flashed a look intended to warn Hope away from any joke she might see floating out there in the cool restaurant air.

Carlos laughed even without a joke from Hope. "He's a mining engineer. He's been at it for thirty some years, so he's pretty high up in the company. More executive than number cruncher at this point, I think."

"Not a rock cruncher?" Hope was standing on the other side of Carlos.

"No. He rarely gets his hands dirty. I'm not sure he ever really did. Back in the day, it was all on computers already. At least his part was. Somebody was getting their hands dirty, obviously."

"Social worker is a long way from mining engineer." Sophie was looking at the menu above the counter as Anthony started ordering for him and Delilah. Sophie figured that left her to buy for Carlos. Software engineer versus social worker, she expected her paying would be appropriate. She also knew Delilah had to get back to the lab soon, so Anthony was expediting her meal for her.

"Yeah. My dad rarely passes up an opportunity to remind me of how far apart those careers are. Especially salary wise. But he's mostly resigned to me being the white sheep in a family of black sheep." He grinned.

Sophie couldn't tell if Carlos was totally joking. Which probably meant he would fit right in with them.

Anthony and Delilah did eat quickly and exit early along with Zeezee, leaving Sophie and Hope with Carlos. He thanked the departing couple profusely again and promised to see them later. And Sophie could tell that all of it was sincere. Everything about Carlos seemed real. And no more specters made an appearance as they ate their lunch and talked.

"So what is it you want me to do?" He had folded his paper products together in the middle of the red plastic tray in front of him.

Hope started consolidating the trash. She let Sophie answer the question.

"Well, you got a little sampler in that meeting room, of course. But, more typically, we have more intense sessions set up with someone suffering serious oppression. Most of the time they're in the care of a therapist already, in combination with a pastor, if possible. Often one or the other. But it would be great to have someone on our team that we know and trust who can keep an eye on the kind of issues a counselor sees and that I don't, and Hope doesn't."

"You'd think I'd have learned something from all the therapy I got." Hope muttered that before heading to the trash chute ten feet away. She pushed the trays into the door that said *Thank You* and slid the trash into the bin before setting the trays on top.

Carlos was watching her. "So you each have your specialties, and you work together as a team. You just wanna add a social worker to the team?"

"We each have our specialties, but we also trust each other completely, so we can blur the lines if something comes up. I believe God sort of distributes gifts in a custom fashion when we're in the middle of it." Sophie sat up straighter, catching herself leaning on the table with her elbows.

Nodding, Carlos played with the dark bristles on the tip of his chin. One o'clock shadow or something. "Good. I believe in that too. I've seen people get a really helpful insight in the middle of a therapy session, like a little treasure dropped from God. I actually count on that sort of thing happening during some of the tougher sessions."

"Nice." Hope was back. She sat next to Sophie, so it felt like they were both interviewing Carlos.

For whatever reason, that was the moment Sophie first clearly saw an angel that appeared to be accompanying Carlos. She tilted her head back and checked out the bright white angel that looked like some ancient scholar or something. "You have a wise angel." She said that before she thought about how it would sound. Of course all holy angels were wise, but that was the strongest impression she received from seeing this particular messenger.

Hope snorted. Maybe she was entertained by Sophie spouting the first thing that came to mind for a change. But she was also looking at the shining angel. "Do you wonder why those guys only make themselves known at a certain moment?"

"What?" Carlos was back to looking over his shoulder, but he didn't do it with the same haunted eyes this time.

"Sometimes angels will just suddenly show themselves to us. I haven't figured out why they do it at those times and not others."

"So you see ... my ... angel?"

"Yup. A real wise guy." Hope bobbed her eyebrows. She was looking just above Carlos with her head cocked to one side.

"That's good, right? That he's there?"

Sophie smiled in a way she hoped was reassuring. "I believe everyone has access to an angel, or maybe is even assigned at least one angel."

"At least one?"

"Some of us seem to need more." Hope backhanded a thumb toward Sophie, though she had been traveling with at least two angels of her own lately.

"We don't know everything. We can only observe. And speculate, really." Sophie didn't mind sounding like the voice of reason against Hope's loose assertions. It worked, as far as she was concerned.

Nodding as he calculated something, Carlos puckered for a second. "So you travel around helping people with these things?"

"I think we can find plenty to do right here in the area. Places around the city. I have a friend who's a counselor and does this kind of ministry with a church group here. They have more to do than they have time for."

"You know a therapist who already does this kinda stuff?"

"Yeah. We've worked with him quite a few times."

"So he's not available for you to keep working with?"

"We might do that on occasion, but he has other responsibilities. He was fully supportive of the idea of us forming another team."

"Huh. I'd like to meet this guy."

"That seems like a wise thing to do." Sophie reached for her phone to text Jonathan.

"Looks like it's not just his angel who's a wise guy." Hope leaned toward Sophie as she grinned at Carlos and his angel.

The Other New Guy

Hope logged off of her laptop and listened to the drum drum of footfalls on the stairway. Could she recognize Sophie's steps? Probably, given the other options. The small Asian couple next door slipped in and out undetected. The young guy across the hall came up the stairs like he was being chased by demons. And the heavy old man down the hall took one step to every three of Sophie's. But hearing the key in the lock was the clincher.

"Hey. Are you ready? That guy is coming by with Delilah and Zeezee any minute."

"No Anthony again?" Hope rocked the office chair forward and stood up.

"He's coming straight from work. Maybe a little late."

"What about Carlos? Are we ready to include him in something like this?"

"I was thinking about that. I don't think it's necessary." Sophie let her messenger bag hang in one hand for a second. "What do you think?"

"It's your place. You can invite whoever you want."

"That's not what I meant."

Hope snorted a laugh. "Yeah, but we have to start thinking about logistics. How many people do you really wanna coordinate?"

"It's a pretty cooperative bunch. Shouldn't be too hard to set things up if we give 'em enough lead time."

"Speaking of lead time, how was work?"

"It's getting there. I like the way the site looks, but the graphics girls are still tweaking."

"Or making you do the tweaking."

"It's not difficult coding. I've done this stuff for years."

"Old war horse that you are."

"Exactly. What about you? Any crazies today?"

Hope laughed. "Yeah. There was this one guy who just couldn't get past the fact that I don't speak Farsi. He tried and tried, like he thought I would catch on if he just kept talking."

"Farsi? Was he calling from … Iran?"

"I don't think so. I only knew it was Farsi because I opened a translation app on my phone. Took a few tries. Not Arabic. Not Hindi. I think Farsi was, like, my fourth guess."

"Good guess."

"Uh-huh. Too bad that translator app doesn't work better. I'm pretty sure the guy wasn't actually telling me to park my car next to the camels."

"You're joking."

"Usually." She stopped herself when a bright angel landed behind Sophie. Hope almost shouted a warning, but the big, winged angel was clearly one of the good guys.

Sophie's three regulars showed up next to him. They formed a blinding phalanx right there in the entryway.

Sophie swung around, maybe catching the heavenly reflection on Hope's face. Was that possible?

"Oh my! Who are you?"

The new angel gave his name.

Wow.

Neither Hope nor Sophie generally asked for a name from the good guys. Hope was worried she would have to be eliminated by some angel hit squad if she ever learned one of their names. Now she prayed that idea was just paranoia left from too many action movies.

The big new angel spoke. "I'm here with Nathan."

"Yo! Nathan is in. That's settled." Hope huffed a laugh at herself.

Whatever ceremony might have followed this angel introduction was interrupted by the buzzer at the bottom of the stairs.

The winged angel said what everyone was thinking. "He's here."

Hope and Sophie looked at each other. Sophie moved her feet first, though she stumbled a bit, her sock feet forgetting how it was done for a second. She kept her eye on the new angel as she pushed the button for the visitors downstairs.

Hope noted that Sophie had bypassed the normal intercom check to make sure it was the expected guests. Clearly she trusted the report from the glowy guy with the big wings.

Most angels Hope had seen did not have wings. This guy definitely did. She suspected Sophie knew what to call one of those angels, but Hope didn't ask. It was enough to let his name rattle around in her head unrestrained ... so far. Could she forget it? Should she be trying to forget it?

Sophie pulled the door open before the three arrivals reached their floor. She was leaning on the door to prop it open and sneaking looks at the angels accumulating in the apartment. A couple that looked somewhat familiar had just joined them. Obviously the angels could do the stairs faster than the humans.

Delilah was the first mortal to appear in the doorway. She let a small wrinkle blemish her brow for half a second, then started looking around the room as if she smelled something enticing.

Zeezee was next, with a guy close behind her. He wasn't as tall as Delilah, but taller than Zeezee by a few inches. He carried a guitar case effortlessly with stout hands and muscular shoulders.

"Hi, y'all. I'm Nathan."

Sophie just nodded.

Hope just watched Sophie nodding.

Zeezee scowled at them and inserted better introductions. "This is Sophie and Hope. Guys, this is Nathan." Of course that last part was unnecessary, but Zeezee was obviously worried about the mute gaping Hope and Sophie were doing.

"Uh, yeah. Hi." Sophie cleared her throat. "We met your angel already."

"Whaaaaat?" Nathan's voice arched musically high. "Are you serious? So you really see ... Wait, are you seeing my angel right now?"

Sophie and Hope nodded in unison.

"Oh my gosh! That is so cool!" He raised a fist, knuckles down.

Sophie stretched to reach the fist bump, speechless again.

The door buzzed. Sophie sidestepped and pressed the button again. Anthony's angel appeared in the doorway at just that moment. Who needed an intercom with the angels announcing arrivals like this?

Hope backed away from the door to allow room for angels and humans. The humans knocked around removing shoes, settling one guitar, and laughing at every little thing.

Anthony appeared next to his angel, and he had another one with him. This one was golden brown, almost copper. A new recruit? Hope was tempted to ask its name, but she held back, still fearing that assassination scenario.

"Hey, Nathan. Good to meet you." Anthony slipped his shoes off. He chuckled at the awkward grins on the faces in the entryway. Then he breezed past the little cluster of people. "My mama wants us all to come to dinner this week or next."

"All of us?" Sophie glanced at Nathan. She was probably thinking what Hope was. How did Detta know it was okay to include the new guy? Or maybe Sophie wasn't teetering as much as Hope was right now.

"Yeah. She seemed pretty clear that she wanted the whole gang. You know how she is."

"Uh-huh. I do, actually." Hope gestured for the others to follow Anthony into the living room.

"Why are you guys all standing by the door? Did something happen?" Anthony took advantage of the hesitations all around him and grabbed the rocking chair, his favorite place to sit in Sophie's apartment.

Hope still called it Sophie's place. She hadn't declared her intention to make the move permanent. She assumed such a decision would mean finding a different apartment that would belong to them both.

"Nathan's main angel showed up before him. Quite an entrance." Hope thought about it a second. "His *maingel*. Ha. I get the copyright on that if it sticks."

Sophie bumped shoulders with her. She was looking at Anthony. "And you came in with a new guy or person or ... whatever, as well. This one is, like, more solid than the one you usually travel with."

"Whaaaat?" Anthony sounded like he was imitating Nathan even though he had missed that part.

Hope nodded her agreement. That was it. Sophie was right. The new one with Anthony seemed more solid.

"Really? What do you think it means if it's more solid?"

"Who knows?" Sophie seemed to stall right there, but Hope suspected that was because she was thinking all these new angels probably meant new trouble. Hope wasn't going to say that aloud either.

Nathan had landed on the couch and was unpacking his guitar. "So is your mother, like, this amazing cook?" He glanced at Anthony.

That got a few chuckles from the knowledgeable among them.

"She's that and a whole lot more. A whole lot more." Hope knew she wouldn't get any argument on that.

Dinner for the New Team

Detta hung up the call with Roddy, not surprised to find he was content to sit out this dinner. She was thinking the crowd of young folks would be a bit much for him. He was still working on getting up to speed. He seemed to get tired more easily than before.

She ran through her list of dishes and thought about how to set up the table. She counted through the guests. Seven all together, two of whom she had never met. Two young men. She knew Zeezee from when she was a girl and her mother used to be part of their church. From what Detta had heard, that girl was at some new progressive church now with mostly white folks. Not the same church as Sophie and Hope though.

That set her to wondering how Priscilla was doing. It felt like there was getting to be too many of these young folks to keep track of. Like when Anthony was in high school, and the cast of friends was constantly shifting. But she had a good feeling about these new boys. Maybe not friends yet, but she expected they soon would be.

Checking the clock, she set to cooking and arranging and praying. The same things she had been doing all her adult life. Though it felt different now. Like she was free in a new way. Maybe it was having her new life with Roddy waiting in the close future. Or maybe the newness was about seeing her boy grown up and taking responsibility. Planning on marriage and digging into a very important ministry. A full-grown man.

She checked the weight of the ham again, not recalling the exact poundage. The oven was preheated already. She could start peeling potatoes next. The dough for the dinner rolls was rising. It would have to rise at least a second time. "Rising again just like you, Lord." She chuckled at her own silliness.

Thinking about Anthony and Sophie and Delilah and their new mission started her praying as automatically as breathing. "Give 'em wisdom, Lord. They're sure gonna need it. Yes, Lord, surely they will. But I know you got plenty. Never in short supply of anything. And never stingy with your wisdom. Just give those young people ears to hear. Ears to hear you. To hear your truth revealed into their own hearts and to hear it from each other. Knit that team together by your Spirit. Yes, Lord."

Praying and cooking had become intertwined for Detta, mixed together in ways that often felt like she was working with another cook. "You think that dough rose enough? I don't want those rolls to be so dense this time."

By the time she had to turn the flame off for the green beans to keep them from getting mushy, the dinner rolls had come out perfectly. "As perfect as an imperfect person can make 'em."

Her phone buzzed. Incoming call from Roddy.

"Hello, sir."

"Hello, my darling. How are dinner preparations going?"

"Preparations are going quite well. Maybe ready a bit early, but twice baked potatoes don't mind that, and I can keep the ham from drying out. Should be just fine."

"Of course. No worries. These young folks all love you. And they would do that even if you weren't a miraculous cook."

"Miraculous? Laying it on a little heavy there, Mr. Harper." She sniffed a laugh. "And not all these young folks even know who I am. There's two young men I've never met in my life. All I have on them is assurance from the Spirit that they're good for Anthony and his team."

"I'm bettin' that Anthony and Sophie have primed those boys real good. They'll be ready to love you even before you feed 'em."

Puffing her skepticism without further comment, a rumble of thunder caught Detta by surprise. She hadn't been paying attention to the weather forecast even if it could potentially affect her rising rolls and the disposition of her guests. She checked the window over the sink. It was getting dark early. She carried her phone with her to the hall closet, where she collected two old green towels to leave on the little table by the front door. "I don't know if they're comin' in the front like guests or in the back like my kids."

"What's that?"

"Is it raining by you? Is it supposed to rain tonight?"

"Could be a lot of rain, I hear. I'm feeling it in my lower back."

"How much rain is your lower back predicting, exactly?" She changed her mind and took the towels to the back door. The guests would probably park cars up the drive and have a shorter run to the back door.

"Hmm. Let me see. Seems like about an inch and a half. Yep. That's my prediction."

"That's a lot of rain. Does that mean you're in a lot of pain? Sorry for the rhyme."

"Not too bad. Only took a couple pills. Just the ordinary stuff, not the prescription pills."

"Well, I bless your back with healing. With freedom from feeling obligated to predict the weather so accurately."

"Ha. Amen."

The first car pulled into the driveway as the first raindrops spattered the kitchen window. Detta turned on the back light in case that car was one of the newcomers who wouldn't know about her backdoor policy. "Okay. Some of 'em are here. A little early. That's good. I guess my green beans knew what time to be ready after all."

"Are your green beans as smart as my back?"

"Oh, I wouldn't presume to compare."

"Ha. Okay, Miss. I love you. Have a wonderful evening. Lots of blessings yourself."

"Thank you, dear. I love you too. Talk to you later, maybe after the kids go."

"All right. Bye."

Detta was saying goodbye as Delilah rapped on the back door before opening it. "Hey, Mama. Looks like we just beat the rain."

"Come in. Come in. Just in time." Detta spread her arms to greet her future daughter-in-law, with her son arriving right behind.

"How are you, Mama? Did we put you to a lot of work, making food for so many folks?" Anthony pressed his cheek to hers for a second and then pulled back to take a look at her.

"I must look tired, or you wouldn't be askin'." She narrowed her eyes as she assessed her own strength. "Food's all ready, so I can just relax and let you two help me with settin' things out and all."

"Absolutely. That's exactly what I had in mind." Delilah surveyed the kitchen with her hands propped on her hips.

"How was work for you two today?" Detta maneuvered around the two slender young folks and turned off the oven.

"I had a pretty smooth day, really." Anthony pushed past Delilah and met his mother by the oven. "Hot pads?" he asked and spotted them immediately after.

Detta handed him one as he grabbed the other.

"We had a leak in one of the containment tanks today." Delilah spread out the serving plates on the kitchen table. "Messed up a couple of big experiments. Equipment failure. Nobody's fault. At least nobody in the lab." She looked up as another car pulled into the driveway. It was really raining now.

"Looks like the early birds avoided the worms this time." Anthony set the ham on the stovetop next to the pot with the green beans.

"He-he. That's right." Detta checked the window above the sink again. "Summer rain is worm time. My robin friends get so excited when the rain comes. Funny I didn't notice that today. Guess I was too focused on the food preparations."

"This looks wonderful, Mama Detta. I love eating at your house. It's like a school for cooking and serving. I'm already better at those things from eating over here."

"You're so sweet. I would love to cook together with you sometime, Delilah. Maybe as I get a little older and slower we can do that more often."

"You feelin' your years today, Mama?" Anthony set the lid of the roaster in the empty sink. He slid the carving knife out of the drawer next to the stove.

"I guess. Roddy was just predicting the rainfall by his back pain. I guess I do feel a bit more achy with a storm comin' in. Hadn't put it together until just now." She caught Anthony looking at her a little too long. "Don't worry, young man. Just a little tired from what's been happenin' with Roddy. We're recovering. He's doin' just fine."

"But you were thinking tonight would be too much for him?" Delilah took the rolls from Detta and dumped them into a wicker basket lined with a cloth napkin.

Sophie swung through the back door along with Hope and a slender young man with dark eyes and a shiny smile. "Hello, everyone. Couldn't somebody hold the rain back for a little bit longer?" Sophie looked toward the drive as another car pulled in. "That should be Nathan and Zeezee."

Detta had heard that Zeezee might not continue with the team much longer, but maybe she got that wrong. Anthony had said something about her nearly running for the door at a ministry session that went badly. Keeping busy with Roddy, Detta was content not to know the details about Sophie and her team. Not every detail, at least.

Introducing Carlos and getting in some hugs, Sophie and Hope moved through the kitchen to stand by the door to the dining room.

"Smells great." Hope grinned hungrily.

"So, Mama, do you have a bottle of champagne?" Anthony was slicing the ham as he had done for her since he was a teenager.

"Champagne? Why would I need a thing like that?" She gestured for Delilah to get the potatoes on the table, hoping that would release some of the congestion in the kitchen.

"So you can launch this team."

"Like with a ship? Well, who exactly do you propose I bust that champagne bottle over?"

"Ha. Any volunteers?" Anthony glanced around at the smiling crew.

Knocking on the back door, Zeezee had clearly read the signs accurately. She had never been over for supper, but maybe her mama did things the way Detta did. Detta hadn't seen Zeezee's mother for a decade at least, but they had been friends back in the day.

"Hello, dear. Come on in. I see you have a musician with you."

Nathan stopped just inside the back door, dripping rain down his face and hugging his guitar case. He had a giant grin on. "Mrs. Washington, I'm so glad to meet you. The food smells wonderful."

"This is Nathan." Zeezee unzipped her red raincoat and patted her soggy friend on the shoulder.

"No umbrellas?" It just occurred to Detta that she would have to figure out what to do with those, but the only one she could see was already leaning against the back doorframe. Maybe that was from Anthony or Sophie.

"No. We relied on our speed to dodge the drops." Nathan pulled at the snaps on his royal blue rain jacket.

"How did you do with that?"

"Not so great, as it turns out." Nathan laughed and shook some rain onto the rug. He did an embarrassed check with Detta.

"There's a couple of towels right there on the edge of that cart. I guess we were saving them for the wettest arrivals."

"The latest arrivals." Zeezee had her jacket off, looking for a place to hang it.

"Just hang it over the back of that chair if you like, dear. You two are right on time. The others just beat you and the rain."

With Sophie and Hope comfortably joining in, it didn't take a minute to get the food on the table. No one showed any interest in sitting around and socializing before the meal. It was time to eat. The food did smell fine, and the young folks were hungry.

Getting Detta's Blessing

Sophie hadn't felt this giddy at any time she could remember. Even holiday meals with her mother or with Detta were not as exciting as this night with her new team. It was really happening. A dream come true. A dream she had only become fully aware of just weeks before these pieces fell together. And the best part was launching this team in Detta's house, with Detta's blessing.

"I hope nobody's keeping track of how many pieces of ham I've had." Nathan was levitating one more slice from the platter to his plate.

"I wish I had been counting now that you say that." Anthony took the serving fork from Nathan. "This ham is perfect, Mama."

"I always get my meat at Jespersen's, you know. Never been disappointed with them."

"Not gonna take any credit for this magnificent meal?" Carlos was leaning back, apparently not planning to keep up with Anthony and Nathan.

"Oh, I'm not denying I did my part. But it's hard to ruin a good ham."

"That sounds like good advice. I'll keep that in mind next time I have to feed a crowd like this." Delilah was finishing a dinner roll. Sophie guessed it wasn't her first. Those things were addicting.

"So does joining up with this ministry mean we get to eat meals over here all the time?" Nathan talked with his mouth full, but he did it with the fingers of one hand over his lips.

"Is that what you promised them, Sophie?" Detta grinned at her, down the full length of the table.

"I may have implied it was part of the benefits package. Hardcore recruiting tactics, ya know."

"Well, I'm glad to feed this lot."

After joking, dinner, and peach cobbler for dessert, they shifted the group to the living room. That required repurposing a couple chairs from the dining room table, but the eight of them formed a cozy circle under golden lamplight. The storm had risen to a roar during the meal, but only briefly. And it had settled into a steady rain since.

Nathan tuned his guitar as the table was cleared and the chairs were arranged. Sophie sat with him to see if they knew the same songs. He and Zeezee went to a different brand of church, but he was familiar with some songs Sophie knew from the church she and Priscilla attended along with Hope now.

After leading an opening prayer, Sophie prompted Nathan to get them started with worship music. As she had learned at their first meeting, his voice was clear and inviting, providing plenty of cover for the shiest among them. The most bashful singer was probably Hope, who might have only been going through the motions of singing.

Sophie noted several in the group wiping at tears during the second song, which alerted her to the possibility that she had been leaning on the handbrake of her own emotions. Maybe she had hit the restraints after noting that earlier giddiness. It probably warned her that she should get a grip to prevent embarrassment. As she worried over this, Sophie noted the gathering of angels, which she had also been avoiding. Another attempt at keeping her emotions in check.

She had never seen this many angels at Detta's house. The walls seemed to bulge to allow space for so many glowing messengers. And Sophie could tell Hope was trying to avoid looking at them as well, like she did during Sunday services. The intensity of the glow might justify those averted eyes, but Sophie had discovered she could stare at a light as bright as the sun when that light came from heaven.

Adjusting her attention away from Hope and the angels, Sophie focused on the King of kings, who had ultimately set all this in motion. The one who rescued her from disaster and depression. And she soon joined those wiping at tears tickling her cheeks as she sang.

Certainly it wasn't just Nathan's voice. It wasn't even the crowd of angels that explained the intensity of the worship time. To Sophie, it felt as if God was as expansively happy about this gathering as she was. Probably even happier.

Checking her phone during a restful lull in the music, Sophie discovered they had been singing for over an hour. She laughed aloud at the discovery, and several heads rose to investigate. She lowered her own head and led another prayer. "Thank you, Lord, for the amazing worship time. We welcome your presence. We welcome your continued direction for this group." She waited for a second, considering whether that was enough.

In the pause Carlos added a prayer to hers. Then Delilah, and Detta, and Anthony, and Zeezee. Nathan prayed and kept strumming. And this went on, around and around, for a while longer.

"Lord, I give up all my reservations. About you, about working for you, and about all these great people. I give all of it up. No more resistance from me." That was Hope, her voice rasping and quivering. Then she started to sob.

Detta slid off her recliner and stood behind Hope, a hand on her shoulder, as Hope rocked in place and cried like Sophie had never seen her do before.

Sophie allowed a longer silence than was comfortable, but it wasn't total silence. Sniffling and small sobs filled the spaces between the sound of the raindrops. Not all the crying was from Hope.

When Hope settled down a bit, Sophie checked her watch again. Nearly forty-five minutes of praying and crying. She snorted her amusement more quietly this time, but Nathan broke the silence by bumping his guitar against something as he tried to set it aside.

"Sorry."

"No problem." Anthony reached for the tissue box that had landed on the coffee table at some point during worship.

"I feel so blessed to be here with you young folks." Detta patted Hope and stepped past Anthony on the way back to her recliner. "This is exactly the way you need to start this ministry. And the way you need to start it is the way you need to conduct it. Always in the presence of God." She lowered herself into her recliner, which was upright for this meeting.

All eyes were on Detta. "Angels are wonderful. Seeing them is a blessing. But it's the presence of God Almighty that sets people free. And seeing you all bathing in the presence here tonight assures me that you are on the right path. That you're going to be a blessing to each other. And the way ahead of you is full of victory and light."

A silence followed, out of which Zeezee blurted an inarticulate word. Her medium-brown face was tinted red around her nose and eyes, and she had blotches on each cheek. "I wanna try to help. I don't know what I can do, but I don't wanna be left out of this group."

No one would contradict or deny her, Sophie knew. But she also suspected that the burning reality of another challenging session of threats and frightful screams might weaken Zeezee's resolve. She was a smart person, probably a good counselor, and was becoming a good friend to Sophie. They would just wait and see what Zeezee could do to help. Surely there was something. Maybe sitting in on initial meetings for evaluating people. That was the sort of meeting they needed to take more seriously than they had with Sean a couple weeks ago.

Sophie nodded and smiled, signaling her acceptance of Zeezee's resolve. But the resolve she really wanted to understand was what had happened for Hope. Her prayer was not only repentance from doubts about ministry, but from holding herself back from God. At least that was how Sophie heard it.

Detta spoke again. "I wanna echo what Zeezee said. I wanna be included, though not necessarily in the room during deliverance ministry. I do wanna cook y'all dinner on occasion. And I'd love to have you meet together over here like this, whether we have time for a meal or not. That's what I would like. Along with keepin' me posted about how to pray."

Again, Sophie knew there was no chance anyone would reject Detta's request. In a way, her appeal was about boundary setting as much as a petition. Though Sophie didn't think anyone was surprised by Detta's proposal, it was good to hear her say it aloud.

"Would you pray for us now, Detta? Maybe a word for each of us? You don't have to get up. You can just bless us from where you are, if you like." Sophie didn't want to further tire her old friend, but she also didn't want to miss this chance to receive her blessing.

"I would love to do that, but I don't think I'd be comfortable doing that sittin' down. Let's see how long these old legs can carry me." She chuckled and surged forward again.

Anthony reached for her as if to help, but she waved him off, having no obvious trouble rising to her feet.

And she did pray for each of the seven people sitting in her living room. The same living room where she had once welcomed a scared young woman who needed assurance that she wasn't entirely crazy for believing she saw angels. The same living room where Sophie had been set free from one thing and another, and where she had seen others set free as well.

Detta's prayers for each one there were unique, guided by the still small voice she heard inside herself. She stood over each one, accompanied by a shifting crew of angels. She spoke blessings, offered inspiration, and even some direction as she felt led.

Sophie did keep an eye on Detta to make sure they weren't wearing her out. Even if her old friend would feel it the next day, she endured through delivering seven long and thorough blessings. Then the meeting ended with one more song and a whole lot of hugs.

Will Wants to Apologize

At first, Anthony didn't know who Joseph was talking about, momentarily confused between Sean and Will, the two young guys he had met a few weeks before. Will wasn't the one they had tried to set free. He was the friend. The one Anthony met first. The one whom Anthony still held in suspicion the most.

"Will wants to apologize?" He squinted at his phone and tried to fit the need for an apology into what had happened that night. And what he and Delilah and Sophie had discussed since. He suspected Will was not interested in apologizing for the problem Hope and Sophie had perceived. So what exactly was he regretting?

Joseph sounded unconcerned by Anthony's question. "That's what he's asking. I don't know him very well, so I can't tell you more than that. I'll leave it to you to decide what to do with it." He sighed lightly over the speakerphone.

"I'll talk to Sophie and see what she wants to do." He could tell Joseph wasn't looking for more of an answer than that.

"He wants to meet with us?" Sophie's voice was a bit muffled, maybe using the speaker on her device in an awkward position. "Meet with who, exactly?"

"Well, he said *you*. But Joseph contacted me. Will has no way to contact you directly. And maybe he included Joseph to gain a bit more sympathy or something."

"Hmm. We've been burned by this guy as far as I'm concerned. But what if it was unintentional? Maybe we should give him a chance to tell us what's going on." She paused. "We have the meeting with that friend of Jonathan's in a few days, so I don't see having time to talk to Will very soon. But maybe you could get his info so we don't have to keep bothering Joseph with this."

"That makes sense. Okay. I have Will's number already and can tell him we'll get back to him soon. That'll give us a chance to think about it for a while."

"Good. Thanks."

"So this guy we're meeting with next week is a friend of Jonathan's? And that's why we're gonna try and help him instead of Jonathan's team doing it?"

"Yeah. I can see how it might be kind of awkward ministering to your friend. Especially for Jonathan, since he's a counselor. They have rules about that—meeting with friends and family or whatever."

"Okay. That makes sense now that you put it that way. For Jonathan. But we're not saying *we* shouldn't help each other when one of us has some kinda cling-on or something, right?"

"Right. I mean, I'm willing to discuss it. I don't think we need to make a rule. Maybe Carlos or Zeezee would feel differently given professional standards. But there's no hard rule for us as far as I'm concerned."

"Ha. Yeah. I don't think this whole group is real interested in making up a lot of rules about things."

"Sure. You're right. But that mess with Will and Sean is a good example of why we do have to pay attention to best practices."

He sniffed a laugh. "Now you're talking my language. Best practices."

"I know the planet you come from, my friend."

"And I, you." He stood up from his favorite chair and glanced at the monitor on the mini PC he used to connect to work. "Okay. I gotta get back to business."

"Working from home today?"

"Yeah. You too?"

"Yep. I'll go in tomorrow for meetings. That's really the only time they require me to be there. With so much going on with Hope moving here and us starting the group, I don't feel like I really need to go in to work to get people time."

"You were going in because you weren't seeing enough human beings before?"

"Sometimes. A few times. Yeah. Is that pitiful?"

"I don't think so. Lots of people have their office as their main social network. I know the guys I work with are like that. Some of 'em, anyway."

"Yeah. Sure. Well, okay. Talk to you later, Anthony. Otherwise I'll see you Monday night for that evaluation session with Tim or Tom."

"Tim. Okay. See ya, Sophie."

Making the Big Move

Back in the hills above LA, Hope set her phone on the door-sized table she used as a desk. "I think I'll get rid of all the big things and just buy stuff when I get back there. Not much of this furniture is worth anything. Flop-house stuff and Salvation Army acquisitions."

"Yeah, that makes sense. Not paying to move old furniture." Sophie seemed to be bending down or lifting something, a tight squeeze to her voice. "You have some kitchen stuff to bring though, and some linens, right?"

"I do have some decent stuff I bought recently, yeah. I've got about half of it in boxes already."

"You must have started packing before you came to visit." Sophie grunted and muttered a mild curse.

"What are you doing, changing diapers or something?"

Sophie snorted a laugh. "Is that what it sounds like?" She laughed some more. "Why in the world did your head go there?"

"Ha. Who knows. Random, I guess. Or maybe I'm ready to start thinking about settling down. At least in the next decade or so."

"Real short term, huh?"

"Hey, it's progress for me."

"Understood, understood. Anyone in particular in mind for this ten-year plan?"

"Someone I want to make me a baby mama?" She snorted. "Well ... what do you think about Nathan? Are him and Zeezee, like, dating?"

"Nathan and Zeezee? I don't think so. I think they just know each other from church. I think he's a few years younger than her. No, I don't see them as a couple. At least from what I can tell."

"Just wondering."

"Cool. I see that as more progress. Even if you don't have it all figured out." She grunted once more. "I really look forward to having you out here again."

Hope shook her head, letting the actual cause of Sophie's noises remain a mystery. "I'm sorry I'm gonna miss that meeting tonight."

"No problem. Just an eval, probably. And there's gonna be plenty of us there, I expect." She took a big breath. "No. Just get your ... stuff together and get back here."

"Yes, dear."

When they hung up, Hope was brushing up against a feeling that some new gift had landed in her apartment or maybe landed in her life in general. After a breath, she guessed that fresh delivery came from the way Sophie didn't make fun of her or sound shocked that Hope was sorta interested in Nathan. That was cool. Nice to just float an idea and not get the Spanish Inquisition about it. It was like being sisters, only better.

That reminded Hope that she should call her brother and tell him about her move. She had talked to her mother already, but her brother, Rob, was out of touch with their parents even more than Hope was. In the linen closet, she set her phone on the shelf closest to her face and hit the speaker button as her brother's phone started ringing.

"Hey, Hope. What's up?"

"I'm cleaning out my linen closet so I can move."

"Really? You're gonna go back to the Midwest on a permanent basis, then? And voluntarily?"

"Yes. It's true. Not home, but back with Sophie. We're gonna look into getting an apartment together."

"Buying or renting?"

"No talk about buying. I don't even know what the condo market is like back there."

"Yeah. You can look at that later. Maybe you won't wanna stay there that long."

"Maybe not. A year of Midwestern weather might be enough to send me back out here."

"Ha. Summer is a sketchy time for making a move decision. Wait till they do the bait and switch. Sunny skies for snow drifts."

"Okay, okay. Stop stealing my joy."

"Sorry." He sighed. "I guess I've been doing that to people lately."

"Hmm. Is that what Amy said when she broke up with you?"

"Something like that."

"Sorry, bro." She stretched to reach the old pillows stuffed onto the top shelf.

"So what's the attraction? Why leave your sunny California?"

"Well, you know I can do my job from anywhere, so there's that. And ... well, I know you won't believe it, but there's a kind of ministry there that I really ... I really feel like needs me. Something I can do with my gifts."

"Hmm. Gifts? Like, you mean seeing ... angels and stuff?"

"Yep. That's what I mean. And, yep, I still see 'em."

"And people there don't think you're crazy for it?"

"Nope. They listen to me. And Sophie sees 'em too." She could hear Rob breathing into the phone, maybe breathing a little harder than normal.

"Well ... I guess ... I guess that's good for you, then. And it makes sense you would move halfway across the country for that. Seems like it might be worth it."

That was the closest thing to an endorsement of Hope's gifts she could expect from anyone in her family. "Thanks, Rob. Thanks for ... for supporting my decision."

"Well, don't go tellin' Mom I said you should do it or anything. They already have me on the naughty list."

"Understood. No problem." She stepped back from the closet to see if she had missed anything jammed into the back of any shelves. That step opened up her perspective to include her main angel standing next to the closet. The feminine messenger looked like she wanted to say something. Hope hit the mute button on Rob. "What is it?"

"Invite Rob to come visit you after you get moved. It will be good to plant that seed with him now."

"Hope? You still there?" Rob grunted almost exactly like Sophie had been doing.

Hope was still there, but she was just staring at her phone. Tapping the mute button again, she cleared her throat. "So, you should come visit me once I get settled. It's not as far from your place."

"Yeah, that's true. I could do that. You should let me know when you get settled in." Another surprisingly positive response from her distant brother. He lived in New Orleans, as far from Minnesota as possible while still living by the Mississippi river. According to Hope's calculations.

"Cool. Yeah. I'll let you know my new address as soon as we find a place."

He breathed heavily into the phone. "Well, I gotta go. Thanks for calling me. Thanks for keeping me posted."

"Of course. Talk to you soon."

"You too. Uh ... love you, sis."

"Yeah. Love you too, bro."

A Time to Mourn

Sophie sat waiting for Delilah to get off the phone. They were a couple minutes early, but everyone was present in Tim's apartment. Sophie, Carlos, Anthony, and Delilah were there. One advantage of a team of seven people was that Sophie could assemble a good group even if not everyone was available.

Delilah had agreed to lead this interview since Sophie would be concentrating on the spiritual atmosphere, and since Carlos was still new. Anthony had deferred to Delilah, thinking Tim might be more forthcoming with her than with him. Sophie didn't question that, thinking Anthony might be getting some direction she wasn't hearing from her heavenly sources.

"Sorry for keeping you waiting. I don't get to talk to my mom very often. She wanted to ask me a couple quick questions. Which turned out to not be so quick." Delilah smiled and shrugged as she rejoined their circle in the living room and sat down.

Already Sophie was noticing something interesting. All the visible angels in the room were bunched around Tim. She decided not to say anything about that for now, letting Delilah open the meeting with prayer and then start the questions.

Tim was a man in his early forties. He explained that he was single and had lived alone most of his adult life. He and Jonathan were friends from church, but not really close.

Delilah was asking the questions, but Carlos had helped formulate most of them. He had spent time talking to Jonathan over the phone. When Tim seemed confused, Carlos was usually the first to respond, explaining the question or digging into the answer. Sophie could tell that, in the future, it would make sense for Carlos to lead this kind of interview. He was more natural at it.

When Delilah got to the question of when the current trouble started—the nightmares and violent images that flashed into his head—Tim seemed to drift away. At first, he squinched his face and gripped the arms of his upholstered armchair. His knuckles began turning white.

"What's going on, Tim?" Carlos leaned forward.

Sophie leaned back, stunned at what she was seeing. Six angels, including two of her own entourage, lifted a body above their heads and carried it away. Like pallbearers at an old-fashioned funeral. "Who died, Tim?"

He flinched without looking at Sophie.

Carlos sat up straighter and twisted his neck toward her.

She shrugged and kept monitoring the actions of the angels. The body they were carrying appeared to be that of a woman, but Sophie saved that insight.

"I ... I think you're talking about my mother. She died. She killed herself when I was a teenager. I was the one who found her."

At that, the angels stopped their pantomime and came back to crowd around Tim. Sophie leaned back again, impressed by so many angels attending to the wounded man.

"How did she do it, Tim?" Carlos's voice was confidingly low.

"She cut herself." He was breathing hard. "I found her shoes on the patio. That was weird." He seemed to calm himself. His eyes were closed now. "There was this little grove of trees right behind our house. We were on the edge of the housing development. And my mom was hiding back there. Or that's what we figured. That's what they figured when the ambulance and fire department and police got there. And my dad." He surged suddenly from a numb monotone to a burst of wrenching sobs punctuated by small squealing wails.

In Tim's quiet apartment, Sophie worried what the neighbors would think of the outburst. She hadn't thought it was risky to have an evaluation interview in a private apartment, but she hadn't accounted for a catharsis like this.

After letting Tim weep for a while, Carlos asked a surprising question. "Tim, is your mother still with you now?"

Sophie recalled that a spirit of death had been following Carlos most of his life. Maybe that was how he knew to ask that question. It certainly seemed appropriate given the funeral demonstration by the angels. If Tim was still carrying his deceased mother with him, it may be time to bury her.

When Tim raised his head, Sophie was relieved to see an expression of recognition and not offense. Carlos's question had been a risk.

"Is that possible? I mean, could that be what's happening?" Tim still held his hands near his face after coming up for air.

Sophie was distracted from Tim's face by an image above him, the ghostly visage of a woman. She supposed it wasn't actually his mother, but some spirit that represented her.

One that had substituted for her when her spirit went where God sent it. What was clear from what Sophie was seeing was that the angels around Tim were prepared to usher that ghostly spirit away.

Carlos nodded his answer to Tim's question and then looked to Sophie.

"It looks like that to me." Sophie glanced above Tim. "It's not actually your mother that I see, I'm sure, but maybe some kind of spirit associated with her, or at least with your memory or attachment to her." She looked at Delilah.

Delilah answered the implied question. "What we can do is help you break that spirit's hold on you. Are you willing to do that?"

"Is that something you can do now?" He looked from Carlos to Sophie to Delilah.

Delilah nodded slowly. "We can do that. The only question is if you're willing."

"You think that's what's giving me the nightmares? And the … violent images during the day?"

"I think it is." Sophie guessed the skeletal face would give her nightmares if she had to carry it around.

Delilah was nodding and waiting.

Tim was looking at his hands. "Her hands were covered with blood. And I took hold of them. I got her blood on my hands. It looked like I had cut myself just like her." Still staring at his hands, he breathed noisily through his nose for a few seconds. "And I thought about that when I was in college. Whenever I got depressed. I thought about how I could do like my mother had done." He paused and shook his head. "I even sometimes felt like I had already done it, in a way. That I had died with her there."

Two of the angels attending Tim knelt next to him and took hold of his arms.

Tim grew unusually still.

Sophie described what was happening. "I feel like they're offering to clean your hands. Others are clearly ready to usher the spirit of your mother's death away. The suicide spirit."

Tim nodded in short sharp movements. "Please. Help me. Get that off me. Please."

And that was what Delilah did, commanding the suicide spirit away and welcoming the washing that Jesus offered through the hands of his angels. She checked in with Tim and led him through a prayer of renunciation and of opening to God's deliverance and healing.

By the time it was over, Sophie was wishing Zeezee had been there. This was the sort of session that would welcome her rather than scare her away. But Carlos filled the therapist role very well. At the end, he spoke with Tim about the counseling he was receiving already and encouraged him to keep that up.

Delilah left it to Tim to test whether they had done enough to banish those haunting images. Then they ended with prayer and thanks and smiles all around.

Small Miracle in Small Group

The church small group Sophie attended met two weeks each month during the summer. They gathered that Wednesday on the back deck of Casandra and Roland's house. Casandra was Priscilla's mentor and friend. The leaders had both grown up in South Africa but had lived in the US for decades. Sophie guessed they were at least in their fifties. Their children were grown and moved away.

Sophie and Priscilla had to cut short their catching up when Roland began strumming his guitar to start the meeting. The idea of adding a worship leader to Sophie's ministry team had seemed obvious given her experience with her church, where any meeting was an occasion for worship music.

During the very first song, Sophie opened her eyes and startled at the sight of a dark and dirty figure lowering itself onto Roland even as he led the group in singing. Maybe he wasn't putting all his heart into it yet as he usually did. But it seemed almost unbelievable that he could lead worship with that slumpy guy hanging on his shoulders.

This left Sophie debating what to do about it. Of course doing nothing was an option, given how disruptive it would be to stop the meeting and describe the grimy ghoul hanging on the group leader. On the other hand, their group was supposed to be open for everyone to participate, to use their gifts as God led. Even if their gifts were ... a little unusual.

Sophie decided to enlist Casandra to help decide what to do. She slid past Priscilla and put a hand on Casandra's shoulder.

The leader opened her eyes with a jerk, clearly not expecting her moment of worship to be interrupted.

"Sorry, but I'm seeing a dark spirit weighing Roland down. What should I do about that?" Sophie leaned back after whispering in Casandra's ear.

Casandra was familiar with Sophie's gifts. Instead of a questioning gaze fixed on Sophie, Casandra turned toward her husband and tilted her head to the side. Was she thinking she could see what Sophie saw if she just tipped her head a bit?

"Okay, that makes sense to me. Let's wait for the first break, and I'll say something. Then you jump in."

Sophie nodded her agreement and tried to relax while still standing next to Casandra during the rest of that song and then another. Her heart doing double time, Sophie took a few breaths she hoped would calm her. She recalled Bruce Albright and his breathing exercises in that moment.

Finally Roland paused his strumming, and Casandra led in prayer. When she was finished, she sounded a familiar note for a small group leader in that church. "Let's rest here a minute and see what the Spirit is saying. Listen for a word or direction."

Allowing two breaths first, Sophie opened her mouth to speak. But someone beat her to it. Roland.

"I feel like some here are carrying a burden that slows them down, that hinders worship. It's like a spiritual presence, even. Like a person you kind of carry on your back."

Sophie blinked hard and tried to get Casandra to look at her. When she did, Casandra just nodded, only the slightest consternation evident in the tightness of her tanned brow. There might also have been a slight smile on her lips as she turned back toward her husband. Sophie couldn't tell at this angle.

"Actually, I was seeing something. A spirit that's like this burden, this heavy obligation that's weighing ... you down, Roland."

He recoiled a bit and then laughed. "That could explain why I was feeling it." He let his shoulders relax and allowed his guitar to slide forward, resting on his knees.

Interpreting his posture as a *go ahead*, Sophie only briefly checked with Casandra before starting to pray. "Thank you, Jesus, for liberation. We welcome that for all of us here now. And specifically, I welcome your release for Roland." She waited a second to see if she could tell what to call that thing.

Priscilla spoke up. "I think it's like an old religious obligation that you've let hold you back and weigh you down at times." She had her eyes closed and her hands open in front of her like she was ready to catch something dropped from heaven.

"Right." Sophie nodded. "Religious burden, I break your hold on Roland. I declare him free to follow Jesus and free from human obligations falsely laid on him in God's name." Again, Sophie paused.

Casandra spoke up. "Yes. Falsely is the key. I break the power of lies. Lies about Roland being unacceptable without performing certain religious duties. I break that in Jesus's name."

The way she said all that led Sophie to suspect Casandra knew specifically what this was about. And, as Casandra finished, Sophie saw that frumpy spirit fold its arms over its chest in disgust. Then it vanished in a puff of vapor.

Roland sighed, still resting his guitar on his knees. His hands and head sagged even farther, much more relaxed. Almost sleepy. "That's good. That's very good." He opened his eyes. "Thanks, guys." He looked at Sophie, Casandra, and Priscilla. He called everyone *guys*.

"Amen." Casandra looked relieved, like she had been carrying one end of that burden. And maybe she had.

The worship after that picked up pace and intensity. During one song, Roland let the others carry the words, only strumming and chuckling from deep in his chest. He was the dictionary picture of a man set free.

Sophie was watching angels swoop in and drop little lights on each of the worshippers. Then she forced herself to close her eyes and focus on the one who sends the messengers and provides the light.

Missing an Apology

Anthony waited in his car in front of Sophie's apartment. How many times had he been in this spot? Maybe he could get his name stenciled on the curb. But, with the price of gas so high these days, he was glad to put his electric car to use for the group. Even Sophie's compact hybrid would cost a bundle to fill with gas this week.

He took a deep breath and tried to focus on the task ahead. When Sophie and Hope came out the front door, he renewed his relief that Hope made it back from California. This time she was here for the long haul. She was a welcome addition, both for the long haul and for this strange meeting.

"Hey. Thanks for coming to get us, Anthony." Sophie slid into the front seat.

"Stuck in the back seat like a little kid again." Hope didn't even bother to say hi.

Anthony grinned at her in the rearview mirror. "You wanna drive? I could trade you places and relive a bit of my childhood."

"You rode in the back even as an only child?" She sounded mildly skeptical.

"When I was little, my mama was strict about that. Of course, it saved me from all those times she would have smashed me in the chest with her arm. You know, the mama emergency seat belt." He mimicked swinging his right arm to block Sophie from banging into the dashboard.

She leaned back. "I recognize the move. My mother let me sit up front eventually, but she had the arm swing down. She was, like, Olympic class at that."

They all laughed, and Anthony hit the accelerator as he checked for traffic. He slammed on the brakes when a cyclist swerved across in front of him, making an illegal and ill-advised right turn. "Dang fool!" Anthony huffed. "Sorry. Trying not to send anyone to the hospital today."

"Seems like a worthy ambition." Hope had a hand on the back of Sophie's bucket seat like she was doing her own version of that mama emergency arm restraint.

Anthony sniffed a laugh and forced his breathing to slow. "So, how are you two doing with the apartment search? Buying or renting?"

Sophie had leaned her right elbow on the door handle after the close call. "Definitely renting. Neither of us knows for sure where we'll be in a year. Not worth it to buy. Mortgages are expensive right now anyway."

"So, you found anything yet?"

"Yeah, maybe. We're looking at one place near Delilah and Zeezee, in fact. And another one not far from my mother's house."

"Two bedroom?"

"Yeah, though one place has a little office too."

"Oh, nice. Who gets the office?"

Sophie said "Hope" at the same time as Hope said "I do."

"Well, I'm glad to see you two agree on that."

"She works from home every day. And she likes cozy nooks. Which that office definitely is."

"Then you think you'll take the one with the office?"

"Maybe not. It's farther from downtown and from church and not close to most of the folks on the team."

"I could just have half my room set up as a little office in a two-bedroom if we can't find an good three-bedroom." Hope was facing the side window as she offered this solution. Her voice was calm and a little distracted.

That made Anthony wonder what was distracting her. "You seeing something out there?" He had a feeling.

"Yeah, like, this secret-service detail of angels flying along the side of the car."

Sophie gestured toward Anthony's side. "Yeah, over there too. High security for this operation, apparently."

"The secret service must've received a tip about a threat." He chuckled. "I bet those guys wish *they* could fly." He tried to make it a joke, but it didn't sound as funny when he said it aloud.

Then his phone rang over the Bluetooth connection in the car. It was Delilah. "Hey, babe. What's up?"

"It's Zeezee. She's, like, having an allergic reaction to something, I think. She's on the floor. Her face is red and swelling up. I don't know, maybe it's a seizure."

"Whoa. You're at home?"

He heard Zeezee next. "Uh ... I'm okay. I feel better now."

"Huh. She does look better. But I gotta take her to the hospital just in case."

"It's an attack." Sophie sounded pretty sure of herself.

"Yep. I can see an enemy in their place," Hope concurred.

"Did you catch that, babe?" Anthony pulled into a parking space near the next corner, one of the last such opportunities before they got onto a busy street with no place to pull over safely.

"Yeah, I can feel it." Delilah said something that was forceful but muffled, like she covered the phone or just spoke away from the mic. "Where are you guys? You're not there yet, are you?"

"Not there. Should we come to you instead?"

"No, don't do that." Delilah's voice was firm even as it faded away from the microphone.

"In the name of Jesus, I send blessing and protection to Delilah and Zeezee. Thank you, Lord." Sophie pronounced those words plainly, her eyes on something outside the car.

"Hey, two of those secret-service angels just took off." Hope was leaning her forehead on the window.

"I'll take that." Delilah's voice was both distant and present. "Huh. I feel something. Something better. Wow, listen to me. I don't even know what I'm saying." She snickered.

Zeezee said something that didn't come clearly over the phone.

"You guys go ahead. We're fine. It feels better here now. Zeezee feels better."

Anthony checked the clock. They would probably be late. "You sure? I could drop the ladies off at the restaurant and come to your place."

"Hmm. I would feel better about that meeting with Will if you were there, Anthony." As Delilah said it, Anthony watched Sophie nod in agreement.

Were they thinking he was needed as a bodyguard? With a crew of angels on the scene, what did they really need him for? "Well, let me know if things change. We're a bit late, but I have no problem canceling this or dividing forces."

"Okay, Anty. I'll call if we need anything."

"You're not going to the hospital?" Sophie was still leaning forward.

"No. Zeezee doesn't want to. Her insurance is a nightmare about emergency rooms, apparently."

"Yeah, but you'll go if she really needs to, right?"

"We will. I'll text you to keep you posted."

"Thanks." Sophie looked at Anthony and raised her eyebrows.

When the call ended, Hope spoke up from the back seat. "Why isn't Delilah with us if she's at home?"

"I thought she was working late tonight." Sophie had questions in her eyes too.

"Yeah, that was the plan. Then her boss had to go out of town, and the meeting was rescheduled. Like, last minute."

"I guess it's a good thing she was at home, with Zeezee having a seizure or something." Sophie nodded and crossed her near leg with her ankle on her knee. She was short enough to do that in Anthony's car, unlike Delilah.

Driving again, Anthony reviewed what had just happened. "Hey, you said a couple of those angels took off when you prayed. Were those some of your regular dudes?"

"And dudesses," Hope amended from the back seat.

"No, not really. I mean, who knows exactly who they all are? But I've been getting this impression that there are, like, angels assigned to different things, different ministries and such."

"Huh. So, like, there's a crew of protectors that are with us because we're meeting with Will?"

"I wouldn't be surprised. There was something off about that guy. I mean, spiritually," Hope answered.

Again, Sophie nodded her agreement.

Anthony contemplated all that as they approached the street on which he would find the Russian deli. Will had described the restaurant as not too crowded early in the evening. Anthony was thinking about a sausage sandwich and hoped the meeting wouldn't ruin his appetite.

He found a parking place on the street just next door, his car fitting into a space that was monitored by a meter. But it was just past six o'clock, and meters in this part of town were strictly nine-to-five.

Hope and Sophie pushed out of the sedan doors next to the curb as Anthony checked for traffic before pushing his door open. No cars. No rogue bicycles either. What about secret-service angels? What difference would it make if he could see those?

Actually, he probably had the best situation. He trusted Hope and Sophie, and he didn't have to see the freaky glowing beings himself. Most of the time.

Stepping briskly up the curb, Anthony hit the lock button on his remote. Still mid-July, the outside was lighter than the inside of the small restaurant. He imagined a creepy guy sitting in there waiting for them. But that imaginary guy wasn't even Will. Like he had sent someone else in his place. Why was Anthony imagining that?

Holding the door as Sophie and Hope led the way, Anthony inhaled a sharp pepper-and-sage aroma that turbocharged his already revving hunger. The scent of freshly baked bread forced a growl from his stomach.

Sophie laughed, standing right in front of him. It was a pretty loud growl. But they all three fell silent as they surveyed the room. No Will. There was an older couple eating at a table for two, and a young woman sitting alone at a larger table. She was staring past them.

Anthony turned to see what that girl was staring at. Nothing there except Hope scowling past him. Scowling back at that girl, maybe. Then Hope's face lit with surprise. Turning back, Anthony just glimpsed that young woman scuttling toward the back of the restaurant. He thought he heard her say something, then he heard another deeper voice. And that was it. Gone. Apparently.

"What can I get you? A table, perhaps?" A man with long gray hair and a bulbous nose smiled at the three of them in a sustained offer of hospitality.

Sophie nodded.

"A table," Anthony answered, still scowling toward the back of the restaurant.

"Yes, please." Hope put a hand on Sophie's back and nudged her forward, so she followed the waiter as he came out from behind the counter.

He gestured grandly toward the booth next to the one where that girl had been sitting. Handing them menus, he said, "My name is Gyorgy. I'll be waiting on you today. Can I start you with some drinks?"

"Uh, just water, please." Anthony poked a glance at each of the women, who affirmed his choice.

Gyorgy nodded and turned toward the back of the restaurant where the girl had disappeared.

"What was that?" Anthony asked just above a whisper. He hoped to avoid the hissing sound of a real whisper.

"I assume you're not talking about Gyorgy." Sophie was looking at the menu, her mouth twisted to the side.

"It was a serious gang of bad guys, that's what it was. That girl had 'em with her." Hope's eyes were wide. She held a menu but wasn't looking at it.

"And there was a guy in the back? I heard a voice."

"There was someone waiting for her. I got the idea that most of the girl's spiritual entourage actually belonged to him." Hope finally started surveying the menu.

"It sounded like a guy." Sophie glanced at Hope and then Anthony.

"Will?" Anthony scoped the restaurant again. "You think they snuck out the back?"

"Seems like it to me. That crowd of critters is gone." Hope sighed and slid herself farther back into the bench seat.

"You think Will was waiting back there to decide whether to meet with us?" Sophie raised her eyebrows at Anthony.

"He could have been. I mean, where is he otherwise?"

"So, that chick was, like, a lookout?" Hope was nodding as if answering her own question.

They studied the menu in silence for a while.

Hope sighed again. "Are we really eating here? This was just where Will wanted to meet."

"Is there something else that's wrong here?" Anthony glanced around. A young couple had just come in. The woman said something to the guy in a Slavic language, maybe Russian.

Hope was nodding more vigorously. "Yes, there is something wrong here. Meat and cabbage. Not my favorites."

"Try the cheese perogies." Sophie quirked a grin at Hope.

"I'm really hungry." That was Anthony's vote.

"Okay. I'm hungry too." Hope stretched her eyebrows and let her eyes settle back onto the menu.

They read in silence for half a minute. "So, what just happened then?" Anthony set his menu down.

"I think she was kind of a spiritual lookout. I think she spotted the security angels with us and called the meeting off. Or reported to Will, who decided to call the meeting off." Sophie only sounded mildly concerned about this possible explanation. "Or maybe it wasn't even him."

"Okay, that's really creepy." Hope winced, still searching the menu for Russian fish tacos, perhaps.

"Well, we already figured out that Will wasn't all he pretended to be. But what is he, then?" Anthony craned his neck toward the back of the restaurant again, then checked out the front window. He felt like they were being watched.

"Does it seem odd that there was that attack on Zeezee while we were on our way here?" Hope had dropped the menu onto the table.

Gyorgy arrived with three waters and took their food orders.

Hope looked at Sophie and Anthony after the waiter left, apparently still wanting an answer.

"And there was the bike that nearly wrecked the evening and that rider's face." Anthony had already noted how inauspicious that near accident was for the start of this little mission.

"I don't like assuming every little bump and setback is an attack from the enemy. But, times like this, it doesn't feel like paranoia." Sophie nodded slowly, watching something outside the front window.

"All paranoids probably say things like that." Anthony tipped his head toward Sophie.

She laughed. "You're probably right."

As much as Anthony wanted everything cleared up, or at least speculated through to the point of a good theory, he didn't mind being interrupted by Delilah calling. She reported peace and physical relief for Zeezee.

The food arrived not long after, and he and Sophie and Hope spent the evening like normal people. Not much more speculation. Not much beyond a question about what they put into that sausage Anthony and Sophie liked so much.

Team Building

Sophie greeted Nathan at the door. He arrived alone this time, unless she counted his guitar, which seemed to accompany him everywhere. But this would be the last time his instrument would come with him to this apartment.

Hope and Sophie had signed a lease on a three-bedroom apartment that was a bit run down but was in a good location and offered a dedicated office for Hope. Her future office had probably been used as a baby's room before. And Sophie would get the biggest bedroom, which she could share with her office computer equipment, including a new standing desk from her employer.

"Almost done packing?" Nathan leaned his guitar case against a neat stack of boxes.

Sophie had Hope to thank for such straight stacks and clear pathways to move around the apartment. "Almost done. This meeting will be one of the last things we do in this place."

"Cool. So we can all say goodbye and thanks for the memories."

"You do Bob Hope tunes?"

Nathan stared at her with his eyebrows high. He glanced toward the kitchen. "Who?"

"Never mind. Old dude in black-and-white movies."

"Oh, okay." He ran his fingers through his wavy brown hair, which was generously highlighted golden.

Sophie wondered if the hair color was natural.

Hope interrupted that thought by bringing a tray out from the kitchen. "Snacks for those in need." She set the tray of crackers, veggies, and dip on the coffee table. It was right out of Delilah's playbook.

"Awesome. That looks great. Thanks, Hope." Nathan was grinning at the food.

Hope was grinning at Nathan.

Sophie shook her head briefly and resisted an eye roll. The door buzzed and delivered her from the temptation to comment on any of it.

Anthony, Delilah, and Zeezee arrived next. Carlos came in the door only a minute later. It was a full house for Sophie's old place. It seemed like a good way to go out. Surely more fun than moving day would be.

Sophie checked out Nathan's bulgy biceps stretching the sleeves of his tight gray T-shirt. She was only assessing his potential for furniture moving, of course.

The whole crew sat nearly shoulder to shoulder around her little living room, brown boxes lining half the walls, and little of her usual decor still visible. But the place felt vibrant and even new, in a way. That was from the people, surely. Not the furnishings.

Sophie asked Delilah to open with prayer and encouraged Nathan to lead them in some songs. "Then we just do what comes. Like praying, singing some more, talking, whatever." It was the kind of meeting people at her church loved. Sophie suspected no one present would mind the open agenda. To her, prayer and worship were great ways to get to know her new team.

During the very first song, the angel Sophie thought of as Nathan's worship angel appeared behind him. The big guy, as big as Sophie's largest angel, was even more handsome than Nathan. Sophie couldn't help staring at him.

She checked with Hope, who was fixated on Nathan, only closing her eyes when she knew Sophie had caught her. Even then, Hope sang with a little grin on her girlish face.

Sophie had given a little thought to what it would mean if Nathan and Hope became a couple like Anthony and Delilah. That would just leave Sophie and Zeezee to fight over Carlos—a very unholy thought she had formulated late one night. In this group meeting, she cut such wanderings off and redirected her attention to the next worship song. She only cast one glance around the circle before lending her voice to the familiar tune.

With her eyes closed, Sophie let the sound of the music saturate her. Nathan's strong voice gave her cover, and the lack of inhibition of all these friends filled her with courage to let loose her own voice.

High into the flight of that song, Sophie felt like the singers had multiplied. It sounded more like a mass choir than a small group. But she decided to keep her eyes shut and focus on the King on his throne instead of possible singing angels in the room. That decision just seemed to make the angel choir sing louder.

She allowed herself to see her own angels for just a second without opening her eyes. They were all three singing. She thought of those three regulars as protectors and messengers. There were angels constantly singing worship around the throne of heaven according to the Bible. But her angels, her guardians, could be worshippers too. Just as the girl who sees angels could be a worshipper.

Nathan was into a spontaneous song by then. "God is a warrior. His victory is real." That was the line he sang over and over.

It was a fitting response to Sophie's thought about being both an angel seer and a worshipper. The line changed then. "God is a warrior. His victory is here."

After a minute there, Carlos altered it. "God is a warrior. His victory is mine."

Sophie was crying by now. She wasn't sure exactly why, but figuring it out didn't seem important. At least not in the moment.

She knew that Anthony was on his knees on the floor next to her. Delilah was standing with her hands raised. Zeezee was sniffling frequently, probably weeping as hard as Sophie was.

Nathan kept it flowing. He seemed capable of constant music no matter how thick the emotions grew in the room. No matter how many angels joined in. No matter how heavy the presence of God.

Sophie blinked away some tears and wiped her face with both hands. She noticed that Hope was flat on her back on the floor. Her eyes were open, however, and she had the biggest smile on her face.

Sophie peeked toward the ceiling. She could tell there was an angel show up there, but she suspected Hope was seeing much more than she was. That was good. Sophie would leave Hope to her private revelation.

Sophie offered one more alteration to that spontaneous song. "We are God's warriors. His victory is ours."

Even with half of them weeping too hard to sing, the song roared on and on with that line. Nathan seemed to be an uninterruptable worshipper. The angels clearly knew no limits to their voices.

That night—with their angels—her teammates were all worship warriors.

A Guide to a Hidden Future

Sophie tossed in bed, kicking the sheet that was her only cover. Most of the work was done, at least for moving out. She was weary from all the packing, not to mention her job as a software developer and now as the leader of a team of spiritual warriors.

Lying there, the image of Delilah as a warrior queen coalesced in Sophie's imagination. And she recognized that as a prayer prompt. A direction as well as a promise. So she started to pray about Delilah reaching toward her potential as a warrior, a servant of God tearing down the gates of the enemy. In Sophie's prayer, as in her imagination, Delilah was not alone. It was all of them, the team supporting Delilah, supporting Sophie. Supporting each other.

In her exhaustion, she must have finally drifted off to sleep even as she prayed. She was probably still sleeping when a golden angel appeared to her. A new angel. Not clearly male or female. Pure and beautiful. For the briefest moment, Sophie recalled a deceptive shining spirit that had come to her in the night a couple years ago. But she was not the same confused young woman she had been then, and she could clearly feel the presence of God as she focused on this new visitor.

"Come with me, Sophie."

"Who are you?"

The angel gave Sophie their name. It was different from any name she had ever heard on earth, but Sophie was pretty sure she was no longer on the earth.

It was no longer night here. They were soaring through a pure blue sky. Sophie was flying. The sensation made her laugh.

The angel turned their smile on her, as if sharing her enjoyment.

Landing on the ground like she had as a girl jumping from her cousins' tree house, Sophie caught the arm of the angel to keep from face planting. In a dream—or whatever this was—she could grab an angel by the arm. She had longed to do that in numerous situations in her waking life. This experience felt more dreamlike for its fulfillment of that girlish desire.

But the angel was drawing Sophie's attention to the ground. They were standing in a meadow thick with unmown grass. Never in the natural world had Sophie stood in such a field, being a life-long city dweller. But she knew it was a pasture for animals. And, as if released by that realization, a large four-legged beast appeared. Lumbering toward them, its head was down. It seemed intent on the succulent greens at its feet.

Then Sophie felt the ground coming up to meet her. Or maybe it was only the grass that was rising, growing rapidly. Or maybe ... maybe she was shrinking. Within seconds, the grass was as tall as her. And it felt like more than her reduced size that linked her with the grass. The grass represented her. These were her people.

Though she didn't see them in their natural forms, she sensed that Anthony, Delilah, Hope, Zeezee, Nathan, and

Carlos were also connected to that grass. They were part of this field.

Above and around her she could still hear heavy footfalls crashing closer and closer. Giant teeth munched the Sophie-sized grass around her. Great dark hooves were sending shadows toward her. The giant beast was devouring the meadow. The meadow included Sophie and her friends. She was in danger. Anthony and Delilah and all of them were in danger.

Sophie startled awake. The sheet was completely kicked aside. Her curtains stirred slightly. The slight breeze brushed her skin, highlighting cold patches where she was sweating. She felt like she had been tossed onto her bed. Tossed like a beanbag. A soft landing after a brief flight. Well aimed, but still thrown.

It was a dream. Only a dream. That's all. "Pretty much a nightmare." She said it aloud. She had used that phrase to describe monstrous work projects, messed up people, and political disasters. But this time she meant it literally.

Then she lay still. Her mind slowed as her heart returned toward a normal rhythm. Her thoughts cooled with the breeze soothing her arms and legs. Yes, it was a dream, but not *only* a dream. It was a dream that included a named angel. It was a real message. A warning. The warning was real. The threat was real.

Sitting up and settling her T-shirt around her neck—draped instead of twisted—Sophie wondered what she was supposed to do with that dream. The clock said 1:13. That was too late to call anyone. Hope was in the living room, probably spilling off the air mattress they had pulled out there after the meeting this evening.

Did the worship time with her team prompt the dream? Were there new angels in play after that meeting's emotional and spiritual blast? It had felt like they were capturing some significant ground as they sang. Maybe that was right. Maybe that experience provoked a new threat. An approaching enemy.

She wouldn't wake Hope. What could Hope tell her anyway? As soon as she formed that internal question, Hope's main angel came through the closed door. She was nodding, a clear sign of understanding, even agreement.

Sophie turned to her three angels, whom she had sensed before but only focused on now. "That was a warning. What am I supposed to do about it?"

"Be vigilant. Know that an enemy is seeking to devour you and your friends." Her big guardian wasn't as likely to speak to Sophie as the female angel, but maybe this was a security matter, and that seemed to be his specialty.

She filed away that thought. "Lord, help me to pay attention to the signs. To accept the messages you send through your angels. And, most of all, protect my friends … from being devoured."

Shaking her head at how dramatic and biblical her prayer sounded, she tried to recall relevant stories from the Bible. Weren't there dreams in the Old Testament about cattle devouring things, people or each other? There was definitely that warning in the New Testament about the devil seeking people to devour.

"Wow."

Her three regular angels joined Hope's main angel in nodding knowingly. Sympathetically.

Sophie was glad to have their sympathy. She was also counting on their protection.

A Moving Experience

Sophie and Hope's apartment move happened the last Saturday in July. The air conditioner was struggling to keep up. Whose idea was it to move at the end of July? Hope didn't ask that aloud. She was one of the coconspirators, of course.

The dream about the munching cow had made it from Sophie's head around to the whole group by now, including Detta and Roderick. Those two were the day's self-appointed cleaning crew, sweeping, mopping, and wiping after the others moved stuff out of one room and then another.

Hope couldn't look at Detta on hands and knees, wearing slacks and an old smock in the warm and humid bathroom. That woman would do *anything* for Hope and Sophie. There was no stopping her. At least Roddy stayed off his knees. He had a hard time standing up, apparently, so he probably stayed upright to avoid a crisis.

"I don't think you should treat it like a curse." Detta was standing in the bathroom doorway now. "If it's from one of God's holy angels, then it's a warning you should heed. No sense in them warning you if there's nothin' you can do to protect yourselves."

Sophie and Anthony were both in the hallway outside the bathroom. The crew was conveying boxes in stages. Now they were stacking them outside the door, on the landing at the top of the stairs. The plan was to move the team to the stairs next and hand the boxes down one floor, continuing in assembly-line fashion. That way no one would wear their legs out trudging up and down stairs.

"I believe you, theoretically. But I feel like I've been looking over my shoulder since then, waiting for some kind of attack." Sophie turned and looked over her shoulder, literally, to get the next box.

"Well, there was that closet rod collapsing and nearly braining you." Anthony sounded like he was joking, though his strain while passing a box complicated the sound of his joking voice.

Hope had heard the scream when Sophie was attacked in her closet by a hanging rod. Anthony and Delilah had been here last night. Delilah brought supper, and the two of them helped with some basic repairs.

"That was more of an attack by you than by some giant chomping cow demon." Sophie could joke about demons more freely than most people. "I don't expect you and your wayward hammer are working for the devil."

Hope appreciated Sophie's humor, but this was real stuff. "No, seriously. I've been doing the paranoid double check on all kinds of things too."

Sophie looked sympathetically at Hope, then wiped sweat off her forehead with the back of her hand. She seemed more preoccupied with the work at hand than the meaning of that dream. But others had taken hold of that message by now.

"Well, for me, it's just another reminder to pray for you folks." Detta tied up a white garbage bag. She looked at Sophie. "You didn't tell me how that time went with the little girl you were telling me about."

"Little girl? Ah, our session with that college girl."

"Oh. Well, young girl, then. What's she doin' at the college in the summer?"

"She took a job working on campus. There are conferences and summer classes, so they still need workers for maintenance and stuff."

Hope answered Detta's original question. "It was good. It went fine. Carlos was super helpful. He got some great tips from Jonathan." She was proud of the way the team helped that girl after those other students had messed up. And meeting those college kids had booted up questions about Hope taking Bible classes at that Christian school. Maybe. Someday.

"It was good. And we were all safe all the way through it." Sophie handed off a box, pausing to step out of the line for a view out the apartment door.

"No chomping." Hope was only half joking. The enemies they'd found plaguing Betsy were more like monkeys than cows, and they were mostly clinging, not devouring. But she didn't say any of that. Probably too much to say to people who weren't there.

"Okay, here's the last. What does the pile look like out there?" Carlos handed a light cardboard box to Hope, who handed it to Sophie, who watched other hands pass it out the door.

Priscilla poked her head in the door. "Looks like a castle out here. Time to move it down."

Kimmy squeezed in the door, which was propped with one of the heavier boxes. "Anything I can do in here that doesn't require lifting?"

"Hey, Kimmy." Sophie grabbed her in a hug despite how dusty and sweaty she was.

"Am I too late?"

"No way. What do you think about going over to the new place to do a little cleaning there?"

"Sure. Who's going over there?"

Crystal came in from the bedroom. "I am. Hey, you look pregnant."

The three of them laughed. Apparently Kimmy was pregnant again. Hope hadn't heard, but it was pretty obvious at this point. That explained the no-lifting clause.

"We'll be comin' over in a few minutes. Roddy and I just need to do the last wipe and sweep in the kitchen." Detta patted Kimmy on the shoulder.

"Oh, great. So we can just go over there and hang out, waiting for the pros to show up."

Sophie's mother came in from the bedroom just then.

Sophie reached a hand toward her. "Here's the real pro, but I made her promise not to do any cleaning. It's her day off."

Her mom smiled, as if unsure what she had missed. "Carlos has gone to get the truck. He wanted me to tell you."

Sophie looked around. Carlos had been in the line a minute ago. "Who did he take with him?"

"He went alone. He said he can leave his car there. He checked with the rental place."

"Man, it's great to have all these responsible adults helping out." Sophie grinned her gratitude toward Hope.

"Amen to that, girl." Everyone was doing more than she expected, which was good, because Hope had never done a proper move before. Running away from home wasn't the same thing. Much less complicated, it turned out. She patted Sophie on the shoulder. "I'll go down and make sure we're clear to move the pile down to the second floor. No obstructions from us or anyone else."

"Great, thanks." Sophie raised her voice to the press of people in the hallway. "Let Hope past, she's scouting the next landing spot."

Hope pushed into the hall, where she started getting high fives from everyone. Not sure where that came from, she laughed all the way to the top of the stairs. She waved to Nathan in that crowd as she stepped down that first step.

Something caught at her toe.

And then she was falling.

Where the hallway above her was full of boxes and people, the stairway was empty. Empty space. Nothing but air. And she had it all to herself.

Then she landed. Catching her weight with the shin of one leg, she instantly regretted it and rolled to catch herself with one hand. She missed and smashed across three or four steps.

Screams and shouts sounded above her.

She hadn't hit her head. Probably. But the world was fading. The pain was intense. A wall of darkness approached at high speed.

Then ...

Getting Patched Up

Detta leaned over Hope and gently touched her forehead. "Heal every bone and joint, please, dear Lord. Heal your servant Hope. Quick and complete recovery. Let it come, in Jesus's name."

Then Hope opened her eyes. She blinked heavily and smiled at Detta. "Must be some good drugs."

Barely shaking her head, Detta sniffed at the joke. "They gave you some painkillers for now. Not too strong ones, though. They were hopin' you would wake up. You're enduring a lot of it on your own strength."

"Strength? I feel like a lump of dough."

Sophie leaned in from the other side of the bed. "Hey, girl. I didn't know you could fly."

"Apparently I can't."

Sophie nodded. "Yeah, I guess you're right. Glad you figured that out."

"Probably were some better ways to discover that." Hope's girly grin faded. "My leg really hurts."

Detta made eye contact with Sophie. Who was going to tell her? They hadn't decided that, not really ready for her to wake up yet.

Sophie accepted responsibility. "You broke your leg, Hope. They're getting you ready to go into surgery. They need to reset it better."

"Oh. That explains why it's screaming at me."

"Yeah. Not happy."

Hope hummed for a second. "What happened to the move?"

"Still going on without us, I guess."

"You guess?"

"Remember all those responsible adults we were talking about?"

"Huh. Yeah. I do."

"They're getting it done. Getting our new place all set up for us."

"Good. Huh. Well, good thing there's an elevator."

Sophie laughed. "Yeah, that's right. Good thing."

Detta looked up as the doctor came in the door. This time he was wearing scrubs.

"Hello, I'm Doctor Hanigan." He was smiling at Hope. "Good to see you awake. We can't find any sign of a head injury, so I suspect you just passed out. Which is normal, given the amount of pain you were in." He had a handsome grin.

Hope stared at him, blinking slowly. "You're gonna put me back together again though, right?"

"That's the plan. Any requests? Taller, faster, stronger?" He raised his eyebrows as if it were a real question.

A little trail of spit made it as far as Hope's chin when she sputtered a laugh. "Taller would be nice, but not too tall." She tried to wipe her chin but found the IV tethering her to a bag of electrolytes. She managed to get one shoulder close enough for a rough cleanup.

"Okay, we'll see what we can do." The doctor patted the rail of the bed and signaled for Detta to follow him toward the door. He waited for her to meet him just in the hallway.

"She seems fine. I'm glad she woke up, just to make sure there was no head trauma that we couldn't detect. How does she seem to you?"

Sophie was close at Detta's shoulder. "She's normal. Obviously in pain. But that's Hope just the way we love her."

"Okay, good to hear that. Well, the anesthetist will be up soon, and we'll get her in right away. No good waiting. She's in a lot of pain, and we don't want the fragment to start adhering in the wrong position."

Sophie winced, and Detta took a deep breath. "Thanks, Doctor. See you when you're done."

"Yes. See you later." He nodded to Detta and Sophie in turn and headed down the hall.

Roddy was standing next to the door, having raised himself from the chair in the hall. "All good?"

Detta nodded at him and led the way back into the room. A nurse was in there checking the IV and recording Hope's vital signs on a tablet computer.

"Does he think I'll live?" Hope was looking at her left wrist, which was splinted.

"You just sprained your wrist," Sophie said.

"Oh, that's good. Would be hard to work with a broken arm."

"Broken leg won't be as bad for work, I guess." Sophie seemed pretty tired.

Hope blinked, looking more childlike than Detta had ever seen her.

"You scared us there for a minute." Sophie was leaning on the edge of the bed as the nurse breezed out of the room.

"The flying part was okay. It was the landing that sucked."

"Yeah. You gotta work on that landing."

Detta shook her head at those two. Such jokers. But she had some serious questions. Like, where were their angels when this girl was tripping over a loose power cord? She breathed a sigh through her nose.

"Sorry I scared you." Hope was looking at Detta now, not Sophie.

"Oh, girl. Don't you worry. I'm fine." Detta glanced over her shoulder at Roddy, who had a hand on her back. "You just relax and let the doctors do their thing. And we'll all be out here prayin' for you."

"Which is easier than cleaning the bathroom, I should point out." Roddy knew he could joke with Hope.

Hope laughed a bit harder, then pressed her elbow to her ribs.

"Oh, yeah. A cracked rib too." Sophie winced again.

"Anything else you're not telling me?"

Sophie laughed, but even she knew not to make another joke.

A New Crew in a New Place

Sophie was sitting at the kitchen/dining room table, eating and watching the angels who were posted by the door to their new apartment. When she glanced at Hope, she could see her looking at the same thing. "Why do you think they stand by the door like that? They didn't used to do that at our old place."

Hope dabbed at her lips with a paper napkin. "Why don't you ask 'em? They talk to you." She scooped some more rice with her fork.

"Not these two. Not these new guys."

"They do look like guys, don't they? Am I crazy, or does it feel like someone sent them over? Like someone gifted us a security team as a housewarming present." She sat up straighter in her dining chair, sliding her cast closer to the edge of the other chair on which it rested.

Sophie slid that footrest chair a little closer and then poked at her faux chicken. "I think I know what you mean. But who do we know besides God who has angels to send over?"

"Well, there is that, I suppose." Hope slipped a piece of meat substitute between her teeth.

"Though, of course, all the angels come from God, ultimately." Sophie turned her gaze from the angels to her meal. "But I've seen it where we pray and an angel takes off as if they're going with the prayer—going to where the person is that we're praying for. Like with Delilah and Zeezee when we were going to meet Will."

"So you think we have, like, some new prayer covering person?" Hope studied the guys by the door as she chewed. She was in a better position to see them.

"Prayer covering? You've been talking to Detta again, I see."

"I know. And she's such a bad influence on me." Hope quirked a grin and picked up her water glass with her healthy hand. Her braced wrist rested idly on the edge of the table, not fully ready for action.

"But seriously, I think that's a possibility. Though, when it comes to all this stuff"—Sophie gestured to the guards by the door—"I don't know enough to say anything for sure."

"Well, telling the good guys from the bad isn't so hard."

"Yeah, that's true. Now. But there was a time when that wasn't the case for me, especially back before I got aligned with Jesus."

"That makes sense. But even when I was drifting, I felt like I knew which was which." Hope shrugged. "Maybe that's from being raised in church."

"Mm-hmm." Too much speculation made Sophie tired, like trying to move boxes that were too heavy.

"Then there's figuring out if something like falling down the stairs was the devil's doing or just me being clumsy."

"Clumsy and distracted by a handsome smile?"

Hope did a double take. "Who told you that?"

"I have my sources." Sophie actually couldn't recall who had mentioned that Hope was waving at Nathan when she took that dive.

Hope's phone interrupted the interrogation. She looked at the name. "Huh. What does he want?"

"Who?"

"Uh, Gerry. That guy from back ... back in the NA group."

"Just checking in?"

"Hmm." Hope tapped to answer the call. "Hello, what's up?" She twisted in her seat like she would go somewhere more private to talk, but her crutches were beyond reach, and she apparently gave up on that.

Sophie focused on finishing up her meal and tried to pretend not to listen. She couldn't remember much of what Hope had said about Gerry, but she got a little twist in her stomach about this call. Or maybe it was just the veggies disguised as chicken that were making a ruckus.

"What? What did you leave in my closet?" Hope was turning red. She swore and then shook her head at Sophie. "No. I will not send you that stuff. I will not commit a felony for you, thanks." She hung up the call.

"What?" Sophies stomach ruckus was threatening to become a riot.

"That ... guy hid some drugs in one of my boots, apparently. Obviously a pair of boots I don't wear very often." She had already slid her cast off the chair, resting it on the wood veneer momentarily while she reached for her crutches.

Sophie just stared in shock as Hope got upright and swung toward the hall closet.

Sophie had noticed a little collection of boots, maybe just two pairs, in their hallway closet. She and Hope each had a closet in their bedrooms. She had assumed Hope's footwear collection required a little overflow space.

Hope got to that closet and opened the door, propping one crutch against the wall, her good arm bracing her weight as she leaned in. Her curses in the closet were muffled, her backside the only part showing out the door. "Sorry." She stood up and grabbed the second crutch, holding a bag of pills between thumb and forefinger. It was a quart bag almost half full. Various sizes and colors, those pills appeared to be sorted into smaller bags within.
    "He was dealing?"
    "It would appear so. I guess he tried to stop by and pick them up a few times before he finally found out I moved."
    "Oh. Dang. And now he wants you to send them to him?"
    "I should flush 'em though, right?" Hope's phone rang again.
    "Technically you shouldn't flush 'em. That stuff messes up the water system. Like, drugs all of us a little, is what I hear."
    "Ugh. Explains why people are so dumb." Hope shook her head sharply. Then she picked up the call. "I'm not sending them to you. I need to turn them in to the cops or a hospital or something." She listened to a sharp reply.
    "But I didn't tell you to fill my boot up with these, you boot violator." Hope huffed and growled.
    Sophie had to clap a hand over her mouth. She had never heard Hope so angry and out of control. "Boot violator?" She kept her mouth covered. *I cannot laugh. I cannot laugh. I cannot ...*
    Tipping as if she might fall over, Hope landed one shoulder against the white wall and rested her head there, the phone still wedged against her ear. "Why couldn't you keep

them at your own place?" She listened. "But I don't wanna see you. And I don't wanna hold your drugs."

Sophie was up and walking across the living room.

Hope listened for another second. "I don't care if the FBI is listening. This all falls on you, not me."

Again, she listened. "Oh. Well, I hope the FBI *is* listening, if you're threatening me. That'll go real well for you." She thumbed her phone to hang up and looked at Sophie. Hope stopped growling. And her eyes stopped flashing. Her face fell toward the floor. "Remember what we were talking about?"

Sophie cocked her head to the side. Then she thought she knew the reference. "About the devil attacking?"

"Yeah, and knowing the difference between the good ones and the bad ones."

"Sure."

"I think I do better with the angels and demons than with people. I'm a terrible judge of people."

"Not always. Just when you're desperate."

"Huh. Okay. Maybe." Hope de-escalated a little more.

"Nathan is a good guy. He really is. You're not wrong about that."

Hope's eyebrows rose to attention. "You think he's interested in me?"

"I don't know, but I wouldn't be surprised. He does kinda light up when you talk to him." She allowed a small smile, recalling that little extra glow from the worship guy.

"Huh." Hope scowled. She looked at the bag of pills. "What am I gonna do with these?"

"Want me to take 'em and stow 'em somewhere safe until we figure it out?" Sophie reached toward the bag.

"You'd do that?"

"For you, I'd do that. Not for Gerry."

"Right. Okay. I guess." She held the bag out to Sophie.

Worried about Hope being tempted by that pharmacy in a bag, Sophie didn't want the pills in the apartment for any amount of time. Hope probably knew that was what motivated the offer.

When Sophie took the bag, Hope turned away. "I gotta go lie down. My leg is killing me." She slowly pivoted toward her room.

Sophie prayed for her friend, knowing there was some supercharged Tylenol in her room for the pain in her leg. She prayed that this enemy attack, even if a result of poor judgment, would not succeed in taking back ground Hope had already conquered.

A Friend in Need

Anthony waited in his car in front of the building where his friend Wesley lived.

Sophie's car rolled to a stop across the street, coming from the opposite direction, the direction of her new apartment. Hope wasn't in the car, but Carlos was.

It would just be the three of them tonight. Would that be enough? Was it reasonable to let Wesley limit the number of people who came to his place for this? Anthony closed his car door and crossed the street.

"Hey, Anthony." Carlos offered the first fist bump as he stepped up the clean new curb.

Anthony met his fist and then offered one to Sophie.

She gently bumped knuckles with him, glancing at the modern apartment building behind them. "This is just a test, like I said. We're just checking to see if there's anything we can do. An eval."

He nodded. "I get it, but at least I wanna try. He's one of my oldest friends. I wanna help if we can."

"Of course."

Carlos was following the two of them. "And what an opportunity, huh? I mean, how many other friends does he have who can help with a thing like this?"

Grinning at Carlos over his shoulder, Anthony nodded. Carlos's words were like the full-volume version of thoughts

Anthony had been streaming to himself. It was at least an opportunity. He should at least *try* to help Wesley.

They stood before a camera in the entryway, and the door lock buzzed. This apartment complex was only a few years old, clean and artfully decorated. The broad-leaved plants in the lobby were clearly all real, arranged among the cushioned benches and the round tables with power outlets and USB jacks in them. Anthony couldn't imagine hanging out in the lobby of his own apartment building, but he'd never hung out in Wesley's lobby either.

"Heather is his new girlfriend?" Sophie stood next to Anthony in front of the elevator door, watching the floor numbers light as the lift came to get them.

"Yeah. They've been together, like, six months."

"Are they living together? Is this her place too?" The elevator arrived, and Sophie stepped in first.

"Actually, I don't know if that's official. I know she stays over here a lot, but I don't know if she still has a place of her own." He knew why Sophie was asking this stuff. Place mattered when it came to spirits and their authority. Ownership and belonging were relevant markers for people and their power over what happened in the spirit world. That still struck Anthony as odd. Like a strange concession God made for materialistic human beings.

"So you take the lead, Anthony, until it seems obvious we should switch to me or Carlos." Sophie almost said it as a question.

Anthony nodded. He didn't mind her saying it, even if she was giving him instructions. Sophie was easily the most experienced at stuff like this. And, as usual, what she said made sense to him.

"If we need to set up a session for her, we'll make sure to have more women present." Sophie kept her eyes on the doors as she said that.

The elevator stopped and dinged, the doors sliding open. Anthony nodded as he led the way into the stone-tiled hall. He shook his head at the contrast between this building and the place where Wesley used to live. Artsy was the best thing that could be said of that old three-story building downtown. Actually it probably was a lot more artsy now after it had been sold and rehabbed. But this place was a big step up. Wesley was moving up in the world, managing a whole region for the cell phone company that employed him. Apparently he had met Heather on the job. She was working for a company that was one of Wesley's corporate clients.

"Hey, Anthony, thanks for coming. Sophie, good to see you again." Wesley was barefoot, wearing linen pants and a loose, woven cotton pullover shirt with three-quarter sleeves. A new look for him.

"Hey, Wesley. This is Carlos, a friend of ours. He's a therapist." Anthony didn't know why he said that last part. Did it matter? What would Wesley think?

"Okay." Wesley hesitated and then met Carlos's offered fist bump. Maybe he was willing to let a therapist into his apartment as long as he fist bumped.

That nutty idea probably only happened in Anthony's head.

"Here's Heather." Wesley gestured toward a slender young woman with very long black hair. She stood in the entrance to the living room, smiling shyly.

They did introductions for Sophie and Carlos. Anthony had seen Heather several times already with Wesley.

"You look like you're feeling okay." Sophie walked with Heather into the living room.

"Yeah, the fever comes and goes. It gets really high, like over 103, and then just goes away."

"You go to the hospital when it gets that high?" Carlos was just behind Sophie's shoulder.

Heather nodded.

Wesley led them into a sort of pit lined with couches, three long sections with a fireplace on the fourth side. Plenty of space for everyone to spread out.

Anthony resisted the urge to relax on one of those couches. He was supposed to take the lead even though Sophie and Carlos had already dipped into the interview process, at least informally.

"So when did these fevers start, exactly?" Anthony was trying to do more than imagine what Sophie or Carlos would ask next. He needed to be actively involved. Surely Wesley would be more comfortable with him asking the questions than Sophie or Carlos.

"Well, first—" Wesley interrupted. "Does anyone want something to drink? Just help yourselves." He gestured to an assortment of soft drink cans and water bottles sweating on the stone top of the broad table in the middle of the sofa pit.

Carlos grabbed a bottle of water, offered it to Sophie, then took another for himself, thanking Wesley. The guy was polite, for sure, but was he interested in Sophie?

Anthony apologized to Wesley. "Oh, sorry to jump right in."

"No, that's cool. I have no idea how this is supposed to go." Wesley raised a palm toward the ceiling and stuck out his lower lip.

"Right. I get it." Anthony hesitated for a second and turned back to Heather. "Well, do you have an idea about when it started?"

"It's been a couple months now, right?" She was looking at Wesley. "It happens a few times a month, maybe."

"Is it that often?" Wesley pulled out his phone. "Maybe I can tell from our text messages."

Heather flinched. "Oh, you don't wanna go through all those."

"I'm not gonna read 'em out loud. I'm just thinking we usually text about it when it starts or when you're feelin' like you need to go to the hospital."

Anthony was trying to imagine the logistics of all that, but also trying to measure the tension between the couple. "It might help to know if there's a pattern."

"Oh. It's so random. I mean, what pattern?" Heather's gaze wandered toward the fireplace in front of her. It was dark. The evening was warm, and the sun was just setting.

"Okay, here's the last one. It was Thursday last week." Wesley thumbed some more.

"Seems like a lot of trouble going through all those." Heather glanced at Wesley.

Anthony felt like he was stuck in the middle of a simmering couple's quarrel. But really it was just Heather resisting. Which wouldn't be surprising if there was a spirit involved in the strange fevers.

"The week before, it was Thursday too. Though earlier in the day, it looks like." Wesley focused on his phone, not even looking up as he reported. "Late Thursday the week before. I didn't realize …" He kept thumbing. "Huh. Why would it only happen on Thursdays?"

"Well, like we said when we talked, it's pretty strange for a fever to come on like that and then go away with a visit to the hospital. I mean, that's what the doctors said, right?" Anthony waited for confirmation.

Heather nodded but said nothing. It was hard to tell what she was thinking, her eyes still rested on that dark fireplace.

"Okay. So that's definitely a pattern, right? I can't find it happening any days but Thursdays." Wesley lowered his phone.

Heather almost seemed to wake up just then. "But I don't have anything except work on Thursdays. I used to watch my shows, but that doesn't …" The steam leaked out before she could finish that, apparently.

"What about Wednesdays? Is there something you do every Wednesday that's new in the last few months?" Maybe Sophie was ready to bail Anthony out. Or was it Heather who needed a rescue?

"Just the spa."

"What kind of spa is it?" Carlos held his water bottle in one hand, his other arm resting along the back of the couch. Clearly a *just hanging out* posture. Was he doing that on purpose?

"It's just … the … The Magic Circle on the west side. Some hot stone massage, some Reiki healing. Just things like that."

There was a short silence.

"You see a therapist there … or …" Sophie sounded like a person waiting for her teammate to get the answer to a quiz question.

"Oh. She's … a practitioner."

"Sure." Sophie nodded.

Anthony was thinking of the sort of stuff Sophie's friend Crystal used to be involved in. He expected Sophie would be familiar with the kind of therapy Heather was describing, but what would she say about it?

Carlos stepped in. Maybe he recognized the delicate place Anthony was in regarding his friendship with Wesley. Carlos cleared his throat. "It seems likely that there's a spiritual element to your fevers, Heather. So we're just looking for possible spiritual involvements during the week. Fever on Thursday, Reiki and that stuff on Wednesday." He shrugged.

"But she's a healer. She's not gonna make me sick." Heather seemed truly confused.

"Have you talked to the practitioner about the fevers?" Wesley was acting like part of the team now, which was pretty awkward.

Heather shot him a look.

Sophie intervened. "I know people have different beliefs, and we're not here to challenge any of that. But our beliefs center on Jesus and the kind of healing he offers. In our sort of ... approach, we might expect that a practitioner of another kind of healing might be making a ... might be involving other kinds of spirits. Maybe unknowingly."

Blinking at her like Sophie had just accused her of kicking small dogs for a hobby, Heather's eyes grew wider and wider. "I can't believe Deirdre has anything to do with that."

This was Tuesday. Presumably Heather would be back at the spa tomorrow. Anthony wasn't going to say anything, but he suspected that next visit would be different for Heather. In what way it would be changed, he couldn't predict. But he had to break the silence. "Well, think about whether you wanna sort of experiment with our approach." He thought of

Delilah in her lab at work. "Then give us a call and we can see what we can do to help."

"But maybe we can just pray for you here tonight and ask for protection." Sophie turned from Heather to Anthony, certainly asking permission of them both.

Wesley was nodding. He certainly knew Anthony was bringing Christian friends with him, but maybe he hadn't made that clear to Heather. He took a second to regard Heather out of the corner of his eye.

All heads turned squarely toward Heather in the silence that followed.

"Well, okay. If you want to. Go ahead."

Sophie nodded to Anthony.

He was thinking, "Thanks a lot," but he didn't hesitate to begin a prayer for protection and continued good health. His own words sounded generic. He didn't think it would work for him to rebuke anything, which made him wonder what Sophie was seeing during all this. Still, revealing some spirits hanging around her would probably not go over well with Heather. So he just prayed that general prayer, and he ended in the name of Jesus, potentially the most offensive part of it.

Sophie hitched onto the end of Anthony's petitions. One part of what she prayed caught his attention particularly. "And we bless Heather's freedom. Her freedom from all sickness. Her freedom from any kind of attack." She ended in the name of Jesus as well.

When all heads were raised, Anthony checked on Heather. Her face was red, especially her nose. He couldn't be sure, but it looked like she had been crying. What was that about? Did *she* even know?

He looked to Sophie next as she slid forward with her hands on the front of her skinny jeans as if preparing to leave. So they were done, apparently.

Wesley followed Sophie's lead, only glancing briefly at Heather.

But Carlos remained seated. "Are you okay, Heather? Do you have any questions?"

If Anthony didn't know any better, he would think Carlos was some kind of therapist or something. He snorted quietly at his own clumsiness.

"I'm fine. I'm ... grateful for the prayers. Thanks." Heather scooted to the edge of the couch and slowly stood, as if gravity had intensified where she was sitting.

The others began sauntering toward the door.

The Woman Who Chases That Strange Girl

Sophie was tired of just texting Carlos and Anthony about what had happened the night before. She called Carlos as she walked down the long open staircase at work. It was late in the afternoon, and the windows along the outside of the stairway were warming the air-conditioned building with patches of bright light.

"You think we screwed up? That I screwed up? Should I have told her about that thing that was hooked onto her head?" She lowered her voice as she noted the sound of footsteps near the bottom of the staircase.

"No one can answer that one hundred percent, Sophie. How would she have reacted? We don't know. And the only way to know is to try. But maybe that would have shut her off from us later. Who knows? I don't think you can blame yourself."

"It's way easier to help when you know the people have faith. Or at least some kind of Christian reference point."

"Oh. I sensed that she had some reference points, but those were probably mostly negative to her."

"Really? You picked that up?"

"Maybe. Again, not a sure thing."

Sophie took a deep breath as she strolled across the lobby.

Carlos broke in. "Well, I have a client coming in. I gotta go."

"Okay. Thanks for talking. It was a good reality check."

"Glad to do it. Take care, Sophie."

"Thanks, you too. Bye." Her goodbye was automatic. Her attention had rushed off toward a vaguely familiar young woman standing across the street from her office building. Sophie slowed outside the revolving door, having trouble recalling where she had seen that girl before. The pale young woman reminded her of Heather, but this girl was younger than Heather, though she had the same figure and long dark hair.

Then the young woman turned directly toward Sophie and made eye contact. She quickly looked away and started off at a brisk pace.

It was the girl from the Russian deli. The girl who took off when Sophie and friends arrived to meet with Will, who never showed up. What was she doing outside Sophie's workplace? Could it be just a coincidence?

Without thinking it through, Sophie sped in the same direction on her side of the street. She checked for traffic and crossed on a *Don't Walk* sign as the girl turned the next corner.

With the young woman almost a block ahead, Sophie could see a pair of spirits fluttering off her like flags. Dirty flags. Maybe dirty flags that had been set on fire. As she noted that, it occurred to Sophie to check with her angels. The big guy was striding next to her but looking at her, not at the way ahead of them, not at that young woman.

Trying to figure out the meaning of the angel's odd posture slowed Sophie, so she set that aside and faced forward to keep up with the young woman. She caught the girl glancing back at her but not increasing her speed as she would if she were really trying to escape. Sophie could feel herself slowing down again.

Curiosity is a powerful driver, though not necessarily a safe driver. Sophie bumped into a man in a suit, who barked a protest. She apologized and had to accelerate again. She began to gradually gain on the girl, who hadn't looked back for a while. Unless she was like someone in a spy movie, checking on Sophie in the reflective surfaces she passed. That uncomfortable possibility reminded Sophie to check with her angel again. He was still next to her. Still looking at her.

"What? Why are you looking at me like that?" She glanced ahead just in time to slam on her brakes at the next crosswalk. Crossing on that *Don't Walk* would have probably been painful. She waited for a car and a scooter to pass before she sprinted across the crowded street.

The girl turned left at the next corner—a maneuver Sophie just barely saw. She jogged at half speed to gain some ground. What she would do if she caught up to the young woman was a question bounding along beside her. Probably jogging on the opposite side of her guardian. Where were the other angels?

She reached the corner of a deeply shaded side street and saw the girl look back over her shoulder before she dodged into a doorway. *Aha.* Sophie thought that, she didn't say it. Because part of her brain was saying, *Hold on a second.* More *hmm* than *aha.* She snorted at her muddled musings and settled her messenger bag on the back of her hip for about the tenth time during this pursuit.

When she reached the half-opened door where the young woman had disappeared, Sophie checked with her angel again.

He stopped and crossed his arms, just standing there.

Waiting? Waiting for what? Before she could ask him, a voice spun her around.

"Sophie, right?" It was Will. "Funny seeing you here."

The shock of seeing that guy after chasing that girl pushed Sophie back half a step into the doorway the girl had entered. Sophie's shoulder bumped into the large metal door, pushing it open a little more.

Then she heard another voice from inside that building. "Sophie, so good to see you again."

Sophie spun again, her feet knocking together on the concrete threshold of the dark doorway.

Maxwell Hartman stood before her. But when she tried to back away from him, Will was pressed up behind her, pushing her the rest of the way into the building and swinging the door shut. He had both of her elbows in his hands. He was stronger than he looked.

Sophie swung hard and wrenched her arms free, whirling to face Will. But he wasn't alone now. Another young guy was there. A heavier guy.

When she tried to squeeze past them, the two young men each seized her by a shoulder and held her in place. She managed to squirm between them to reach one hand to the door, but the old brass handle didn't budge. Locked.

She could hear Hartman's appeals for calm. He seemed to be getting closer, just behind her now. As she wrenched one arm free from Will, she felt a sting in the back of her other arm.

"It doesn't have to be like this, Sophie. I just wanted to talk." Maxwell Hartman was right next to her. She didn't believe a word he said.

She tried to spin toward him one more time, but those young guys had a good grip on her. And she was suddenly feeling very tired. Very ... very ...

Have You Heard from Sophie?

Hope did the one-crutch hop out of the bathroom. That method was meant to allow her to check her phone. Theoretically. She stopped when she almost tipped sideways, banging the crutch against the wall. She swore and then apologized to the wall and to the angels in the room.

After a few more hops, she plunked onto the couch. She leaned the crutch next to her and checked her text messages again. The last thing from Sophie was still that funny meme of the little kid with the hat over his eyes. Peekaboo. No replies to Hope's texts since then. Hope sent a few question marks back at Sophie and waited. Still no answer. Then Hope tried another message. **"You coming home soon. I'm hungry."** She realized that text was shy one question mark and missing all evidence of patience.

Keeping herself off the pain meds was making Hope perpetually crabby. She was glad Sophie had taken care of Gerry's illicit pills. If they had still been in the apartment, those drugs would be calling her name right now.

"Hope. Hopie. Come and get us. We want to make you feel better." She tried it in an animated pill-like voice. She was both cranky and crazy these days. And don't even start to think about the itch inside the cast.

Throwing her gaze around the room in search of anything, she noticed Sophie's woman angel by the front door. "Is Sophie right behind you? Why isn't she texting me?"

"They took her phone away." The angel's voice was calm and motherly.

Hope froze. Had she actually taken the pain meds? Maybe she had taken lots of them. Because, otherwise, that lady angel had actually talked to her. No angels besides her regular girl angel ever talked to her. Usually. She struggled to recall exceptions. But that was beside the point. "Wait. This is real. You're serious."

The angel nodded.

Like an angel would try to punk her. Of course she was serious.

"Sophie's in trouble?"

The angel nodded again and then disappeared.

Hope started to shout for her to come back but realized that Sophie might need all the angels she could get if she was in trouble.

"What did she say? They took her phone away? What the ...?"

Hope looked at her cast, now resting on the coffee table towel. The towel was a standard living room feature with that monster cast just waiting to scratch up the table. "Dang. I'm a gimp. What can I do?" She still had her phone in her hand. She dialed Detta.

"Hello, Hope. How are things?"

"Sophie's in trouble."

"What? What kind of trouble?"

"Uh, well, I don't know, exactly. I expected her home an hour ago. And she's not answering texts. And then her lady angel showed up and said Sophie wasn't answering texts because they took her phone away."

"Who took her phone away?"

"Well, the angel didn't share that part." Hope puffed her frustration. She had probably botched the angel interview part of this challenge.

"The angel ... she talked to you?"

"Yeah. That was unusual. Also unusual to see her without Sophie. I asked her if Sophie was in trouble, just to clarify, and she nodded and disappeared. And I figured Sophie needed her, so ..." She didn't need to go on. Detta was already praying. That was probably the main point of calling her. Not to give the sweet old lady a heart attack. Or to send her out beating the bushes for Sophie.

"Who would take her phone? Has there been trouble I don't know about?"

Hope thought about Gerry and his drugs. She had been waiting on edge for a door buzzer to invade their new place at some odd time of the day. Gerry coming all the way here to get his drugs back. "Did Sophie give you a package to hold for her?"

"A package? No. What's that about?"

"Oh. Something else. Maybe ... I don't know." Hope wasn't only trying to save Detta from heart failure, she didn't want to get her tied up in some kind of drug crime. Clearly Sophie hadn't wanted that either.

"What's going on, Hope?"

"All I know is what the angel told me." That wasn't entirely true, of course, but not telling Detta everything was probably best at this point.

"Well, I'll get the prayer group on it." Detta hesitated. "Thanks for letting me know." She breathed hard into the phone. "Keep in touch, Hope."

"Of course. Thanks, Detta."

The hollowness at the end of that call was unavoidable. What was important was that Detta knew to pray. But Hope now realized she had originally called her for more than that. She needed someone to help her figure out what to do. Who should she call next?

She thought of calling Sophie's mother, but that nearly stopped Hope's heart. She didn't want to tell Mrs. Ramos what the angel had told her. "Lord, send someone else for that." One of the sincerest prayers of her life, no doubt.

Hope tried calling Anthony. He was maybe still at work. He didn't pick up. She called Delilah. It went right to voice mail. Then she tried Nathan. Maybe that was desperate. As much as she was crushing on him, she didn't really know Nathan as well as the others. He had been over once this week to bring her flowers, but they were surely *Get well soon* flowers, not the other kind. Still, she really wanted to talk to him.

"Hey, Hope. Okay if I call you back in a minute? I gotta finish something up."

"Oh, sure. Yeah. When you get a chance. It's important." She hung up. Of course she didn't have to say it was important to get him to call her. She shook that off.

Going to the police was supposed to only be an option after, like, twenty-four hours. Or maybe forty-eight. She had gathered that from the movies. But she also had a girlfriend that went missing in California. That waiting period was a thing in the real world.

Nathan called. "What's up? You said it was important."

"I did. Something weird is going on. And I need someone to listen to me and believe me."

"Heck, I can do that."

So she told him the whole story, including the part she didn't tell Detta, in case Gerry was somehow mixed up in what was happening to Sophie.

"Help me, Jesus." That was Nathan's response during the breath Hope took after dumping the whole load on him.

"My thoughts exactly. I called Detta to get her praying. Though I didn't tell her the part about the drugs."

"Yeah. She might not understand. And ... well ... it's illegal. So ..."

"Aagh. I know. I just included you in this weird conspiracy to do something bad or something."

"It's okay. I'm here to help. I don't think I'm in trouble yet." They both waited for a few seconds. "So, this California guy, is he, like, a criminal type?"

"Well, I didn't think so when I was hanging out with him. But I didn't know he was dealing drugs then either, and I didn't know he would use one of my boots for a stash. I mean, I didn't—you know—I didn't have him stay overnight or anything. So he had to sneak it in there ... like, I don't know when."

"Okay. I understand. But is he likely to come here and grab Sophie so he can get the drugs back?"

"Well, I wouldn't have thought so. Before. And before Sophie went missing. Though I was worried he would show up out of the blue and demand his pills."

"Hmm. It might be worth telling the police about that part in case anything happens to you."

"Really?"

207

"I don't know. I don't normally deal with this kinda stuff, to be honest."

She breathed hard through her nose for a few seconds. "One thing I know for sure is that we won't be able to get the police to believe what an angel told me."

"No, you're probably right about that. You think I should go looking for her? Do you have any idea where I should look?"

Hope's heart was melting in her chest like dark chocolate on a summer day. "Thanks, Nathan. You're awesome to offer. But I have no idea where to look. If she was still at her office, she would have emailed me, at least. Even if her phone was dead, she could do that." She huffed. "I think I'll try Anthony again. He might know. And maybe she stashed the drugs with him. He and Sophie are like brother and sister."

"Yeah, that's true. Okay. Just let me know what I can do. Maybe I should come over there later if she doesn't show up soon."

"Oh. Huh. I mean, maybe. Uh, well, I'll ... I'll get back to you. I'll call you when I know something." When she ended the call, she could feel sweat dripping in her armpits. Hope snorted her disapproval at getting all steamed up at the idea of Nathan coming over to comfort her. She had to stay focused on the beasts that took her best friend's phone away.

She tried calling Anthony again.

The Whole Network Is Down

Anthony assumed the string of messages hitting his phone had to do with the major outage on the network he'd just witnessed at his workstation. Now he pushed the network room door open and saw more than half the servers had gone dark. Three-quarters of the uninterruptable power supplies were dark. How was that possible? Multiple simultaneous failures? Really?

He glanced at his phone, drawn by some microscopic hope that whoever was flooding his phone had an answer.

But most of the messages were texts from Hope.

"Have you heard from Sophie?"
"Hello?"
"Sorry to bug you at work"
"Anthony?"
"Help!"
"Has everyone been abducted?"
"Is this the rapture?"
"Did I get left behind?"
"Anthony!!!!"
"Help!!!"
"Sophie is in trouble."
"Her angel told me"

"What the—" He aborted that curse even before his boss called his name.

Anthony spun around and saw John with his hands raised shoulder high and his eyes big. "What happened?"

Anthony was thinking "*All hell broke loose*," but that might actually be too close to the truth to use it as a euphemism. "Power is out on at least one circuit, and we had failures on, like, four of the backup power supplies."

"How is that possible?"

Sighing and shaking his head, Anthony just turned back to the network room. At least one electrical circuit was still lit. He could move power cables for essential items to that one. He looked over his shoulder at John. "Can you have building engineering check on the circuit breakers?"

"Yep. On it." And then John was gone.

Anthony glanced at his phone. Sophie was in trouble, and Anthony was too. But maybe Sophie's was worse. He thought about that packet she'd asked him to stash. She would owe him for the rest of her life for doing that. Did this new trouble have to do with what was in that packet?

He wrenched his attention back to the crisis right in front of his nose. The room was rank with ozone. "Dang." Anthony leaned in to see behind the server rack, checking for smoke. He could smell it more clearly back there, like a small electrical fire, but he couldn't see anything. Definitely nothing still burning.

As he pulled cables and replugged servers and switches, he tried not to think about what might be happening with Sophie. Praying was all he could do right now. No amount of texting back to Hope would calm her down, obviously. And Anthony didn't have anything to tell her. Who would know about Sophie?

When he realized he had unplugged and replugged the same electrical cable the second or third time, he prayed for himself and for some grace to focus on the task at hand.

It only took a few minutes to move the cables, and another five to power up the most important equipment. That would get most people back to work. Some services would still be offline, but the staff generally wouldn't notice those. At least not at first. Once the basics were up and running, a switch still connected to the downed circuit kicked on. Someone must have reset the circuit breaker. That was the solution to the original problem. That crisis had passed now.

He texted Hope. "Having a problem here at work. Maybe through the worst. I'll call you in a few."

She replied with praying hands. Maybe to signal gratitude. Though praying was a good thing to keep at even as he talked to his boss and reported on the failed equipment.

Fred, the other network tech, was in the room now testing the battery backups.

Anthony told his coworker he needed a short break.

Fred grunted in reply.

"Anthony, thanks for calling. Sorry to bug you at work, but it might be serious." Hope sounded unusually subdued.

"You said Sophie's angel talked to you?"

"Yeah, that was shocking. And she scared me with what she said. She told me Sophie wasn't responding to my texts because they took her phone away."

"Who took her phone away?"

"I know! That would be helpful to know. What I do know is Sophie is definitely in trouble. She and I are supposed to be out to supper now, but I've had no word from her. Then her angel woman said Sophie can't answer because they took her phone away."

"But who would do that?"

"Did Sophie talk to you about something we found in ... we found after we moved?"

"Are you talking about the package she left at my place?"

"Uh-huh. Did she say what was in it?"

"She said I didn't wanna know."

"Oh. That makes sense."

"So you *do* know?"

"Yeah. But she's right. You don't wanna know."

"I figure it's some kind of controlled substance she didn't want to ... keep at home."

"Okay, I guess that's obvious. And you probably should know what you're holding." She puffed a few times. "It's my fault. I ... it's better for me not to have that stuff around. And it was from this guy I know who hid it in my shoe, who also thought he shouldn't have it around." She groaned.

"He hid it in your shoe while you were in California?"

"Yeah. Apparently he's been trying to contact me to get it back. I was ignoring his texts. And he didn't want to admit what he did. Until he found out I'd moved all the way back here. Now he's mad as ... heck and wants his stuff back."

"Wait. So you think this guy grabbed Sophie because he thinks she has the stuff?" His voice cracked embarrassingly, but he needed to be upset at this point. Not only had he gotten tangled up in some drug thing, but Sophie was in trouble because of it.

"I don't know. I really don't know. But what else could it be? Who else would take her and take her phone away?"

"Maybe it's just some random crime. Have you called the police?"

"They want somebody to be gone a day or two before you report it."

"I guess. But that's stupid. A lot could go wrong in a day or two."

"Clearly."

Praying like Bible Saints

Detta called Hope before she sat down in the prayer circle.

Roddy was already seated, his cane propped against his leg. He was filling in the most recent arrivals with what they knew.

"Hope, have you heard anything?" Detta cleared her throat after asking, pacing into the kitchen.

"Nothing. Not even from angels." Hope sounded even smaller and younger than usual.

"Maybe we can come get you so you can stay here with me."

"Oh, that's nice of you, Detta. But I think I wanna stay here in case Sophie comes back."

"Okay. I understand." At least Detta understood part of what was going on. "Keep us posted, dear."

Hope promised to do that, and they hung up.

The part Detta didn't understand was why Hope was lying to her. Or at least not telling her everything. What was it that Hope couldn't tell Detta? How was this group supposed to pray if they didn't know everything?

But Detta stepped away from that thought and right back into the living room and the prayer circle. She didn't have to know everything in order to pray. The Spirit would tell her all she needed to know. She didn't need to hear from Hope or from an angel to get started praying.

"You wanna lead out, Detta?" Roddy asked as if he knew the answer. Which, of course, he did.

Settling into her chair, she began an opening prayer, five of her closest friends around her, along with a couple more from Roddy's church. Her living room was full of people. The people were full of the Spirit. And the enemy was going to have to back down.

Detta offered her petitions for Sophie's protection and safe return. And others followed that path, the same road that led to the throne, where every one of them was welcomed.

Then Sister Candace got an inkling. "I believe Sophie is safe right now, but she is in the hands of Satan's servants. They mean her no good. They want to have her. To have her gifts in their service."

That silenced the room after a short chorus of exclamations.

But Detta could feel the truth of Candace's impression, strange as it sounded. Her words rang like urgent church bells in Detta's head. "Lord, have mercy. Christ, have mercy. We come against the power of the enemy and all those who use that power to oppress others. I speak now to the spirits influencing Sophie's captors and bind their power to keep her captive. I bind your power in the name of Jesus."

And she went on, and others went on like that, for half an hour. To Detta, their prayers were fueled by divine truth. Every brother and sister there was sensing the trouble Sophie was in. That it wasn't trouble of her own making, but a plot of the enemy. That certainty lit their prayers and kept their focus true.

After that full frontal attack on the enemy stronghold, they turned again to petitions. These were more personal. Prayers for Sophie's comfort and care. For her provision and peace.

As she listened to her brothers and sisters ministering to Sophie's personal and emotional needs in prayer, Detta felt certain that what Anthony and Hope weren't telling her was irrelevant. She had a deep confidence that she knew what was happening to Sophie. She knew all she needed to know. And that realization set her at peace. It was the peace of a hunter who has come upon a clearing, spotted the prey, and calmed her breathing in preparation to loose her arrow.

When there was another lull, Detta led out in a new direction. "Lord, bless the young people who are part of Sophie's ministry team. Bless them with peace. Give them assurance. Show them how to pray, and show them what is required of them. Speak to them and comfort them. Especially, comfort Hope. Let her not despair. Fill her with hope, Lord, according to your greatness and according to her name. Send her your comforter, Lord. And perhaps also send her others to comfort her as well."

She realized she'd said the word comfort a few times. It seemed like the thing Hope needed most tonight. And, of course, others added their voices, stepping up next to Hope even if she wasn't in the room with them. And though several had never met her.

When that stream had run its course, Roddy opened his Bible and coughed once. "I believe the Lord has led me to this passage. And I trust it will guide us in how to pray for our sister." Then he read out of the book of Acts.

Detta knew immediately that he was right. It was the right word. Roddy was seeing the way they should pray. Just like in that story from the New Testament, they would pray. She smiled at Roddy when he finished, and others added hearty amens.

Another Gathering

When she heard the buzz of the door, Hope's mind leaped to her fear that Gerry had come looking for her. But she knew who it was, really. In the real world. Outside her head filled with paranoid panic.

She hit the button to let Nathan up. But when she opened the front door, leaning on one crutch, she could hear Nathan talking. Maybe he was just on his phone. But, no, there were other footfalls. The fear monger in her head groped around for who would be with Nathan.

Clearly, Hope was tired. Not thinking straight. Maybe some pain meds would help. But that thought vanished at the sight of Zeezee and Carlos accompanying Nathan.

"Oh. Hi, guys."

"I called in the troops. I hope you don't mind. Anthony and Delilah should be here soon." Even as Nathan revealed his devious machinations, he lifted his eyebrows toward his hairline. Apology and inquiry both, probably.

"Great idea. We need all the reinforcements we can get." Hope noted a couple of jokes dangling in the corners of her brain, but she left them there. Too tired. Too worried.

Eventually, the whole crew took seats around the living room, except Delilah, who was assembling a drink tray in the kitchen. The others started asking questions.

"Has Sophie ever done anything like this before?" Carlos was leaning forward, his elbows on his knees.

"You mean get abducted?"

"Is that what it is for sure?"

"That depends on if you believe her angel." Hope scowled at herself as much as at Carlos. "I guess it really depends on how much you believe in my sight. And me being able to hear a message from somebody else's angel."

"The angels all work for God though." Nathan had unpacked his guitar but had rested it against the side of the couch. "So I don't have any problem with you getting a message from Sophie's angel." He didn't look at Carlos but focused on Hope, who was in the armchair with her cast propped on the coffee table. Nathan had moved her towel over there, willing to play the role of nurse to her neediness.

"Just checking. I'm new to this group. Just wanted to cover all the bases." Carlos stayed steady, no wince on his face or taint of defensiveness in his voice. He was being the clinician. Someone had to be.

Hope sighed. "I get it. And the police will be thinking that way too, I expect. But the fact is, the only reason I know—or believe—she was abducted was from what the angel told me. I would be totally freaked out even without that though, because she was due home hours ago, and she hasn't contacted me at all. Calls to her phone go right to voice mail. But even if her phone battery was out and she was gonna be late, she would get me word from her laptop."

"Or maybe get you word by angel messenger." Anthony raised his eyebrows and cocked his head, a very tight grin on his lips. But his eyes sagged a bit.

Hope didn't grin back. "Maybe that's not a joke. I mean, she would contact me. And, really, God would want me to know, right? So God could send an angel even if Sophie didn't send it per se."

Delilah walked in from the kitchen balancing bottles and glasses on the tray that Hope had shown her. "Maybe Sophie knew you would be worried, and she was praying for you. I think she said something once about seeing angels heading out when people prayed for some distant person."

Though Hope had not thought of calling this gang together, her gratitude for the gathering was expanding every minute.

Then an angel appeared. This was one of those new guard guys Hope often saw standing at the door. Had he been there all along? Was Hope just ignoring him in the middle of stressing out? He was looking straight at her. "You need to pray for Sophie. Pray together. Pray now."

She let her mouth droop open but closed it before a string of drool escaped. "Dang. That door man guy just told us to pray. Pray for Sophie. Pray together. Pray now."

"Thank you, Jesus." Delilah was still standing.

"Then that's what we should do." Anthony leaned forward in the rocking chair, his elbows on the arms, his hands clasped in front of him.

Everyone else was nodding, eyes closing. Hands clasped or heads raised. Whatever fit a serious prayer meeting in the respective churches represented.

Nathan started an a cappella song inviting God's presence, welcoming the Spirit to guide them.

Then Delilah led out in prayer. She started solemnly, but she built volume and intensity. She was definitely going boldly.

The tone was set and the battle engaged. Everyone took a turn praying for Sophie's safety, for her deliverance from the hands of the enemy, both spiritual and human.

Then Hope tried to combine intercession with confession. "Lord, I don't know who grabbed Soph, and I'm sorry if it has anything to do with stupid things I've done. But I'm glad to set that aside if you just want to set her free from whatever creeps have her. I hand all of it, even potential guilt on my part, over to you."

The silence that followed prompted Hope to raise her head. Anthony was looking at her, as was Nathan. Delilah had her head cocked a bit to one side as she threw suspicion toward Hope. Zeezee and Carlos looked more confused than suspicious.

Carlos spoke first. "Is there something else we should know about?"

Hope heaved a massive sigh. She looked at Nathan, who was looking at her from under the shelter of his ample brown eyebrows. Then, as if repenting from that posture, he sat up straighter and offered a small smile. Encouragement.

Anthony nodded to her. He, after all, was already implicated.

Telling the whole story to this group of new friends was scary at the start and a giant relief by the time she finished, though another silence followed her telling.

Delilah responded first. "So we know that Sophie helped you dispose of, or at least hide, the package …"

Hope had left out the detail about Anthony taking the package.

He raised his hand. "Just to do, like, full disclosure here, I took the package from Sophie and hid it at my place. She didn't say what it was, and I didn't ask. She just said she needed me to hide it for Hope."

Hope had been thinking Sophie was hiding the stuff *from* her, so she appreciated the generosity of Anthony's explanation. Maybe everyone else could figure that part out. Full disclosure didn't actually include having to explain everything. Probably.

Delilah stared at Anthony longer than would have been comfortable to Hope if she were the target. But what Delilah said next became the real focus. "I don't think this is about that. It just feels like a distraction. Like a confusing coincidence. Maybe even the enemy trying to mislead us."

As soon as Delilah said all that, Hope recognized a feeling she had been ignoring, thinking it was just about seeking cover from her guilt. She didn't actually know that Sophie's disappearance had anything to do with Gerry. She had just assumed it. Or maybe leaped to the conclusion was a better description. And Gerry grabbing her was really very unlikely, as far as Hope knew.

"So there might be someone else who wants to harm her?" Carlos looked worried.

"You know, there was this new-age guru or whatever who was, like, haunting Sophie with astral projections when we first met her." Anthony paused there.

The staring silence was back. Confused eyebrows and rapid blinking had infected a few more folks in the circle.

"Astral projections?" Carlos was doing bug eyes that Hope would have previously assumed were beneath his clinical dignity.

"We're talking about a girl—a woman—who can see and hear and talk to angels. And you have a problem with astral projections?" Anthony was queuing a mischievous grin but holding it back, as far as Hope could tell.

The arrival of Sophie's lady angel, again, sat Hope up. She could feel eyes turn to her as she snapped to attention. The angel pointed to Anthony and nodded. Then she disappeared.

That angel finger point and nod took Hope back to games of charades she had played as a young teen. With all eyes on her now, Hope relayed what she had seen.

"Whoa. That's cool." Nathan sat up abruptly, thumping against the back couch cushion.

Blinking at the revelation, Anthony shrugged. "Okay. So that changes things ... a little. But only a little, really. I mean, Hope can stop beating herself up about that guy stowing drugs in her boot and getting Sophie involved. I guess that's not such a small thing that we know that now. But even though we think it's not about the drugs, Sophie is still missing. What does it mean that some Satan-worshipper dude has abducted her instead?"

"You said 'new-age guru.' That's not the same as a Satan worshipper." Carlos was good at challenging someone without an argumentative tone. He would be a good negotiator, Hope was pretty sure. Might be a killer card player too. Note to self. She turned to Anthony for his response.

"I'm not sure what difference that makes."

"Well, me neither, really, but it will probably make a difference to the police if they consider putting a special investigation unit on this." Carlos's eyes did a lap around the circle.

"You sound like you know something about that." Delilah was sitting next to Anthony, though maybe not as close as normal.

Hope was trying to figure out how mad Delilah was that Anthony hadn't told her about the drugs.

Carlos nodded and took a deep breath. "Some of the kids we work with at the agency have been abused by cults and pagan practitioners and even Satan worshippers. But the latter aren't so common, at least from what we're seeing." He looked at Anthony and shrugged. "I guess it feels better to me if this guy who has her is not a Satan worshipper per se. But you're probably right. It might not make that much difference for us and for Sophie."

Anthony nodded. He had a recalculating expression on his face. He leaned back and looked at Nathan. "Aren't we supposed to be praying?"

Nathan nodded deeply. "Yes, we are." And then he started that a cappella song again.

The rest of the group followed him out of their wheel-spinning troubleshooting and back toward the throne of heaven.

Guarded on All Sides

Sophie opened her eyes, then forced them shut immediately. Her head seemed to be expanding exponentially. And opening her eyes might have started it. Or not. Where was she? What was happening? It felt like she had survived an accident. She ached all over, like she had been beaten up or knocked around. That happened in accidents, didn't it?

Then something became clear through the fuzz of interference in her brain. Some*one* became clear. Maxwell Hartman. Had she seen him? Had she heard him? She felt like she had at least heard him. A replay of his voice pleading with her echoed in her head. Hartman trying to persuade her ... again.

Opening her eyes once more didn't hurt as much, though her ballooning headache hadn't shrunk at all. The place she was in was dark. She was lying on some kind of cot. The wall next to her was rough brick, like in a city loft. Though this room was too dark for a loft. Unless it was nighttime. She thought it should still be daylight, but she didn't actually know how long she'd been unconscious.

She heard the replay of Maxwell Hartman's voice. His actual voice, not just a distant memory of it. She was fairly certain about that part.

Sophie tried to turn onto her back. That simple maneuver had become more difficult since her body had been turned to stone, apparently. "Crap." She heard her own word travel farther than she had expected. Maybe it was a loft. A high ceiling. Maybe it really was nighttime. She forced those stones to move, including the ones that used to be her shoulders and hips. "Oh, man. What happened to me?"

That was when the angels appeared, as if they couldn't show themselves until she turned away from the wall. Like they wouldn't fit between her and the bricks next to her. That was a random thought, but it was blotted out by a sudden gusty storm in her head. A swirl of angels. Real angels all around. Spinning and shining, but not lighting up the room. Where was she? How did she get here? The storm started to settle.

"You are being held here by Maxwell Hartman and his associates." The lady angel had landed, as if answered some of those questions. Though *associates* raised a bunch more questions.

"Were Will and that other guy—what's his name? Were they working with Hartman all along?"

The angel nodded. Her pacific face invited Sophie to join in her peace. "Rest. We will keep watch. Your friends are praying."

Okay. More questions. The prospect of an actual conversation with one of her angels woke Sophie a bit more. "Which friends?"

"Many of them. As many as know about your capture."

"I've been ... captured?" Further proof that she wasn't all connected yet. Of course the angel had already told her ... something like that. "Why are they holding me?"

"They hope to study you, to learn from you. And perhaps to persuade you to work with them." As soon as she finished, that angel joined the other two in turning to face away from Sophie as if standing guard.

Immediately, a huge flaming beast burst through the far wall. It roared at her, or at the angels. Or both. The thing was gigantic, angry, and extremely scary. But her angels didn't flinch even though they seemed determined not to turn their backs on that beast. Maybe their defensive postures were just to assure Sophie.

Two more angels appeared, one at the foot and one at the head of the cot. And the wall beside Sophie began to glow. The very-Anthony thought that entered her head was that the glow was from a forcefield. She came close to grinning at that idea, but the urge passed quickly.

She surveyed the five visible angels. Then she glanced at that massive balrog thing. There was one big beast roaring at her. Five peaceful angels on guard. Plus, there was that forcefield or whatever. Was that monster trying to intimidate the angels? Probably just trying to scare Sophie. It wasn't working so well. Her heart rate had already started to settle back to normal. At least *toward* normal. Her hands were only sweating a little.

"I'm safe." She took a deep breath. "Thank you, Lord, for keeping me safe."

Then the flaming demon disappeared.

Sophie released a long breath and tried to stretch her legs. They were slow about it but cooperated eventually. "They must have drugged me." She noticed an ache in the back of her right arm like a bee sting.

The three most familiar angels turned to face her. She looked at them, so grateful she could see this watchful crew. "Thank you ... Lord." She detoured from thanking the angels to thanking the one who had sent them. The one who had been sending them from the beginning.

When that monster demon had barged through the wall, Sophie had noticed the door of this room. A conversation outside that door now rose and fell. Anger. Rebuke. Badgering. That much she could hear. But the exact words were getting lost. It must be a thick door. The slimmest line of light shone at the bottom.

Sophie thought she heard the people on the other side of that door walk away. A shadow sliding past. At least one of them gone. How many were out there?

Telling Mrs. Ramos

Anthony took a sip of the fruit-flavored sparkling water in the purple can. The group had drifted around the room like leaves pushed around an alley. In fact, there was an image of a dark alley streaming into his head just now. Where was that little video from?

"Has anyone told Sophie's mother?" Delilah had met Mrs. Ramos once, as far as Anthony could recall.

He had also thought about a mother's need to know her daughter was missing, if not abducted. But the idea of calling her seemed like a very important thing for someone *else* to do. Not something he would volunteer for.

He shook his head and checked with Hope. She was looking a little guilty. The group had been together for well over an hour. It was dark outside now. Sophie was missing. And the image of a shadowy metal door in an alley or narrow street was looping in his head.

"You should do it, Anthony." Delilah sidled up to him.

One of the most frustrating things about loving Delilah was how often she was right. Right about all kinds of things. Including the foolishness of not telling her about hiding the drugs Sophie gave him. He checked Delilah's eyes for lingering resentment over keeping that from her. Had his apology been enough? The fact that he had done it to protect her, given the likely illegality of holding that package?

"She deserves to know. And to start praying."

"She might already be praying." Hope was up on her crutches, headed toward the bathroom. Maybe she would hide in there while Anthony had to make the call by himself. But Hope wasn't like that. "I'll be back. Don't call till I get out." She ducked into the bathroom.

Anthony could tell that Delilah was usually right because everyone around them usually agreed with her. Setting that elemental reality aside, he decided to tap his fiancée's wisdom about something else. "I have this picture of a dark alley, shadows like late in the afternoon. A metal door. Maybe it's just a narrow street. Does that make sense?"

Delilah's shoulders convulsed visibly. "Whoa. Do you know what street?"

He shivered right back. She was taking him seriously, him and his psychic insight. Or whatever his mother would call it. Maybe Anthony should call his mama. "No. It's not really familiar from, like, real life."

When Hope hobbled out of the bathroom, Anthony could avoid his foisted responsibility no longer. She was looking at him, waiting. Delilah was looking at him from much closer. Expectant.

He pulled out his phone. For a second, he entertained the brief possibility that he didn't have Mrs. Ramos's number. But there had been that time when Sophie had to go to the emergency room, and it wasn't clear how serious it was. Not serious, it turned out. He had probably gotten her mother's number then. How long ago was that?

Distraction.

No more avoiding. He hit the name *Sophie's Madre*.

"Hello? Is this Anthony?"

He thought he heard a tremor in her voice. She must know. At least she knew that he wouldn't be calling her unless there was something wrong ... with Sophie.

"Mrs. Ramos, I have some news. We haven't seen Sophie tonight even though she was supposed to be here a few hours ago. She hasn't contacted us. Her phone goes to voice mail."

"I tried to call her. She wasn't responding to my texts." Mrs. Ramos was quiet for a second. "I didn't want to bother her."

Anthony almost burst into tears. He quickly offered the phone to Hope as he caught his breath. She didn't accept it immediately, but she didn't refuse either. He pulled the phone back. "Hope is here. You should talk to her." He was thinking it was better for her to tell the part about what the angels had said.

Taking the phone from his hand, Hope leaned on one crutch, her chin almost resting on it. "Hi, Mrs. Ramos. I'm sorry I didn't call sooner, but we didn't know what was happening. A couple of Sophie's angels have come and given me messages—given us messages, really—and now we think we know what's happening."

"What do you mean?" Her alarmed voice came clearly over the phone even without the speaker enabled. It was more adamant than Anthony had ever heard Mrs. Ramos.

"It seems like some new-age guru guy she used to know has probably grabbed her. The angel first told me someone had taken her phone away. And another angel later confirmed that it was a guy Anthony knew about. I guess this person used to send, like, a spiritual projection to Sophie at night. When she first met Detta."

Anthony could hear her voice but didn't catch what Mrs. Ramos said next. Then she spoke more forcefully again. "Do you know for sure it is this person? How can you be sure?"

"Well, I only know from what the angels are telling me. I'm pretty confident myself, but I can understand that it might be hard for other people to believe me. Of course we can't go to the cops with this …" She let her voice diminish.

"Oh, I believe …" Mrs. Ramos said more that he missed. Anthony only now wished he had set the phone to speaker, but maybe that wouldn't have been fair to Mrs. Ramos. This was her daughter. Missing. It couldn't get more personal than that.

"Yeah. It seems pretty certain that something is wrong. Something has happened to her. We just don't have the kind of evidence the police would want. And they won't wanna hear about it until she's been gone for a day or two."

"They won't start looking, but you can still report …" Mrs. Ramos raised the intensity of her voice again, but the last of what she said got lost to Anthony.

"Okay. So I'll call and report. Yeah. That makes sense." Hope listened a few seconds. "Sure, I'll tell them what I know for sure. But I don't wanna tell them about the angels. Then they really won't take us seriously."

Murmurs were all Anthony heard after that, until Hope handed him the phone back.

"Mrs. Ramos, we'll file a report." He hesitated. "And we'll keep praying. We have a group gathered here praying. I know my mama and some of her friends are praying at her house too."

"Yes. Thank you. I'll call some of my church friends to pray as well." She came across more resolutely. "And, Anthony, tell me what you know as soon as you know it."

"Even if it just comes from Hope talking to an angel?"

"Yes. Even that."

"Okay. We will."

"Thank you, Anthony."

"Blessings, Mrs. Ramos."

Reluctant Interviewers

Another little gathering outside the door stopped Sophie's breath for a few seconds. She shifted around and managed to sit up. She didn't want to be lying down if they finally came in. This was at least the third time someone had come to the door and not entered. The humans had stayed out, anyway. An assortment of demons had poked their heads in several times, as if trying to spook her. Or maybe they were spying out what was going on in the darkened room. The answer to what was going on in here was *Not much.* Just a groggy woman on a cot with a few shining guardians. And a need for a bathroom.

The dark gray or green door swung open, and a whitish light divided the room. Two people stood in the doorway.

Sophie wished she had more confidence in her legs. The hesitation of those two visitors seemed an opening for her to run. Neither of the male forms in the door looked particularly big or strong. As the fog continued to lift, she cast a thought toward what had happened to that young woman she had been following.

One of the silhouettes in the door held a phone. He touched something on it, and an overhead light illuminated.

Nice trick. Sophie wished she knew that trick. She wished she had her phone.

"Sophie. Good to see you again." It was him. The real Maxwell Hartman.

She wasn't seeing him entirely clearly, however. Was he really here? She reconsidered. Maybe he was just projecting his image. There were swirling and fading shapes around him. Then she realized she was seeing the real man but seeing him with an intense accompaniment of spirits, obscuring him as they surrounded him. His version of guardians, perhaps.

"Can't say it's good to see you though." She knew her line was supposed to have been "*What do you want with me?*" or maybe "*You'll never get away with this.*" She had seen those movies, but she didn't have to do those lines. She knew what Hartman wanted with her. The angel had told her. She blinked hard instead of giving in to the urge to rub her eyes. She had really slept hard.

"I know those drugs were intense. I'm sorry I had to do that. Not much lasting effect though. Only a few brain cells lost. You have plenty to spare." He was in the middle of the room now.

The other guy, someone she didn't recognize, stood by the door, which was now closed behind him. To her left, she noted another door. A smaller one.

"Only a few brain cells? That's comforting to hear."

Hartman had been grinning all along. His grin twitched. She could see his face more clearly now, but the mantle of monsters wrapped around him remained in place. "Can you see them all? How many do you see?" He bobbed his thick dark eyebrows.

Sophie checked out a feminine snaky thing winding in and out with some other things that had no heads, and still others that seemed to be all eyes. Then one of her angels, one of the new guardians, reached into that tangled mess, and several of the beasts disappeared.

Barking his disapproval, Hartman backed up. His pale face flushed red.

She wanted to laugh at what the angel had done, but she wasn't sure how to take all this. "Are you testing me?" Her main angel had told her something about him evaluating her gifts. "Only God has the right to test me." Sophie scooted a little higher against the rough brick wall and tried to relax her shoulders. She could at least pretend to be relaxed.

His voice was like honey. "I believe in God, you know. I know who created all these beautiful creatures, including you and the lights that surround you."

"Are those lights the reason your people keep arguing outside the door? Afraid to get too close?" That idea had just popped into Sophie's head. Again, she checked with the angels to see if it was all right to say it. Then she remembered to listen in her heart, the way Detta had taught her. To listen to the Spirit of God. As soon as she did, a chuckle got loose in her gut. She let it out.

That was unexpected.

Clearly it was unexpected to Hartman. He lost his arrogant grin all together. His pale eyes flashed. "You need to take me seriously, Sophie. I can disrupt your entire life. You have no idea how much trouble I can bring down on the people you care about. I think you've seen some of it by now. And that's only the beginning."

The threat called to mind Hope's tumble down the stairs, and the threat of that guy from California coming to pick up his drugs. Sophie knew she couldn't draw any conclusions about those events based on Hartman's words. "When he lies, he is speaking his native tongue." She couldn't remember the context, but she knew Jesus had said something like that about the devil.

As if resetting himself, Hartman stood perfectly still. Only then did Sophie realize how much he had been swaying side to side and leaning forward and back as he spoke. Whatever that was about, she had apparently interrupted it.

"I'll leave you to think about your responses, Sophie. I know your mother is missing you by now. She'll be worried, of course. And maybe she should be."

Sophie smothered a twitch at the plucking of that string in her heart. Like a low bass string, the reverberation lasted. But she kept it inside.

Hartman turned toward the door and signaled to the guy there, who used his phone to unlock the door. High-tech henchmen. Why not?

She heard a pair of voices in the hallway when Hartman left. Maybe those were the ones too afraid to enter her cell. She finally had a chance to look around at her cell. The light was dim, but it was definitely better than total darkness.

Tell Me What You Know

Detta stood up, her knees cracking and her back complaining a little. Her phone was ringing. A call from Anthony.

"Mama. We've been praying over here at Hope and Sophie's place, and we've been getting visits from Sophie's angels."

"Praise the Lord for all that. What have you learned?" She looked over her shoulder at Roddy, who watched her as she drifted toward the kitchen. It was time to refill the kettle for more tea.

"Well, this whole thing doesn't have to do with that package Sophie gave me."

"A package she gave *you*? Hope didn't say anything about you and a package."

"She didn't know I had it. Sophie was keeping things on the down-low, for obvious reasons."

"Mm-hmm. Keepin' it quiet. I understand. But anyway, *that* whole problem is just a distraction, isn't it?"

"That's right. A distraction. You already knew that?"

"We were getting a feeling about Hope being upset that part of this is her fault. That didn't seem right. Seemed like the enemy wanted her to think so, but it wasn't about that."

"Okay. That's exactly what we're hearing. The angel seemed to confirm that it has to do with that guy who was, like, haunting Sophie when she first came to see you."

"Oh, Lord. That's not good. I didn't know he was still in the picture."

"Neither did any of us. I don't think Sophie did either. I haven't heard her mention that guy for years."

"What was his name?" She let her voice coast.

"I don't remember."

"I'm pretty sure Sophie said his name at some point. I mean, we had to lead her through breaking off that man's power from her. I'm sure we named him when we did that." She stood in the kitchen breathing through her half-stuffed nose. It was getting close to her bedtime. "It doesn't help to have this old brain when it comes to remembering things like that."

He cleared his throat. "I'm not sure if I was there when she said the guy's name. Maybe I was, but my young brain doesn't recall either."

"I can pray about it, have the folks here pray over my memory. But is this the kinda thing where you could give that man's name to the police?"

"We filed a missing person's report. Or whatever they call what you do before the police officially consider her missing. We left out the angel parts though."

"Is that how you know it's this man?"

"Yeah. I mean, I got this feeling. You know, like a leading. And then one of Sophie's angels showed up, and it told Hope somehow that I was right. I think part of that was so Hope would stop blaming herself."

"Well, you could at least google that man, if we could remember his name. Or maybe just telling the police about Sophie's history with him and his group would be worth something."

"They never abducted her before. That wasn't part of her history with them, was it?"

"No, but she was afraid of something like that back then. I think he was mostly trying to intimidate her, to draw her in with his evil spirit guides or whatever he called 'em."

"I doubt that kinda intimidation's gonna work on Sophie now."

"Oh, I agree. She's seen too much and grown too strong in the Spirit to be intimidated by some demon. At least not for long. But these people might have other things they can do. I was thinking maybe that fall Hope took was possibly an enemy attack. And now this thing about her and a package. Awful coincidences, it seems."

Roddy had limped into the kitchen by now. Curious about the call, or just anxious for tea? He patted Detta on the arm and kissed her cheek. Maybe he was just in here to support his fiancée. That was a nice thought.

Having Roddy right there reminded her of the promise they had found in Scripture. "Anthony, we've been praying a particular Scripture over Sophie."

"Yeah? What's that? Maybe we should be praying the same thing."

"It's the story of when the apostle Peter was held in prison, and he had a dream where an angel came to him and loosed his chains, and opened the door to his cell, and led him right out the gates of the prison. Only he discovered it wasn't a dream. It was really happening. It was a real angel leading him out of captivity."

"Thank you, Jesus." Anthony said that like he was at a late-night prayer meeting. "Okay, Mama, that gave me serious chills. We'll pray that over here too."

"All right." She let her satisfaction spread a grin on her face. Then she thought of something. "Anthony, have you talked to Sophie's mother yet?"

His answer started with a low moan. "I did. Wasn't easy telling her, especially with us only knowing what the angels are telling us."

"Oh, she believes in all that. I know she does. I'll call her in a bit. She'll still be awake, with Sophie missing and all. Maybe she'll wanna come over here."

"She said she'd call some of her prayer partners."

"Did she call 'em that?"

"Well, maybe not. But that was the gist."

"Right." She paused. "That was a *man's* job you did, Anthony, having to tell a mother something like that about her only child."

She could hear Anthony sniff a laugh. "It was Delilah and Hope who made me do it."

Detta chuckled briefly. "Well, sometimes a man needs a woman to remind him what his job is."

"Huh. Do me a favor and don't tell that to Delilah."

As Detta chuckled some more, she thought she heard Delilah's voice in the background. Then she got serious and said goodbye to her son. It was time for her to call a worried mother.

A Door in the Shadows

When Hope looked up from her phone—another call to Sophie gone to voice mail—she could see Delilah and Anthony debating something next to the dinner table. "What's up?" She worried they were arguing about going home.

Anthony looked at her, but Delilah kept looking at Anthony.

"What?" Hope's voice cracked.

"Anthony has an idea of where we can look for Sophie." Delilah was still focused on Anthony. Pretty intimidating.

Hope never wanted Delilah to look at her like that.

Nathan was standing next to Hope. "Like a rescue mission? Do we tell the cops?"

Delilah turned her eyes toward Hope now. "Well, it's really based on something the Spirit is telling Anthony."

"What? What are you hearing?" Hope sat up straighter, delaying the awkward climb off the couch.

"Not hearing. Seeing, more like." The whole group had gathered around by now, and Anthony ran a wary gaze over the eager faces.

Hope knew he was uncomfortable being the seer of such things. More used to following what Sophie saw. Or Hope, even.

"It feels real to me." Delilah glanced around at the waiting faces. "But not, like, something we can tell the police, of course."

Carlos looked as alarmed as Hope had ever seen him. Which was to say, a little alarmed. "So you're proposing we go to this place and look for her?"

Zeezee seemed to swell with an intake of air. "Actually, as strange as it sounds, I'm kinda feeling like this is ... real. I don't know how to explain it."

"God is moving. God is leading us." Nathan was so excited, his voice boomed. And he showed no regret at the excited volume.

Hope grinned at him, then turned to Anthony. "Where is it?" Even as she asked, she feared *she* would not be going wherever it was. At least not if two good legs were required.

"I feel like it's near where Sophie works." Delilah squinted slightly, like someone aiming a gun, maybe.

"I thought it was Anthony that ... saw ... something." Carlos had his hands buried in his tan pants pockets.

Anthony nodded loosely, then rubbed his neck with one hand. "It was me. I had this picture of a dark green metal door in an old building. It was down an alley or a narrow street."

"There are streets like that around where she works." Hope could picture them but couldn't name any of them, of course, not being from around here. She had visited Sophie's work before the move.

"Yeah, there are." Anthony assessed his audience, or maybe more like his team. "We can keep praying, but maybe we can take it on the road. Like, drive around that neighborhood and see if we get some kind of leading or something."

"And break her out?" Hope glanced at Carlos to see if she was the only one freaked out by this part of the plan.

Delilah answered. "Well, we can count on God to show us what to do. And if *you* come along, you can spot what the angels are doing and whatever else is going on."

Hope tried to imagine the kind of spiritual activity happening around an evil lair where a new-age guru was holding Sophie captive. Actually, she could sort of picture it. "Okay. Let's go."

Nathan looked down at her cast. "You sure you're okay to go on the road?"

"I won't lead the foot chase, I know, but I can spot things from a car. We should be able to drive close to wherever this is, shouldn't we?"

Anthony and Delilah both nodded but didn't say anything. Were they having second thoughts?

Carlos gave half a shrug. "I can stay in the car with Hope while you guys chase the bad guys." His boyish grin probably implied a joke. He was clearly up for this, whatever *this* was.

When they agreed, they all gathered the stuff they had brought with them. Mostly Nathan and his guitar.

Hope had only gone down the elevator twice since she came home from the hospital, and that was to go see doctors. That fact was a tribute to the wonders of working from home and of food delivery, not to mention telemedicine. But Sophie got some credit too, helping with anything Hope needed brought in or carried out.

"We can carry you when we get to the ground floor." Nathan stood next to her as they waited for the elevator.

Hope let a little skepticism show on her face.

Nathan looked at Anthony. "Me and Anthony can do it. You're light. We can do a fireman's chair. We'll go easy."

Delilah looked a little skeptical too.

"I can use the crutches. Maybe you guys could go get your cars." Hope was assuming Nathan and Anthony had driven.

Carlos corroborated. "I can walk with her. I'm used to walking slow, like with toddlers."

Hope laughed as the elevator came to a stop. "Gee, thanks. Now I'm a toddler."

Zeezee smiled at her. "And a child shall lead them."

Hope laughed again.

Another Prison Guard

Though not much else was clear, Sophie could tell she had fallen asleep again. What time it was now, how long she had slept, and what her future held, were all mysterious. She heard a disposable bottle of water slosh and crinkle when she tried to sit up. That fleeing girl had brought the water. Not a word passed between them. Sophie had been half asleep at the time.

She had checked out that other door. It led to a small toilet room. The best news she had received so far, up there with the angels and her friends praying.

She wondered again about that young woman who'd brought the water. A glowing pair of spirits had wafted in after her, their illumination a dark sparkle. Only in the spirit realm did Sophie ever see what she thought of as a dark glow.

The door clicked and then swung open. Two silhouetted figures came through the gap, the light behind them brighter than the small bulb in her cell.

The slimmer of the two men carried a tray. He crossed the room and set it on a small table Sophie hadn't noticed next to the wall opposite the toilet closet.

She paused to worry that there might be something in that water bottle. And what was on the tray? She hoped the tray was the source of a faint foody odor and not the repository for surgical torture instruments. She struggled to get into a less slouchy sitting position against the wall.

"Sophie, I hope you had a good sleep." The stouter of the two men was Maxwell Hartman. "I know you've met my protégé, Will Costanza." He gestured toward the younger man, who now approached Sophie's cot more aggressively than Hartman had yet.

"Are you done with the water? Need a refill?" Will stopped just short of the cot.

Shaking her head, even more concerned about the contents of that water bottle now that he was offering a refill, Sophie looked hard at Will. She could see no accompanying spirits. That had fooled her when they'd met before. She couldn't help her curiosity. "How do you hide the spirits you carry?"

"No preliminaries. Just how do I do that?" He smirked at her. "Maybe we can learn from each other. You have your tricks, I have mine. You might benefit from what I have to show you. What we have to show you." He gestured vaguely toward Hartman with one hand.

"I have no tricks. Just a gift. But maybe you know something about that." She recalled that Will had fooled at least one assistant pastor into trusting him. How did he do that?

"I was in church when I was a kid. That was where I learned how to use the spirits to get what I want."

"Witchcraft in church?"

"They didn't call it witchcraft. They called it ministering to those in need."

After a brief taste of gratitude that she had never been in such a church, if one really existed, Sophie didn't want to pick up the hot plate he had just set before her. Figuratively.

She assumed the plate on that tray wasn't nearly as scalding as Will's assessment of his childhood church experience.

As Sophie hesitated over responding to his claim, a monstrous face flashed over his head, as if a giant beast had been riding on Will's back and had suddenly become visible.

Immediately, Sophie's guardian leaped in front of her and thrust a hand up to block that demonic face.

Will recoiled, stepping back a few inches.

Sophie recoiled too, startled by Will's hop away from her as much as the thrust of the angel. She allowed her hands to settle back onto the cot as that demon faded. Its threat was just a bluff, of course. The equivalent of saying *boo!* Not an actual attack. The dark spirits in this room knew they couldn't touch her. She whispered a brief prayer of thanks for that fact, hoping she would keep a grasp on that confidence.

She was not so certain about her safety from the *people* in the room, however. While Hartman maintained his position in the center of the square room, ten feet away, Will stepped forward again, almost knocking his knees against Sophie's cot. She couldn't help sliding back a little to gain a bit more personal space.

"How do *you* do it, Sophie? How do you see so much?" He had been studying her shamelessly during the pause.

"God gave me the gift. Ask God."

"You think I don't? You think I don't talk to God about this? About everything?" Will took a deep breath, his narrow chest swelling.

Sophie let her eyes rest on his untucked button-up shirt, gaping slightly as Will folded his arms. She thought she saw something there. Something inside him, which was rare.

Usually she only saw spirits that hovered over or hung onto people. She knew it was all mostly symbolic. But what was the significance of seeing Will's spirit pals contained inside him?

"I welcome them there." He answered her unspoken question, or so it seemed.

"That's the secret? The trick? You welcome them inside? What about him?" She raised a hand toward Hartman.

Will turned his head and looked again at Sophie, sharply executing the maneuver as if he worried she would try to run while he was distracted. Run where? Maybe to that toilet room? She was feeling the need again.

"Maxwell welcomes the ones he wants around him, the ones you see. He likes the way that looks. He likes the way the spirits fill the eyes of others."

After a pause at the creepy way Will was talking about Hartman, who was standing right behind him, Sophie cleared her throat. "But most people don't see that show, of course. Is that why I'm here, so you have an audience to show off to?" She knew it was cheeky, but the idea had just slipped into her head and then out of her mouth like a fish swimming downstream.

Grinning appreciatively, Will glanced over his shoulder again. "Maybe so. Someone who really appreciates what we can do. Unlike the whole blind world out there." He flipped a hand toward the unseen masses he accused so universally.

"Maybe you need to move to another culture where they believe in spirits."

"Oh, we have our own culture. Our own society. And you'd be surprised how many people believe in the kind of power we're exploring."

"Power? Spiritual power?"

"All power is spiritual power."

Sophie huffed a skeptical laugh but stifled her response. She knew he was right in a way, but she wanted to avoid a debate. Even one in which she and Will agreed. Especially one in which she and Will agreed.

"You want something to eat? More water?" He gestured toward the tray.

"What's in the water?"

He laughed. "Wouldn't *you* like to know?"

She glanced at her woman angel. That guardian surely would have warned Sophie if the water was tainted. The angel bowed her head slightly. The water was fine.

"I'm not really worried about it."

Will was watching the space where Sophie's female angel stood. "Wish I could see what you see." He sighed in a way that seemed entirely sincere.

"We can always ask God to give us spiritual gifts. Maybe you want it because you're supposed to have it. But you're going at it the wrong way." She hoped no one would ask her to explain all that. It seemed to be streaming from a source beyond her. Maybe from a teaching by Julius, her pastor.

"Enough. This is getting us nowhere." Hartman's voice startled Sophie. She had begun to think of him as a piece of furniture. The grandfather clock had suddenly spoken.

Will lowered his head, resigned.

Sophie shook her head at herself. And her two jailors turned to leave.

When Sophie made eye contact with her angels, she was startled to see stern looks on all their faces. They looked like warriors preparing for battle. What kind of battle?

Never Would Have Believed It

Anthony was recalling what his mother had said about him taking on a man's job. Leading this little team out into the night to find Sophie, and somehow liberate her, felt like one of those adult responsibilities. Even above and beyond what most people would do, men or women.

Delilah was in the front seat of his car, Hope in the back. Delilah was on the phone to Zeezee, who was in the other car with Nathan and Carlos, following close behind. Anthony checked the rearview, noting that Nathan was keeping up without a problem. Not much traffic. It was nearly eleven o'clock.

Downtown, most of the foot traffic passed in couples and small packs, arm in arm and joking, one trio even singing. The bars were doing just fine, apparently. Recovered from the lockdowns, it seemed. Anthony had driven past Sophie's workplace a minute ago and started a sort of grid search beginning to the west of that building.

Hope was watching out the window. Scouting for spiritual evidence, presumably.

Delilah was watching the map on the car's display. "What about that street? Benson. It looks narrow and runs at a funny angle. Maybe it's dark and shady."

Anthony nodded and turned at the next corner, pausing for two young women who were weaving carelessly across the road, ignoring the crosswalk.

"Be careful." Delilah reached toward the dashboard briefly.

"Tell *them* to be careful. Just stick your head out the window and let 'em know there are still cars on the road at night."

"Okay, calm down."

"Sorry. I thought that was calm."

"Moderately calm, I'd say." Hope offered that over his shoulder.

Anthony and Delilah both snorted a laugh. Hope might not be the ideal mediator to keep peace in his relationship with Delilah, but she was pretty funny. Anthony slowed and turned down Benson Street. Immediately he knew it was wrong. New shops with glass windows. It would be light and glistening at various times during business hours. Not a dark alley by any stretch.

"No. Let's go down that way." He pointed south with his head, and Delilah started zooming the GPS map for options in that direction.

"Okay. How about head for Hamilton? That one faces mostly north and south, so it would be darkish in the afternoon. And maybe those streets down there are more industrial." She glanced out the window.

"Yeah, that sounds about right. Industrial." Every time Delilah said something about his inkling or leading, Anthony felt as if she had seen it too. Or at least had fully absorbed what Anthony had seen.

"Lord, have mercy." Hope was muttering in the back seat.

"Amen." Delilah turned to watch a small gathering of people on a dim corner. A few of them seemed to be teenage girls. Girls with bare arms and legs and lots of other skin showing too.

Anthony didn't look directly at them. Those girls were not their mission this evening. He knew Priscilla and some of her friends went around to street corners late at night offering to pray for the young girls waiting there ... waiting for whatever trouble they sought. That wasn't a ministry Anthony would likely get into, though he could imagine Sophie, Hope, and Delilah doing a lot of good there. He would save that suggestion for another time.

Stopping at a red light, he glanced in the mirror at Nathan's car. They were singing back there. Okay. Well, Nathan was driving. Maybe that was what you did in his car.

"Did you know they're singing back there?"

Delilah nodded. "Just started a minute ago. Zeezee put her phone on mute." She smiled dryly. Anthony couldn't tell if she was amused or jealous. She was focusing on this task with her usual self-discipline.

"That Nathan is a wild man." Hope was watching the crew behind them. "But, really, he's being serious. I can tell. They're doing, like, serious warfare worship."

As he pressed the accelerator to cross the next intersection, Anthony glanced at Hope. "You sound like my mama. 'Warfare worship.'"

"Guilty as charged."

Anthony felt left out. "We could sing."

"Turn here." Delilah nearly caught him with an elbow, pointing toward the corner he should have been aiming for.

He nodded slowly, allowing his singing proposal to dissolve and disappear. Another time, maybe. Then they had to stop behind a double-parked pickup truck, occupants arguing with folks on the sidewalk.

"Let's hope none of them have guns." Anthony checked both groups, looking for intent.

"Funny you should say that. There's a battle going on over that parking space. A demon fight. Like, pow, pow, pa pow!" Hope sounded more fascinated than worried.

"Huh." Delilah said it idly. She was praying under her breath when Anthony looked at her.

"Hmph. That was weird." Hope wasn't watching the battle for the parking space anymore.

Anthony tracked her gaze ahead of the pickup obstruction and found a darkish corner, a smallish street, and a bit of a spine tingle. "That may be it."

"What, where?" Delilah leaned toward him to see around the pickup.

The driver of the truck slammed it in gear and burned rubber before settling down to a merely dangerous speed and taking a quick right at the next corner.

Anthony and friends watched the noisy exit before rolling toward the intersection past that. "What did you see?" Anthony couldn't see anything weird.

Hope was leaning forward, her face close enough to hear her breathing. "This big spirit came roaring into view, like, penetrating all the buildings. Or showing itself, like, 'Whoa, here I am. Look on me and tremble.' That sort of thing."

"Oh. Okay."

"That feels to me like a good place to check out." Delilah was focused on that corner, though Anthony was sure she wasn't seeing some giant spirit defying God and all his servants.

"I'm not trembling, just so you know," Hope said flatly. Dry humor or calm reassurance? It was hard to tell which.

"Yeah, this looks like the right area." Anthony had to slow for a young guy who jogged out of the way, apparently aware that he was walking in the street. Not everyone seemed so well aware.

When he reached the corner, Anthony checked for pedestrians before making the left turn. "Maybe. What I saw was kinda like this. It could be it."

"How are we gonna see a dark green door? It's all too dark." Delilah was surveying the brick buildings as Anthony slowly cruised up the little incline of the bumpy street. Probably brick pavement. A really old road.

"The defiant giant was around here, but I'm not sure he came from this street. Maybe the next one." Hope was leaning back so she could see out the back window toward the sky.

Anthony surveyed the buildings on the left, but it felt like the mental image had been of a door on the other side. "Should we get out and walk?"

"Let's try the next street first." Hope's face was reflected in the back passenger side window, the light from Delilah's phone and the car display giving her a bluish complexion.

"Okay." Anthony checked their friends in the car behind them. They looked more subdued. No sign of singing this time. He felt like he made eye contact with Carlos in the mirror, if that was possible in the dimness of their two cars. He signaled right and started a turn, slowing to allow a stray cat to gallop out of the way.

"Run, kitty." Hope, of course, rooted for the underdog, as it were.

"Is it crazy that I feel like Sophie's gonna be all right?" Delilah said that to the window, her eyes still glued there.

"Crazy? I don't know. I'm not feelin' it myself, but I'm glad you are, I guess." Anthony muttered that as he focused on driving down a street with lights the color of a manilla file folder. As little as he wanted to be driving here, it felt like they were getting closer to the scene in the sort of vision he'd had.

"You see the corner?" Delilah surely asked that because it was hard to see the next corner. Construction on the sidewalk or something.

Anthony had almost turned into an open parking space, mistaking it for the next street. But he was going slow enough to avoid crashing. The street corner, at least, had a dim streetlight to mark it. But the road around that corner was dark, much like the parallel road they had just left. He could feel his breath shortening. "We should stop here."

"This feels close." Delilah was practically panting through her nose.

"Yeah." Hope looked out the back window.

The other car pulled to the curb behind them. It was a *No Parking Anytime* side of the street. Anthony hoped no cops would come by and check, though he was also wondering if there was any way they could get cops to come back them up.

"You okay to stay here alone?" Delilah had just opened her door but turned to look at Hope in the back.

"Yes, Mom. Don't worry. I won't call the cops for being abandoned in the car."

Clearly everyone had cops on the brain.

"Maybe I'll leave the window open." Hope sounded a little more serious, hitting the power window button.

Nathan's car had emptied, and he and his passengers stood as if waiting for instructions.

Anthony climbed out even as he heard Hope exclaim "Whoa!"

"What?"

"Angels."

Angels behind a Prison Door

Sophie was monitoring her angels, who took turns vanishing and reappearing. If that view of their activity was instructive, what was she learning from it? That they were on the job? Yes, and that they were in touch with what was happening inside and outside of this room. That was all good. But the comings and goings were starting to worry her.

"Am I in trouble?"

Her big guardian stepped closer. "It's time to get you out of here."

"What? Why? Wasn't it time ... before?"

He gave his usual *I'm-not-answering-that-question* grin. Keeping top secret info under wraps was second nature for him, of course.

The woman angel did offer an answer, of sorts. "Your friends are praying. The enemy is weakened. We can get you free now."

A fringe faction of Sophie's brain wanted to dig through all those pieces, especially when they were combined with the nonanswer from the other angel. But she silenced that fringe element as she slid off the cot, grabbed her bag, and slipped into her shoes. She waited for instructions.

Her third angel, the one with the impressive armor, strode to the door and took hold of the handle. He pulled it open.

"Wait. What?" She silenced her exclamations at a sign from her big guardian. A finger to his lips. A pretty clear sign.

Sorting through the possible explanations that she was likely never to receive, Sophie considered that the bad guys might have forgotten to lock the door. Really she couldn't recall them doing that on their phones this last time. Not exactly. Then there was that story in the Bible where an angel got Peter out of jail by doing some kind of trick with the door. She was hazy on the details of that story.

While tiptoeing toward the hallway, Sophie decided to believe the last explanation. It would probably be the one Detta favored. That was good enough for Sophie.

Outside that door, all the angels disappeared except Sophie's main guardian. Why? Another gaping mystery. Someday someone would explain all this. But maybe not before she got to heaven.

The hallway was lighted, which she knew from the times the door had been opened. She squinted and checked for exits. Since she had no memory of being brought to her cell, she had no idea which way to go. Except, she suddenly remembered following that strange girl in through a door. Maybe it was the door to her left.

Her warrior angel reappeared standing near that door. As the angel checked something over Sophie's shoulder, the reinforced metal door swung inward. If anyone was touching it, they were invisible. And as far as Sophie was concerned, that was entirely possible.

Just then, she understood why Saint Peter thought he was dreaming in the middle of his rescue.

The angels both shooed Sophie toward the door and looked behind them.

When she stepped out onto the street, Sophie found her woman angel. Then she nearly fell over.

That dream feeling seized her and tried to lift her off the ground.

"Sophie?"

"Sophie!"

"Sophie!"

Those were the exclamations of her friends. At least the ones who were not dumbstruck. Sophie fully sympathized with Zeezee, who mutely stared with her mouth open.

Reflecting back the mute stare was tempting, but Sophie forced herself to focus on moving. "We should get outta here." She scooted over to where Anthony was gaping at her, the whites of his eyes showing all the way around the brown circles in the center. "Go, Anthony!"

Suddenly reanimated, Anthony turned, grabbed Sophie's hand and then Delilah's, leading an awkward little line across the street.

A car door opened before Sophie had even noticed it was Anthony's car. Hope stuck her head out and then slid away from the opening.

Sophie wanted to scream her friend's name but held on another moment. She checked as Nathan and his crew arrived at his little sedan, parked right behind Anthony's. Then she turned to her left and saw one of Hartman's underlings do a skidding stop outside the door she had just exited.

"Go! Go! Go!" She dropped onto the back seat of the car as Anthony arrived at the driver's door. He paused for a second before diving into his seat. Delilah's door slammed right after Sophie's. Then Anthony's. Bang. Bang. Bang.

Sophie prayed those would be the only bangs they would hear tonight. She had no idea if Hartman's people carried weapons—other than syringes of sleeping potion.

As soon as Anthony navigated away from the curb and hit the accelerator, the questions started.

"How did you guys know I was here?" Sophie got hers out first.

Hope had started a question. Delilah finished one about how Sophie had gotten out. And Anthony said something Sophie missed entirely. They all laughed. But Anthony stopped laughing when he checked the rearview mirror.

"There's guys running. They might have one of those cars up the block. Are they serious? Really?" Maybe Anthony was trying to talk those guys out of a car chase. Or maybe he was just mind blown that any of this was happening.

"What are those guys gonna do?" Delilah looked at Sophie.

Sophie turned to see if she could find pursuers behind Nathan's car. "I have no idea. I guess anything is possible with these people."

"Who are they?" Hope sounded almost as frantic as Anthony.

"Followers of this guy named Maxwell Hartman. He's the guy who tried to recruit me into his group of psychics and angel worshippers years ago."

"And he came after you again?"

"Yeah. That guy, Will, was working for him."

"Oh dang." Anthony surged the car to a higher speed.

Sophie looked behind to see if Anthony's exclamation was about something other than her story. There did seem to be a car or two behind Nathan's. "Are they really following us?"

"It looks like it. Whoa!" Anthony swerved.

Sophie started to turn forward but was captivated by the action behind them. Nathan had stopped his car at an angle that prevented the vehicles behind him from passing. There was a construction dumpster on one side and a fire hydrant on the other. Horns were blaring. Sophie thought she saw someone in Nathan's car on the phone.

"We should call the police in case Hartman's people keep coming, and in case Nathan and those guys get in trouble."

Delilah looked at her phone. "Zeezee says Carlos is already talking to the cops. She says we should keep going."

Sophie laughed hard. "What a great team!"

Shaking his head and maybe chuckling, she could only imagine what Anthony was thinking.

Everybody Just Take a Breath

It was the older cop who said it when they were all trying to speak at once, and Hope thought it was pretty good advice in general.

"Everybody just take a breath here for a minute, okay? Relax. You're all safe now. And we can start looking for this guy and see where it goes from there." He had pushed his hat back so the visor aimed toward the ceiling. Maybe he had forgotten he still had it on.

"Like, arrests and trials and all that?" Hope was high on caffeine early in the morning. She didn't really look forward to any of those legal things. She was just saying whatever popped into her head.

An hour later, after the two officers left, she still had to force herself to slow down and take a breath. She knew she needed to settle down when she realized she'd been ignoring the pain in her leg for hours. No meds at all and way too much thumping down sidewalks and halls, etc., etc.

Sophie was in bed, the last of her friends having left after two in the morning. Groggy goodbyes, foggy farewells. Lots of relieved smiles.

With her foot propped on an extra pillow, Hope slept in her bed for a few slices, probably about forty-five minutes each. Sleeping while the sun was rising had always been a struggle. After the third round of restless sleep, she lay listening for signs of life.

Sophie had gone down before the cops even left. They were still finishing their root beers and talking to Anthony and Delilah at that point. The younger cop seemed to know some of the people those two knew. She could tell they weren't talking about Sophie's abduction anymore by then.

Hope got the impression early on that the cops were weirded out by the story. But the fact that there were so many witnesses, to at least part of it, seemed to keep them from rejecting it entirely. Or maybe the younger cop was a church kid. Maybe that was how Anthony knew him. Either way, neither of the cops spent time speculating aloud on the motive behind the kidnapping. At least not while they were still in the apartment. They seemed glad to talk about something else as soon as another topic came along.

Nightshift cops. They were probably glad for the excitement. Excitement that didn't involve blood or breaking up a drunken fight.

They seemed pretty impressed by Nathan. His maneuver to stop the pursuers was risky, but clearly he had been right about the goons in the chaser car. Apparently they only wanted Sophie and weren't willing to harm the three strangers blocking them nervously in that little sedan.

Hope was still picturing Nathan holding the bad guys off with his guitar. Would he fend them off by swinging it like a club, or by playing powerful worship music?

From what Nathan and Carlos said, Maxwell Hartman wasn't part of the pursuit. That made sense. Crime lords and supervillains didn't do their own car chases.

No wonder she couldn't sleep. Her brain was still in action-movie mode.

Lying there amid her thoughts and speculations allowed Hope to home in on something—those creeps had grabbed Sophie because of her skills. Even if it was never entirely clear what they wanted from Sophie or what they planned to do to her if they didn't get it. Now Hope could put herself in Sophie's place. She had skills too. Was she in danger from people like that? And was she also in danger from Gerry?

Yeah. No wonder she couldn't sleep.

Swinging her gimpy leg off the side of the bed, Hope winced at a stabbing pain below her knee, just above the fiberglass cast. She must have overworked it hopping out of the car, rushing to keep up with Sophie and the others when they got home, so anxious to hear the whole story.

Sophie seemed okay, really. No torture. One small bruise. One drugging that she had recovered from. At least until she passed out while the cops talked to Anthony and Delilah. Hope assumed being abducted was exhausting, drugs or no drugs. Even more exhausting than worrying about what had happened to your best friend.

Hope thumped into the kitchen, recalling the looming beasts around that building where Sophie had been held. Was it worth it? Seeing those things, risking provoking people like this Hartman guy? All that talk about being warriors and battling the enemy was supposed to just be a metaphor. Symbolic. Or at least limited to the realm that was invisible to most people. Right?

"Ow! No! No! Let me go!" Sophie's voice boiled over from behind her bedroom door.

Hope froze for a second. Could someone have gotten into the apartment? She zoomed in on the spiritual population in the place. One of Sophie's usual trio was standing by her bedroom door looking at Hope.

"What? What am I supposed to do?"

The angel raised his eyebrows toward Sophie's room and disappeared from view.

That guardian angel hadn't looked alarmed, really. And he made no kind of show of fighting off some spiritual enemy. So maybe it was just a nightmare this time.

As Hope crutched toward Sophie's room, she struggled to recall whether you were supposed to wake someone from a nightmare. She had hardly ever babysat for anyone. She had very little nightmare experience beyond her own and that of an occasional fellow addict. Flopped in some random house or apartment somewhere, she had often heard other people battling monsters in their dreams. But she was usually too out of it to even consider doing anything about those drug-addled night terrors.

She arrived at Sophie's door and waited. She focused on the angels again. All three of Sophie's regulars were in there. Hope's two most likely partners were waiting with her outside the door. A perverse scheme about faking like she would go in, to see if her angels would go without her, dried up quickly. She slowly swung the door open for real and saw that Sophie's eyes were open.

Sophie turned toward her and smiled weakly. "Bad guys in my dreams."

Along with exhaustion, Hope assumed such dreams were part of the aftermath. She stepped into the room, stuff still not totally organized in there. "I was worried that someone was actually in here. You sounded pretty convincing."

"I said something?"

"You were shouting. You know, the usual stuff."

"No! No! Don't do it?"

"Yeah. Like that." Hope grinned. "You ready for breakfast?"

Sophie twisted her neck to look at her bedside clock, which sat atop an unopened packing box. "Pretty late. Time for you to start work."

"I messaged Tracy that I'm taking the day off. I have plenty of time accumulated. Being stuck in this apartment hasn't hurt my work hours."

"Chasing after your loony friend has hurt though."

"You think you can convince me that *you're* loony? Ha. I was part of the crew that went out looking for you at an address none of us knew. A crew consisting of one musician, two therapists, a network geek, and a water scientist. And half of us held off a gang of bad guys with only phones and a guitar."

Sophie belly laughed. "Ha. Okay. Associated with loonies, it is." Then she stretched and groaned, one foot escaping from her covers. Her toenail polish needed updating, a couple nails entirely unpainted, and chips apparent on the others.

"I could paint your nails if you want." Hope heard herself say that and wondered what movie she was quoting, because she couldn't remember ever offering such a thing before.

"Really? Huh. Yeah. We could, like, have a girls' day at home. And I could do *your* nails. Or was that what you were aiming for all along?"

Hope looked down at her cast. The exposed toes were no longer purple, only red, and hardly swollen at all. "I can reach 'em, but bending my knee that much isn't easy."

"I'll bet." Sophie sat up with the kind of vigor that might start momentum toward a new day. But she stopped and pressed a palm to her forehead. "Okay, gotta go slow." She shook her head gingerly. "Definitely need a quiet day at home."

Safe with the Ones She Loves

Detta released Sophie from the bear hug and looked at her to check for signs of wear and tear. Then she looked at Mrs. Ramos, right behind Sophie. "You must be so relieved, dear."

Mrs. Ramos nodded and squinted a quivering smile that threatened to release a flood. But she seemed to choke that off. "Thank you for praying, Detta. I know your prayers helped get her free."

"Did she tell you about the verses Roddy found? We took it as a sign and prayed right into that," Detta said.

"And it happened." Sophie had her mother's arm now, smiling consolingly at her.

"Praise God for that." Roddy was behind Detta.

She turned and smiled at him where he stood in the doorway of her kitchen. Detta didn't envy his restraint, having to stand back and just watch the hugs. In time, she guessed that would change as Roddy and Sophie got more used to each other. Maybe after the wedding when Detta moved into his house.

"Well, dears, why don't you all take a seat in the livin' room while I get things on the table?" She had set the kitchen table since it was just the four of them. And just family.

After waving off propositions of kitchen help, she herded the others into the living room. Surely all three of those folks could use a sit. Roddy was much improved, but not ready to spend long periods on his feet. He had helped her get meals together when it was just the two of them, but mostly he did that while sitting down. His hands were working better than his feet.

As Detta turned her attention back to her work, she heard Sophie asking about Roddy's recovery and recognized his familiar upbeat assessment.

"Getting better every day. I sure am glad for Detta's patience. She's helpin' me, and lettin' me help her, and doing it all without lettin' on how frustrating it is."

Detta snorted at that, deciding to keep her disclaimers to herself for now. The roast chicken came out of the oven golden brown, the carrots and potatoes just about perfect. She landed the roasting pan on the stovetop, then stepped to the fridge and grabbed two of the wedge salads and set them on the table.

Sophie's mother was asking about Roddy's revelation about how they were supposed to pray for Sophie. "Were you really confident that it would happen like it happened in the Bible?"

"Oh, well, I believe that faith doesn't always start with confidence. For me, it often starts with a stirring in my gut that feels a lot like fear, really. I mean, I'm declaring to my brothers and sisters that we ought to pray this way, thinkin' I probably got the idea from the Holy Spirit, but I'm not sure. Not confident, really. Kinda excited that it might be so, but not what you could call certain at first."

"So you do it anyway, and that's faith," Sophie tagged on.

"It sure is part of it. Doing it even before you're certain. That's a big part of faith for me."

With a cautious tone, Mrs. Ramos seemed to drill deeper. "And what about now, about Sophie being safe from those bad people? The police haven't taken anyone into custody. Do you have faith for that in the future?"

Detta winced. She could imagine Roddy restraining his own urge to do the same. Detta wasn't fully confident about the intentions of those wayward people or of the police. She uttered another prayer for Sophie's continued protection as she pulled a carving knife out of the drawer.

"I am confident that God wants to keep us all safe. And I believe we're safest when we're doing God's will. But I know folks are free to do what they want, and even God won't always stop people from doing evil. We get free will even when we're working against God." There was a longish pause. "I do believe Sophie's work is God's will. And I'll continue to pray for her protection. You can count on that."

"Don't worry, Madre. The police haven't arrested those people because they don't have enough evidence. It's just my word and what my friends saw when I was outside. The cops still haven't found out what Hartman's people did with my old phone. I guess there isn't anything they can do without more evidence that I was there against my will. But if those people try to touch me now, that would be just what the police need."

"Did you ever figure out what it was they wanted from you?" Roddy had asked Detta that before.

Detta could imagine Sophie shrugging.

"I do know they're fascinated by what God has given me. They were asking about my gift. And they said they wanted me to consider working with them." She smacked her lips. "As impossible as it is for us to imagine, they don't think there's anything wrong with the way they work with what I think of as evil spirits. So they don't see the big gap between what they do and what we do."

"I wonder, though." Sophie's mother started with a skeptical tone. "How could they really not know the difference? Maybe they're just saying that to make themselves look good. Maybe they really know that what they do is wrong, and they don't want to admit it."

"I don't know. They seemed convincing to me at the time, at least. Though I gotta admit I was a bit stressed out and groggy." Sophie paused, maybe for another shrug. "I think that's why the police were slow to arrest anyone. Even though I know it was an abduction, I can't really prove they threatened to harm me. I worried that they would, but I can't really prove anything."

"It's not okay to detain a person like that, that's for sure." Roddy's indignation came through loud and clear.

"Okay, folks. Come on in and get it while it's hot." Detta placed the dish of carrots and potatoes in the center of the table next to the carved chicken. That was when she remembered the other two wedge salads. "Or cold, as the case may be," she muttered as she sidestepped to the fridge one more time.

As the other three settled into their seats, Detta retrieved the gravy from the top of the stove. The conversation in the living room had obviously hindered her usual routine in the kitchen. "Well, I do hope that's everything." She wiped her hands on her apron and realized she had forgotten to take it off.

As she reached around to untie it, Roddy stopped her. "I got it, dear." Reaching from his seat, he pulled on the bow he had tied at the small of her back when she started cooking. Handy to have an extra set of hands for things like that.

She chuckled as she pulled the apron free and tossed it on the counter across the kitchen. Detta sat down. "Will you lead us in grace, Brother Harper?"

"I will indeed, Sister Washington."

Another Escapee

Sophie paused as soon as she stepped off the elevator. Her hiking sandals squeaked on the super shiny lobby tiles. Someone was peeking at her from behind lush potted greenery that looked like a banana plant. It was a young woman. She looked familiar. Sophie flashed back to the last time that same girl was waiting for her to leave this office building. That connection shuddered Sophie's shoulders vigorously enough that the girl probably saw it from across the lobby.

She was coming right toward Sophie, casting glances left and right. What did she want?

The police still hadn't gotten back to Sophie. Not even on whether she qualified for a restraining order against Hartman and Will and their crew. That suddenly seemed like a much more important omission.

"I'm sorry for bothering you, but I need help, and I don't know where else to go." The girl with the giant cat eyes, hollow cheeks, and lank dark hair was either an award-winning actress, or she was really in trouble. The spirits Sophie could see on her looked like refugees from some ancient war. Battered, depressed.

"What kind of trouble?" Sophie was uncomfortable meeting this girl but not as uncomfortable as the girl appeared to be.

She shifted in her flip-flops and kept glancing around the lobby. "I need to get away from them, but they won't ... They—they don't want me to talk to anyone about the things they did."

"Have they harmed you?"

The girl looked confused by that question, brows knit and eyes blinking as she searched for something. "What they did to *you*. I'm talking about what they did to you. I need to get away from them ... and their, like, criminal activity." She glanced over her shoulder in the way she might if she could see the spirit hovering behind her now, something like a haggard old man clinging with dirty claws.

Sophie had to ask. "Can you see him?" She waved a hand all around the girl. "See them?"

The girl just raised one shoulder. "Can we go somewhere more private?"

Sophie blinked for a few seconds, letting her heart slow down. She had driven her car today, parked in the city garage up the street. She had only come into the office for two hours to attend a meeting and get a tech to look at her laptop. She hefted her messenger bag. "We can go to my car."

The girl nodded, releasing a breath she had been holding back. "I'm Mara, by the way."

"Nice to properly meet you, Mara." Sophie almost retracted what was an obvious falsehood. Nice? Not really. But it was, at least, good to have a name to go with the frightened face.

Sophie led the way out the tall glass doors, checking their surroundings almost as vigilantly as the younger woman was.

The Woman Who Welcomes Angels

Mara huddled close to Sophie as if she thought she might find physical shelter there. Or perhaps it was the spiritual shelter of Sophie's angels she was seeking. There were four of them visible to her now. One of the doormen, as she and Hope were calling them, had shown up about the time Mara introduced herself. Sophie interpreted that guard's arrival as divine provision for helping this young woman. Of course Sophie was supposed to help. How could she not?

They bustled up the street, Mara's flip-flops slapping the pavement. She wore yoga pants and a crop top, three inches of midriff showing. She looked like she hadn't had time to get dressed before escaping. She did have a small purse slung across her chest.

"Oh no." Mara muttered under her breath as Sophie led her across the last intersection before the public parking garage.

"What?"

"Eric." She pointed her nose across the street and bumped hips with Sophie, as if she thought she could get even closer.

"One of Hartman's guys?"

"Yes. I was hoping they wouldn't see me with you. I don't wanna get you into any more trouble."

Even though Sophie was pretty sure Mara was actually in trouble, she wasn't ready to believe everything she said. This could still be a trap. Sophie would need to manage their movements as much as possible to keep from falling into their hands again. "Let's get to my car. We can decide what to do from there." She was thinking that going to the police was the best option. How much could this girl tell the authorities?

Sophie checked again and found the guy watching them from across the street. The same refugee kind of spirits were hanging on him. That was her first clue about which person over there was him. The second clue was that he was staring at them.

Mara bumped into Sophie repeatedly on the way into and out of the elevator and along the concrete ramp on the third level of the garage.

"He's not the kinda guy that's gonna try to grab you, is he?" The skinny young guy probably wouldn't be much of a match for her and Mara. She knew for sure that his raggedy spirits would get nowhere past her angels. Not to mention the angel that seemed to be following them at a distance. She assumed that one was attached to Mara. But maybe distantly related was more like it.

"No. Eric isn't that kind of ... muscle. There were only a couple guys like that, that I ever saw. Eric's just like me. Drifted into Hartman when he didn't have anywhere else to stay."

Sophie hit her car remote. "You ran away from home?"

"Not really. I was in college when the lockdowns first happened, and my mom was paranoid about me getting her sick. Which she did anyway—got sick. And I couldn't find a place to stay right away. The dorms closed, so I had to scramble for a place. I knew this girl from work who said I could stay with her. She was one of Hartman's followers, it turned out. I guess his people sort of scoop up homeless kids."

Wincing at that revelation even though it wasn't entirely surprising, Sophie unlocked the passenger door as she slipped into her seat. When Mara opened her door, Sophie asked another question. "So why are you leaving him now?"

"It was too much—when I saw you in that room and could tell you were, like, a prisoner, and they drugged you." Her voice arched with incredulity. "That was way over the top. No way was I okay with all that."

"You didn't know they did things like that?"

"I didn't. I mean, I'm not sure how much they do that. I think Hartman's kinda obsessed with you especially."

"Obsessed enough that he thought he could actually get away with grabbing me?" She started the car and checked windows and mirrors and the rearview camera. Was that guy, Eric, still following them?

"Well, I heard them talking about people in the police department that would help them. Like, keep them from getting in trouble as long as they didn't really hurt anybody or something. I wasn't there for the whole conversation, just overheard part of it before I went into that meeting room."

Sophie took a deep breath. She was still measuring how much she trusted this girl. She looked in the rearview to get some hint from the two angels seated back there. They looked sedate, not alarmed. Instead of talking to them, she uttered a silent prayer for wisdom. She knew that was a safe prayer. But how safe was it to be driving around with this girl?

"I really don't think they were gonna hurt you. Definitely not kill you. But I think they might have planned to take you somewhere else. I'm not sure where or why, exactly. That was part of what Hartman was saying about the police. Like, maybe it was better to stay in the city where they had people to protect them from inside the department."

"Do you think they would harm *you*? I mean, will they, now that they know you're with me?" Sophie glanced at Mara as she slowed for the parking garage ticket booth.

"I don't know. I had no idea they would drug someone and hold them prisoner. There was never anything like that before. At least not that I saw." She pushed her hair behind her ear with a slender finger. "I heard them threaten one guy once. Not Hartman, but Will threatened to tell the cops that this guy was dealing drugs." She shook her head. "I thought the guy must have been dealing at first. But then later I wondered if they were saying—if Will was saying—he would tell the cops the guy was a dealer even if it wasn't true. I never really trusted Will."

"But you trusted Hartman?" Sophie checked up and down the street before finding Eric waiting behind a bike rack. They made eye contact. "He sees us."

Mara started to slide down in her seat, but it was too late for that. She gave up and pulled at her top as she sat up straight again.

"You look like you took off in a hurry." Sophie nodded at Mara's outfit as she pulled onto the street.

"I did. I was looking for a chance, and suddenly I was alone in that place where they took you. I guess most people were getting out of there in case the cops came back. I know Hartman was going to take a plane somewhere." She shook her head. "Anyway, I didn't know how much time I had. I just grabbed my purse and escaped with what I had on. I have some money in the bank if I have to get some clothes." She breathed heavily through her nose. "I don't wanna go to my mother's house. I don't want Hartman's people to go there. She can't know about any of this."

Sophie noted that Mara was about Hope's size, but she hadn't decided yet if she would take the girl home with her. She figured she should contact someone from church or from her team to help her make that kind of decision. She thought of Carlos as she turned onto the street that led toward his office. It was a couple miles away in a near suburb. She could probably get there even if there was a car chase involved. She checked her mirrors again.

Mara apparently saw that vigilant glance. "Eric doesn't have a car. And I don't think he would chase us anyway. At least he wouldn't do it himself."

"So there were guys with Hartman that you thought of as 'muscle,' you said?"

"Kind of. Mostly it seemed to me like they were Hartman's bodyguards, sort of. I guess he has some enemies."

Sophie wasn't surprised to hear that.

What We Signed Up For

Anthony tapped on Sophie's text message.
"That girl who was with Hartman is with me now. Escaped."
He replied, **"That girl?"**
"The one I followed into the trap."
"Is she reading what she's writing?" He spoke aloud but didn't thumb type that. He had been working from home. Now he was at the pharmacy, picking up some essentials. He forwarded the original text to Delilah, noting that Sophie hadn't started with the whole group. Maybe this was too sensitive to blast out to seven or eight people.

Sophie texted again after a few minutes of silence. **"Going to see Carlos."**

The first thing that entered Anthony's mind when he saw that was, *Why Carlos*? But then he realized Carlos might know something about abductions. Maybe that girl had been abducted like Sophie. Anthony had no idea how old the girl was or much else about her, really. All he knew was what she looked like and that she was one of the cult leader's tools for trapping Sophie. Who was to say she wasn't being used for that again?

He texted, **"Want me to come?"**
"You available?"
"I could do it. Carlos's office?"

"Yeah. I'm in front of his building."

Maybe it didn't make sense for Anthony to charge over there now. What would he bring? And he would be late to the meeting. "I'll wait. Let me know if you need me."

"Okay. Maybe pull you in on a call if we have decisions. Forgot to include Delilah. Please forward."

"Already did."

"Cool."

He continued gathering meds and supplements and headed to the cash register. A text from Delilah came back. He waited until he paid at the register before he responded.

Anthony called her. "Hello, beautiful."

"Hello, handsome. Has our girl, Sophie, gone out of her mind?" Delilah's prosaic tone hinted that she assumed the answer was no. Maybe she was just imagining what Anthony was thinking. In some ways, he was more cautious than her.

"I mean, she can see the girl's spiritual cling-ons, presumably. So she has to have some reason to think it's okay. She took her to Carlos's office." Anthony was sitting in his car by now.

"Huh. Okay. That sorta makes sense. Maybe the girl was abused or abducted."

"That's what I was thinking. But Carlos will be helpful in evaluating her even if that isn't the issue."

"Yeah, more than evaluating the size and color of the demons she carries."

"Uh-huh." Anthony rolled down both front windows. It was a windy day, like a blow dryer switched on high, but it wasn't as hot outside as the interior of the car. "Is this part of what we signed up for with her?"

"I think so. I mean, Sophie's skills make it easier for her to tell what's going on with people who carry serious spiritual oppression." Delilah paused. "I can see God using her to help lots of really troubled people. Troubled in all kinds o' ways."

He started his car to get the air-conditioning going. "That reminds me of this thought I had the night we were looking for Sophie and saw those girls on the street corner downtown."

"Those girls?"

"You know the ones I mean."

"Really? Tell me what you were thinking about when you saw those ladies of the night."

He huffed at her and shook his head. "Settle down, girl. You got nothin' at all to worry about." He took a deep breath. "Seriously, I know some folks who do ministry on the streets with girls like that. Like, going to where they are and offering to pray for them for healing and protection and stuff. Mostly women doing it, actually."

"I've heard of that, yeah. And, of course, you're thinking Sophie's skills would be pretty good for that sorta thing?"

"I am. And with a strong, godly woman like you to offer wisdom to those girls, it almost seems like a no-brainer. Add in Zeezee and Hope, and you guys are a force to reckon with."

"Hmm. What about you? You gonna let us girls take the risk while you just stay home and stream a movie?"

He snorted another laugh. She knew better. "Well, maybe Nathan and I could wait in the car somewhere close by in case you girls need some help. Carlos could ride along in case they need therapy." He snickered, powering the windows back up. Then he turned serious. Sort of. "Or maybe we would be there if you needed a getaway."

"I can see why that night going after Sophie got you thinkin' like that. You like the car chases."

"No, dear. I'm just sayin' us boys won't stay home and sip beers while you girls bring light to the darkness on the city streets."

He heard Delilah laugh. "It *is* a good idea, Anty. I think God laid that on your heart, actually."

"Yeah, easy for me to hear God telling *you* all to take a big risk."

"Oh, our bodyguards better not be far away if us girls do that kinda ministry."

"I know. Okay." He checked his rearview camera before backing up. "Hey, Sophie said she might call us to get in on deciding what to do with that escaped girl."

"I wonder how she escaped. Maybe angels opened the doors for her too."

"It seems like she was allowed to walk around on her own before, but who knows?"

"Okay. I'll head home a bit early in case we need to get on a call or come to the rescue."

"Good. Talk to you later either way."

"Love you, Anty."

"Love you too, Delilah."

In Prison You Visited Me

Sophie stood up when Carlos entered the meeting room, a well-lit space just down the hall from his private office. He had been meeting with someone when they arrived, so she and Mara had to wait in this little room lined with several cushy chairs and one love seat.

"Carlos, thanks for seeing us." Sophie turned to Mara, who was standing now too, clutching her purse in front of her. "This is Mara. She was at Hartman's place. She decided to get out when she saw what they did to me."

Mara waved. "Hi. Uh, what kind of counselor are you?"

Offering his hand, Carlos said, "Well, this is a child welfare agency supported by area churches. That's what I do for a living. But I also work with Sophie on things that are kind of outside of my regular job."

"Huh. Okay. I mean, I guess I heard *counselor*, and I was thinking lawyer." She shook his hand.

"Do you think you need a lawyer?" Carlos gestured to the seat behind Mara, and she backed up and sat down.

"I don't know. Maybe. I'm wondering if it would be safe to go to the cops without one. I mean, there are supposedly people in the department who are friends of Hartman. People who might help him. They might even … help him get at me if I report him."

"Then you'd better go to the FBI instead. And if it's related to Sophie being kidnapped, I think the feds would be willing to get involved."

"And you're not a lawyer?"

Carlos smiled, then turned that into a brief grimace. "Once in a while we help kids who have been kidnapped. Usually I see them after they've been free for a while, but sometimes we hear about the process that got them free. That's why I know something about kidnappings."

"Not because you're a kidnapper in your free time?" Mara kept her voice and her eyes low. To Sophie, it was obvious she was flirting with Carlos, but maybe that was just part of Sophie's overall suspicion about this girl.

For his part, Carlos didn't smile at Mara's joke. He had probably picked up on the flirting, maybe more readily than Sophie had. That was more his field.

Sophie's field of expertise included the coquettish little spirit that had just appeared next to Mara as if standing on the arm of her chair. The little imp was inching her skirt up to show more leg. Sophie shook that off and focused on the humans in the room. "Are you willing to tell the FBI what you know about Hartman kidnapping me?"

Mara did a big intake of air, a little more midriff showing for a second. "I was thinking I couldn't tell the police because of Hartman's connections with them, but if it's the FBI ..." She seemed to drift a bit. "I don't know. It seems kinda dangerous. Hartman might get nastier if he thinks I can get them all thrown into prison."

"That might be true." Sophie slowed her response. Did she really expect Mara to risk her own life to get charges pressed against Hartman? What if Mara was right that they didn't normally abduct people?

Carlos spoke up. "Don't you think you owe it to the next person they might capture?"

Mara squinted around the room. "I never would have thought they could do that before I saw *her* there." She poked a finger toward Sophie. "I still don't know if they abduct people regularly. I mean, you're special." Mara looked at Sophie. "That's what Hartman kept saying."

Carlos grinned just briefly. "Well, that's true. Sophie is special." He paused as if letting that dissipate from the room. "But I'm guessing a group that would abduct one woman would be willing to kidnap others later, especially if they got away with it the first time."

Mara took another of those big breaths. She looked toward the door. Was she considering running? "I don't know. Would it be possible to talk to the FBI and just find out what might happen?"

"Maybe." Again, Sophie hit pause after releasing her initial answer. What if the FBI saw Mara as part of the kidnapping? She had taken part in it to some extent. They might hold her in order to force her to implicate others. If this was just about Sophie, she might let it go. But Carlos had to be right. Hartman might try to grab someone else.

"I think there would definitely be some risk for you, to be honest." Sophie fiddled with the strap of her smart watch. "Since you took part in the trap, they might not let you go until you told them more. So maybe going in just to see what might happen would be risky."

"I guess I do need a lawyer, but I don't wanna call my mother to see if she can help me pay for one."

Carlos pursed his lips thoughtfully. "I could put you in touch with a lawyer that our agency works with to see if she has some advice. That would be free, at least for one phone call."

"And no matter what you decide, we can pull together a few people who could help you get rid of the spirits that are hooked onto you. Would you like that?" Sophie raised her eyebrows in offer.

Mara stared at Sophie, her eyes shifting slightly as she calculated. "I don't know. I guess I'm just used to them."

"Do you see them?"

"Not clearly. I just know they're with me."

"How many?"

"Four right now." She didn't hesitate.

"That's how many I see, but that's no guarantee there aren't more."

"Getting rid of them should make it easier for you to make a good decision about how to deal with Hartman and his crimes. Spirits like that can feed you fear in a way that serves people like him." Carlos flicked his eyes toward Sophie as if wondering whether she would agree, but he kept his sympathetic gaze mostly on Mara.

"If *you* think I should do it, then I will." She glanced from Carlos to Sophie and back. "Get rid of those four, I mean."

As enchanting as were Carlos's good looks, Sophie suspected it was his obvious gentleness and sympathy that really persuaded Mara.

"Is it okay if we sort of lock those spirits down for now without totally getting rid of them? We can usually limit their power for a while." Sophie was glossing over a whole list of complexities, but she suspected Mara would understand enough of what she was saying—at least what she was implying.

"I don't mind. It would be interesting to see what difference it makes." Again, she settled her eyes on Carlos.

Sophie knew Mara's attraction to Carlos would be a hindrance in a real deliverance setting, but she was just proposing locking the spirits down temporarily, not prying them loose. "Okay if we pray? Then I'll forbid them from interfering with you."

"You can really do that?"

"With your cooperation, we can." Sophie waited.

Mara nodded slowly. "Okay. Tell me what to do."

"Just sit back and relax and agree with what I say so far as you can. If there's something I say that bothers you, we can talk about it."

"Hmm. Okay." Mara folded her hands in her lap and bowed her head.

Though Sophie had not advised that posture, she decided to let it be. She checked with Carlos, then started a prayer for protection and wisdom before commanding the four spirits to be bound and not to mess with Mara. It wasn't elaborate or dramatic. She watched Mara for any drama she might bring. That would give Sophie a sense of how much control the spirits had over the young woman. If they were deeply entrenched in Mara, they were holding back, not showing any resistance.

Carlos added a prayer for safety and peace of mind for Mara, and Sophie watched the younger woman's toes curl and uncurl as if savoring Carlos's voice and attention. Clearly Mara had issues that Carlos triggered. Though, of course,

Sophie wasn't blaming her for being attracted to Mr. Dark and Handsome.

They let Carlos get back to work after Mara thanked him with a hug.

Sophie decided not to follow her example, just offered a small smile as she left Carlos by the elevator.

Sophie and Mara were alone on the way to the lobby. "How do you feel?"

Mara shrugged. "I like him a lot."

"I mean after we bound those spirits." Sophie was watching the four imps sort of float idly around Mara now. That they hadn't gone invisible was a good sign. They hadn't pretended to leave to get her to stop bothering them.

"Oh. No problem." She leaned on the back of the elevator. "So, Carlos is gonna have that lawyer call me?"

"Yeah. Or I'll get her number, and you can call her. We'll wait to see what Carlos finds out about her availability." The elevator door opened, and Sophie let Mara step out first.

When they reached Sophie's car in the parking lot behind the building, they let the doors stand open for half a minute to clear some of the greenhouse heat. "You don't have anywhere to go?"

"Not if I'm staying around here and not going to my mother's place in Kansas."

"I'll contact my roommate and see what she says about you staying with us."

"Oh, that would be nice." Mara took a jittery breath, a threat of tears not far off. "That's so nice of you, Sophie."

"Well, we escaped from the same prison. We owe it to each other." After saying that, she tried to imagine whether Hope would agree.

A Little Crowded for a While

Sophie only apologized to Hope once about how long Mara was staying with them. She let that early apology stand for four days.

Mara slept on the couch. She had a job that got her out of the apartment each day. Hope was able to work almost as usual. But when Mara discovered a Hartman underling watching the clothing shop where she worked, she took a leave of absence. Or maybe just quit. Sophie couldn't tell for sure which.

"Is she gonna go to Anthony and Delilah's engagement party with us?" Hope's doubtful tone hinted at her opinion on that question.

Sophie didn't attempt to fulfill or disappoint Hope's expectations. She was focused just then on getting Mara to the meeting with the lawyer at the FBI office downtown. Sophie hadn't even known there *was* an FBI office downtown, though it made sense. Maybe they had one in all cities of a certain size.

When Mara settled into the passenger seat of Sophie's car, she glanced back toward the apartment building. "Hope's getting bugged by me being around. I can tell."

"She's okay." Sophie knew part of the problem was the spirits that seemed to feel free to wander into their place at random intervals. None seemed to do any harm except to reiterate some claim they had on Mara. Maybe the claim was something Hartman had on Mara. Or just something he *wanted* to have on her.

Would those spirits know about this meeting? Would they report to Hartman? That would certainly raise the stakes for Mara and anyone harboring her. Those questions rode downtown with Sophie.

The woman who served as the legal consultant for Carlos's agency had connected Mara with someone else in her firm. An average height athletic man with black hair and caramel skin met them in front of the FBI offices. He looked good in a medium-blue suit.

"Sophie? Mara?" The guy had good enough instincts to tell who was who.

Sophie shook hands with Mr. Patel and thanked him.

"Oh, this is a very interesting case. I'm curious to see where it leads. We won't have to discuss fees until we talk to the people in here. It's not clear to me yet whether you'll need representation." He turned his attention from Mara to Sophie. "You, of course, don't need representation unless you want to bring a suit against the local police for failing to sufficiently prosecute your case. Seems like you might have grounds for that."

Sophie shook her head. That wasn't something she was interested in. While Mr. Patel seemed a fine person, she didn't relish the notion of spending much time with lawyers, especially in court.

In the FBI office, they were ushered to a conference room that would fit a dozen people. Sophie could identify that many spirits in there. Five of them were angels with her and Mara. Mara's guardian had apparently gotten more comfortable around her in the days since Sophie invited the girl to stay with her.

Mr. Patel traveled with an inspiring angel that appeared to be made of pure gold. That angel had a more sober persona than Mr. Patel.

Mara's oppressor spirits weren't visible, but there were at least half a dozen other demons making this meeting their business. Sophie couldn't tell who they were associated with.

Two agents entered the room bringing no apparent accompaniment with them, though some of the spirits already in the room might have been assigned to either or both of them. Handshakes and polite greetings started the meeting. Then the two agents took turns perusing pages from a file and asking clarifying questions.

"And you don't know the name of the police officers or staff who are familiar with your Mr. Hartman?" The younger agent, a ruddy man about the same age as Sophie, raised his eyes toward Mara.

"No. I just overheard Hartman talking about them. It seemed like he was keeping their names out of it, like maybe he didn't trust the people he was talking to."

"Or he knew you were listening." The older agent, a gaunt woman with medium-brown skin and her hair in a tight bun, arrowed her eyes at Mara.

"He might have. He can see things beyond what's visible to most people." Mara said that as if she wasn't aware of how it might sound to crime investigators.

The woman, Agent Anders, replied briskly. "That's what he claims, anyway. I can see that from our research on Hartman. He claims to be a psychic with powers in that area."

"The spiritual context is what he calls it," Mara said, as if trying to be helpful.

Anders scowled. "But what you do know for sure is that Ms. Ramos was abducted by Mr. Hartman, who either instructed someone to drug her or did so himself."

Mara nodded. "I thought he would just surprise her and try to get her to talk to him. I had no idea he was going to hold her against her will. I was freaked out when I heard they had her locked in that room. And then they asked me to take water to her. I mean, I was scared. I had no idea those people would commit crimes like that. I thought they were only concerned with the spiritual context."

"But they wanted Ms. Ramos to help them with that. Wasn't that the reason for the abduction?" The younger agent, Murphy, seemed to be doing the good cop part when it came to Sophie and Mara's supernatural explanations.

Sophie was thinking, *Wait until I tell them how I got out.* But she didn't have to reveal that just yet. The agents seemed content with Mara's story. The key question for them seemed to be whether it was okay for Mara to go home to Kansas.

"In fact, I think it would be a good idea," Agent Anders said after some discussion and one intense phone call. "We can have you check in with our office in Kansas City so they're aware of your presence. Though we don't have any evidence of Hartman or his associates planning something against you, it would be prudent for you to get away from here."

Though it would be nice to get the living room back, Sophie wasn't relieved to hear this proposal. Mara, on the other hand, brightened at the prospect of escaping even farther from Hartman.

With an extensive exchange of email addresses and phone numbers, Mara, Sophie, and Mr. Patel left the office and headed out to the breezy, warm street.

"The best news is that they're not considering you a suspect, only a person of interest. Though you should know they'll be tracking you. Keep that in mind, especially when you communicate with anyone electronically." Patel squinted in the bright sunlight on the sidewalk, which shone nearly white at this time of day. An American flag snapped above them, casting a sharp shadow on the concrete.

Mara shifted her weight from one foot to the other. She was wearing sandals from Sophie's closet, her feet closer to Sophie's size than Hope's. Glancing up from the radiating pavement, she seemed unconcerned. "I'm not gonna do anything I'm ashamed of. I'm actually glad to think of them keeping an eye on me and watching out for any of Hartman's people."

"Hmm. I wish they could do more." Sophie didn't know what more—this wasn't her realm. "But at least we can be praying for your protection." She was more confident in the angels than the agents.

Mara's fluttering eyes seemed to signal less of that confidence.

Another Surprise Visitor

"I had to wait until I could get a cheap flight to make it worth it. Never tried flying standby before."

Hope shook her head, disbelief streaming through her earbuds and into her brain. Gerry was in her ears. Gerry was at the airport.

"You should have called before you bought a ticket. You think I'm coming to pick you up like this?"

"No. I assume you're still mad at me. I'll get a rideshare. Just tell me where to meet you."

"Good call on me still being mad." As unhinged as the guy was, at least he didn't assume she would tell him her home address. Though she wondered how long until her new address became a data point a guy like Gerry could find on the internet. "I don't know. I gotta think about this."

"Well, I came all this way. You gotta see me. And you gotta give me my stuff."

"Pretty careless of you to let it get away." Hope was thinking he had been careless about letting *her* get away, but probably that wasn't all his fault.

"I know." A little whine tainted his voice. "You know I regret it. But I didn't tell you 'cause I didn't want you to get in trouble. I just had to get that stuff out of my sight for a while. You know ..."

She sort of did know, but she wasn't feeling forgiving, nonetheless. "And still, you stowed it at my place."

Even Gerry knew an unbeatable argument. He grunted. "Look, I'm tapped out. I spent my last dollar to fly out here. I need that stuff now. I owe people money. Can't you just meet me?"

She checked her girl angel, who seemed unconcerned. "It has to be in a public place."

"Of course." He snorted a laugh. "You can buy me lunch."

"Ha. Pretty audacious." But she probably would buy him lunch, truth be told. She wasn't entirely cold toward him. "Okay, there's a food court at a mall not far from the airport." She flipped to a rideshare app on her phone. As she did, it occurred to her to see if any of her crew could come along. It was the middle of a workday, so that was doubtful.

"Yeah, sure. I can see a big mall on the map. That's fine. You're gonna bring the stuff with you?"

"I don't have it. A friend stowed it for me."

"Oh." After a considering pause, he swore. "I need that stuff, Hope. No messin' around. I need it." The words weren't threats per se, but his tone was becoming more threatening.

Hope envisioned gangsters coming to her place to toss it in search of the missing drugs. But that wasn't what he was saying. Did Gerry have any kind of backing? For the best answer to that, Hope focused on her bigger guardian angel, The Ranger. What did he think from a security perspective?

As if in response to her unspoken question, two ragged spirits appeared next to that guardian. His calm turn toward them implied he not only knew they were coming, but he had allowed them in.

As he and Hope watched, the closest spirit reached into the rags that passed for its clothes and pulled out pockets on both sides. Empty. Nothing there. The second spirit revealed its pockets to be empty as well.

As Sophie liked to say, the visions of these spirits were symbolic. The point was clear. Gerry didn't have any backing. He wasn't making any kind of real threat. Even the implication of a threat was empty.

"Come on, Hope. I need this."

"What if I could get you some money instead?" The image of the two impoverished spirits seemed to verify Gerry's claim that his own pockets were empty. "I just don't think I can see any way to justify giving you illegal substances even if they did once belong to you. But what if I could raise some cash?"

"I'm not looking for charity, just what's mine."

"I believe there's this saying about possession being a big part of legal ownership, right?" She opened her texting app and started a group message to Sophie and the team. "So I don't have to give it to you. And it's not like you're gonna report me to the cops. But I am willing to help you to, like, not starve."

Gerry swore. "I'm stuck." He swore again. "What can I say? I got—I got nothin'."

"Well, I can sympathize with that. I've been desperate before. And I have some friends who know what that's like too. I also know none of them are gonna say I should give you the pills." After the night of Sophie's escape and that friendly conversation between Anthony and one of the cops he knew, Hope could picture turning the drugs in to that particular officer. He would know Anthony was legit.

Gerry huffed over the phone. "Okay, okay."

"Let me talk to my people and get back to you."

"Sure. I got a flight at eight tonight. I'm not going anywhere for a few hours."

"I could send you money with an app even if you have to leave before I get it together."

"Yeah. I ... I appreciate it." He breathed hard over the phone. "Now I feel even worse about sticking you with that stuff."

"Well, I've learned that guilt without real change is worthless, so if you're not getting out of that racket, then you may as well skip the guilt." Harsh words, she knew, but she kind of had him trapped. Hope looked at her guardians again. The impoverished imps were gone, and her ranger didn't seem particularly vigilant.

As her friends started replying with cash offers, Hope looked at her bank account and did some math. One part of the calculation was how much was enough to keep Gerry from starving versus how much was enough to get him set up with more pills to sell. They didn't teach that kind of equation in math class, so Hope resorted to prayer instead.

Then she had an idea. She sent a text to her old sponsor in California.

When she called Gerry back, she had commitments for $2,500, including from herself. "But there's a catch. I'm sending it to Bernice. You have to go to her to get the money."

Gerry had a favorite curse word. That was his first response. No surprise. "Man, Hope. You're a hard case." Then he laughed. "I guess I knew you were tough. That's why I wasn't really worried you'd get hurt when I stowed that stuff with you."

"Hmm. I have no idea how to respond to that. But what do you say? I send the money to Bernice, and you go see her. And maybe you get back into group?"

"Hmm. Maybe."

Relief before Going Home

Anthony sent the electronic transfer to Hope and then called the police precinct where he thought his old friend Garret worked. It felt like important business to settle before going into a deliverance session for Mara. Maybe there wasn't any real connection, but Anthony assumed not every spiritual connection would make total sense to his computer-networking brain.

And then there was his mama's voice inside his head. Preparing for an intense ministry session always raised his esteem for his mother. He would call his mama after he got through to Garret.

By the time he was picking Delilah up at her place along with Zeezee, Anthony had heard back from Garret, and they had an appointment with Hope to turn over the pills. The friendly officer even said they would get a receipt for the package. Like they could change their minds and reclaim their illegal drugs later? Well, maybe not that.

"Everything okay with your friend Garret?" Delilah asked after Anthony kissed her.

Zeezee was putting on her shoes right there in the entryway where Anthony was propping the apartment door open.

"Everything's good. Hope and I will see him the day after tomorrow. No problem." That last phrase was supposed to be code, to assure her that Garret believed Anthony's story about how he came by the pills.

"Good. It'll be good to have that taken care of."

"You talking about the drugs?" Zeezee stood up next to Delilah but addressed Anthony.

He grinned at her. "No secrets around here, huh?"

"I could tell by what you two weren't saying."

"I guess we're not as sneaky as we think." Anthony held the door as the two ladies stepped into the hall.

"That can be a good thing." Zeezee grinned at him and slipped ahead of them on the way downstairs.

Delilah tilted her head to the side as if to say, "*Good point*," but she just smiled at her man.

He took the chance to kiss her again. Any chance would do.

Relieved at the pending solution to the pills, Anthony still felt his stomach tighten when he thought about their destination. The whole team would gather to help Mara before she headed back to Kansas. Sophie, Zeezee and Carlos had done a couple of interviews with her. Apparently one thing they figured out was that Carlos would have to sit back because Mara had a crush on him. Zeezee would take the place Carlos might have in a normal session. Well, in a different session. *Normal* probably wasn't even a thing.

"What are you worrying about, Anty?" Delilah had her window open and her elbow propped on the door.

He suspected that window would go back up once they got rolling at speed. Wind in his hair was no issue for Anthony. It was different for Delilah.

"How do you know I'm worrying?"

"You have this thing you do with your lips. Like you're trying to seal your mouth shut permanently or something."

"Humph. Yeah, I can see that." But he hesitated to admit what was worrying him.

"What is it? You suspect she's more entangled with Hartman than she lets on?"

Taking his foot off the accelerator, Anthony stared at his fiancée for a second. "Dang. I can't even have a secret inside my own head." He tried a teasing smile, not sure he pulled it off.

She did roll up her window at that point. "I just say that 'cause that's what I've been sensing."

"Oh, does that mean another one of those big scary monsters?" Zeezee was leaning forward, her voice coming from right behind Anthony's ear.

"Don't know, but it'll be good to have the whole team there." Delilah tightened her lips down. Maybe she was hoping to seal away her fears so they didn't add to Zeezee's.

"Gotta start with some worship." Anthony said that aloud without intending to.

"Your mama and her friends will be worshipping upstairs. And interceding." Delilah's tone was meditative. Perhaps she was consoling herself with those thoughts.

"Yes, they will." When they'd arranged all this, Anthony's first thought had been *overkill*. But, right now, overkill was exactly what he wanted. Less drama, more victory.

When they arrived at the church, Anthony hugged his mama in the foyer and shook Roddy's hand. Roddy was looking stronger, though maybe he had lost some weight. Anthony wasn't sure about that.

"You all have everything you need?" His mama pushed her glasses up and surveyed the gathered team. Nathan and Carlos were still on their way.

Hope hugged Detta and said something about the hug being all she was missing. Anthony thought he saw a year or two drop off Hope's face after that embrace from his highly huggable mama. Then Nathan and Carlos entered the front door of the church looking uncertain about where to go next.

Gesturing for them to join the crowd, Anthony glanced at Mara, who was wedged between Hope and Sophie. He had probably been avoiding eye contact with her, though Anthony knew that wasn't right. The vulnerability that came with submitting to this kind of ministry still made him uncomfortable. And his sense was that Mara really wasn't prepared for what was coming. Though it had to be different than the ambush they'd experienced with Sean and Will.

Sophie led the way down the stairs to the fellowship hall. Some couches and chairs had been arranged in the corner opposite the kitchen. Sophie headed to that corner as Anthony turned off the extra lights that made the place look like it was ready for a potluck. He left a third of the room illuminated with bluish fluorescence. That looked friendlier to him, though he had no way of knowing how it looked to Mara.

Delilah clicked the switch on a standing lamp in the corner. The youth group met over here sometimes, so some homey touches had been put in place. No one set that up with this kind of ministry in mind, Anthony was sure.

A long table by the wall had been arranged with snacks and cups, a water cooler standing past the far end of the table. "Feel free to help yourself to anything you want here." Anthony stopped by the table and got himself a few crackers with some cheese and a cup of water. It was nervous eating. He had finished supper about an hour ago.

Mara shook off the offer of provisions and followed Sophie to a comfy chair near the wall, which had been painted a coffee-with-cream color recently. That was way better than the radiation green it had been painted for years before the upgrade.

Sophie and Anthony conferred quietly as they decided on assigned seats for each of the team members. They decided Sophie and Delilah would sit right in front of Mara. Zeezee and Anthony would flank them. Hope would be next to Anthony, where Sophie could see her, and Carlos would sit where Zeezee could see him. Nathan could sit on the far right from Anthony, not facing Mara directly.

Anthony knew Nathan would capture some of the focus of the gathering when he started leading worship. That might relieve some of the pressure on Mara at the beginning.

When he checked with her, Delilah was sipping water and gesturing for Anthony to slide his chair closer to hers. He felt like her consultant or her legal partner in court. She had the lead seat because Mara was attracted to men and had clearly demonstrated a tendency to be distracted by that, particularly by Carlos.

Hope settled in with a plate full of food in one hand. Anthony saw her make eye contact with Sophie, who nodded and pursed her lips. Noting that exchange between the two seers alerted Anthony to a feeling that the room was filling up with beings he couldn't see. Another glance at Sophie confirmed that feeling. She did a sweep of the wall behind Mara as if assessing what stood before her.

"Ouch! Oh, that hurts! Stop that!" Mara rose from her seat as if someone were poking her from behind with a needle.

Sophie nodded. It had begun.

Delilah commanded all unholy spirits present to stand down and leave Mara alone. Then she signaled to Nathan to start the worship music.

He was leaning on his guitar by then, tuned and ready. The first thing he did was not strum his guitar, however. Instead, he closed his eyes and took a deep breath.

That reminded Anthony to relax and focus. When he took a few seconds to do that, it felt like everyone was in their place, and the whole room was filling with peace. All the way to the church kitchen. Even Mara's shoulders settled lower, though she seemed a bit confused about what Nathan was doing.

Then he began to play.

Dealing With Family Business

Sophie had been praying all day about what would happen at the church tonight. She worked from home and monitored Mara, who spent the day in the apartment messaging family and friends and watching movies on a tablet computer Sophie had loaned her. And Sophie had avoided eye contact with Hope most of the day for fear they would say something to each other or even flash a look that would frighten Mara away.

She knew it was good to have Mara in sight to be sure she was safe and at peace. To shelter her from people or spirits who might try to draw her away. But all that made it hard to concentrate on work. Sophie was glad no one was micromanaging her progress with the rewrites for the organization's staff webpage. She envied Hope her constant stream of support calls, the demands of customers that kept her focused. At least more focused than Sophie was today.

When the three of them arrived at the church, Sophie was already tired. The burden of anticipation had drained her. Hugging Detta was like visiting a filling station. She felt an infusion of inspiration and energy. She could see Hope gather the same from her contact with Detta. In a way, it was Detta and the prayer group that would carry them. Sophie and friends just had to ride the Spirit and fight off anything that was oppressing Mara.

Maybe this spiritual work wasn't so easy as that, but it helped Sophie to simplify their task. Simplicity and focus. That had to be good.

Once they were all settled in, Sophie counted the crowd of enemies lining the wall behind Mara. It was unusual to see more than one or two spirits at the beginning of ministry like this. The spirits generally favored stealth and deception. But maybe this crowd of spirits *was* the deception. Meant to intimidate. The appearance of a dozen visible demons was fairly intimidating.

After Delilah bound the little imps that were poking Mara in the back, Sophie looked at Hope as Nathan started the worship music. Hope had stopped chewing midbite, as if starting to catalog the gathering of enemies. Turning to follow the aim of Hope's stunned attention, Sophie noted a sort of screen. It was more solid than a smoke screen but more fluid than a projector screen.

Perhaps noting the silent communication between Sophie and Hope, Delilah leaned toward Sophie. She paused as if waiting for Sophie to speak, then filled the silence. "I feel like we need to get started—to get ahead of their games."

Sophie nodded deeply. "Exactly. I think you're right. Let's you and I just start binding the things I see and sort of establish how much Mara is tied into them."

Delilah ran a questioning appraisal from Mara to the wall behind her as if hoping to see connections.

Sophie knew Delilah might be sensing even if she wasn't seeing.

Interrupting Sophie and Delilah's private deliberations, Mara started fidgeting in her seat again. Nathan's voice, accompanied by guitar and the voices of four or five others, served as background as Sophie and Delilah took turns praying and binding spirits that were presenting themselves.

Sophie was hoping to find the connector, the controller spirit. She glanced at Hope, who nodded toward something directly above Mara. There stood a man, or a spirit disguised as a man. Sophie had noticed him before. Now he had his arms crossed over his chest. His face was severe. His gaze aimed to the side, off toward the distance.

Sophie signaled for Zeezee. The counselor was singing quietly with Nathan on a contemplative worship song. She stopped singing and leaned in.

With the three women only a foot from Mara's face, that stern male spirit disappeared. Sophie took that as an answer to the question she was about to ask Mara.

"Mara, tell me about your father and your relationship with him."

Still squirming as if her little brother were pestering her in the backseat of the family car, Mara moaned. "Not much of a relationship. He took off when I was six."

"Took off?"

"Left my mom and me and married another woman. Started another family. Then totally disappeared from my life."

It seemed that he was back now, at least as a spiritual representation. "Have you seen a counselor about all that?"

Shaking her head loosely as if she didn't understand the point of the question, Mara said, "No. Is that important?"

Sophie knew the little group of blue and green goblins still poking Mara weren't helping her understand the question. "It's not gonna stop us, but it's something for you to look at later." Then she turned her attention to those goblins and shut down their annoyance campaign. That was easy. They complied. Sophie's two newest guardian angels elbowed in among them, and the little beasties disappeared.

"What's this one that keeps going away and coming back?" Delilah glanced above Mara's head, not landing her eyes there long enough for Sophie to think she actually saw the spirit's image.

"The absent father."

As soon as Sophie said that, Mara leaped from her seat and spun around. She lunged at the space behind her chair, nearly tripping over it. Was she seeing that abandoning father spirit? She foraged in the air as if she knew he was there but couldn't clearly reach him.

"I command the abandonment spirit to stop haunting Mara right now. Stand back. Be silent and don't communicate with her in any way." Sophie hadn't heard the demon speak but sensed that Mara had.

The worship music continued. Nathan's steadiness and endurance would serve them well, as would his sensitivity. His voice could go big and fill the entire social hall, but he was keeping it small and intimate. Carlos and Anthony sang with him, a guys' trio for now.

Mara sat back down and folded her arms over her chest, an exaggerated pout on her lips. "I want my daddy. And I want him right now."

That started a new struggle. Hope identified the spirit speaking through Mara as Abandoned Girl. Not so clever maybe, but functional. That spirit seemed dependent in some way on Absent Father, as they labeled the surly male spirit.

At one point, Sophie looked at Zeezee for help. Without hesitation, Zeezee began to affirm the little girl's need for her father and her attachment to him. But she also pointed out that Mara was grown up now and could decide the nature of her relationship with her father even in his absence.

As in most other sessions Sophie had done, the person they were helping had an array of wounds and attachments, spiritual and emotional. She seconded Zeezee's affirmation of the real emotional issues and the real need. Then she insisted on sending the absent father away as an interloper. Not Mara's real father. And not really helpful.

But the abandoned girl didn't want him to go, which clarified that Delilah needed to send her away first. Again, the psychological roots connecting those two spirits were obvious to Sophie. Counseling might be required before those spirits could be banished, but they had to try before concluding that.

"Mara. Mara, please talk to me." Delilah had commanded the father and the girl spirits to be silent. "Mara, these are not helping you. You can get real help for the abandonment. These two spirits are not helpful."

"Okay." That sounded like Mara. Compliant and a bit feckless.

"Are you willing to tell the girl to go away?"

"But, isn't she part of me?"

Delilah looked at Sophie.

This was where Sophie had an advantage. The wounded little girl that really was part of Mara would not appear as a ghostly child with dead eyes. Even if she did speak with a girl's voice and pout a lot, the spirit they were seeing was not a real girl. "The loss in your heart is part of you, but this girl trying to take control of your mouth and making you squirm is not part of you. She is your enemy." Sophie glanced at Hope, who affirmed her assessment with an emphatic nod.

Even as Mara began to relax visibly, the scene behind her changed. That odd mix of spirits milling behind her suddenly became one huge many-headed creature. And Mara stiffened before releasing a scream that nearly stopped Sophie's heart.

The beast pounced on Mara. Her scream intensified.

"Occult ruler, I command you to be silent. To sit back and not touch Mara in any way." Her voice was louder than she wanted, but Sophie expected she sounded calm enough for the other people in the room. She uttered a silent prayer for protection, knowing the spirits could sense her fear.

The tone of the worship music elevated. Nathan's voice expanded. Maybe that increased volume was his version of whistling in the dark. But if that was the case, it was a very inspiring tune he was whistling.

Principalities and Powers

Hope braced her good foot on the floor preparing to run for it. Mostly she wanted to run toward Mara, to grab her and get her out of there. Another part of her longed for a quiet evening at home. Or at least a quiet evening anywhere other than this church basement.

The beast that filled the wall and even seemed to raise the ceiling was as visible to Hope as any of the humans in the room. Her teammates were cowering even if they couldn't see what looked like a dragon with multiple heads and claws stretching over the whole team. Nathan was the only one not cringing, as if the music he played was a shield big enough to completely obscure the threat of that beast.

When Sophie tried to shut down that multiheaded dragon, a bigger spirit appeared. An almost-human face filled the entire ceiling, also defying the true height of the basement room.

"Help us, Lord Jesus." Delilah was gripping the arms of her chair and looking just above Mara.

Sophie added to Delilah's prayer, a petition for protection from the large beasts looming over them. "We're here on your business, Lord. I know these interlopers are no problem for you. Get us into the shelter of your wings. Increase our faith to know you are Lord of all this. Lord of all of us."

Mara let out another of those screams, and this time, she changed colors.

Hope couldn't tell at first whether the girl had literally changed colors, but Mara had turned deep red in Hope's eyes. And then Hope realized it was blood red. That idea registered as important, but it took a second for Hope to conclude that it was only an image. Something imposed by the spirits that were oppressing the girl. What did it mean?

"Blood! Blood! Covered in blood!" Mara screeched in a voice clearly not her own.

Anthony spoke up. "It's fake. All deception." He was shaking visibly, but his eyes were clear, and he was leaning forward.

"It's the blood." The voice changed to a boomy, ghoulish sound. "She's covered in the blood."

Sophie commanded the spirits to be silent. "The blood of Jesus is all we're impressed with here. The blood of the true Lord Jesus Christ shed on the cross of Calvary."

Hope breathed a heavy sigh as Mara's color faded toward normal, if not all the way there yet.

From there, Delilah and Sophie spent a good deal of time trying to sort out who was in charge. Especially important was trying to decide what connection Mara had to the huge ruling spirits that were manifesting in the room.

As Sophie and Delilah took turns binding various spirits that presented themselves, Zeezee always seemed poised to talk to Mara. She checked in with her whenever Sophie or Delilah opened a space for her to do so.

After an hour, Sophie and Delilah called a break. They had settled on a theory that the ruling spirits were not deeply attached to Mara herself. The real trouble was still with the abandoned girl and the absent father spirits. Zeezee supported the notion that the dragons and giants were just there to keep Mara from addressing those real issues.

When they took a pause, Mara inhaled several long, slow breaths, at Sophie's advice. A few of the team left the room, perhaps for the bathroom. Hope wondered if Anthony left to go and talk to his mother. That seemed like a good thing to do at this point, but Hope stayed in the room, propping her cast on a chair. She was interested in something that was roiling in place of the giant and the dragon whenever they pulled back. It was like a cloud layer those monsters sank into. Her attention landed on Mara, however, as Zeezee slid her chair close and leaned in to talk.

"I'm fine, really. I just feel so ... so loved by you all. It's so great to have you on my side. I don't feel so alone anymore."

A shiver prompted Hope to turn in her chair. She wanted to be ready to duck for cover if she started crying. She could hear her young self in Mara's relief and wonder. She could remember what a powerful relief it was to see people like Sophie dedicated to her freedom even at obvious risk to themselves.

Delilah, Sophie, and Zeezee weren't spending any time actively declaring their love for Mara. They were just showing it. Demonstrating it in their patience and persistence. In their gentleness and honesty. No one was posturing, pretending to know everything or to be immune to the threats of the massive spirits. They were just there to help and determined to make a difference.

"How are you doing?" Hope asked Sophie when she came back from the restroom.

"Fortunately I'm getting some inspiration. I was pretty drained when we came in here, but I feel like there's an opportunity to make some real progress. I know we're not gonna solve everything, but I can sense an opening."

Hope nodded. "Yeah. I'm with you." She tilted her head toward the wall behind Mara. "Have you noticed this cloud thing going on behind those two big ones?"

"Mm-hmm." Sophie looked up in a way that seemed more about contemplation than discovery. "We need to address Hartman, I think. He's probably sending the interference."

As soon as Sophie said that, Zeezee grabbed her head and winced, her eyes shut tight. "Oh, oh, ouch! Oh my Lord." She was wearing her hair in an Afro bleached golden these days. She squashed her hair down hard with her fists. "Help me."

Hope stepped past Sophie and stuck her hand right into the clench of hair and fists. "Let go of her right now in the name of Jesus. You have no right to any part of Zeezee's body. Let go of her head." She watched something like a spear being withdrawn from Zeezee's head.

Though she had survived the screams and the scary beast stuff tonight, Zeezee still seemed like the most vulnerable member of the team. It was hard to forget what had happened in the session with Sean and Will. And maybe that still affected Zeezee's expectations for herself. Second string to Carlos. Not a worship warrior like Nathan. Not a leader like Anthony or Delilah. Not given X-ray vision like Sophie and Hope.

"You are blessed by your Father in heaven." Sophie seemed to be sensing those same issues. She had an arm around Zeezee's shoulders. "You are meant to be here,

Zeezee. You are not vulnerable to the enemy. God has you."

Sophie pulled back and checked on Zeezee.

Zeezee's panting respiration had slowed considerably.

"Huh. That was good. I felt something shift inside when you said that." She raised her head. "Thanks, Sophie."

Hope noticed Mara watching all this. She had a serene admiration on her face, perhaps appreciating seeing more of that love she had felt toward herself.

"Does anyone feel like we need to get an angel choir going to fend off some interference coming from, like, far away?" Nathan settled his guitar strap over his head and remained standing, ready to play with that angel choir, it seemed.

Hope's instant internal response was, "Out of the mouths of babes." His suggestion fit perfectly with what she was seeing.

Not that Hope thought of Nathan as a babe. Only, she kind of did. But in a different sense of the word, of course.

Clearing the Atmosphere

Worship filled the basement of the church as a total of twenty people joined in, unified in place as well as purpose. Sophie grinned as she sang, nearly elevated off the floor by the voices ringing all around her. Detta and her prayer group were with them in the fellowship hall, providing close cover now. That was Nathan's idea.

Sophie looked at Anthony, his hands raised toward the ceiling, tears streaming down his face. She loved that guy. And she loved Delilah, standing next to him with her hands raised in fists. A fighting posture. Triumphant.

Feeling her responsibility for the ministry and this meeting, Sophie kept an eye on Mara. At times, the young woman appeared adrift, as if the music lifted her and floated her to a place she hadn't expected and maybe wasn't fully willing to go. Then she would lean back and watch and listen. Maybe she was feeling some of the affection Sophie had toward the friends around her.

Adjusting her eyes from Mara to Hope, Sophie redirected her gaze toward something that had grabbed Hope's attention. There was a split in the cloud that Hope had pointed out during the break. The gray-blue bank was torn, allowing in shafts of golden light. One of those rays landed on the sinister giant who seemed to be the backup to the multiheaded dragon. And that giant looked a lot more familiar under that beam.

Checking on Mara, Sophie signaled to Hope, and they approached Mara as the music continued.

Mara's face contorted from curious to fearful to some other emotion that was too much to show on one face. "I feel something coming or going. I can't tell which."

Hope shifted her eyes beyond Mara and nodded. Sophie saw the absent father spirit there. He was being stretched like a comic that had been copied onto a piece of Silly Putty. It was as if forces were pulling on him even as something stronger than him forced him to stay in place.

Then Mara crumpled forward in her chair. She clutched at her stomach and leaned her head over her knees.

Hope and Sophie dropped down next to her. Delilah squatted in front of her. Hope stretched her cast past Mara's chair.

Delilah seemed to know what was happening. "I command the abandoned girl spirit to release Mara's gut and go where Jesus wants you to go." Delilah had a hand on Mara's shoulder.

Sophie wasn't certain they were in a safe place for that kind of physical contact with Mara. She and Hope were close but not touching her.

Mara sat up and roared, "Nooooooo!"

Sophie could imagine Delilah's ears flapping in the force of that shout, her curls billowing behind her. But that was only in her imagination. She could still see the absent father spirit being stretched out of recognizable shape. Now she knew what she had to do. "I command the absent father to leave here and take the spirits sent by Maxwell Hartman with him. I break the power of Maxwell Hartman over Mara in the name of the Lord Jesus Christ."

Mara tumbled off the chair and landed under Delilah, who scrambled to avoid either sitting on Mara or stepping on her. Her feet were bare, so they probably wouldn't have left a mark. That was Sophie's profane impression before she was rocked back by a blast of something. Whether there was actual force to it and not just the appearance of it, she couldn't tell, but the absent father spirit launched away from Sophie and disappeared through that rip in the clouds. Then the cloud distorted and flowed away before vanishing in another flash.

"Leave now. You have no power here!" Sophie pointed at the dragon, which flared its eyes at her, at least a dozen eyes alight with flame. But that fiery glare seemed to be the last bluff from the creature before it went the way of the vanishing cloud.

When Sophie tried to face the sinister giant, she found it missing. She turned to Hope for a check and saw a relieved smirk from her friend.

Mara was curled fetal on the floor, a gray throw rug her resting place. Delilah settled cross-legged next to her. Zeezee followed suit. Hope dragged her cast back to her chair.

The worship music continued, but the tone had changed. Celebration was the mood as well as the theme of the songs Nathan selected.

But Sophie knew their evening wasn't over. She sat on the floor next to Mara and began to struggle again to move that abandoned girl away from Mara's soul. Angels were crowding around, providing a sort of shelter for the four women on the floor.

After going back and forth with the abandoned girl spirit for another ten minutes, Sophie was ready to call it a night. But Carlos stepped up to their little enclave, and Delilah and Zeezee gave him room to sit down.

Mara didn't look up. She remained curled around the pain of her history. Wrapped around herself in a fetal attempt at shelter. And she didn't react visibly when a male voice entered their little space. Maybe she could sense him there. Maybe she knew what she needed. Maybe she had known all along that Carlos would help set her free.

"In the name of Jesus, I declare Mara perfectly loveable. There is nothing about her that prevents her from being loved. She was never abandoned by her Father in heaven. And her earthly father was a fool to let her go." He said those words with confidence and firmness, a warm quaver around the edges.

"Spirit of abandonment and spirit of lies, you must leave now." Sophie used the same warm tone as Carlos. Calm and steady. Firm and confident. "She doesn't need you. She is no longer an abandoned little girl. She is a woman, free to love and be loved."

A burst of bawling sobs from Mara rocked all four of them back, but the worshippers still standing around them stayed strong.

And the grace of a loving God landed on that lost girl who was now a woman, finding herself.

Summer Celebration

Detta put the finishing touches on the flower arrangement in the center of the head table. She was so happy for the perfect summer weather that she dared not even say thanks, lest she spoil its perfection by pointing it out. "That's a nutty idea, you crazy old lady." She chuckled at herself.

"Who are you talking to?" Coming out the kitchen door, Roddy set the pan of pork chops on the end of the table closest to the grill. He regripped the cotton towel beneath that pan. When he stepped to the grill, his limp seemed exaggerated by his load.

"I'm talking to my constant companion, of course. Myself." She grinned at him.

"Can she make room for another constant companion?" He grinned back at her.

"I already have." Detta decided to stop referring to herself in the third person before someone heard the two crazy old people.

Sophie came out of the house with a pan of sauce, going straight to the smoky grill and setting it on the redwood side shelf closest to the back door. "Delilah and Anthony just arrived."

"Don't they know they're not supposed to help set up their own engagement party?" Roddy chuckled as he adjusted the pan of chops on the other side shelf.

"He's my boy." Detta shook her head as she stepped around the table toward the kitchen. She was anxious to greet one of her special guests.

In the kitchen, she found Delilah and Anthony with Delilah's mother.

"Glenda, my dear. I haven't seen you in so long, but you've hardly changed at all." Detta wrapped her arms around the younger woman, chortling her pleasure at seeing her again, and on such a happy occasion.

"Well, I'm counting on the eyesight of old friends to be faded at least a little to maintain that impression." Glenda snickered into Detta's neck and patted her on the back. "I'm so glad to see you, Detta. And congratulations on so many things. These young ones making such a momentous commitment, and you finding a love of your own."

Roddy had come in the back door at some point during the hugging. His round laugh behind her alerted Detta to that fact. She backed up and presented him with a welcoming gesture. "Here he is. The man of my dreams. This is Roderick Harper."

"Roddy, please. So glad to meet you, Glenda."

That little glowing greeting in the kitchen was just about the most peaceful moment of the evening. Fifty people came through the house—or up the driveway if they knew where they were. Old friends of both Anthony and Delilah were there, and new friends of the two together. Laughing, eating, drinking, and lots of talking.

Detta was interested to see Wesley and his current girlfriend there. That young woman seemed quite friendly with Sophie, lots of private conversation between them and a few hugs as well.

The Woman Who Welcomes Angels

Sophie's whole team was there. Carlos gave the most inspiring toast. He was a young man Detta hardly knew, but she truly wanted to get to know him better after he raised his glass and said, "To Delilah and Anthony. May the grace of our Lord Jesus Christ fill your hearts and warm your home in the winters and breathe fresh breezes on summer days like this. And let there always be peace and unity between you even as you break down the gates of the enemy whenever you get the chance. Blessings!"

Detta and Roddy competed for the loudest amen to that one.

Roddy's barbecued pork chops were almost as good as the toasts and as delightful as meeting new folks. Detta's potato salad wasn't too bad either. All the food was good. And she didn't mind so much serving wine—something she normally wouldn't do. Just for this occasion.

Roddy had agreed. "Otherwise one of Anthony's friends just might turn the water into wine."

"Oh, that would be worth seeing." Detta had laughed at Roddy's joke during their shopping trip.

And Detta was still chuckling as the last of the guests began to find their way back down the driveway late that night.

Late-Night Ministry

Sophie had done her best to console Hope. "We're not just gonna do this once. There will be other chances."

Hope climbed into the back of the car, Nathan and Anthony in the front. "Still cursing my clumsiness." She looked up at Sophie, frustration and understanding crisscrossing on her face.

"Sorry, Hope." Nathan was turned in his seat. "But we won't be far away. You can still help out. Text stuff, maybe."

"Yeah. Be sure to text me or Delilah if you see something." Sophie stood up, waving dully at both Nathan and Hope.

Hope's new walking cast wouldn't be up to the concrete sidewalks and asphalt streets of downtown. Especially if the girls had to make a run for it. Instead, she would ride in what was essentially the getaway car. Or maybe the first responders' vehicle.

Sophie really felt for Hope, sidelined from this particular ministry. When Anthony had first suggested it, Hope had nearly fallen on the floor, she was weeping so hard.

"That is exactly what Jesus would do." Hope was becoming a more and more vocal fan of Jesus all the time.

And Hope's focus on Jesus was inspiring Sophie. It certainly put a fine frame on their plans tonight. What would

Jesus say to, and do for, the young women standing on downtown street corners peddling their bodies?

Sighing as she stepped onto the curb to join Delilah, Zeezee, and Priscilla, Sophie forced a nervous smile. Zeezee was twisting a finger through a clump of her hair when she suddenly stopped as if catching herself, dropping her hand to her side. Delilah had the solemn mask of a mourner on. Nervous solemnity, perhaps.

"Okay, Lord. Show us the ones you want us to meet and to serve tonight." Priscilla prayed those words as if she had said them before, which Sophie assumed she had. Her friend was a veteran at this ministry compared to Sophie, Delilah, and Zeezee. Brave rookies, all.

Striding on her sneakers with the pure white rubber around the sides and over the toes, Priscilla was either fearless or doing a great job of faking it. "Come, Lord Jesus. Be with us in this dark place."

Sophie was seeing what Priscilla was apparently feeling. An inky darkness hovered over three girls standing at the corner of Coolidge and Third. One of the girls dropped a cigarette butt and ground it out with a high-heeled boot. Another stepped vaguely toward the four approaching women while keeping her eyes raised like she didn't see them.

Sophie guessed that she and her friends—all over thirty and wearing sneakers and jeans—would not appear to be competition for these young girls. She suspected her crew looked more like lost tourists to them. This corner hosted bars and restaurants, but this late at night, there weren't a lot of pedestrians.

"Hi, I'm Priscilla. These are my friends. Is there anything we can pray for you about?"

The pale skinny girl wearing a straight blonde wig stopped her line walk, heel to toe. Her shoulders suddenly slouched, and her bare knees leaned toward each other. "What did you say? Did you say pray?" She glanced over her shoulder at the other two girls, but they were pretending not to notice what was going on. "Pray for me?" That last question came with a small throat squeak.

"Of course. I'm Sophie." She offered a fist bump, which the girl met automatically.

"Taffy."

"Is that what your mother calls you?" Delilah said that with a little grin and her lids lowered halfway.

"My mother?"

"Because the name I'm hearing is Beth."

"Hearing? How do you ... are you cops?"

The two girls pretending to ignore them started walking in the opposite direction.

Taffy watched her friends over her shoulder but made no move to follow. She did glance at a passing car but didn't seem to find anything interesting there. "I don't get it. What is this?"

"I'm Delilah. This is Zeezee. We just wanted to offer to pray for some of the girls out here tonight. We know things can be tough. We just wanted to offer what help we know how. We know how to pray."

Sophie was listening to all this while watching a raggedy blackness morphing above the girl's head, whether her name was Taffy or Beth. "Has someone died lately? Someone close to you?" It was a stretch, but that looming darkness felt like death to her, like a shroud. A funeral cloth.

The young woman, apparently still a teenager, blinked her heavily painted eyes, her lashes like little combs fanning the night air. "My mother told me she wished I was dead. That's what you make me think of when you ask that. But I don't really care about that. She was always angry at me, so I got outta there."

Sophie glanced up at the dark spirit again. "I think we can send that death feeling away from you. It's like something sort of haunting you."

Beth nearly sat on the ground, knees buckling, butt falling fast.

Delilah was faster. She grabbed one arm.

Zeezee grabbed Beth's other hand.

"God wants to help you, Beth." Priscilla spoke in a warm, motherly tone, her face drawing close to the girl who was being steadied by the other two women.

"Why me?"

Sophie sensed something in the question. "We would be glad to pray for any of you girls. Does one of your friends have something you're worried about?"

Beth nodded like a little girl caught talking to herself. "There's Cherry. She's got some kind of mouth cancer. I think it's from tobacco."

"A doctor told her—?" Priscilla stopped when Anthony's car pulled to the curb.

Hope's window was down. "That other girl who just left has, like, a metal hook through her mouth. Is that something you're gonna go after?"

"Her mouth?" Beth wobbled atop her too-high heels.

"Which girl?" Sophie bent her neck to see Hope better.

"The dark one. There's something with her mouth."

Beth swore. "That's her. That's Cherry." She goggled her big eyes at all five of the women now. "Who *are* you people?"

Sophie could hear Nathan snigger before he bellowed, "Your guardian angels." His window was still up, but his voice came out of Hope's open window loud and clear.

"I guess so." Beth settled her eyes on Sophie as if considering their original offer to pray for her. She reached around and massaged her lower back. "My back hurts. Can you pray for that? They tell me it's 'cause of these shoes." She looked past her knock knees toward the spiky heels.

"Okay, let's pray for that healing." Priscilla stepped a little closer.

"And send away that death thing I'm seeing," Sophie said. She watched Anthony's car start to roll away.

"You got that right," she heard Hope shout before they were too far away.

Sophie snorted and then nodded to Priscilla to start the prayer for Beth. They could go try to find Cherry after that.

Just a Walk in the Park

Hope could feel the knock of her foot against the pavement all the way up to her head. Some nerve firing with each step of her new brace.

"You look tired." Nathan looked pretty tired himself.

"Yeah, I guess I am. Battling with spirits seems to take something out of me. And we had a late phone call last night with Mara. She wanted to tell us all about her talk with the FBI and how she's been doing in Kansas."

"She going to that church out there?"

"She's still looking around, I guess. We tried to help her figure out what she was looking for in a church."

They had arrived at the park near Hope and Sophie's new apartment. Their first walk together, but Hope felt like she was dragging her bad leg. More *galumphing* than walking. That was a word her mother had probably taught her. It was a good word for what it was like walking in this brace. But she was supposed to do a little exercise every day now.

The park was full of children on this warm Saturday in late September. The array of family units was entertaining, including some grandmother and grandfather types on benches under the trees.

As much as Hope was enjoying those homey family scenes, her attention kept turning to a guy tucked back from the playground under the shade of a locust tree. The leaves were turning yellow. But the shade glowed bluish with some kind of spiritual presence. Hope got the idea the guy was actively working in cooperation with that spirit.

She gestured toward the lone man, and Nathan narrowed his eyes a little. Probably just trying to see into the shade, not evaluating the metallic monster perched on the shoulders of that man.

"What's up with that guy?" Nathan slowed as they rounded the curve in the path toward that stand-alone tree.

Hope tried to evaluate the man without obviously staring at him. But the guy was focused on the kids on the playground, so he didn't seem to notice the attention he was getting from the two walkers on the asphalt path.

The spirit on him, however, turned and glared at Hope. He raised a hand and pointed it at her like he was holding a gun.

When she stopped her galumphing to discern the meaning of the spirit's posture, the man turned his head toward Nathan and Hope.

Nathan did what Nathan would naturally do, of course. "Hey, dude. What's up?" He took a few steps toward the guy.

The man wasn't much older than Hope or Nathan. He wore a medium-weight jacket despite the seventy-degree temperature. His hair was dark and longish, especially dark against his pale forehead, over which it was hastily swept. His eyes bored into Hope and then landed on Nathan.

The demon was in full fight mode. At least that's how Hope interpreted its posture. She reached for Nathan's arm where he had stepped off the path ahead of her. And then she remembered to pray as her hand missed Nathan's elbow. "Oh, Lord. Help." Initially it felt like she was asking God to help the guy under the tree, given that beast on him. Then she was hoping for something like wisdom for Nathan.

That was when she saw the gun. The real gun.

Raising his hands chest high, Nathan froze. "Whoa, dude. I come in peace."

Hope's next instinct was to step up and smack Nathan on the shoulder for kidding around in this situation, but that urge faded when the guy with the gun blinked hard. Maybe stunned. Maybe stunned at Nathan's stupid response.

The demon on that guy's shoulders surged toward Nathan, but Nathan's big worship angel appeared directly between him and the gunman. The demon slammed into the angel and then slammed again. It was like a kid trying to batter his way through an NFL lineman. It wasn't working.

But the guy with the gun raised it higher, pointing it directly at Nathan.

"Wait. Don't do it. You deserve better than this." Hope blurted that like she was channeling Carlos or Zeezee or some other source of therapeutic wisdom.

When the gunman diverted his attention toward Hope, he seemed to be blinded for a second, his free hand reaching for his eyes.

Nathan seized the opportunity, lunging forward and grabbing the gun. He forced it toward the ground.

A shot sounded.

Kids and parents screamed in the background.

Hope screamed right there next to the two struggling men. The sound of running feet on the path behind her was like a drum track to the wrestling match under the tree.

Size and strength were probably on Nathan's side, but he was hopping awkwardly on one foot, apparently in pain but still trying to get control of the gun.

Someone shouted, "Stop! Police!"

The gunman let go and dodged past the tree, fleeing with impressive speed.

Thundering boots grew louder and then sped past Hope. A man in blue.

Nathan crumpled to the ground, dropping the automatic pistol near his feet.

Another cop stopped near Nathan. He grabbed a handset attached to his body armor. "Shots fired. Civilian down. Send ambulance."

"Nooooo!" Hope didn't want any of it. No ambulance. No shot fired. No civilian down. No Nathan rolling on the ground gripping his leg.

"It's okay. I'm okay. It hurts like ... heck. But I'm okay."

"What did you do? What were you thinking?" Hope started the interrogation before the cop could get into it.

The cop knelt next to Nathan. "Pretty brave thing, from what I saw. That guy had a gun, right? What was he doing?"

"He was watching the kids." Nathan squinted toward the playground.

That playground was abandoned. Like squirrels spotting a circling hawk, the families had scattered. Maybe some were hiding in the equipment or behind it. Hope sensed an intense spiritual presence in that direction, but she wasn't focused on that. She was stretching her sore leg on the grass and figuring how to sit next to Nathan without tearing a ligament.

The cop was tying something around Nathan's thigh. His jeans were dark purple below the knee.

Nathan winced and then forced a smile at Hope.

"Nice little walk in the park, huh?" She shook her head at him.

"You saw something on him? You knew he had a gun?"

Thinking it would be good to distract Nathan from the pain, Hope was glad to answer, but she hesitated with the cop right there. "I could tell there was something ... bothering him. Disturbing him. Like, stirring him up." How to say it without saying it? "But I was not proposing that you go and confront him."

"I just said, 'What's up.'" Nathan laughed and winced some more.

Sirens were drawing closer, apparently coming from all sides. A police car skidded to a stop at the far corner of the park. Several more followed. Then a large firetruck and an ambulance.

Hope reconsidered her earlier rejection of that ambulance. It was a good thing, of course.

Nathan was down. Hope scootched as close to him as she could, and she clung to his near shoulder. Silently she uttered prayers for healing. Silently she thanked God for the angels.

And she asked for a little more wisdom to know what to do about the spirits she saw in the future.

Maybe a lot more wisdom.

Book One in the series is available on Amazon: https://www.amazon.com/dp/B08NGRJ278

You might also enjoy, *Seeing Jesus*: https://www.amazon.com/dp/B00D8KZH0M

Sign up for our newsletter if you're interested: Subscribe | jeffreymcclainjones

Thank you!

Printed in Great Britain
by Amazon

THEN THERE WERE ... TWO MURDERS?

AN AMATEUR FEMALE SLEUTH HISTORICAL COZY MYSTERY

P.C. JAMES

To be kept up-to-date with future Miss Riddell's Cozy Mysteries, sign up for my newsletter here.

Or if you prefer a QR Code:

And to pre-order the next Miss Riddell book, follow this link: The Dead of Winter

1

NEWCASTLE-UPON-TYNE, ENGLAND, DECEMBER 1953

Pauline stared at the letter in her hand, hardly daring to believe it possible. Only minutes ago, she'd been wondering how she could change her life to make it more exciting and here it was. A letter from a woman, Mrs. Elliott, who wanted her help and all because she'd been mentioned in the newspapers as having solved a murder when the police had given up. The glow from that praise had already begun to wear off, the world, even the local world, had moved on. Marjorie's death, only months ago, was forgotten and even the 'deaths' of the two culprits, Murdock and Wagner, were fading in the public memory and that was only weeks ago. The spotlight that newspapers shone on places and events was like a wartime searchlight sweeping the sky, momentarily highlighting a plane before moving onto another. Nothing lasted long in the news – unless someone wanted it to.

If it wasn't for the letter, which she could clearly see and feel in her hand, even she might have thought she'd dreamt it all. A dream from which she'd wake and be disappointed. Already, it felt like there'd been no murder and she hadn't exposed it. When everyone was crowding around, shaking her hand, praising her to the skies, she'd hated it. It made her uncomfortable. Now those moments were gone, she found she missed them. Or, more accurately, she missed the feeling she had achieved something more than just office work.

It was ridiculous, she knew. She was twenty-one years old, hardly out of secretarial college, in her first job and had already been promoted. That should have been cause for pride, real pride, enough. Searching for a meaning beyond that was pretentious and smacked of false pride, which was a sin she tried hard to avoid. She smiled as an image formed in her mind of herself holding out a bowl, in true Oliver Twist fashion, and saying, 'Please sir, I want some more.'

She held up the letter so she could see it better in the light streaming through the window from the nearby streetlight. The words seemed to float on the page, drawing her in.

Dear Miss Riddell,

I saw the article in the Herald yesterday and your amazing success in unmasking those killers. I have a puzzle the police won't look at, but somebody should. I thought, hoped, you might like to. I can't pay very much. I'm not rich but it may interest you. It's not a serious thing like murder but it is puzzling, and it worries me. Sorry if you think I'm rambling. I just can't get it out of my mind. Maybe it would be better if I explained a little, then you'd see.

First, you should know I live in an old house on the outskirts of Mitford. It's very quiet, or at least it was. Recently, I've heard noises, particularly at night. I have a good security alarm system and I lock up carefully, so I don't believe I'm in any danger. However, something is going on.

A week ago, I was crossing a stream on my daily walk by a bridge I've used every day, twice a day, since I retired. There's never been any trouble. On this occasion, the bridge had come loose and it tipped me into the stream. Fortunately, though I'm old, I'm not frail and while I'm cut and bruised, I'm not seriously hurt. But I could have been. I showed the bridge to the police and told them about the noises, but our local policeman says the bridge is old and the bad weather broke the bridge and has driven a lot of animals to find shelter in and around houses. What he said is true, but it doesn't explain it. I've lived in this house nearly forty years now and I know every creak – and so does Jem, my dog.

I have more to tell you, however, you may not be interested. If you are, please phone me at this number and I'll explain more fully.

Yours Sincerely,

Doris Elliott

Pauline put down the letter and walked to the window, where the cold December night was lit by the lights of houses opposite and a nearby streetlamp. She told herself she wanted to think about this invitation. Should she raise this woman's hopes and then dash them because she couldn't provide answers or because the answers were as ordinary as the local policeman said? She shook herself. What on earth was she thinking of? Of course she'd phone and accept the cry for help. After all, it wasn't just Mrs. Elliott who needed her to use her gifts, she needed to use them as well. The new life she'd wondered about was stretching out before her. There could be no question about turning away. She glanced at her watch. It was too late to call now. She'd phone Mrs. Elliott after church in the morning.

2

SCOUTING THE GROUND

Mrs. Elliott didn't answer when Pauline phoned, and she hung up the phone with a strong feeling of foreboding mingled with disappointment. Perhaps church services were later or ran longer in Mitford. She'd call again after Sunday dinner. Even an elderly widow, and Pauline was sure she must be for there was no mention of a Mr. Elliott, would be home for Sunday dinner. Everyone in the country would be. She wished, as she had all through church, she'd called last night or earlier this morning. Now she'd decided, she couldn't wait to start.

The result was the same at 1:30 when Pauline tried again. It seemed Mrs. Elliott was out for the day, which was truly annoying, for Pauline could have visited her today, but now it would have to be next Saturday afternoon at the earliest. Her full-time job at the armament factory as an Executive Secretary, the youngest in the company, didn't allow much in the way of opportunity for detecting on the side.

"I'm going out for a drive," Pauline said to the Bertrams, her landlords and would-have-been parents-in-law, who were settling down in their armchairs to let their roast beef digest.

"It isn't a very nice day, dear," Mrs. Bertram said. "It would be much safer to stay inside. It looks like snow soon."

"I'll be very careful," Pauline said, smiling. Mrs. Bertram had taken on the role of mother in their relationship. "But I really need some air and activity."

"Be back before dark, then," Mrs. Bertram said.

Knowing she'd worry, Pauline assured her she would be back long before then and set off through the sleety rain that spattered the windshield. As always, the wipers hardly seemed to make a difference.

She drove up the Great North Road toward Morpeth, wondering if she had time to take her reporter friend, Poppy, along with her. She decided against that. The light was already going because of the low, thick clouds. It would be dark by three and she had only about an hour of daylight left. At Morpeth, she left the main road and headed west along the narrow road to Mitford. She soon found Mrs. Elliott's house, set back from the road and surrounded by shrubs and trees at the back.

Pauline stopped the car in the driveway, pulled up her mackintosh coat's hood and walked quickly to the door, where a small porch provided some shelter. She rang the bell, which clanged inside the house in a way that said 'no one home' more eloquently than the lack of lights in the windows. After waiting for a few minutes to be sure, Pauline returned to the car.

She drove slowly through the village, noting its principal features of the old stone bridge over the river, the pub, and on the western outskirts, up a steep hill, the impressive gates to the local manor house. Returning, she drove back along the only street and turned right onto a side lane that passed the ruins of an ancient castle on its earthen mound, the Motte in the 'motte and bailey' style of castle used by The Normans when they conquered England in 1066. Mitford would be a pretty village -- on a summer day.

Reluctantly, for there were still no lights in Mrs. Elliott's house, she drove away from Mitford and back to the Bertram's house in time for afternoon tea. As she'd predicted, the light was completely gone when she arrived back, and she could see Mrs. Bertram at the window looking out anxiously for her return. Pauline decided soon she would have to find a place of her own to live.

3

CONTACTING HER CLIENT

PAULINE PHONED AGAIN on the Monday night after work and this time was successful. "Mrs. Elliott?" Pauline asked, when she heard the phone picked up.

"Yes. Who is this?"

"It's Pauline Riddell, Mrs. Elliott. I'm phoning about your letter and request for someone to look into the odd things that have been happening to you."

"Can you help, Miss Riddell?"

"If you'd tell me more, I will be able to judge better," Pauline said. "As it is, I don't fully understand the whole picture."

"It will be an expensive phone call if I tell you everything now," Mrs. Elliott said. "Could you visit me here? I'll explain and show you. That would be better."

"I will certainly visit you as soon as I can, Mrs. Elliott, but that will be Saturday afternoon because I still have to work to live."

"I see. Then I'll expect you on Saturday."

"You must tell me more before you go, Mrs. Elliott. When did these noises begin, for example?"

"It isn't just noises. Things have been moved. I'm sure someone is prowling around outside the house."

"They haven't broken in though, have they?" Pauline asked.

"I don't think so," Mrs. Elliott said. "I'm sure Jem would create a hullabaloo if someone was in the house."

"Your dog?"

"Yes. I thought I'd said in my letter. Jem is a golden Labrador, and he guards the house with zeal. No one has been in, I'm sure."

"When did this start?"

"About a month ago."

"Did anything happen that you can link to the start of this?"

"I don't think so," Mrs. Elliott said. "I've been puzzling it out and I can't find anything."

"So, you have no ideas of what might be behind it?"

"None."

"Has anything happened recently, maybe not to you, but in the village that might be a link?"

"As I said," Mrs. Elliott replied. "I've thought a lot about it and there's only one thing, but it was too long ago to be relevant."

"What was that?"

"About six months ago, a good friend of mine, Mrs. Churchill, died suddenly and her adopted son inherited her house and money. I was horrified to learn, only days later, he had married a young woman whom I know my friend had absolutely refused to let him marry. She and I discussed this more than once and I know she'd told the boy that if he married that girl, she'd cut him off without a shilling, as the saying goes."

"You haven't been telling other people about this

recently, have you?" Pauline said, alarmed at the thoughts this raised.

"Of course, I haven't," Mrs. Elliott said sharply. "What good would it do. The will has been read, the boy has the money, and the girl. My complaining wouldn't change anything." She paused, and then added, "I did mention it to a friend in confidence when I first heard Frank Churchill was getting married but that was months ago."

"Your thoughts wouldn't mean anything unless your friend didn't die naturally," Pauline said, thoughtfully, "but..." she let the sentence end unfinished.

"That's a wicked thing to say, or think," Mrs. Elliott said. "Though I must admit I thought the same thing at the time. But Dr. Turner is a very trustworthy man and a good doctor, he signed the death certificate without any hesitation."

"Then we can rule out this possible link," Pauline said, though in her mind she added *for now*. "There's nothing else?"

"Nothing," Mrs. Elliott said. "I've wracked my brains until I'm exhausted, and nothing comes to mind."

"Why are you sure the local policeman is wrong about the noises?" Pauline asked.

"Because Jem knows what animals sound like, and he ignores them. He always reacts to these noises so I'm sure it's a prowler."

"Have you looked out to see if there is a prowler?"

"Of course, I have," Mrs. Elliott said, "but... Well, you'll see when you visit on Saturday. The shrubs come up too close to the house."

"Have them cut down," Pauline replied.

"Oh no, dear. I can't do that. Arthur planted them. They were his favorite and they are so beautiful in the spring. They lift my spirits just gazing at them."

Deciding the call had already cost her the best part of her week's wages, Pauline thanked the woman and rang off. This wasn't going to be as easy as she'd hoped.

The phone conversation had, however, given Pauline plenty to think about and lots of new questions to ask when she and Mrs. Elliott met on the coming Saturday. Some she could start looking for answers to right away. Or, at least, Poppy, her friend – her now dead fiancé Stephen's cousin and a local reporter – could start looking right away.

Poppy, however, wasn't inclined to start right away when Pauline suggested it to her. She had a story running that was going to catapult her from provincial backwater to the heights of Fleet Street in London. She couldn't stop to investigate the natural death of an old lady in the sticks.

"When might you be able to help me?" Pauline asked, using precious minutes of yet another phone conversation that threatened to send her into bankruptcy.

"Maybe never, Pauline," Poppy said, excitedly. "If this goes right, I'll be enjoying the high life in London when it's over."

"Do reporters get to enjoy London's high life?" Pauline asked.

"I've heard about parties that would make your hair curl, Pauline."

"I've heard of parties here that make my hair curl," Pauline said. "You don't need London for such behavior. People are all too prone to indulge themselves when let off the leash."

"You need to live a little," Poppy said. "The war's over. It's a new world."

"Perhaps," Pauline said, "but while this new world is unfolding, do you think you could look into the paper's archives and find Mrs. Churchill's death notices? You know, a death in this old, real, world?"

"All right but that's it!" Poppy said. "You've had your chance for promotion and took it. This is mine and I'm not letting it drift away from me chasing your wild imaginings."

With that, Pauline wished Poppy well and rang off. She hoped Mrs. Elliott wasn't as poor as she'd suggested in her letter for the phone bills alone were going to be horrifying.

That week, Pauline spent each night in the local library reading old newspapers from the past year. Nothing in them was linked in any way to the strange happenings in Mitford. In fact, nothing at all happened in Mitford. She wasn't surprised, only disappointed. If there was a case here, something must be moving the events. If it wasn't the death of Mrs. Churchill it had to be something else.

By Saturday, when she left after finishing work at midday, Pauline was sure the local policeman was right. The sounds around Mrs. Elliott's house were animals or young people. Animals sheltering from the awful winter weather they were having or children looking for a way to pay back an old lady who'd angered them in some way. As she set off from work, heading north, she once again wondered if Mrs. Elliott would pay the phone expenses she'd already spent. Pauline rather thought not.

4

HER CLIENT IS DEAD

The house was quiet and there were no lights on inside even though it was a dark, overcast day when Pauline once again parked in Mrs. Elliott's driveway. She hoped the woman hadn't forgotten that she was coming.

She locked the car and quickly ran to the porch to escape the incessant rain. Ringing the bell produced the same empty sound it had the last time she'd done it. Pauline fished a plastic hood from her coat pocket, flipped it over her head and tied it under her chin. She hated wearing these things – she looked ridiculous in them – and walked to the large bay window that she knew graced the lounge.

Mrs. Elliott was slumped forward, asleep in an armchair in front of a four-bar electric heater with all bars on. Pauline rapped on the window with her knuckles. It hurt and did little good. Mrs. Elliott slept on.

"All that heat has sent her into dreamland," Pauline grumbled, using a pebble to rap on the window.

The woman still didn't stir. A cup and saucer sat on the table beside her.

"She's been asleep since her bedtime cocoa last night,"

Then There Were ... Two Murders? 13

Pauline said to herself. An uncomfortable feeling began in her middle. It looked like Mrs. Elliott was dead. Pauline rapped again, harder, pressing her face against the window and calling to attract the woman's attention. Mrs. Elliott remained motionless.

Suddenly, there was a thump that shook the window and two large paws, and a gaping jaw smacked against the other side. Startled, Pauline leapt back. Then she grinned. Jem at least was alive. They stared at each other for a moment, Pauline trying to reassure the dog, who looked like he was crying out for help. He was probably starving, she realized.

Pauline ran back to her car and backed it out of the drive. The police house wasn't far along the street. No doubt a doctor would be somewhere nearby too.

Police Constable Jarvis seemed unwilling to venture out on such an afternoon on the say-so of a young woman but was persuaded to accompany Pauline by the offer of a dry trip there and back in her car.

"And you say she was exactly like this when you arrived half an hour ago?" Jarvis asked, as they stood together under his umbrella gazing at Mrs. Elliott through the window.

Pauline nodded. "Exactly like that," she said.

"We need Joe Moffatt, the mechanic," Jarvis said. "He does locks too. And we need Dr. Turner."

"You give directions," Pauline said, "and I'll drive."

An hour later, Pauline, Jarvis, and Moffat waited impatiently for the doctor to pronounce his findings. She already knew what he would say. There were two empty pill bottles on the kitchen table and another half empty bottle of sleeping draught beside them. Along with them, the empty cup at her chair side pointed all too obviously to the cause of death.

"She's been dead about twenty-four hours," Dr. Turner said, straightening up after his inspection of Mrs. Elliott's mouth and chin, "and I have to conclude she died by poisoning herself with aspirin, after taking a good slug of sleeping draught. Poor soul, I didn't realize how hard she'd taken the death of her husband and then her friend."

"When I spoke to her on Monday evening," Pauline countered, "she showed no sign of grieving excessively over her friend. Quite the reverse, I'd say."

"Ah, but Mrs. Elliott wasn't a woman to wear her heart on her sleeve, as they say," Turner replied. "Very stoical, she was."

"I should have guessed when she called me in to investigate noises around her house," Constable Jarvis added. "There was no sign of anything being disturbed beyond what a cat or rat could have pushed aside."

"Why were you coming to see Mrs. Elliott, Miss Riddell?" Dr. Turner asked.

"She asked me to look into the strange things that had been happening around her," Pauline replied, glaring at PC Jarvis.

"Are you a private investigator?" Jarvis asked suspiciously.

Pauline shook her head. Mitford, it seemed, was farther out in the country than even she'd thought. "I had some success in solving a murder case in Newcastle," she said. "It was in all the papers and on the radio news. She read about it and asked if I could help her."

"I knew the name was familiar," Dr. Turner said, nodding.

PC Jarvis also nodded but his expression suggested the memory, now it was recalled, didn't please him at all.

"It was less than a month ago," Pauline said.

"Yes, but in Newcastle," Turner interjected. "We take little note of anything that happens there. City folk, you know." He shook his head. The doings of city folk being too inexplicable to warrant the attention of regular people.

"It is the edge of the world," Pauline agreed, trying not to sound too sarcastic.

"Oh, I'm sure they're good people for the most part," Turner said, hurriedly. "They just live in a city, which crams them in and makes them anxious. I'm surprised how few murders they have, to be honest. That's how I know they're generally good people; there'd be more murders if they weren't."

"People should live in the country. I agree with you there, doctor," Moffatt said, joining in the condemnation of the vices of city life. "It's the only place for people."

The three men nodded. Pauline sighed.

"Someone should tell her daughter," Dr. Turner said.

Jarvis agreed and said he'd do that after the body was moved for safekeeping until a postmortem was arranged.

"You need to secure this area, constable," Pauline said, when it was clear that wasn't going to be done. "Even a coroner will require assurance this was a real suicide before pronouncing."

"Yes, of course," PC Jarvis said.

"And you doctor," Pauline said, "have you seen enough to be sure of your conclusion?"

"Ah," Turner said, "you think because she called you in and was expected to meet you today, she wouldn't have killed herself."

"Quite so," Pauline replied. "Even if her intention was to have me as witness to her suicide, I think she would have left a note saying why."

"They generally do," Turner agreed, "but it isn't something you can rely on. After all, the balance of the mind is disturbed at a time like this."

"If she wanted me to find her body," Pauline said, "it means she planned it. She's had since Monday evening to write a note."

"She may have sent it to you through the post," Jarvis said.

"Then it's strange I haven't received it, though I agree it may come Monday," Pauline replied. "The Royal Mail provide a very prompt service. It couldn't be later than that."

"It certainly isn't here, if she wrote one," Jarvis said, after a careful inspection of the room. "It may, of course, be in another room. We will have to do a proper search."

Pauline felt pleased that her gentle prodding had brought the others to consider this a possible murder scene. Now, how was she to keep them thinking that way until she was sure herself one way or the other?

"Perhaps we could search now," she said. "There's nothing we can do for Mrs. Elliott and we came in one car so we can't contact her daughter or the undertaker without us all leaving."

"We can contact her daughter," Dr. Turner said, reaching into his bag and drawing from it a notebook. "I have her phone number in case I should ever need it. And now it seems, that time is here." He flicked through the pages and found the number.

"Please use a handkerchief when you call, Doctor," Pauline said. "There may be fingerprints on the phone that Constable Jarvis will need for his evidence."

Turner grimaced. "I hadn't thought of that," he said, "but I'm sure this is a suicide so I think it unlikely there will be fingerprints that can't be identified as proper."

"Nevertheless, Doctor," PC Jarvis said, "I think Miss

Riddell has made a good point. We don't want something to turn up later that casts doubt on poor Mrs. Elliott's death when we could have done a more adequate job collecting evidence to settle the matter."

Pauline made her way upstairs to find Mrs. Elliott's bedroom, followed by Jem who appeared to have adopted her. If a note was left, that was a likely place to find it. She found the room but not a note. The room appeared as it should; nothing was out of place. The nearby bathroom was also undisturbed. Mrs. Elliott had even closed her medicine cabinet door carefully after extracting the medicine bottles. No sign of a disturbed mind at work here either. In fact, the house seemed to be that of a sensibly tidy woman who managed her affairs as a sensible woman would.

Pauline pondered this conundrum as she returned downstairs. Sensible, level-headed, and yet she appears to have committed suicide without a word to anyone, before or after, if a note could be said to be 'after.'

"What say you, Jem?" Pauline said, quietly. She didn't want the others to think she talked to dogs. Jem however, said nothing. He continued to look forlorn and hungry.

"Before we do anything else," Pauline said. "We'll get you fed." They made their way to the kitchen where Pauline soon found canned dog food, an opener, and a clean bowl.

Jem cleaned the bowl thoroughly in no time. She gave him water to wash it down and left him to it.

Returning to the living room, where Mrs. Elliott's body still sat upright in the armchair, Pauline began inspecting the room with even more care than she'd viewed it before. If the woman hadn't killed herself, then someone else did it for her and they may have left some trace of themselves behind. There was nothing that Pauline could see to suggest another person had been there when Mrs. Elliott died, and she was forced to admit it had all the elements suicide. The house doors were locked, the windows were shut, and their handles fully engaged. But there were key features of suicide missing, like the note, for example, and that set her senses tingling. As Pauline was finishing her inspection, the daughter and her husband arrived.

Dr. Turner greeted them and led the way into the room. Pauline watched them both with care, hoping for a glimpse of something that might raise suspicion. She knew nothing against them but when people die in unusual circumstances, it's best to follow the money; hadn't she heard and read that somewhere? There was nothing about them or their behavior to suggest wrongdoing – no elation at coming into money or nervousness about what the police might have found. Both seemed genuinely upset, the daughter, Evelyn, particularly so. Was that a sign? Pauline felt it more likely it was a sign she was genuinely grieved at losing her mother suddenly.

After a hurried conference, the local cottage hospital was chosen as the place for Mrs. Elliott's body to be kept while awaiting the police report and the coroner's decision. This roused the son-in-law to enquire when they could expect to bury Mrs. Elliott.

Constable Jarvis told him there should be no difficulty if the post-mortem showed no evidence of foul play. This wasn't well received.

"My wife will be distraught if this drags out," the son-in-law said. "I hope there'll be nothing like that. Does there have to be a postmortem? Isn't it obvious how she died?"

"All deaths that aren't natural have to be investigated, Mr. Boothroyd," Jarvis said. "It's just a formality."

This seemed to mollify him. An ambulance was called and, thirty minutes later, the body removed. The grieving couple followed the ambulance. Pauline wondered why he was unhappy about an autopsy and so anxious to have his mother-in-law buried. Was it just nerves, shock at seeing her dead? Or was it something more sinister?

Before the couple had left, Pauline had asked them if they would take Jem. Someone must look after him. They both shook their heads. They weren't dog lovers, they said, and in return Jem didn't care for them. This too alerted Pauline's senses. She firmly believed dogs knew good from bad people and Jem seemed an eminently sensible dog.

As Pauline had no idea if the Bertrams were dog lovers, the subject had never come up, and she felt she couldn't take Jem though she would have dearly loved to have him when she explored the neighborhood, which she fully intended to do over the coming days and weeks. Until she was satisfied, she wouldn't accept Mrs. Elliott killed herself.

PC Jarvis said he'd take Jem until they could find a suitable home for him.

"I'd be happy to take him for a good long walk tomorrow," Pauline said. "If that will help."

"That's kind of you, Miss," Jarvis said. "Mrs. Jarvis isn't much for walking and she likes to have me busy about the house on my day off. She wouldn't take kindly to me disappearing with a dog. She says she sees little enough of me as it is."

Pauline laughed. "You're a fortunate man, Constable, to have a wife who is still keen to have your company after so many years married."

Jarvis grinned sheepishly. "I think it's more I'm out all day on my rounds and the household jobs a man is supposed to do get delayed."

"I think we've all been absent too long today," Pauline said. "I suggest we lock up and I'll drive you all home. It will be tight with the one extra passenger." Jem, who'd finished his meal and was watching the group anxiously, seemed unconcerned at sharing with the four humans.

"We should leave everything as it is," Constable Jarvis said. "My superiors may want to have a more experienced man look at the scene." As he'd already told the grieving couple this, Pauline wasn't surprised, but it did give her one idea that she intended to waste no time in acting upon.

5

ADVICE FROM INSPECTOR RAMSAY

"Miss Riddell," Inspector Ramsay said when he heard her voice. "This is a pleasant surprise."

"I hope you'll think so when you hear why I called you," Pauline said.

"Oh dear," he replied. "You aren't meddling in police business again, are you? It isn't a month ago you were almost killed."

"I'm not," Pauline protested indignantly. "I'm passing this on to you so the police can manage it themselves." She quickly explained the events of the previous week, culminating in the sad scene played out the previous day.

"I'm sure there are officers at Morpeth who can handle this quite adequately, Miss Riddell," Ramsay said, when she finished.

"I've no doubt but I'd like someone who knows and, I hope, trusts my judgment enough to look more closely into this," Pauline said.

"I'll see what I can do," Ramsay said. "Do understand, Miss Riddell, this isn't in my jurisdiction and I won't tread on a brother officer's toes."

"I do understand, Inspector," Pauline said. "But I'm sure you have the tact and diplomatic skills needed."

"Too much flattery, Miss Riddell, is always suspicious."

Pauline laughed. "It's no more than you deserve, Inspector," she said. "Really."

"I suggest you provide me with a written statement today, so I have something to work with. Can you come into the station?"

"I'll be there after church."

"So, Miss Riddell," Inspector Ramsay said, when she was seated in his office visitor chair. "You've decided to become a private detective."

Pauline was pleased to see him. He'd been a good friend throughout her chilling experience during the summer, particularly in helping rather than stopping her when she provided herself as bait in the trap that had unmasked the murderer and spies.

"Not really, Inspector," Pauline said. "Mrs. Elliott just asked me if I could help her understand what was happening to her as I seemed to have a talent for this kind of thing."

"And when you arrived, you found her dead?"

"Exactly," Pauline said. "It may be suicide but it's quite a coincidence if it is."

"What was happening to her?"

Pauline told him what she'd been told and handed him the letter to read. Ramsay read the letter and handed it back. "It still could be the imaginings of a lonely old woman living on her own out in the countryside," he said.

"It could," Pauline agreed. "The shrubs do come up to the house and I imagine they scrape on the wall and windows when the wind blows. And I can accept animals live in them after dark, particularly now the winter is here.

The bridge is undoubtedly old and could have come loose any time. All this is true."

"But you think too many coincidences?"

"I do. Then the final coincidence, she asks me to call and is dead when I arrive," Pauline said. "Apparently by her own hand, though there's no note and no letter."

"It may still be in the mail," Ramsay reminded her.

"And if it is, I will be pleased to find my suspicions are unfounded. Until then, I'd like you to look at it and tell me what you think."

"Here's pen and paper," Ramsay said, pushing pad and fountain pen across his desk. "Take your time and write down everything you can think of. It will provide me the reason I need to approach my colleagues in Morpeth and push myself into at least one visit to the scene."

"Should I include my suspicions around Mr. Churchill as well?" Pauline asked, looking up from the notepad.

"Say no more than what Mrs. Elliott told you," Ramsay said. "They may suspect you of being too eager to point fingers; you know how people are."

Pauline nodded and continued writing, copying from the notes she'd brought with her. Notes she'd spent much of the previous evening collating to fix the scene and her conversation with the dead woman in her mind. Finally, after a long pause to read through what she'd written, she handed the notepad and pen back to Ramsay.

"Two large pill bottles," Ramsay said. "That must have been difficult to take, even with the nighttime cocoa you say was beside her."

Pauline laughed. "I agree. I find two aspirins difficult enough to take," she said, "let alone two bottles full."

Ramsay nodded. "I do too, but we're the exceptions to

the rule, Miss Riddell. I regularly see people who've overdosed one way or another and they managed just fine."

"I looked through Mrs. Elliott's house, Inspector. She was a very traditional woman and, I think, a Catholic. She was extremely High Church if she was Church of England. She wouldn't commit suicide."

"I'll elbow my way into the initial stages of this investigation, Miss Riddell, but if, as I suspect, the evidence clearly points to suicide, and the coroner agrees, then there's little else I can do."

"I understand," Pauline said. "I'm just looking for another opinion really. Someone with expertise and no axe to grind."

"And you shall have it," Ramsay said, rising from his chair and ushering Pauline out.

Leaving the police station, Pauline drove north to start getting a better understanding of what had been bothering Mrs. Elliott and to renew her acquaintance with Jem. The Bertrams, it turned out, were happy to have Jem, provided he didn't bring dirt into the house. Pauline would look after him until a proper home was found. With luck, Pauline thought, she may have a canine partner on this investigation. Someone who could follow a trail if necessary.

PC Jarvis was happy to let Pauline take Jem for a walk when she arrived at the police house. He was even happier to hear Pauline would be taking Jem away with her after the walk.

Jem too was happy to see her; he clearly remembered her as the woman who fed him the day before. He pressed against her legs, threatening to knock her over.

Pauline petted him, saying, "Yes, Jem, I'm happy to see you too. Now into the car and let's go for a long walk." She held open the passenger side door and Jem leapt in.

However, when she arrived at the Elliott house, Pauline felt a sharp pang of guilt. Jem ran straight to the door, whining to be let in. She joined him quickly and ushered him away.

"I'm sorry, Jem," she said. "You can't go home. Not today, anyway."

She walked quickly to the gate at the back of the house. For a moment, it seemed Jem was going to return to the door but then he rallied and waited impatiently while Pauline opened the gate. When it was barely open wide enough, Jem pushed through and trotted out onto the well-worn path that ran from the gate to the left and right.

"Which way, Jem?"

Jem set off to the left and they made their way along the edge of a deep ravine at the bottom of which ran a fast-flowing stream, or 'burn' as it was called in these northern parts. Almost immediately, Pauline could see the bridge, or what was left of it, lying half-submerged in the water against the farther bank. They reached the point where the pathway once crossed the burn by way of the bridge and Pauline was able to study the broken footings still upright in the stream.

She saw at once why PC Jarvis had said the bridge's collapse was an accident. On either side, the grasses and reeds were broken and bent horizontal by the force of the water, swelled by the recent rains but now left above the receded water as evidence of its passing. Pauline had no doubt the old wooden bridge could easily have been overthrown simply by the floodwaters.

She began to clamber down the bank side to get a closer look at the nearest broken post, but Jem pounced and grabbed her coat between his teeth, growling a warning as he pulled her back.

Pauline frowned. Then she laughed. "You've seen one

woman dumped in the burn here already, haven't you?" she said. She stroked his head and ears until he let go of her coat. "All right," she said. "I agree, it is too dangerous." Certainly, the vegetation underfoot was wet, the bank steep and muddy. It would be easy to slide right into the stream. Though it wasn't so very deep now, she'd still get an unpleasant drenching in ice-cold water.

She studied the three remaining posts whose broken tops were above the water that swirled around them. They looked like natural breaks. There was no sign of them being cut or damaged by human action. The fourth post had snapped lower down and wasn't available for inspection, so she turned her attention to the remains of the bridge itself. Unfortunately, the stump of the fourth post on the ruined bridge was also underwater so she couldn't be certain that it too had broken naturally. Maybe, on a future walk, the broken post would be visible.

"We'll keep walking, Jem," Pauline said, and Jem trotted on ahead of her.

They'd only gone a minute or two further when Jem stopped and growled at someone in the garden to the left of the path. Pauline arrived to find Jem and a man locked in a staring contest. It was hard to tell which of them disliked the other more. The man wasn't quietly growling the way Jem was, but he could well have been.

"Good morning," Pauline said over the hedge to the man brightly, hoping to break the intense stand-off. "You clearly startled Jem."

"He doesn't like me nor I him," the man said. "I don't know why. He hasn't from the moment we met."

"Oh dear," Pauline said. "How odd."

"Odd?" The man said. "It's damn awkward. It got so Mrs.

Elliott couldn't bring him here when she visited my mother."

"That is awkward," Pauline said. "Well, I'll be taking Jem away with me this afternoon so the two of you aren't likely to meet again."

"Good," the man said. "I know Mrs. Elliott's daughter and son-in-law weren't fond of the dog either. It should have been put down years ago."

"Well," Pauline said, "so far he's been fine with me. We mustn't keep you. Come on, Jem, let's continue our walk. Good day to you," she added, nodding farewell to the man.

"Good day, and good riddance to that dog," the man replied, and abruptly walked back to his house.

"Well, Jem," Pauline said, when they were out of his hearing, "who is that and why do you dislike him so much?"

Jem turned to face her, and Pauline felt that if he could speak, she would learn a lot about that man and none of it to his advantage.

They crossed the burn at a stone-built bridge higher up the stream and made their way back down to where the wooden bridge lay. The bank on this side wasn't so steep so, with Jem's permission, she carefully made her way down to examine the ruins. The three posts still visible had indeed broken naturally, as she'd thought from her previous examination. So, everything hinged on the one post she couldn't see. Had it been tampered with so that when it was hit by the raging floodwaters it had broken leaving the remaining three posts unable to cope? Even if that were true, how would anyone other than a structural engineer know that it would? It really seemed Constable Jarvis's explanation was the correct one and Mrs. Elliott had been letting her imagination get the better of her.

It was an hour before they returned to the house. While

Jem snuffled and whined at the door, Pauline examined the shrubs that had grown wild around the walls and lower windows. Here too, she could see no sign of human activity. As Jarvis said, there were no human footprints in the wet soil. There were prints that looked like cat, fox, rabbit, maybe even badger, but nothing sinister.

'Come along, Jem," she said, holding his collar and dragging him away as gently as she could. "There's nothing here for either of us anymore."

During the drive back, Pauline examined her options. If Mrs. Elliot had indeed become a client – no agreement had been reached before the woman's untimely death – based on what she'd seen today, Pauline suspected she'd have advised the woman there was nothing to be investigated. The suicide, however odd it's circumstances, was genuine on the face of it. Which left her without an investigation. Her disappointment surprised her. She hadn't realized how much she was depending on this mystery to brighten her life, to help her forget Stephen and that life together they were never to have.

"And where are you to sleep, Jem?" Pauline asked. The winter night had already closed in and her thoughts now returned to practicalities. She had no dog food and no bed for Jem and there'd be no shops open until tomorrow when she would be at work. She'd have to try to get something on her lunch break for the shops would be closed when her workday finished. She hoped Dr. Enderby would be willing to give her time to get into town and back on an extended lunch break.

Jem's sleeping arrangements, however, were easily settled.

"Stephen had a Lab when he was a boy," Mr. Bertram said. "I'm sure the basket is still in the attic somewhere." He left the room to get a stepladder with which to reach the trapdoor in the ceiling at the top of the stairs. "I hope it's still serviceable," he said. "It should be. Moths don't eat whicker."

The basket was soon found and handed down from the loft to Pauline waiting below. It looked perfectly sound to Pauline and she took it downstairs where Mrs. Bertram said, "We have some old pillows upstairs. I'll get them. I think it best if he sleeps in your room, dear. I don't altogether trust him near the pantry."

They both looked at Jem who gazed back in the manner of an innocent who was being wrongly accused of a heinous crime and clearly slandered.

"I think it would be best," Pauline said, grinning. "Anyone who looks that innocent is acting."

When the pillows were placed in the basket, and the basket placed at the foot of her bed, Jem hopped inside, turned himself around to press the pillows down and curled himself into a comfortable position.

"It seems he's found his home," Mrs. Bertram said, smiling.

"I do hope so," Pauline replied. "He was upset today when we returned to Mrs. Elliott's house. I thought he might fret when we left."

"If he was with her all those hours after she died, I'm sure he knows she's dead," Mrs. Bertram said. "Animals don't need to be told the way we do."

As they turned to leave, Jem sat up and leapt out of his bed. He followed them downstairs and into the living room, taking up a place at the side of Pauline's chair.

"I wish he could tell us something of what happened," Pauline said. "I'm sure something untoward occurred but can't yet see what it was."

"It's best you leave the police to sort that out," Mr. Bertram said. "It's what we pay them for."

Pauline nodded. "I'm sure you're right," she said. "I just hope they *can* find out what happened."

"They have all sorts of clever tools and techniques," Mr. Bertram said. "They'll get to the bottom of it, never fear."

But Pauline did fear. If someone had been as clever as it looked like they had, the 'tools and techniques' wouldn't work. Everyone knew what the police did in investigations, it was in books, movies, and she was told, though she'd never seen one herself, television shows. With so much working against them, the police's tools were too easily subverted by ordinary well-informed people.

While she waited for the police to sort it out, Pauline decided she'd try once again to interest Poppy in the investigation.

6

RAMSAY REPORTS BACK

Because Mrs. Bertram had promised to buy dog food for Jem, Pauline was able to slip out of work at lunch time and call Poppy. Unfortunately, she was out following up a story. Pauline left her name and number and phoned Inspector Ramsay, where she had more success.

"Miss Riddell," he said, "how nice to hear from you."

Pauline could see his smile just from the tone of his voice. "How nice of you to say so, Inspector," she replied, "when you must know I'm calling to encourage you to continue pressing Inspector Pringle and his investigation."

"I'm continuing to show an interest, Miss Riddell. If I were to 'press' Inspector Pringle, he would tell me where to go, and rightly so."

"Whatever you have to do," Pauline said. "Only don't let it get swept under the carpet."

"Do you have some new evidence for us to look at?"

Pauline had to admit she didn't.

"Then I don't think you're going to get the result you clearly want," Ramsay said. "Detectives, even amateur ones, need to guard against prejudging the issues. Inspector

Pringle has found no evidence that suggests anything other than suicide."

"That doesn't mean the evidence doesn't exist," Pauline said. "Please, just keep being interested while I find something that will get the inquest adjourned."

"There will be a brief inquest next week when the police will ask for an adjournment until after Christmas," Ramsay said.

"I'd like it to be pushed back further than that," Pauline said. "It isn't going to be easy finding the evidence we need."

"You must understand, Pauline," Ramsay said. "People need to get on with their lives. The state can't hold bodies indefinitely in the hope something will turn up one day."

"But this one is odd—" Pauline began.

"It's not so very odd," Ramsay interjected. "You mustn't imagine murders where there are none. You'll go mad if you go down that path."

The following days were purgatory for Pauline. She longed to phone Poppy, who had not returned her call, and Ramsay, to urge them both to faster endeavors but knew it would be counterproductive. They could both rightly refuse to do anything if she annoyed them. The evenings after work were too dark to drive to the Elliott house, let alone walk around the area; she'd miss any clues that might be there. At the local library, she read, and re-read, the local papers for anything pertaining to Mitford in the past year of which there was very little. She read and re-read Mrs. Churchill's obituary and the details of her adopted son's wedding until she knew all the minute details of their published lives. It was pitifully little.

On Wednesday evening she had to work late on an important report her boss, Dr. Enderby, was preparing to deliver to the board in the following days. Her normally patient temper was stretched to the limit when, on returning to her lodgings, she learned Inspector Ramsay had called and asked her to call him back.

"I hope you have good news, Inspector," Pauline said, when he answered the phone. "I've had a tiring day and I need some cheering up."

"I don't know if it's good news, Miss Riddell," Ramsay said. "I visited the scene today with Inspector Pringle who has the case. Your description of the scene was very accurate; I must commend you for it."

"Never mind the soft soap, Inspector," Pauline said. "What did you learn?"

Ramsay laughed. "You know I can't divulge police business to you," he said. "It would be most improper."

Pauline gritted her teeth and checked the sharp retort that had sprung to her tongue. "Very well," she said, "tell me what you can."

"The only fingerprints on the pill bottles and the cup beside her were hers," Ramsay said. "The doors and windows were all locked. The heat from the electric fire is causing the forensic folks some difficulties with an exact time of death but it may have been twenty-four hours before she was found."

"I'm sure you've already thought that the killer may well have had a door key and you've seen that the windows had those old-fashioned rotating handles that are easy to jiggle closed from the outside," Pauline said.

"Yes, I did," Ramsay said. "However, there were no footprints in the soil outside any of the windows, except yours, of course, so we think that closes off that line of enquiry."

"Has a post-mortem been done?" Pauline asked.

"It has and it answered the question we both had on how someone could swallow that many dry tablets with only one small cup of cocoa," Ramsay said. "The tablets had been ground up into a fine powder and mixed into the drink. Also..." he said quickly, to cut off Pauline's interjection, "also, she'd taken a sleeping draught either before or along with this slurry of aspirin."

"Do you think she was drugged and then, while drowsy, fed the lethal dose?"

"It's possible," Ramsay said, "and if she was drugged by someone else, then your murder theory is true. However, there's no evidence anyone else was in the house."

"The inquest is still going to be pushed back, isn't it?"

"Inspector Pringle says he's asking for that and the coroner will agree, I'm sure."

"Thank you, Inspector. Maybe I can find something to raise enough doubts to have this treated as a murder enquiry."

"Inspector Pringle will be contacting you soon, probably tomorrow, to go through your statement," Ramsay said. "I hope you'll remember you know only what you've seen. I wouldn't like it thought I was interfering in another man's case."

As Pauline wanted Ramsay to remain as a friend and supporter, she assured him she would be extremely careful and wished him good night.

7
MISS RIDDELL GIVES HER STATEMENT

The following evening, the phone rang in the hall and Mrs. Bertram picked it up.

"It's for you, Pauline," she said, leaning around the door jamb and looking into the living room where Pauline was reading.

Pauline grimaced. She was sure she knew who it would be. She put down her book and walked the short distance to where Mrs. Bertram was holding out the handset.

"Hello?"

"Miss Riddell, Inspector Pringle here," the voice said. "I hope Inspector Ramsay warned you I would be calling."

"He did," Pauline said, shortly. She wished it was Ramsay on the case. She didn't think anyone else would be anywhere near as friendly.

"Good," Pringle said. "I won't take up a lot of your time. Your statement is very comprehensive, but I would like to sit down with you and walk through the events you described."

"I'm not home from work until after six in the evening, Inspector," Pauline said, "but any time after that will find me here."

"Maybe I could drop by this evening," Pringle said. "You're not so far away and I'd really like to hear it from you directly, Miss Riddell."

Pauline looked at the grandfather clock standing farther down the hall. It was already seven o'clock and it was a good half hour drive from Morpeth. Still, it would get it over with.

"Very well, Inspector, but please be quick. I don't want my friends inconvenienced by late hours. Here's the address." Pauline quickly gave him directions and he promised to be there within the hour.

True to his word, Inspector Pringle arrived before the hour was up. Pauline ushered him into the best room, the one kept for special occasions, where she and Mrs. Bertram had lit a fire to warm it up.

"What is it you want to discuss, Inspector," Pauline asked. "I believe I made it all very clear in my statement."

"You did, Miss Riddell," he replied. "I just want to understand why you thought Mrs. Elliott's story was more believable than what seems obvious to everyone else."

"You mean the noises she heard and the bridge tipping her off when she walked across it?" Pauline asked.

"Exactly," Pringle said.

"Mrs. Elliott has lived there for decades and struck me as a sensible woman. One not given to flights of fancy. Therefore," Pauline said, "I judged it wise to take what she told me at face value until I learned otherwise."

Pringle nodded. "When you saw the bushes growing up against the house, didn't that convince you that the noises had a perfectly natural and normal explanation?"

"Are you a gardener, Inspector?" Pauline asked. "If the bushes had looked like they'd just grown up against the house, they would have convinced me. But they haven't, have they?"

He nodded. "It's true. Her husband was the gardener. The bushes haven't been trimmed since he died."

"Quite so," Pauline said, "which means Mrs. Elliott would have been used to their normal noise and was aware something different was happening. As for the bridge, it's true the recent rain and floods may well have loosened the bridge, but Mrs. Elliott walked that way daily. She knew the bridge and its state of repair. Again, something hidden was different."

"I'm not so sure I go along with you there, Miss Riddell," Pringle said. "But why do you mention the earlier death of her friend when she herself told you she'd told no one of her suspicions?"

"She said she'd told no one of her suspicions *recently*," Pauline replied. "So, she didn't think that could explain the sudden events. However, there's nothing to say she didn't tell someone months ago and that person just told someone else recently."

"Which is why you suspect Mrs. Churchill's adopted son?"

"It's too early to say I suspect anyone, Inspector," Pauline replied. "I just felt there was enough doubt to warrant me looking into it. I thought it most likely that all these things were a series of coincidences and Mrs. Elliott was placing too much emphasis on them. Then she died suddenly."

"Surely," Inspector Pringle said, "if the son had killed his mother, though Dr. Turner is positive she died of natural causes, he wouldn't want to raise suspicions by killing Mrs. Elliott. Particularly, if it was generally known she believed him responsible for his mother's death."

"I had thought that too, Inspector, and, as I say, I felt there would be nothing in this," Pauline said. "My investigating may possibly have been all that was needed to set Mrs. Elliott's mind at ease."

Pringle nodded. "And then she died," he said.

Pauline nodded in agreement. "Precisely," she said. "I wonder if she told anyone I was visiting."

"You think if the person responsible knew she'd called in outside help, he wouldn't have acted?"

"That's what I think," Pauline said. "I think she didn't tell anyone, so the perpetrator felt confident enough to continue their already existing plan."

"Why would they have been planning her death?"

"I think because they did know she'd told people of her suspicions and, when the fuss died down, they acted to prevent her resurrecting the story in times to come," Pauline said.

"They didn't want it hanging over their head. Never sure they were safe?"

"Something like that," Pauline said.

"You've given me plenty to think about, Miss Riddell, and I thank you for that, but I must ask you not to interfere until after the inquest," Pringle said.

"I won't, Inspector, for there's nothing now for me to do. If Mrs. Elliott was hoping I would keep her safe, it's too late. Will you be asking for an adjournment at the inquest?"

"For now, yes," Pringle said. "I want to follow up on what you and others have told me before providing a final report."

"I hope you're able to find something, Inspector. I really do. On both counts. That suicide scenario looks solid but there are many peculiar aspects of it."

"Suicides aren't all neat and tidy, Miss Riddell. I fear this may be one of those."

Pringle took his leave of the Bertrams and said goodbye

to Pauline at the door. Pauline returned to the living room to the enquiring gazes of Mr. and Mrs. Bertram.

"Surely you aren't mixed up with the police again, dear?" Mrs. Bertram asked plaintively.

"As I told you," Pauline said. "They were sure to question me because I was the one who found the body."

"But you gave your statement to that nice Inspector Ramsay," Mrs. Bertram said.

"He's not the officer on the case, unfortunately."

Mr. Bertram frowned. "Do you have doubts about the fellow who was just here?" he asked.

"Not at all," Pauline replied. "I just know and feel comfortable with Inspector Ramsay. I'm sure Inspector Pringle is every bit as good."

"This isn't going to spoil Christmas, is it?" Mrs. Bertram asked.

"There will be an initial inquest very soon," Pauline said. "I believe the police are going to ask for the full inquest to be adjourned until they've finished their enquiries. I think that should make the Christmas holidays safe."

"I do hope so," Mrs. Bertram said. "You need a proper rest after what's happened. I'm surprised you'd even entertain the idea of investigating this old woman's imaginings."

Pauline buried her nose in the new Agatha Christie novel, *A Pocket Full of Rye*, and let the conversation end without it going further. Mrs. Bertram would be seriously worried if she knew Pauline was planning to spend the best part of the following weekend walking all over Mitford and the paths and land around Mrs. Elliott's house. She felt she needed a better understanding of the village and its people before the inquest. Anything she could do to help the police get their adjournment, she intended to do. Her best hope for that was Poppy and she was missing in action.

The following day, Pauline slipped out from her office at lunch time and called The Morpeth Herald's office. Poppy answered the phone.

"This is something new," Pauline said. "You're usually out when I phone."

"I'm wrapping up a story," Poppy said, "and I haven't much time. What do you want?"

Pauline recognized that tone. Poppy had nothing to tell her and wanted this call to end, but she said, "I was hoping you'd made some progress on that research we discussed."

"Your work you asked me to do for you, you mean," Poppy replied.

Pauline was taken aback. She hadn't quite expected Poppy to be quite so hostile. "There's a story in it for you," Pauline said. "When I get to the bottom of it."

"Pauline, there have been two deaths of old people in a small village in the country," Poppy said. "You're the only one in the world who thinks there's a story and you think that because you want it to be so."

"I was right last time," Pauline replied, "and you got a story that has helped you. You said so yourself. This time will be the same."

"I'm working on a story that has ten times the legs of the story you're trying to create," Poppy said. "The story I'm working on will run. Yours is a non-starter."

"Very well," Pauline said. "There was a reporter from the Newcastle Journal who was pressing me for a follow-up on 'living with fame' just last week. I'm sure he'd do some digging for me."

There was a brief silence. "All right," Poppy said, at last, "sorry. I'm just so wound up on this story. It's big, Pauline, really big and it's making me snap at everyone. Sorry. What was it you wanted again?"

Pauline smiled triumphantly; pleased Poppy couldn't see her gloating. Maybe she was beginning to get a grasp on how the world worked and how to make it work for her in future.

"It was to find and research the death notices of Mrs. Churchill," Pauline said. "But now I also need anything you can find on Frank Churchill, his wife, and Mrs. Elliott's daughter and son-in-law."

Pauline thought she could practically hear Poppy's brain working, calculating the odds of Pauline being right again against the work and time she'd waste if Pauline was wrong.

"I'll be as quick as I can," Poppy said, "but my present story comes first."

"I need something before the inquest, Poppy," Pauline warned her.

"All right, all right. I'll get you something," Poppy said. "Now, get lost and let me finish this article."

Pauline returned to her office deep in thought. It looked like Poppy may not be the help she'd been expecting. There was no Journal reporter looking for a story, that hadn't been true, and her conscience would give her heck over it, but there *could* be a Journal reporter who would be interested. She'd fobbed off enough reporters these past weeks to know how hungry those people were. Poppy wasn't the only shark in this particular sea.

8

THE INITIAL INQUEST

Though the initial inquest was on a workday, Pauline made sure to be there. She had evidence to give and intended to give it in person. It was a fine winter's day, frosty in the morning with a clear blue sky overhead. Even her car seemed to feel the excitement as it sped along dry roads between leafless hedgerows. She parked near the hall and quickly made her way to a seat near the front of the room where the coroner's desk was placed.

Once the inquest began, Pauline listened intently to the evidence being given before she was called to give her own evidence. Focused though she was on the proceedings, she took care to observe the crowd that filled the small village hall. There was considerable local interest in this unexpected death.

She'd hoped to see the man who said he and Jem didn't get along, but he wasn't in attendance. She recognized only Inspector Pringle, Constable Jarvis, Dr Turner, and the handyman-cum-locksmith, Joe Moffatt. She wanted to interview him the moment the inquest was over.

The coroner seemed to have already made up his mind.

Then There Were ... Two Murders?

The witnesses quickly gave their statements, and the coroner asked few questions. Finally, it was Pauline's turn. She recounted the events that had brought her to Mrs. Elliott's house that afternoon.

"And you felt, from reading the deceased's letter and your conversation on the phone, that there was sufficient merit in what she said to warrant your involvement?" His tone suggested she was an interfering busybody, but Pauline remained unmoved. She wasn't going to be provoked by a jumped-up country justice of the peace. She'd faced down real villains and lived to tell the tale.

"What I'd been told by Mrs. Elliott could be explained by normal events," she said. "However, I judged Mrs. Elliott to be a level-headed woman and my investigating may have been enough to convince her she was mistaken or that she should press the matter further with the authorities."

Pauline was dismissed and the coroner summed up his judgement for the day.

"We have heard that Mrs. Elliott had become something of a recluse in recent months, particularly since the death of her good friend Mrs. Churchill. That the loss of her husband had depressed her. That she'd asked for and been given a sleeping draught by Dr. Turner to help her sleep. We've heard that she became convinced something or someone was threatening her. I feel I have enough evidence now to give a verdict of suicide while the balance of the mind was disturbed; however, the police have asked for more time to rule out other possibilities and I feel that would be for the best. This inquest is adjourned until January 15, 1954."

Pauline breathed a sigh of relief. When the coroner had begun his summing up, she was afraid he was going to close off the investigation today. Seeing Joe Moffatt preparing to leave, Pauline rose and quickly crossed the floor to where he was standing.

"Mr. Moffatt," she began, "can I have a word in private?"

"What about?" he asked bluntly.

"Can we talk somewhere quieter?" Pauline said.

They walked together out of the hall and Pauline ushered him away from the crowd streaming out of the door until they were well away from the chattering throng.

"Has anyone asked you to make any keys of the sort on Mrs. Elliott's door?" Pauline asked.

He laughed. "Nay," he said, "and it wouldn't be much good to ask me. I have a cutter to make the Yale-lock type of key. But you saw what old locks and keys her house had. You'd need a furnace and forge to make them."

Pauline nodded. "I did notice," she said. "Do you know any locksmiths in the county who still make those?"

He shook his head. "I don't. There's no call for those great heavy things nowadays."

"Well, that's one idea gone," Pauline said. "I wasn't very hopeful, but it needed clearing up."

They walked back to the road where Pauline's car was parked with Jem peering eagerly out of the window.

"You've taken Jem?" Moffatt asked.

"For now," Pauline said. "Mrs. Elliott's daughter didn't want him, PC Jarvis's wife doesn't like dogs, and there were no other volunteers."

"It's a shame," Moffatt said. "He's a right friendly dog. But my missus is a cat person and won't let dogs near the house."

Pauline laughed. "He's not friendly to everyone," she said. "When we were walking the other day, Jem and the man in that house over there," she pointed to the end terrace house across the way, "obviously didn't like each other."

Moffatt nodded. "Aye," he said. "I heard Jem didn't like Frank Churchill. To be honest, not many folks do, and his missus is even less likeable."

So that's who it was, Pauline thought, well, well, well. "Is there a reason for that dislike?" she asked.

Moffatt shook his head. "Not really," he said. "They're just an awkward, strange couple who don't mix well with others. They're not wrongdoers or anything like that."

"They weren't at the inquest," Pauline said, as she opened the car to let Jem out.

"Well, he'll be at work likely," Moffatt said, "and they weren't particular friends of Mrs. Elliott. I imagine they just weren't interested."

Pauline fixed the leash to Jem's collar. "We're going for a walk," she said, as Moffatt was preparing to leave. "I don't know if it's good for Jem to be here when he may never live here again, but he does enjoy it."

9

MISS RIDDELL MAKES A FRIEND

PAULINE STRODE down the road toward where she knew she could get into the land behind the houses that ran along the roadside. She wanted to time how long it took to walk from Frank Churchill's house to Mrs. Elliott's house. He was the one who had the most reason to be upset with Mrs. Elliott, especially if he'd learned what she was thinking, perhaps saying, about his good fortune in having his adopted mother die so he could marry his wife. A woman Mrs. Churchill clearly disapproved of.

But Pauline knew there were many holes in this possible line of enquiry. First, Frank Churchill and his now wife didn't have to marry immediately. They could have simply waited it out, unless she was pregnant, of course. Pauline needed to know if they had a child. Second, Jem hated Frank Churchill and would never have let him in the house that night and would certainly have intervened if he'd seen Churchill harming Mrs. Elliott, unless Jem had been drugged as well. Third, how could Frank Churchill have obtained a key to the house? It was unlikely Mrs. Elliott would have given him one.

She sighed as they cut through the narrow alley running from the road to the old stone bridge across the burn. She unclipped Jem's leash and he trotted on over the bridge in search of rabbits to chase.

"Your evidence here would be useful, Jem," Pauline said, as he looked back at her dawdling along in his wake.

Jem set off again as she got nearer to him. He clearly was used to watching older humans who couldn't keep up.

"Not that way, Jem," Pauline called, as he took a small track off to the left instead of the broader path to the right that they'd followed on their earlier walk. It was no use. He was gone, hidden among the tall grass and hedgerow. Pauline followed, vowing to keep him on the leash in the future.

The track entered a small, wooded area surrounding an older house, a cottage really, where smoke lazily rose from one chimney. Pauline approached warily. It didn't look a very nice place, in her opinion. It looked the kind of house where the local ne'er-do-well lived: rundown, unkempt, and dirty.

Jem barked at the window facing the path where, after a minute or two, an old woman appeared. She smiled when she saw Jem and waved at him. Jem trotted back to the door and waited. It opened and a fox terrier rushed out to greet Jem. While they were chasing around the yard catching up on lost time, the old woman came out and greeted Pauline.

"Hello," Pauline replied, pleased the house was not what she'd imagined. "You and your dog know Jem, I see."

The woman nodded. "We walked together with Dorothy and Jem, when we could," she said. "I'm not as strong as I once was but even when I couldn't go, Dorothy took Ranter with her and sat with me after. I'm going to miss her, as Ranter has missed Jem these past days."

"I am sorry," Pauline said, and she meant it, but her mind was already forming the question she hoped she could now get answered. "If you like, Ranter could come with us today. I won't be too long."

"That's very kind of you. I'm Betty Johnstone, by the way," she held out a thin, wrinkled hand, which Pauline shook.

"Pauline Riddell," she said. "Would you be strong enough to join us today?"

The woman nodded and looked at the sky. "I believe so," she said. "The weather looks promising and it's dry underfoot, for a change. Let me get a coat and hat." She disappeared indoors, returning a few moments later, dressed and carrying an umbrella and dog leash.

"Perhaps," Pauline said, "you can choose the route. I don't know the village at all, you see."

The older woman nodded. "The dogs know the way," she said.

"Did you and Mrs. Elliott walk together often?" Pauline asked.

"Almost every day since Arthur died," Betty said. "I lost my own husband only the winter before."

Pauline felt she could understand why. The cottage, surrounded by trees, looked dark, damp and would be a horror to heat.

"Then you may be able to help me," Pauline said. "I found Mrs. Elliott and everything in the room pointed to her taking her own life. Do you think that likely?"

"Nay," Betty said. "That's nonsense. She would never leave Jem like that and she would have told me, even if it was just to say, 'I can't walk tomorrow.' No, it's murder right enough and I hope the police catch him and hang him."

"Do you think you know who did it?" Pauline asked.

"That son-in-law of hers," Betty said. "He's no use to man nor beast and she knew it. I imagine he decided to act before she changed her will."

"Was she going to change her will?"

"She was coming around to the idea of a trust that would pay an income to her daughter only. No free cash for thon waster to spend," Betty said.

Pauline laughed. "I take it you don't like him much either," she said.

Betty grimaced and shook her head. "He's a wrong un, that one," she said.

"Does he work?"

"Not what you'd call work," she said. "He's an artist. An artist who has yet to sell a picture. His wife keeps him." This last was said with all the contempt of a northerner for a man who didn't provide for his family.

"Would he know Mrs. Elliott was planning to change her will, do you think?"

"I'm sure he would have guessed," Betty said. "Their frequent heated discussions about his status would have warned him, I'm sure."

This was promising, Pauline thought. While Frank Churchill might have been angry at Mrs. Elliott for suggesting his mother hadn't died naturally, it would be madness for him to kill Mrs. Elliott and open the whole question to village gossip. But a son-in-law who may well be in desperate need of money that he expected to come soon but who learns it may not be forthcoming was a likely candidate. The example of Frank Churchill and his good fortune would be a powerful motivator. She needed to learn more.

As Pauline was thinking about next steps, Betty said, "I usually rest on that seat over there." She pointed to a bench set off from the pathway. "And, if you don't mind, I shall turn around here. I don't want you carrying me home."

Pauline smiled. "Of course," she said. "I'll sit with you for a while." She thought Betty looked even more frail now than when they'd set off.

"Oh, don't worry about me," Betty said. "I'll be right as rain in a few minutes."

"What's Mrs. Elliott's son-in-law called?" Pauline asked. "He came to the house with the daughter when I found the body, but I don't remember him being introduced."

"Boothroyd," Betty said. "Eustace Boothroyd. Did you ever hear such a silly name as Eustace?"

"I've never thought about it," Pauline said. "Perhaps that's why it isn't common nowadays. Did Jem like him?"

Betty looked shocked. "Nay," she said. "Jem's a good judge of character."

Pauline felt Jem probably just picked up on Mrs. Elliott's dislike of her son-in-law so held her opinion, only saying, "They do say dogs can always tell."

"Ranter didn't like him either," Betty said. "If we met him in the street, Ranter would lunge and growl. It was the same with that Frank Churchill."

"I've already witnessed Jem's dislike," she said, and recounted Jem and Churchill's standoff on their previous walk.

"Frank Churchill is the kind of man who is as nice as ninepence when there's only women about but as quiet as a mouse in the company of men. That's how my husband described him. He warned me to keep out of his way and I always did."

"They seem to be the village's dark side," Pauline said, frowning.

"Oh, I don't know," Betty replied. "Others seem to get

along with them. It may just be we are of an older generation and they're hard for us to understand."

"You mean artists?"

"Frank Churchill isn't an artist, dear," Betty said. "That's his wife. He's a clerk in the local government."

"Two artists in one small village," Pauline laughed. "It must be one of those artists' colonies we read about."

"She's a more practical kind of artist," Betty said. "She makes jewelry and knick-knacks for the home. People do buy her stuff."

"I should look in and see if there's anything I like," Pauline said, sensing an opportunity to peer into one of the possible suspect's lives.

"She has a workshop behind their house," Betty said. "You'll find her there most days. It's just there," Betty pointed to where Pauline could see a house roof and chimney above the hedge and shrubs. "You go and see if she's there while I rest."

"What about the dogs?" Pauline asked, suddenly aware Jem and Ranter weren't in sight.

"Don't worry about them," Betty said. "There are no farm animals in the fields, and they know their way home."

Pauline laughed. "They may bring us home a rabbit," she said.

Betty smiled. "If they do, it will be the oldest, slowest rabbit that ever lived," she said. "Still, if they do, it will help my meat ration go further."

"This rationing is difficult and depressing," Pauline said. "The end of it always seems to be soon and never quite here. Like Alice in Wonderland, always 'jam yesterday and jam tomorrow but no jam today'."

"Then here's to the dogs and their hunting," Betty said, pretending to raise a glass. "Maybe we'll get a rabbit each."

"Or a pheasant," Pauline added. "I like pheasant."

"Ah," Betty said, shaking her head. "The human condition. No sooner do we have a thought of some small thing that would help, we start desiring things beyond our reach. An old, tired rabbit is just possible but neither Ranter nor Jem can fly."

Pauline sighed. "It's true," she said, "our hopes always grow faster than our needs." She rose from the bench. "I'm going to meet our local jewelry artist and see what I learn there."

"You'll not learn much from her," Betty said, laughing.

"Why?" Pauline asked. "What's her name, by the way? I never thought to ask."

"You'll see why," Betty said, "and her name is June."

10

MRS. JUNE CHURCHILL

It took a moment for Pauline to realize the entrance to the woman's studio was not, as she'd imagined, through the back gate of the garden but off a narrow lane that ran alongside the house. Opening the door, which clanged to announce her arrival, she stepped inside. There was a strong smell of fire, soot, and ash, even in the small room that constituted the sales side of the business. Before she'd even begun to admire the jewelry on display in glass cases, a door opened at the back of the counter and an elegant young woman came through it.

Pauline was amused by her own reaction to the woman. The old workshop, the smell of soot and cinders, had all led her to imagine the artist as a blacksmith.

"Can I help you?" the woman asked in a studied, measured speech that sounded a bit unnatural.

"I've only just discovered your shop," Pauline said. "Are all these your own work?" She gestured to the pieces in the cabinets and under the glass-topped counter.

"Yes," the woman replied. Again, that voice.

"You're very talented," Pauline said. "I love all of them, I think."

"Thank you," the woman said.

Pauline decided the woman's talents clearly didn't extend to marketing her products in a meaningful way.

"Do you do all the work here, in the shop, even the metalwork?"

"Yes."

Pauline continued her study of all the items on display while she tried to think of a way to draw the woman out into talking about herself or even just her work.

"I had no idea we had such talented artists in our area," Pauline said. "I live not too far away, and I've never heard of, or seen, your work anywhere. I'm Pauline Riddell, by the way." She held out her hand, but the woman remained motionless.

"I know who you are," she said. "You're that busybody who got famous. The one Mrs. Elliott wanted to hire."

This was the longest speech she'd made, and it gave Pauline a sense of the difficulty. The woman had some kind of speech impediment – a lisp or stammer, perhaps – and she'd trained herself to articulate slowly to hide it.

Pauline smiled. "She contacted me, yes," she said. "Unfortunately, she died before I learned what it was all about. Were you at the inquest?"

"No."

"Oh, I wonder how you knew who I was."

"Everybody in the village knows," the woman said.

"It was like that where I grew up too," Pauline said, smiling. "Anything that happened, or a stranger in town, it was all around the neighborhood in a flash."

The woman nodded.

"Well, I won't keep you chatting any longer," Pauline

said. "I can see you're dying to get on with your work. I'll look back when I've made up my mind about which piece I like best." She smiled in what she hoped was a friendly way, though she didn't feel friendly, and returned to find Betty stroking and petting the two dogs.

"They're telling me all the exciting things they've seen on their ramble," Betty said, when Pauline sat down.

"More exciting than my conversation with Mrs. June Churchill, I hope."

Betty laughed. "She's one who likes to keep her own counsel is that one," she said.

"She does indeed. The phrase 'blood' and 'stone' came strongly to mind," Pauline said. "Is she a local girl?"

"Nay. He met her at college. She's from the Midlands somewhere, I believe."

"She has no accent at all," Pauline said.

"I heard she had to learn to speak again, after an accident of some kind."

"Poor woman. How awful."

Betty nodded. "It is and many have wished to be helpful, but she doesn't like people getting close, which puts people off her."

"She isn't very welcoming to potential customers," Pauline said, grinning.

"She's like that with everybody," Betty said, "Take no heed. Now, I think I should be getting back. The cold is seeping into my old bones."

"And, sadly, no rabbit to warm our tummies later," Pauline said.

As they made their way back to Betty's cottage, the dogs trotting on ahead, Pauline said, "The accident and what it did to her voice seem to have made her withdraw from people. It's understandable but sad."

"If you knew her better, you'd know it has also made her bitter," Betty said. "She's not shy or withdrawn; she's angry at us all."

"I can see how that might be."

"There's no 'might be' about it," Betty said, sharply. "She lashes out over the smallest things, even toward children."

"Oh dear," Pauline replied. "That is sad. What will she do when she has her own?"

"They say they aren't having children. I think that would be for the best."

Gathering Jem into her car was a trial Pauline found herself almost unequal to. Jem would much prefer to stay with Ranter, but Betty shook her head.

"I can't," she said. "I'm finding it harder to walk every day, and even Ranter may have to go soon."

"I am sorry," Pauline said. "I'll be returning here once or twice over the coming weeks, perhaps I can call in and Ranter can walk with Jem and me."

It was agreed and Pauline drove home with a disconsolate Jem in the passenger seat casting resentful glances her way.

"I can't help it, Jem," she said. "This is the best I can do right now."

He seemed to accept that and turned to watch the world go by out the side window, while Pauline considered everything she'd learned. She had a new and credible suspect and now knew how a key for Mrs. Elliott's old door lock could have been made, which made her earlier suspicions more credible too. She wondered if there were any other suspects in that one small village.

11

CHRISTMAS AND NEW YEAR'S EVE, 1953

CHRISTMAS WAS FINALLY HERE, and Pauline drove home to Yorkshire immediately after work on Christmas Eve. In the urban areas, the roads were well cleared. Once she entered the rural lanes, however, they wound around sharp bends with slushy piles at the curbs and down steep hills into valleys where the sun had already set, and the surfaces were slick with newly forming ice. It needed all her concentration to keep the car from sliding into a ditch.

As she'd discovered every year at this time since she'd left home for secretarial college, she was in two minds about going home for the holidays. She loved being home, loved Christmas, and loved her family but... There was always that but. Her mother fussed. There was no other word for it. Being the baby of the family had serious drawbacks, one of which was the firm belief in her mother's eyes that she hadn't yet left the nursery and shouldn't be out without parental supervision. Pauline vowed she would do her best to be patient, but she knew in her heart that sooner or later her mother's over-attention would make her snap.

Fortunately, that evening, when her nerves were still on

edge from the drive, many of the family visited and the room was noisy with the excited laughter of children and the gossiping of their parents. For Pauline, the scene brought bitter reflections of what might have been if Stephen had not gone to Korea or had not been killed before the war was brought to that peculiar stalemate. She was blinking away tears when her mother, seeing her isolation, grasped her arm and dragged her off to join an animated discussion between her sister Freda and a neighbor.

"You need to stop these two coming to hair-pulling," her mother whispered, too loudly.

"Mam," Pauline protested but she was profusely welcomed by the two women who, she felt, had also realized the discussion was getting too heated.

The conversation turned to what Pauline was doing in Newcastle and how she enjoyed her work, which allowed Pauline's attention to wander as her replies were oft repeated by now. The radio was playing the Christmas hits, (Pauline had just learned Britain now had a top ten songs chart) and the melody of the present song gave her another painful moment.

Across the room, she could see her father chatting to the men, amused and slightly detached as he always was. The song was *Oh Mein Papa* and it struck Pauline just how much she relied on her father for support when her mother became too much. He looked up and saw her watching him and he smiled. She smiled back and hoped he understood. Stephen too might have been considering fatherhood now if he'd lived.

Fortunately, there were enough visitors over the whole two days to divert her mother's attention from Pauline and the days slipped by without the scene Pauline dreaded.

Then There Were ... Two Murders? 59

Christmas and Boxing Day came and went, and Pauline was able to return to Newcastle on Sunday afternoon without a hard word being spoken by anyone. It was a relief.

The days between returning to work on the Monday after her drive back to Newcastle and the New Year's Day holiday on the Friday were slow and Pauline wished she'd had vacation to take but all of that had been used up solving Marjorie's death. And now she had another murder, perhaps two, and no time of her own left in which to do it.

On New Year's Eve, the phone on her desk rang. It was Poppy.

"Have you a date for tonight?" Poppy asked immediately.

"A date?" Pauline cried, upset at her friend's insensitivity. Considering Poppy was Stephen's cousin, Pauline expected better. "This is my first new year without Stephen," she added. "Do you think I can forget that?"

"Sorry," Poppy said. "I wasn't thinking. But if you're free you can come with me and the others tonight. You shouldn't be alone."

"I like alone," Pauline said, still not mollified by her friend's casual apology and refusal to take no for an answer.

"Nonsense," Poppy said, "get yourself to the Black Bull here in Morpeth at eight o'clock and then on to the clock tower for ringing in the New Year."

"Poppy—" Pauline began, but was interrupted.

"Don't Poppy me, Pauline," Poppy interjected. "Eight o'clock, Black Bull, and wear a warm coat. It gets cold waiting for midnight when the pubs close at ten-thirty."

Realizing Poppy wasn't taking a refusal, and unwilling to lose her friend's goodwill, Pauline agreed. At least, Pauline thought, I might hear something of Poppy's research.

Poppy was right, the evening air was cold, even with the crowds milling around the old clock tower waiting for midnight, greeting friends, neighbors, and making new acquaintances. As the minutes ticked away, more and more people arrived, leaving pubs and private parties full of holiday spirit – in Pauline's view, too many holiday spirits. However, the crowd was a happy one; it seemed everyone was here to celebrate the end of the old year and the birth of the new. Occasional bursts of Auld Lang Syne began and ended in raucous laughter as people prepared for their annual moment of singing in public.

"Wake up," Poppy said, suddenly arriving at Pauline's side with a bearded man in tow.

"I was watching everyone," Pauline said, "and thinking of those who didn't make it to this night."

"Morbid stuff," the bearded man said, thrusting a bottle into her hand. "Here, have a drink. It'll make you feel better."

Pauline grinned, returning the rum bottle to him. "It really wouldn't," she said. "It would make me ill but thank you anyway."

Poppy and her companion drifted away, and Pauline was once again alone among a noisy, happy crowd in which everyone knew everyone else. Occasionally, passers-by would wish her a Happy New Year and she'd respond as enthusiastically as she could, but her heart wasn't in it. Stephen's death had felt like the end and now, these last few minutes of the year in which he died seemed like the final nail in his coffin. She let the tears flow down her face without making any attempt to stop them.

The crowd counted down and the deep notes of the clock's bell rang out. The crowd began to sing Auld Lang Syne in a surprisingly good unison and Pauline turned away, returning to her car and her future. She shivered. Maybe it was colder than she thought.

12

A NEW YEAR, 1954

THE FOLLOWING DAY, January 1, was a local holiday and Pauline drove to Poppy's flat after lunch. She suspected that if she arrived before lunch Poppy may not be alone. She rang the bell vigorously until Poppy stuck her head out of a window to see who was at the door.

"Oh, it's you," she said. "You're very bright and bushy-tailed. Did you find someone last night? I missed you after the midnight bell was rung."

"I wasn't looking for someone," Pauline said. "I left right after. It seemed best."

"So why are you here now?"

Pauline got straight down to business, "With everyone around us last night, we couldn't talk about what you've learned. What *have* you learned about our suspects?"

Poppy shook her head in disbelief. "And Happy New Year to you too, Pauline," she said. "Give me a minute to dress and we'll find a pub that's open."

Pauline waited patiently, pacing up and down outside the door, until Poppy emerged wrapped in what looked like every piece of clothing she possessed.

"You do know it's freezing out here," Poppy grumbled, correctly interpreting Pauline's quizzical expression.

"Only if you've just fallen out of bed," Pauline replied, unmoved by her friend's unhappiness. They walked up Bridge Street until they found somewhere open and entered a room warmed by a blazing fire. Poppy chose a seat as close as she could get.

"I can hardly afford to heat my place," she said. "Electricity is so expensive, and the electric fire just eats up my shillings. Being in bed is the only way to keep warm. It helps to have someone in there with me as well. I'm not cut out for this climate. I'm thinking of emigrating to Australia."

Pauline bought drinks at the bar and brought them over to Poppy. "You would be better with a hot drink," Pauline said, handing over Poppy's pint of Amber ale.

"I had enough of that last night," Poppy said, grinning. "Rum keeps the cold out wonderfully well."

"I meant tea," Pauline said, primly.

"You are very odd," Poppy said, after she'd taken a long gulp of beer.

"I'm a woman on a mission," Pauline said. "Now tell me what you've learned about our possible suspects."

"Frank Churchill is everything he seems to be, so far as the records go, which isn't far," Poppy replied. "He's a fine upstanding citizen who went to college after school and now works in local government. He has no criminal record at all."

"He's popular with the older ladies," Pauline said. "They think him well-meaning and charming. The men say he's sly."

"And you clearly believe the men?"

"In this case, yes," Pauline said. "What about his wife? She seems the more interesting of the two."

"Not really," Poppy said. "Going by the public records, she's also an honest upright citizen without a blemish on her character."

"She's uncommunicative and cold," Pauline said.

"Possibly," Poppy said, grinning, "but that isn't yet evidence for murderous tendencies. In fact, I've never heard of a murderer described as anything but being kind to animals and his or her mother, so I think that lets both these two off the hook."

"All right," Pauline said. "Now for the serious ones, the son-in-law and daughter."

"The daughter is also all that she seems," Poppy said, "as far as the records go."

"You are being deliberately infuriating and you might well be murdered by me if you don't stop smirking like an idiot and tell me what I want to know," Pauline said.

Poppy laughed. "I blame the sherry," she said. "If you drank a long, slow, pint of beer instead of that foreign muck, you'd be a more relaxed woman."

Pauline fixed her with what she hoped was a baleful stare and said nothing.

"All right," Poppy said, "the son-in-law did it. There, I've solved the case for you."

Pauline growled in frustration. "Poppy," she said, warningly.

Poppy nodded her head, sadly. "The sherry," she said. "All that hot-blooded Spanish temperament in a bottle."

Pauline kicked her under the table.

"Ow," Poppy said, rubbing her shin. "All right. Here's the scoop. He was sent down to reform school after fighting with a teacher at his regular school. At the reform school, he was involved in another fight. He really is a hot-tempered man. Maybe he drinks sherry too," she added mischievously.

"I thought as much," Pauline said, triumphantly. "Two credible suspects."

"So where do we start?"

Pauline noted Poppy was now sounding like the old Poppy, the Poppy she'd expected to have at her side, and was pleased but kept her expression and voice neutral. "We have to find enough evidence to make the coroner postpone the inquest until we have the case solved, or failing that, have him declare Mrs. Elliott unlawfully killed by a person or persons unknown."

"I'm sure the police are looking into Boothroyd's movements at the time in question," Poppy objected. "How can we do better than they can?"

Pauline frowned. "I wish I wasn't now so well known in the village," she said. "Then I could have asked innocent questions. As it is, it will have to be you."

"I'm a reporter," Poppy said. "They will be as wary of me as they are of you."

"Not if you're doing a nice memorial piece on Mrs. Elliott, praising her for her civic virtues et cetera."

'I didn't know she had any,' Poppy said.

"All matronly women in villages are members of this and that charity or committee," Pauline said. "It will be easy."

13

POPPY LOSES FAITH

IN THE DAYS THAT FOLLOWED, while Poppy gathered information for her 'memorial,' Pauline began focusing her attention on the Churchills and in particular, Mrs. June Churchill. The woman had to be a suspect in one or both murders and the fact the police didn't seem to be pursuing that angle left her free to do so.

"Betty," she asked, on her next visit to the village, "what can you tell me about the Churchills?"

"There's not a lot to tell, dear," Betty replied, as they sipped afternoon tea. The dogs lay in front of the meager fire, warming themselves after their walk. "He lived with his stepmother since he was a boy, right up to her death, and he met the present Mrs. Churchill at college. She moved here to be near him, though they never gave any sign of being a couple because the word would have been carried back to old Mrs. Churchill and she'd taken a dislike to her from the moment they met."

"She forbade him to marry her, I heard."

"She did." Betty said, "So strongly I was surprised her will didn't include a requirement for him to inherit only if he didn't marry her, but you must remember, I didn't know her well. We didn't move in the same social circles, as you might imagine." She grinned. "Not even when my husband was alive were we grand enough for Mrs. Churchill."

Pauline smiled. She could imagine. Her own village had just such a woman in it. "Clearly, her will didn't have such a clause," Pauline said.

"Clearly," Betty said, and then added with a mischievous grin, "If this was a murder-mystery I'd have expected to learn she was about to add that to her will before she was killed."

"Do you think she was killed?"

"Nay, love," she said. "I were just saying, in books or radio plays that's what happens. In this case, she was well past her dying day. Everyone could see that."

Pauline nodded. "You never suspected anything untoward? After all, Mrs. Elliott did."

"Aye, but she and Mrs. Churchill were friendly," Betty said. "She would feel the loss keenly, I imagine. And she too was getting on in years and you know how people begin to see things darkly when they grow old. They think everything was better when they were young." She laughed, and added, "I feel that way myself sometimes, but I know it's just my age talking. Most old people don't."

"So, you're sure Mrs. Churchill died a natural death?"

"I do, why? Do you think there was something odd about it?" Betty asked, genuinely puzzled.

Pauline shook her head. "It's like you said about murder-mystery books. Her death was just so convenient for her adopted son and his now wife. Too convenient," she said. "It makes me suspicious."

"But I can think of two other cases in my own life where someone's death came at a good time for the beneficiaries,"

Betty said, "and I don't think they were murders. It must happen all the time, really. We all struggle in life and then when someone leaves us a legacy, it looks like Providence answered our prayers, but it was just their time."

"You're probably right," Pauline said. "My suspicions are odious. I just can't help it."

"That's because you unmasked those two murderers in Newcastle," Betty said. "Now you think we're all murderers."

Pauline laughed nervously. Betty's words almost seemed like they were her own thoughts. Still, she wouldn't give up quite yet.

Pauline rose to take her leave. "I'll come back next week to take Ranter out, if I may," she said.

"Do, dear," Betty said. "It's good for Ranter and it's good for me to have someone to chat to."

"Well, Jem," Pauline said, as she walked briskly back to the car. It was growing cold as the light went. "Can you help me? You don't like Frank Churchill, and that's good enough for me, but what about the woman?"

Jem gazed at her as he trotted at her side. He seemed puzzled how to answer her question.

"I shall bring you and her together," Pauline said, "and you can tell me what you think. Meanwhile, you and I are going to look at that bridge. The water's lower now; we should be able to see that fourth post."

When they reached the spot, Pauline could see the fourth post, which was now visible in the stream. Like the other three posts, it too looked like a natural break. So, Constable Jarvis was right. An old bridge had been damaged by the floodwaters and Mrs. Elliott was just the person unlucky enough to walk on it when it was ready to fall.

"I'm getting bad feelings about this, Jem," Pauline said,

as they walked back to the car. "I think they may be right, and I may be wrong. All of this is a wild goose chase."

Jem, sensing her unhappiness, closed the gap between them and nuzzled her hand.

The following day, Pauline phoned Poppy to arrange a meeting. But Poppy said there was no point.

"I have nothing to tell you yet," Poppy said, "beyond what you already know."

"Find a way of asking if anyone saw anybody hanging around Mrs. Churchill's house near the time of her death," Pauline said.

"How would that fit in with questions about her public service and general philanthropy?" Poppy said indignantly. "Be sensible, Pauline."

"Find a way," Pauline said. "And what about the Boothroyds?"

"Pauline," Poppy said, seriously, "I have a job that keeps me very busy and I'm working on a story that any reporter would die for. I'm busy so I haven't found anything to help you yet. Give me time."

"Sorry," Pauline said. "I'm just so anxious to have something to say at the inquest."

"Why not just tell Pringle what you think happened to Mrs. Churchill and leave it to him and his men to do the work?"

"Because it sounds crazy without evidence," Pauline said. "I know. I explained it to Betty Johnstone, but she still didn't buy it. Pringle won't either."

"But there's no way for you and me to get evidence, is there?" Poppy said. "Whatever we find will be just as circumstantial as it is now. Tell Pringle."

14

INSPECTOR PRINGLE DELIVERS A LECTURE

PAULINE COULDN'T. She struggled within her own mind about possible ways of getting the evidence, and good enough evidence that would persuade Inspector Pringle to investigate. It was useless. Mrs. Churchill's death was months ago and the woman she suspected of doing it now lived in the house. If she couldn't show Mrs. Churchill's death to be a crime, there was no way Pringle would accept her proposed link to Mrs. Elliott's death. To go to him as things stood would be to invite humiliation.

By the Wednesday evening, however, her other self, the one she thought of as being a 'better, more civic-minded' self, had once again reminded her that if Frank Churchill did die suddenly in the near future, and she'd done nothing to stop it happening, it would be on her conscience for the rest of her life. With a sinking feeling inside, she called Inspector Pringle and arranged to meet him at his office after work.

When the time came, Pauline almost didn't go. She knew it was going to be a disaster. In a depressed state of mind, she greeted him and explained her theory and her fears. He listened impassively at first, but she could sense his growing anger, which became clear when he finally spoke.

"Miss Riddell," he said, "I took a statement from you because you had a small part in the tragedy that was Mrs. Elliott's death and because my colleague, Inspector Ramsay, spoke highly of you. However, casting such wicked aspersions on innocent people who have done you no harm is outrageous. Do you know these people and their lives?"

Pauline shook her head. "I've barely met most of them," she said, "and I'd never been to Mitford before that day."

"Yet you accuse this poor woman of two murders and planning a third?"

"I'm not accusing anyone, Inspector. I'm only asking you to consider the possibility that Mrs. Churchill was murdered and now Mrs. Elliott has been murdered also," Pauline said.

"And now you're suggesting we were negligent in not investigating Mrs. Churchill's death, though the doctor signed the death certificate as natural causes and we weren't involved, and now we're doing a poor job with Mrs. Elliott's death," he said.

Pauline took a deep breath to keep hold of her emotions, before saying, "I'm doing none of those things. As I've thought about the events that have happened in Mitford, I realized there may be a complicated answer to explain them and it may have future consequences if nothing is done."

Pringle shook his head in disgust. "We get a lot of daft ideas thrown at us in these cases," he said, "but yours is frankly little more than malicious. When there's a police investigation everybody thinks they can hurt someone they dislike by falsely using the police, but you want us to harass people without you even knowing them."

"I'm only asking you to consider this in your investigation, Inspector. Nothing more than that."

Pauline was preparing to leave but paused when Pringle said, "Miss Riddell, Inspector Ramsay may have been impressed by your part in that Newcastle murder, but I'm not impressed by this wild accusation and the complete lack of anything to confirm its merit. You were lucky before, now you're just being unpleasant and unhelpful. Good day."

Pauline returned to her car where Jem was eagerly waiting to be released and taken for a walk. "A walk would do us both good," Pauline said, as she clipped the leash onto his collar. "I won't be safe to drive for an hour at least."

They walked into Carlisle Park and toward the raised mound, the motte, which was all that remained of Morpeth's old Norman castle. The motte was lightly covered in snow. Dark channels where children had tobogganed down it stood out starkly against the white. It reminded Pauline of winter days of her own childhood and how simple life had been for her then. The path was well-lit and almost empty, apart from other dog walkers so Pauline talked out her frustration to Jem.

"I knew it would be awful telling them without any evidence," she said. "I just didn't realize how awful. He'll never trust another word I say and will probably stop working on her death just to spite me."

Jem seemed to nod as they walked and that was good enough for Pauline.

"The thing is," she said. "I couldn't do nothing because, even if the inquest does say suicide, if something happens to Frank Churchill in the future, Inspector Pringle will remember what I told him and there'll be a better investigation then. That won't be much comfort to Mr. Churchill, but it will make me feel better. Do you see?"

Jem looked at her. He obviously understood he was

being talked to but had no idea how to respond. There didn't seem to be much about him in all this.

Pauline laughed and tickled behind his ears. "You're right," she said. "It's not your problem. Still, I'm determined to get your opinion on all the people involved."

She drove home in a better frame of mind than when she'd left Pringle's office and determined to at least hint at some of this at the inquest. Not accuse anyone or point fingers in any way, just make sure the coroner understood there were possibilities other than suicide. Meanwhile, she would continue to make enquiries and hope for something helpful from Poppy.

She heard nothing from Poppy but walking Jem and Ranter the next Sunday afternoon, she had the good fortune to meet with Mrs. June Churchill in the street where she had just parked her car.

"Oh, hello," Pauline said, smiling, hoping it would disarm the woman. "Do you remember me? I looked at your jewelry a few weeks ago."

The woman nodded. "I remember," she said, not even pausing in her stride. "You were looking to point fingers at us then and you're doing it again now."

Pauline and Jem walked toward her. Jem's hackles were rising with very step.

"I'm only interested in what happened to Mrs. Elliott," Pauline said. She stopped but Mrs. Churchill swept by without pausing. As they watched the woman walk away, Jem's hackles sank and the tension in his stance subsided.

"You don't like her either," Pauline said, quietly. "I wonder why not. Is she unkind to dogs as well as people?"

There was a new thin covering of snow on the ground and puddles were ice-rimmed pools, so Betty said she wouldn't join them in their walk today. Pauline walked the dogs beyond what had been Mrs. Elliott's house, hoping she would have the same good fortune in meeting the Boothroyds as she had with Mrs. Churchill, but it seemed she'd had all her luck for the day.

Returning to Betty's cottage after their walk, Pauline told Betty about her brief meeting with June Churchill earlier in the afternoon.

"She's allus on her own," Betty said. "You hardly ever see her and her husband together. I hear they're at odds most of the time. It's as they say, 'marry in haste, repent at leisure.'"

"I thought they'd been together since college?" Pauline said.

"Going out for a drink or a dance isn't like being married, dear," Betty said. "You only learn about each other when you're living together. That's when you know. Clearly, they didn't know and now they do. Or so I hear."

"Is that what they say in the village?"

"Aye, it is. You can't keep a secret like that in a place as small as this," Betty said.

"It's rather sad, I think," Pauline said. "They are neither of them so desirable they'd do better by separating."

Betty laughed. "That's true enough," she said. "Though there's plenty of silly women who'd fall for him. Her…" she broke off with a shake of her head.

"She is so cold and controlled," Pauline said. "It isn't attractive in anyone. I don't feel a desire to even be her friend."

"She wouldn't thank you for trying," Betty said. "Believe me, she's sent a number of folks off with a flea in their ear who offered her the hand of friendship. It's not natural." She grimaced to reinforce her words.

Pauline drove home mulling over Betty's words. What did June Churchill have to hide that she needed to prevent anyone coming close enough to find out? And Jem not liking her was further proof of something wrong, Pauline was sure. She stroked him as he lay curled on the passenger seat, dozing.

The road to Morpeth ran alongside the River Wansbeck, in summer a slow, gentle stream, now a fast-rushing torrent from all the recent rain and snow. Pauline shivered. It was almost a year ago when the worst flooding in living memory had killed hundreds of people along England's east coast. She hoped the Wansbeck wasn't giving a warning of worse to come.

15

INSPECTOR PRINGLE IS ANGRY

"Pauline," Mrs. Bertram said, one day the following week when Pauline entered the house after work. "Inspector Pringle has asked that you go and see him."

"Did he phone today?"

"Yes, this afternoon, about an hour ago. He thought you might be home from work."

"He doesn't understand how hard those of us who aren't policemen work, does he?" Pauline said, smiling.

"I'm sure he thinks nothing of the sort," Mrs. Bertram said. "He said phone him when you got in."

"I will, after we've eaten," Pauline replied. "He only intends to shout at me again, I'm sure."

"You don't know that at all. He may have discovered something and wishes to thank you for your good information."

Pauline laughed. "Even Inspector Ramsay never went that far," she said.

Later, she phoned and was put though to his office.

"You wanted to speak to me, Inspector?" Pauline asked.

"I did," he replied. "I'm sure after our chat at the

weekend you would think I wasn't going to follow up on your outrageous theory and I wanted to be sure you knew that I did. Despite my dislike of your finger-pointing, I take all information I'm given very seriously."

"I'm sure you do," Pauline said. "I've no doubt about your conscientiousness or integrity."

"Then let me assure you, we have investigated the possibility you raised," Inspector Pringle said. "And, as I already told you, if you recall, we investigated the whereabouts of Mr. and Mrs. Churchill at the times of both deaths, and they had strong alibis. Yet you chose to continue hounding them, prying into their private lives for no reason other than your own wish for fame and adulation. We appreciate that you were instrumental in bringing those two murderers to justice in Newcastle last year, but this persecution of innocent people is, as I've already said, little short of wickedness."

Pauline flushed at the stinging rebuke. It hurt because he was saying all the things she'd thought about her motives and rationalized away. Nevertheless, she felt his accusations were unfair and needed a response.

"I've thought about my actions and motives carefully throughout this, Inspector, you can be sure," she said. "Nothing I have done has been done without much soul-searching on my part. However, I was convinced that Mrs. Elliott was murdered, and the present Mrs. Churchill was a credible suspect and what I presented to you was a possible, and not incredible, scenario. What you told me was they were each other's alibi, which I feel is worthy of fuller investigation considering the powerful motives they jointly have."

"Miss Riddell," Pringle said, interjecting before Pauline could continue her defense, "Mrs. Churchill is not a likeable character, I grant you, but you don't give enough thought to the difficulties she experiences from her unfortunate condition."

"Inspector," Pauline said, angrily, "I do not believe Mrs. Churchill to be guilty because of her condition, whatever that is. I don't even know what might be 'her condition' and if I did, I would never do such a thing as you've just suggested."

"I'm pleased to hear that," he said, "but it doesn't absolve you from harassing innocent people in the street when you knew they couldn't have had anything to do with it. We had confirmed their innocence, and I'd told you of that confirmation, though really I shouldn't have done so."

"You told me you had evidence," Pauline said. "That evidence was they were together the whole evening. I assume from this discussion you have since checked further. If that is true, though I haven't heard you say that you have, but if it is, we've both done our jobs, distasteful though it may be to both of us, and uncomfortable as it must have been for the Churchills."

"My point is, Miss Riddell, that the Churchills should not have been treated this way and wouldn't have been but for your nasty snooping."

"I have been asking questions in the village, in pursuit of justice for my client, Inspector, not snooping."

"You aren't a private detective, you haven't got a client and the woman you call your client is dead, probably by her own hand, Miss Riddell," Pringle said. "I must ask you to desist from this unpleasant mischief-making. If you don't, I will consider what the law can do to protect these innocent people from you."

"I think everything that needs to be said has been said, Inspector. Good night," Pauline almost slammed down the handset, seething with indignation. Throughout her investigation, she'd felt guilty because she might have been pointing a finger at an innocent woman, but now all she could feel was a renewed determination for justice. If the police had dug deeper into the alibis the Churchill's had given in the first place, she wouldn't have felt the need to ask them to do more, and she would have been spared this lecture.

She returned to the living room and slumped down into her chair. Jem, who'd been resting on the floor when she came in, placed his head on her lap with such a mournful expression she almost laughed.

"Not good news, then?" Mr. Bertram asked.

Pauline shook her head, not daring to speak until she was in command of her tongue.

Finally, she said, "They think I'm being vindictive. I don't know any of these people so how could I be?"

"So, what will you do now?"

"I'll attend the inquest and explain why I'm sure Mrs. Elliott didn't kill herself," Pauline said, "and hope that is enough to have the inquest adjourned again."

Mr. Bertram nodded. "You must do what you think to be right, Pauline. Though that is never an easy path to take."

Pauline laughed, a little unsteadily. "I thought last time was bad," she said, "this is already much worse. He even suggested he'd set the law on me if I didn't stop."

"Then maybe you should stop," Mrs. Bertram said. "Why ruin your life for people you didn't know and make others' lives miserable when you have no evidence that they did anything wrong?"

"I'm sure those two women were killed," Pauline said obstinately. "As my great-uncle Thomas would say 'I feel it in my bones.'"

"Is your great-uncle a detective?" Mr. Bertram asked.

Pauline shook her head. "No," she said, "he's a retired sea captain. He went around Cape Horn on a sailing ship, you know."

Mr. Bertram laughed. "That is impressive, I grant you, but how does it relate to the mysterious deaths of these two old ladies?"

Pauline grinned. "It doesn't. I'm just saying my great-uncle knows when the weather is going to change by a feeling he gets. That's how I know what happened isn't natural."

"The coroner will not be impressed," Mr. Bertram said. "I wouldn't mention great-uncle Thomas in your evidence."

"I won't but I will try to persuade the coroner to wait, nevertheless."

Jem nudged her hand with his nose, and she turned her attention to him. "You're like 'tat doggie in the window the Beverley sisters were singing about a few minutes ago," Pauline said. Unusually for the Bertrams, tonight they had the radio playing popular music and the Christmas songs were still being played.

"The Beverley Sisters were singing *I saw mummy kissing Santa Claus*, dear," Mrs. Bertram said, displaying more knowledge of popular music than Pauline would have expected. "It was Patti Page who was singing about the dog in the window and that was some time before."

Pauline laughed; all her upset was gone. Between Jem and Mrs. Bertram, the world had righted itself.

16

THE INQUEST

THE DAY of the inquest was a bad one for Pauline. First the weather was awful. January in northern England is rarely good, but this was poor even by its low standards. A driving wind battered icy sleet against the car's windshield as she drove through the gloom. Low clouds blotted out what little sun there might have been. The car's wheels slipped and slithered through the slush building up on the roads, until Pauline wished she'd never set out. She was still a new driver and was struggling to get used to driving in these conditions.

When she arrived at the village hall, where the inquest was to be held, she found nowhere to park. Everyone had come out to watch the proceedings. She parked about a quarter of a mile down the road and walked back, getting drenched in the icy deluge in the process. Inside, the dozens of people, still in their coats, hats, and scarves, were as chilled as she was for there was no heating on. The custodian couldn't get the ancient boiler lit.

Worse was to follow as she heard Inspector Pringle outline the results of the investigation. There was no doubt how the coroner would decide. If her own testimony couldn't turn the tables, suicide was going to be the inquest's finding.

She did her best, reiterating everything Mrs. Elliott had told her and the peculiar circumstances of her finding of the body. She suggested several ways that Mrs. Elliott might have been killed that could still fit in the information the police had provided, but it made no difference. The coroner, without actually being sarcastic, brushed her 'possibilities' aside. Truth be told, as Pauline listened to the coroner's finding of 'suicide while the balance of the mind was disturbed,' she was just pleased to see it ended so she could get home, get out of her wet clothes and into a hot bath. She had no doubt the coroner felt the same way.

Driving home was, in some ways, the exact reverse of her drive to the inquest. Then she'd been hopeful, and the weather had been lousy. Now the weather was better, the roads drier, but her mood was lousy. Her mood wasn't improved when she entered the Bertram's house and Mrs. Bertram began fussing before Pauline even had her coat off.

"I'm fine," Pauline said sharply when told to go straight upstairs and change out of her wet clothes as if she were a five-year-old.

'You're not fine," Mrs. Bertram said. "You're blue and your teeth are chattering. You get undressed while I run you a hot bath."

Pauline wanted to scream but looking in the hall mirror she could see why Mrs. Bertram was anxious. She did look ill.

"I can run a bath," Pauline said, making one last bid for some measure of independence. It was too late. Mrs. Bertram was already halfway up the stairs. Pauline followed, shaking her head in frustration. She must find somewhere to live before she and the Bertrams were locked into this parent and child relationship she could already see developing. It was hard on them when they'd lost their only child, but Pauline couldn't let herself become his replacement.

She lay in the bath brooding. What was it about her that made elderly women believe she was a child? Her mother and now Mrs. Bertram. Did she seem childlike to them? Was she presenting herself as being incapable? As the warmth soaked into her, her gloom dispersed. A place of her own was what she needed. The sooner the better.

Over their evening meal, Pauline told them what had happened at the inquest.

'I am glad it's over," Mrs. Bertram said. "I don't like the idea of you investigating any more murders. You could have been killed last time and this time, if there had been a murderer, could have ended the same way."

When the meal was over, Pauline said she wanted an early night and retired to her room, wishing she could talk to someone who understood her wish to be something more than a secretary. She considered phoning Inspector Ramsay. He would also prefer she didn't involve herself in dangerous crimes, but he at least wouldn't say so.

17

RAMSAY GIVES HOPE

NEXT DAY, after returning from work, she did call him.

"I'm not at all happy with the coroner's verdict," she told him.

Ramsay laughed. "When I heard from Inspector Pringle what the finding was," he said, "I expected to hear from you immediately. You've disappointed me. It's been almost twenty-four hours."

Pauline smiled in spite of herself. "I couldn't call earlier," she said. "I was at work."

"I didn't take that into account," he agreed. "What is it you hope I can do for you, Miss Riddell?"

"Advise me on how I can overturn that inquest finding."

"As always, find evidence to show it is wrong," Ramsay said. "It will be hard in this case. The evidence supports suicide. Only suppositions point in other directions."

"The police won't be continuing their investigation?" Pauline asked.

"Not unless new evidence is brought forward."

"Then I'll find some," Pauline said.

"Are you really so sure?" Ramsay asked. "You never met

the woman. Even if you had met her that day, you still would have no idea what was really going through her mind."

"I may not know what was really going through her mind," Pauline said, "but I'm sure of what was *not* going through her mind and that was suicide."

"Oh dear," Ramsay said. "I was hoping for a quiet winter without serious unpleasantness. A nice little shoplifting or the like."

"After our adventure last autumn," Pauline said, in mock surprise. "You can't want that. I don't believe it."

"This isn't the best place to talk," Ramsay said. "Where shall we meet?"

"The teashop in the Central Arcade in an hour," Pauline said. "If anyone sees us, you can say I'm an informant."

He laughed. "Informants aren't usually seen so publicly," he said. "One hour, it is."

Inspector Ramsay had barely taken his seat before Pauline said, "I would like your advice on how to proceed."

"Pauline," Ramsay said, almost despairingly, "why can't you accept the evidence and conclude you were wrong?"

"Because I'm not," Pauline said. "She was killed, and I will get justice for her."

Ramsay sipped his tea as he gazed at her across the rim of his cup. He placed it carefully on its saucer before saying, "I talked the case over with Inspector Pringle and I promise he did everything he should to find wrongdoing. There are oddities about her death, it's true, but nothing points to someone else being involved. There were no fingerprints that shouldn't have been there. The doors were locked, the windows too. Nothing to show anyone other than Mrs. Elliott caused her death. I urge you to leave it and get on with *your* life."

Pauline shook her head. "Mrs. Elliott reached out to me," she said. "I won't fail her."

Ramsay sighed. "I suppose," he said, "it's easier for the police. We always have too many competing cases that we can turn to. For you, there was only this one. But I do urge you to stop before you get yourself into trouble or cause some harm to other people."

"I think I will have to keep going in order to stop harm happening to other people," Pauline said. "I'm growing more convinced that there will be another murder."

"Why would there be another murder?" Ramsay asked.

"It's my third option," Pauline said. "Mrs. Elliot was killed because she'd told people Mrs. Churchill had been killed. Someone was afraid their next murder would be linked to the earlier ones."

"But that person can only be Mrs. Frank Churchill," Ramsay said. "No one else qualifies. And why would she do anything? Killing Mrs. Elliott only raises awareness in the village. Another suspicious death that benefitted her would put her right in the frame. No, it doesn't make sense."

"It does if you consider she's sure the first death is accepted as natural and the second is accepted as suicide," Pauline said. "A third, equally explainable death would be just bad luck. Isn't that what they say? Bad things come in threes?"

"They do indeed say that," Ramsay said. "Has it occurred to you that, if you're correct and you continue to upset everyone, the third death may be your own?"

"That's where you and Inspector Pringle come in," Pauline said. "If it is known the police know what I'm doing and are watching me like a hawk, I should be safe."

"I'll ask Inspector Pringle to make it known," Ramsay said. "But right now, I think you're in more danger of being murdered by Pringle. The Churchill woman tore quite a strip off him after you accosted her in the street. Turning to a more pleasant topic, what do you make of these date squares?"

'Not enough dates," Pauline replied. "You?"

He nodded. "The same," he said, and then continued. "And too fancy by half. Now I like the humble date square. It's simple yet it symbolizes our far-flung trade in its recipe. The dates come from the Middle East, the sugar from the Caribbean, the wheat from Canada and the oats from Scotland, amazing don't you think?"

"I hadn't given it much thought," Pauline said, "but I agree. And so many of our recipes do – have ingredients from all around the world, I mean."

"We're fortunate in the times we live," Ramsay said. "Though sometimes we forget."

"If all of this is to make me give up my determination to find Mrs. Elliott's killer, Inspector," Pauline said, "I can assure you it won't. No matter how wonderful the times we live in, people can't commit murder and get away with it."

Ramsay laughed. "I wasn't trying to influence you," he said, "just ruminating on a subject I hold dear, the perfect date square."

"Good, because I want to know if you're with me or not," Pauline said.

"I'm with you until I'm convinced there is no murder here," Ramsay said. "But this isn't my case. You have to convince Inspector Pringle."

"And I will," Pauline said. "You remember to have him tell the local bobby I'm on the killer's trail. I want to smoke him or her out."

That evening, as she and the Bertrams read their newspapers and books with the radio playing softly in the background, Pauline was startled by Mr. Bertram saying suddenly, "Those idiots!"

"Which idiots in particular, dear?" Mrs. Bertram asked, smiling. Mr. Bertram had little time for half the world he read about in the news and no time for the rest.

"Our Houses of Parliament," he said. "It was bad enough they agreed to commercial television but now they're giving out licenses to any Tom, Dick or Harry who wants to broadcast nonsense to the country." He shook his head in disgust. "It will end badly, you'll see. It will make the cinema look positively highbrow once they get going."

Pauline had only seen brief glimpses of television in the windows of shops selling, or renting, the sets. She hadn't cared much for what she'd seen. She rather agreed with Mr. Bertram.

"I don't know," Mrs. Bertram said. "I think it would be more restful for my eyes than reading and knitting. And we'd see shows from other places, which would be interesting."

"It will lead to the ruination of the land," Mr. Bertram said. "You mark my words."

"Then we have a precarious future ahead of us, dear," Mrs. Bertram said, grinning at Pauline. "Because everything you read in the paper leads to our ruin."

Mr. Bertram harumphed and hid behind the paper, leaving Pauline glad she hadn't been drawn into the discussion. Her own thoughts leaned toward Mr. Bertram's view. Would men strive to achieve when they spent their time watching game shows and the like? Would Edmund Hilary and Sherpa Tensing have conquered Everest last year, if they'd grown up on a diet of frivolous nonsense? Would she be willing to risk her own comfort, her life even, if her days were spent watching advertisements for mundane products? She thought not.

She gave herself a shake. On the other hand, would John Christie have murdered eight people if he'd had more to entertain him in his apartment at Rillington Place? Perhaps Mrs. Bertram was right to be in favor, after all.

18

AN ADMIRABLE YOUNG MAN

THE FOLLOWING SUNDAY AFTERNOON, Betty was in better shape to walk part of the way with Pauline and the dogs. It was fortunate because it gave Pauline the chance to meet another of the villagers.

"Betty, who is that young man watching us?" Pauline asked, as they walked slowly through the village, keeping to the pavement because their usual walking trails were so muddy and slippery.

"Ted Watson," Betty said. "He's Frank Churchill's half-brother."

"I didn't know Churchill had a brother."

"It's a long story," Betty said, waving to the boy as he watched them from the relative comfort of the bus shelter.

"We have all afternoon," Pauline said. "Jem and Ranter won't mind a longer walk." In truth, Jem and Ranter seemed inclined to cross the road and go to the boy.

Seeing Jem's obvious inclination, Betty said, "Ted gets on well with the dogs. He's a nice boy, always helpful, and he loves Ranter. Jem and him get on really well too. I think it's because Ted always gives the dogs treats when they meet."

Pauline laughed. "And I have the job of stopping Jem from going and getting more goodies," she cried. "I'll be in Jem's bad books all the way home."

"We could just walk over and let Jem and Ted say hello."

"We'll do that," Pauline agreed. She checked the road, which was quiet on this January Sunday afternoon, and they crossed.

"Where are you off to, Ted?" Betty asked, as they joined him in the shelter, where Jem and Ranter were investigating Ted's coat pockets.

'Nowhere, Mrs. Johnstone," the boy said, disbursing dog biscuits to the two dogs, while he spoke to the women. "I was at Frank's for dinner and heading home when it looked like rain. I came in the shelter, in case."

"Is your mam all right?"

"As well as can be expected," Ted said, guardedly.

"Jem seems to like you, Ted," Pauline said, watching the lab nuzzle Ted's hands for attention.

"This is Pauline Riddell, Ted," Mrs. Johnstone said. "She's looking after Jem until a good home can be found for him."

Ted nodded, his expression grave. 'I wish I could take him," he said, "but you know how we're fixed."

"Aye," Mrs. Johnstone said. "Your poor mother couldn't manage, that's certain."

"I'll be old enough to work soon," Ted said, defensively.

"And you'll be a good worker and a great help to your mother," Betty said. "We all know that."

Seeing Ted was looking embarrassed by this topic, Pauline asked, "Are you going to join the other boys?" She gestured to the nearby field where two younger boys were kicking a ball at the goal, where an older-looking boy saved it and kicked it back, making the youngsters run the length of the field to retrieve it.

Ted's expression was disdainful. "Nay," he said, "they're nought but bairns."

Amused, Pauline said, "You're hardly an old man, Ted. What makes them so childish you can't join them?"

"All they think on is football, collecting birds' eggs, and petty thieving," Ted said.

"What Ted's referring to," Betty hastily interjected, "is the younger of them over there, the one in the pale jumper, was caught stealing cigarettes at the Post Office."

"Oh dear," Pauline said, "Maybe you're right to avoid them, Ted, but it does seem a shame not to mix with people your own age."

"I've friends at school," Ted said. "They just don't live in our village."

"That's good," Pauline said, smiling, "Now we should be getting on, Betty. Jem and Ranter will eat all Ted's treats and leave none for anyone else if we stay any longer."

"That we should," Betty said. "Give my regards to your mam, Ted."

"Two suspicious deaths and petty theft," Pauline said, grinning. "Mitford seems to be a hot bed of vice."

Betty shook her head. "Nay," she said. "It's nought like that. The youngster was probably trying to get his dad a birthday present and didn't altogether understand why he shouldn't. He's only nine years old, after all."

"Probably," Pauline said. "It always bothers me when I see how much money poorer people spend on cigarettes," she added. "It shouldn't because it isn't my business, but it does."

"Oh, they don't spend so very much," Betty said. "They all roll their own with those little Rizla machines and what use is living if you can't enjoy what gives you pleasure, particularly when you can afford so little of life's luxuries."

"I just know it's bad for people and that bothers me," Pauline said.

Betty laughed. "My Tom had a bad chest," she said. "Every winter I was always trying to get him to go to Dr. Turner, but he rarely did. And why? Because the doctor would lecture him on giving up smoking because of his bronchitis."

"My father refuses to go the doctor when he's ill too," Pauline said. "Says the doctor fusses like an old woman."

"Tom said much the same. He always said they want you to give up all life's daily pleasures so you can live miserably for a year longer."

There was a sadness to Betty's story that made Pauline pause. She was about to find a more productive topic of conversation when Ted's prophecy came true. It began to rain.

"I'm too old to get wet through," Betty said, calling Ranter back to her side. "We'll go back to my place and have a cuppa."

"I'd like that," Pauline said. She particularly wanted to know more about Ted and Frank and how they got on and hoped she could steer the conversation in that direction.

When Betty had stoked up the coal fire, they drew their chairs close, sipped their tea from what was once Betty's best tea service, and Pauline asked how Ted came to be Frank's brother.

"Frank's mother died in childbirth," Betty said, nibbling her Bakewell tart between thoughts, "and Frank's dad was a seaman. Old Mrs. Churchill was childless, and she was the child's aunt, so she offered to look after Frank while his father went back to work. This was 1933 and jobs were too precious to lose, you understand."

Pauline nodded. "I was born then," she said, "though I don't actually remember, I know how it affected my own parents and uncles and aunts."

"Well," Betty said, "old Mrs. Churchill grew so fond of young Frank, she offered to adopt him and that was agreed. It seemed sensible. Frank's dad was always away at sea and there was no one else."

"Frank was fortunate," Pauline said. "He might have ended up in an orphanage or a government care home."

Betty nodded. "And he knew that, "she said. "He was always most fond of his new mother. Anyway, war broke out in 1939 and Frank's dad was on a ship that was torpedoed, 1940, I think."

"Poor man," Pauline said, "I assume he must have survived?"

"He did but his health was gone," Betty said. "He swallowed a lot of oil when he was in the sea waiting for rescue and he couldn't work after."

"When I hear of people like Frank's father, I realize how fortunate I've been in my own life," Pauline said.

"You're young yet, my dear," Betty said. "Don't tempt providence."

"I won't, you can be sure of it."

"Anyway, Frank's father came back to the village to live and he met and married Edie Watson, a nice woman, though a little old and set in her ways by that time. They had a son, Edward, Ted, who we just met. He was their only child because Ted's father died less than a year later."

"Leaving Edie to bring up the boy on her own?" Pauline asked.

Betty nodded. "And she's done a good job. Ted is a treasure. He does odd jobs around the village to help because Edie is living on her widow's pension and the bit she gets from cleaning and laundering for others. They both work hard, and they get by."

"Ted said he'd been to Frank's for his dinner. Is that a regular thing?"

"On Sunday, yes," Betty replied. "Edie's too proud to go but I'm sure it helps her housekeeping to have a growing teenage boy fed one good meal a week."

Pauline laughed. "I remember how much my brothers ate at that age," she said, "so I can believe it is a help."

"It's only since old Mrs. Churchill died, mind. She kept Frank on a tight leash in every way," Betty said.

"She didn't want to share him," Pauline said, smiling.

"That she didn't," Betty said. "Well, one shouldn't speak ill of the dead, so I won't say more but Frank has done the right thing by Ted since she died. He has the lad around quite a lot and often for a square meal."

Pauline considered what she'd heard. Did young Ted resent the way he'd been treated? Unfairly treated by a fate that had made one brother comparatively rich, in this small neighborhood anyhow, and by Mrs. Churchill, who robbed him of a brother's companionship?

"But they are getting along as brothers now, aren't they?" Pauline asked.

"I think so," Betty said. "As far as I can tell."

"I'm glad," Pauline said. "It would be terrible if Mrs. Churchill's insecurity estranged them forever. Family is everything for most people."

"You've an old head on your young shoulders," Betty said. "Many folks don't understand that until they're old."

Pauline smiled. "Perhaps adversity, of the kind Ted has experienced, will spur him on to do great things," she said.

"I'm sure it will," Betty replied. "No one works harder. He runs errands and mows lawns for folks, and he does all the usual country jobs, beating the bushes for the guns in the shooting season and, in the autumn, picking rose hips for the syrup manufacturers and potatoes for farmers. That young man will be rich one day, you mark my words."

Pauline drove home before the darkness descended, mulling over her new information in some disquiet. It seemed wrong to be suspicious about such an estimable character, but she couldn't help it. She stroked Jem's head as he sat in the passenger seat watching the world flashing past in the headlights.

"I wonder, Jem," she said, making him turn to look at her, "is it only because you weren't found dead by Mrs. Elliott's side, and therefore no postmortem was done on you, that we didn't find sleeping draught in your stomach too? You take treats from that young man without considering the consequences. It isn't wise, you know."

Jem chose not to dignify this rebuke with an answer and, as it seemed no further involvement was required from him, he returned to gazing out the window.

"You're right," Pauline said. "There's no motive and how would he get in even if he had a motive. I'm just so keen to prove myself a master detective, I'm now slandering perfectly innocent, and entirely blameworthy, people. I must do better, as too many of my school reports said."

19

PAULINE AND POPPY

As always happened, when Pauline phoned Poppy to meet, they ended up meeting in a pub, which wasn't Pauline's preferred choice. However, she guessed Poppy's flat was unlikely to be a model of good housekeeping and she could hardly ask Poppy to get on a bus and visit her at the Bertrams' house. The Black Bull pub near Poppy's flat was at least clean and respectable.

"The thing is, Poppy," Pauline said, when they'd taken their drinks to a table in the Snug. "There are only three real possibilities here. The first is neither of these deaths is a murder. Mrs. Churchill really did die naturally, and Mrs. Elliott did commit suicide – though I can't for the life of me see why."

"Then she probably didn't," Poppy said.

"Well, I don't think she did, but you have to admit there's that possibility."

"All right," Poppy said, "I'll accept it as a possibility. What are the other two?"

"The second is, Mrs. Churchill died naturally, and Mrs. Elliott was murdered," Pauline said.

"Which is much more likely," Poppy interjected.

"Yes, and that leads to the culprit likely being her daughter or son-in-law. I hope it's him because I didn't like him one bit."

Poppy grinned. "Nowadays, here in the West, we generally try to avoid executing people just because we don't like them," she said.

"Well, I think exceptions could be made," Pauline said, laughing.

"And the third?"

"The third is complicated," Pauline said, serious again. "Both old ladies were murdered and that leads down two different paths. Two separate murderers with two separate killers or one murderer committing both."

"Two separate murderers seem incredible in one small village where the last murder likely took place in the eighteenth century," Poppy suggested.

"I know but I think it is still plausible. What if the death of Mrs. Churchill, and the ease at which it was accepted as natural, encouraged a person into thinking they could kill someone and make it seem, if not natural, at least not murder?"

"Flimsy, if you ask me."

"I just say it isn't as outlandish as two murderers in one small village might otherwise seem," Pauline said.

"And your other 'path' is equally strange," Poppy said. "What connection is there between Mrs. Churchill and Mrs. Elliott that would require them both to die? Unless it's a quarrel from the church parish council or the Women's Institute committee, I don't see anything."

"I think Mrs. Elliott told someone of her suspicions and the killer wanted to shut her up before carrying out another murder. The final victim of her plan – Frank Churchill."

"You've said this before, Pauline," Poppy retorted, "and as I've said before, the idea Frank's wife would kill Frank's mother who was standing in the way of her marrying him, and then go on to kill him to get his house and money is too convoluted to exist anywhere outside a novel."

Pauline shook her head. "I don't agree. It isn't convoluted at all. Once she'd found how easy it was to kill the mother to marry the son, the idea of killing the son to get everything for herself would have grown naturally in her mind. It didn't need to be planned at all."

"I hate to tell you," Poppy said, "but of your three options, I'm now leaning toward the first one. No murder. Just a suicide that is hard to explain."

"It's more than hard to explain," Pauline retorted. "It's impossible."

"Only because you think you're so important even people who've never met you would hang around just so they could. Why can't it be she was desperate when she wrote, grew more desperate as the days passed, and then when you spoke on the phone, realized she'd made a terrible mistake in writing to you and ended it all before she had to take it any further."

Pauline blushed at Poppy's jibe and said sharply, "I'm not as conceited as you imagine. She would at least want to tell her daughter why she wanted to go. She would leave an explanation."

"Yet Inspector Pringle says many don't."

"And she wouldn't have left Jem alone like that," Pauline added.

"Then, we have to look at your second option," Poppy said, "because the third one is too much."

"Good," Pauline replied. "I hoped you'd say that. What can you find out about the daughter and the son-in-law?"

"Pauline," Poppy said. "I'm busy. I keep telling you and you don't listen. We have something big."

"In Morpeth?" Pauline exclaimed. Then seeing the hurt look in Poppy's eyes, said, "Sorry. I know it's important to you, but this will be too, when we discover the truth."

Poppy sighed. "I am getting around to it," she said, "but it won't be easy. These aren't public figures."

"You do the research into what there is in the records," Pauline said. "I'm going to ask around the village."

Poppy's expression showed her alarm. "You'll stir up a hornet's nest if you do that," she said. "It's a small village. They'll soon hear you're asking about them and, if they are murderers, you'll be their next target."

"Pooh," Pauline said. "I've been targeted by trained spies and lived to tell the tale. They don't frighten me."

"It isn't just violence though, Pauline," Poppy argued. "They can rightly say you're slandering them or whatever and turn the police on you. You can't go around pointing fingers that way."

Pauline frowned. Poppy was right. Asking questions in a village as small as Mitford would cause trouble.

"I have one contact who won't tell," she said, at last. "I'll see what Betty knows and hope you can dig up some dirt."

"Dirt? They're two ordinary people in a small village, Pauline. Everybody would know if there was any dirt," Poppy said.

"The son-in-law isn't local. His name's Boothroyd. That's from Yorkshire or Lancashire," Pauline said stubbornly.

"His family could have moved here any time these past five hundred years. I should remind you, not everyone from Yorkshire, or even Lancashire, is a monster. I'm told they've settled down over the centuries and some of them are quite civilized. The Riddells, for example."

"Yes, yes," Pauline said, grinning. "I wasn't suggesting he was bad because he came from outside, only that he may have things in his past that the local people don't know about. That even his wife may not know."

"This is all going to be thin gruel," Poppy said. "We haven't the resources for a proper search."

"Which is why I'm going to set Inspectors Pringle or Ramsay onto it."

"You do know they don't do work for private individuals, don't you?" Poppy said. "They'll send you off with a flea in your ear."

"I'll approach them carefully," Pauline said. "Explain my lines of enquiry and offer to share if they will reciprocate. It will be fine." She spoke confidently but she knew Poppy was right. The police would not help unless she could needle or cajole them into doing it.

20

WINNING OVER INSPECTOR PRINGLE?

"Inspector Pringle," Pauline said, as she was shown into his office at the Morpeth headquarters after leaving Poppy. "I hope you don't mind me dropping in like this after what you said last time I was here, but I've been thinking a lot about the deaths of those two elderly ladies, particularly that of Mrs. Elliott, who requested my help."

Pringle's expression was as unwelcoming as she'd expected but he asked her to sit down, and Pauline felt that was a good start. He hadn't thrown her out without listening, after all.

"What is it you wanted to say, Miss Riddell," he said, when she was seated.

"Well," Pauline began, "it's like this. I can't believe Mrs. Elliott committed suicide and that leads me to wonder who benefits. There's only her daughter and husband. I wondered if you'd considered this?"

"We have to consider all possibilities, Miss Riddell, and we have considered them," he said, "including the unlikely ones you are continually raising."

"Is it so unlikely though?" Pauline persisted. "They're

not rich and coming into Mrs. Elliott's estate sooner rather than later must have been blessing for them, don't you think?"

"But they weren't really poor either, Miss Riddell," Pringle replied, "and very few people murder their parent to get an inheritance early."

"But you have looked into it?" Pauline asked.

"We looked into the possibility, yes," Pringle said. "They were together, at their home, at the time Mrs. Elliott died and there's nothing in their backgrounds that would suggest murderous tendencies."

"I am glad," Pauline said. "That will save me a lot of work."

"You shouldn't be doing any 'work' on this, Miss Riddell. It's a police matter."

"She was my client, Inspector. I can't let her death release me of all responsibility toward her."

"She was not your client Miss Riddell. You have no need to do anything on her behalf. She is beyond your help now," Pringle said severely.

"Are you so convinced it was suicide, Inspector?" Pauline asked, deciding not to correct his mistaken understanding of what she considered a contract.

"I was skeptical at first, I admit," Pringle said, "but with every passing day I become surer it was suicide, however unusual the circumstances."

"Is your look into the background of the beneficiaries part of that growing belief, Inspector?"

"Miss Riddell," he said firmly now, "I'm not going to tell you private details of their lives any more than I would tell them about your private life. Suffice to say, they are both what they seem. Ordinary, decent people struggling with life as it is in the aftermath of a horrific war. There's nothing to suggest anything more. Now, good day. I have work to do."

Pauline left the building and headed back to her car, parked opposite the building. She was pleased with the results of her first effort. It didn't entirely convince her that her two suspects were innocent but there didn't seem to be a large dark secret waiting to be revealed for it sounded like the police hadn't found one. But her continued pressing would surely keep the police looking too. They wouldn't want to have her solve the case and it come out they weren't even working on it.

Maybe Poppy would have better luck. She wondered if Inspector Ramsay would also be in his office in Newcastle on this Sunday afternoon. He usually was.

21

RAMSAY PROVIDES BALANCE

"Miss Riddell, what a nice surprise," Ramsay said when she was ushered into his office.

"I thought we'd dispensed with the formality, Inspector," Pauline said. "I'm more than an ordinary member of the public to you now, surely."

"Ah," Ramsay said, grinning. "I'm being formal because I have a good idea why you're here and I want to formally warn you I will not be used to further your private investigator credentials."

"Inspector Pringle phoned you, did he?"

"He did."

"Ah. I thought he might," Pauline said, smiling despite herself.

"And you hoped he hadn't," Ramsay said.

"Yes, that too."

"You wanted him to look into the beneficiaries of her will, I guess," Ramsay said.

"I did and he tells me he has done that, which was a great relief for I couldn't easily manage. I don't have access to all sorts of files," Pauline said.

"But do you really think they killed her?" Ramsay asked.

Pauline outlined the different theories she'd shared with Poppy and, when she finished, said, "You can see the most plausible theory, if there's no suicide, is that the daughter and or her husband killed her."

"It's not my case," Ramsay said, "but why isn't your first option the most likely? After all, everything points to one natural death and one suicide."

"This is why I came here," Pauline said. "I wanted to hear what you would think most likely and your thoughts on how to proceed if the first option wasn't the preferred one."

"What I think is, it isn't my case and it's not yours either," Ramsay said, "but, if it were my case, I'd start with your second option because the third seems extremely unlikely."

Pauline nodded. "And how would you proceed with investigating the possible murder of Mrs. Elliott?"

"Exactly as Inspector Pringle is doing," Ramsay said. "Look into the background of those who have a motive, attempt to discover if there are others with a motive, and see who had the means and the opportunity."

"The obvious people with motive are the daughter and son-in-law," Pauline said, "but I see the possibility of a third party if Mrs. Churchill was also murdered."

"And what did Inspector Pringle think about that?"

Pauline grimaced. "He sees no reason to believe she was murdered so that rules out the Churchills."

"And if we're following the second option," Ramsay said, "then you have no reason to imagine a motive there either."

Pauline frowned. That was true but she couldn't shake off her suspicions. "Do you know what I find most frustrating about this?" she said. "There's nothing physical for me to do. Last time, I could follow the culprits, secretly watch them, eavesdrop on their doings, and so on," she finished lamely, suddenly remembering she was talking to a police officer who might take exception to confessions of trespassing, housebreaking and burglary.

Ramsay laughed. "As I recall, you complained bitterly at the boredom of watching houses," he said.

"It's true," Pauline agreed, "but only because I didn't know any better. Now there's nothing and nobody to watch and it is maddening."

"It's too cold for all that surveillance stuff anyway," Ramsay said. "I suggest you confine yourself to the Public Records Office where you may learn something interesting and keep warm while doing it."

"All that will tell me is dull stuff. It won't tell me if the son-in-law has a criminal background, for example."

"Your friend Poppy can find that out," Ramsay said.

"So, he does?" Pauline said. "What for?"

"Miss Riddell," Ramsay said sternly, "I thought I'd explained my position quite clearly at the start of this conversation."

"Poppy will find out anyhow, so it isn't as if you're telling me anything I won't know soon enough."

"Moving right along," Ramsay said, "the Public Records can tell you about wills once they're over and done with."

"Would that help?"

"I've no idea, Pauline. I'm just trying to keep you safely indoors and prevent you provoking someone to righteous anger, to be honest."

"I could also confirm the aspirin and sleeping draught she took was sold to Mrs. Elliott and not the daughter and her husband," Pauline said, "but maybe that has already been done?"

"It has. You needn't annoy the local chemists with

enquiries of that nature. They wouldn't like the thought of some busybody trying to make it their fault."

"It's going to be suicide in the end, isn't it?" Pauline said, despondently.

"I'm afraid so. I don't see any other outcome."

"Even if there are people with a motive? A good motive?"

"There are always people with a motive and often means and opportunity, but that doesn't mean they actually did anything wrong," Ramsay said. "You'd be surprised how many people I murder in my mind daily. I suspect everyone feels the same way."

Pauline grinned. "There are people at work..." she said and stopped. "Perhaps, you're right. I'm reading too much into what is really quite a simple affair."

"I think you saw Mrs. Elliott's letter as a chance to relive the excitement, and dare I say it, the fame you garnered on solving your friend Marjorie's murder. Now that there is no mystery, you're clutching at straws to invent one."

Pauline was about to vehemently deny this rebuke but didn't. It was likely the truth. Poppy's words came back to her, 'I doubt they've had a murder there since the Eighteenth Century.'

"From your experience," she asked, "are there many murders in Northumbrian villages in any year?"

"I'm a city cop," Ramsay said, "but from my reading of the annual crime figures for the surrounding areas, they are very rare. And two in one village in one year is unheard of. I doubt it's happened since the border wars ended in the Union of the Crowns."

"Your words of good sense have depressed me a little," Pauline said, rising and gathering her gloves and bag, "But you have not dissuaded me. I shall continue searching for evidence, and when I find it, you will have to re-open the case."

She left his office and headed home, not as despondent as she'd led Inspector Ramsay to believe. She did have people she could interview, and she would start with Dr. Turner. He signed Mrs. Churchill's death certificate. Was he as sure now that he got that right as he was on the day he signed it? Now that another old lady in his practice had died mysteriously.

22

MISS RIDDELL LOSING FRIENDS

"Good evening, Dr. Turner," Pauline said next evening as she entered his surgery. She'd driven straight from work to be in his surgery early, since noting the times on her last visit to the village.

"Good evening, Miss Riddell," he replied. "This is a cold, blustery night to be out and about."

"I've been visiting Mrs. Johnstone," Pauline lied, "and I saw you had an evening surgery, so I called in."

"Aren't you feeling well?"

"I'm perfectly healthy," Pauline said. "I wanted to ask you about old Mrs. Churchill's death."

"Why?" he replied, his expression hardening and the tone of his voice growing decidedly colder.

"I wanted to know if you had doubts about her death being of natural causes or if you've had doubts since?"

"Miss Riddell," he replied, "I'm a qualified doctor and have served this community for many years. Mrs. Churchill's death was not a surprise to me or anyone, quite the reverse, in fact. The fact she lived as long as she did was a constant surprise to all of us."

"I'm not questioning your credentials or competence, Doctor," Pauline said. "It's just when we expect someone to die, and then they do die, we're not as inclined to look for other possibilities."

"She died peacefully in her sleep and there were no signs to suggest otherwise," Turner said, his voice low and his anger barely in check. "She'd already lived longer than I would have imagined possible, kept going by her love of her son and his care and affection for her. To suggest any kind of wrongdoing and particularly wrongdoing by him is a monstrous allegation without any foundation in truth."

"Yet Mrs. Elliott thought otherwise."

"Mrs. Elliott was upset at the death of her friend," Turner said. "I think we all understand that in grief we imagine and say things that are not true, but we would like them to be true. Allowances have to be made."

"There was no postmortem?"

Turner's anger at this was blindingly clear. "There was not and there was no need for one," he said. "Now if you've nothing sensible to say and you aren't here as a patient, leave and let me get on with attending to people who are ill."

"I'm sorry to have upset you, Dr. Turner," Pauline said, "I'm not questioning your abilities. I only want to be sure there was no other explanation for her death."

"Your professions of sorrow are as insulting as your questions were," Turner said. "Please, leave and don't come back. Go!" He vehemently pointed at the door.

Pauline left, wondering if his anger hid an unquiet conscience. Or if he was just angered at having his competence questioned. She thought probably the latter and couldn't help feeling she understood how he felt. She didn't like it whenever someone suggested she wasn't a true detective. After all, she was just starting out, not well into a respectable career.

23

WHO KNOWS THE VILLAGE AFTER NIGHTFALL?

SUNDAY AFTERNOON, bright and frosty, was a pleasant change from the usual leaden skies with downpours that had been her lot on her previous visits to Betty. Here, away from the city, the hoar frost that had coated every branch, twig, and blade of grass in the morning delighted her as she'd walked through the churchyard to the service, and still lingered thanks to the shade cast by the trees and bushes. Where the pale sunlight caught it, light twinkled or glowed in the ice crystals like fairyland in a children's book, she thought, with a sad smile for days long since lost.

As Pauline approached the cottage, she saw Ted Watson carrying a bundle of logs into the coal shed.

"Hello, Ted," Pauline said. "Are you helping out?"

"Aye," he replied. "Mrs. Johnstone needs more fuel than she can afford. Coal being so expensive these days."

Pauline smiled at the idea of a thirteen-year-old having any idea of the price of coal now or in the past. "It's certainly expensive," she said. "I don't buy it but the couple I rent from do and they tell me it is."

Then There Were ... Two Murders? 113

Betty appeared at the door, dressed in an old army greatcoat and thick boots. "I thought I heard voices," she said. "Hello, Pauline, come in."

Pauline followed her into the living room where a larger than usual fire glowed in the grate.

"You've always told me you didn't like the heat," Pauline said, concerned now that she'd accepted the old woman's words as being the whole truth and, unlike young Ted, she'd made no effort to enquire further.

"Well, it's true but I do like it warmer than I've been able to afford this winter. The coal man charges such a lot for delivering up the small lane to my house."

"And Ted came to your aid," Pauline said.

"Someone told him of my difficulty," Betty said. "He collects dead wood for his own mother. He says it's no bother to collect a little more for me."

She'd just finished speaking when Ted entered the house. "I'm finished for now, Mrs. Johnstone," he called from the door.

"Come in and get warm, Ted," Betty shouted.

"Nay, you have visitors, I'll come again another day and we can chat then." The door opened and closed again, and he was gone.

"This is new," Pauline said.

"Yes," Betty replied, "he came by yesterday to ask if I needed help. I said no, of course not. Poor lad, he has no time for himself, but he insisted. I'll pay him something."

"And I'm here to help you by taking Ranter for his Sunday walk with Jem," Pauline said. "Will you be joining us today?"

Betty shook her head and laughed. "Look at that fire," she said. 'I haven't seen a blaze like that since I don't know when. I'll stay and enjoy it. You go. Maybe Ranter and Jem will make the day complete with that rabbit we always talk about, but never appears."

"I think the dogs are actually friends with the rabbits," Pauline said. "I've never known such well-behaved dogs. On the farm, we were always plagued by visitors and their dogs worrying the sheep."

"From what I hear on the radio," Betty said. "We shouldn't eat them, even if they were to catch one. There's a disease been found in rabbits down south and it's killing them."

Pauline nodded. "I heard that too," she said. "It's called myxomatosis, or something like that. Very nasty, so they say. I don't think we have it up here though."

"Well, you and the dogs should keep away from them just in case, and don't be out too long," Betty said, "I have a nice Dundee cake to go with our afternoon tea."

"How did you afford the ingredients?" Pauline asked, laughing, "or did Ted bring those too?"

Betty shook her head. "Neither of those," she said. "My daughter visited yesterday and brought it."

"Then I'll be sure to be back in good time," Pauline said, rising and heading for the door where the two dogs were waiting patiently to go. She opened the door and they scooted out.

"They will catch a rabbit today, now we've been told not to eat them," she said, waving goodbye to Betty. "There was a lot of energy in that exit."

Pauline had no intention of allowing the dogs anywhere near the fields, however. The Boothroyds were now living in Mrs. Elliott's house and she wanted to learn what she could about them. When she'd spoken to Poppy and Ramsay about surveillance not being possible, she'd meant in a formal way. But passing a house and discovering what she could about the new owners from it was a normal, even natural, thing to do.

Her passing surveillance of the house, however, proved to be as dull as Poppy and Ramsay would have told her it would be. Without leaves on the surrounding trees, it was easy to see there weren't even new curtains at the windows to signal a change of ownership. It seemed Evelyn Boothroyd wasn't in a hurry to make changes from her mother's taste. Or perhaps, they just didn't have the money to spend. Calling the dogs to heel, Pauline made her way back to Betty's cottage. The sun may have been shining but a sharp wind had sprung up, making its way straight down from the North Pole, Pauline thought, as she quickened her pace in anticipation of hot tea and fruit cake.

"Betty," Pauline said, when they were sat in front of the fire eating an excellent Dundee cake, "if I wanted to know what went on in the village after dark, who would I speak to?"

"Why would you want to know that, dear?" Betty asked.

"Mrs. Elliott died late in the day on the Friday before I was to meet with her," Pauline said. "This is winter so few people were out and about, I'm sure, but maybe someone was and could tell me if anyone else was."

"You'd best talk to Len, our resident poacher and general ne'er-do-well," Betty said. "Or Ted, he's always about."

"Where would I find Len?"

"He lives in the old smithy now," Betty replied. "He moved in when June Churchill moved her workshop out."

"So, she had her workshop elsewhere before?"

"Of course, dear. Old Mrs. Churchill had no time for her

and would never have allowed her to use the outhouse she uses now."

"I'll talk to Len before I leave today," Pauline said.

"Be sure you have Jem with you," Betty said. "Len's all right generally but if he gets money, he gets drunk and he isn't a nice drunk."

"I will. You say Ted is often out and about after dark too? Is that wise? He's only a boy, after all," Pauline said,

"Oh, Ted can look after himself. He already does the same work as a man, they say," Betty said. "Lots of the small jobs he does don't stop when the light goes."

"I suppose. How will I find the old smithy?" Pauline asked. "I don't think I've seen it."

"It's along the road past the old castle ruin," Betty said. "It's no more than a tumbled down shed now but they say it was once a blacksmith's workshop."

"I'll go the moment I've finished my tea," Pauline said, "before it gets too dark."

"Aye, he'll be about then, right enough," Betty said, laughing.

Betty was right. Len was outside his home, almost sniffing the air, as she and Jem arrived.

"Hello," she said brightly, "are you Len?"

"And who might you be?" the man asked suspiciously.

"I'm Jem's walking companion," Pauline said, pointing to him, "until he finds a new home."

"You're that nosey parker from town," he said. "I recognize you now."

"Then I hope you'll also recognize I'm trying to do right by Mrs. Elliott," Pauline said.

"And you've come to lay the blame on me, I'll warrant."

"No, I have not," Pauline said, brusquely. "I thought you

might have seen something the night she died that would help me explain her death."

"Why would I do that? She was nothing to me," he said.

"Nor to me but I think suspicious deaths need to be explained," Pauline said. "After all, if one person living on their own can die in mysterious circumstances, why not another?"

"I can look after myself," he said, but then added, "but I see what you mean."

"I'm glad. Perhaps then you'll think about that night for me," Pauline said. "Were you out and about?"

"I'm out and about most nights and most nights are much the same as the others," he said.

"All right," Pauline said, "have there been nights where you saw or heard something or someone that you didn't expect to see? Someone you never saw out before or since?"

The man thought, his face twisting as though just the effort was painful. Pauline waited, stroking Jem to keep him quiet. She noticed Jem had accepted her approaching Len without any complaint. Jem at least didn't dislike him.

"There are sometimes things," the man said, at last, "but I think the one that you want to hear is I saw yon Useless Boothroyd out around then. He's often out and about late. Only I can't recall which night."

Pauline, still smiling at Len's name for Eustace Boothroyd, said, "Was it the night before you saw me, the doctor, the police, and the ambulance at Mrs. Elliott's house?"

He shook his head. "That's the thing, I can't be sure. It likely was but I can't say for certain."

"Did you tell the police about this?"

"The police?" he asked. "Nay, they didn't ask me ought and I told them nought."

"They didn't question you?" Pauline said.

"Nay, why should they?"

"Well, you're known to be out on an evening, I thought it likely they would," Pauline said. "Was there anything else about the night you saw Boothroyd that you remember? Maybe that could help establish the date."

Len once again thought deeply, before saying, "Nay, nought comes to mind. It was a regular Friday night."

Pauline's heart leapt but she kept her expression calm. "You know it was a Friday?" she asked.

"Oh, aye. I went to the Angler Arms, which I do on Friday if I've got money to spend."

"You don't always have money to spend?" Pauline asked.

He laughed. "That I don't," he said.

"So how did you have money that night?"

"Ah," he said, "on account of two pheasant I'd sold."

"Can you remember when that was?"

"It were a Friday," he said, "but that's as far as I remember."

"The person you sold them to may remember which Friday that was," Pauline said.

He nodded. "Aye, I reckon they would."

"Can you ask them for me? I'm sure they won't want me asking about them buying pheasants," Pauline said.

"I could, if it was worth my while," he said.

Pauline was tempted to say she would tell the police what they just discussed but realized the information would never come out if she did.

"One pound, if you give me the date when you sold those pheasants," she said. "I'll be here tomorrow night."

He shook his head. "Not tomorrow night," he said. "You walk the dog every Sunday, I've seen you. Next Sunday and bring the money."

"I will. Thank you, Len," Pauline replied. "I hope this is to both our benefits."

Walking back to her car, it was all Pauline could do not to sing, she felt so elated. Jem too seemed happier; pleased to be on the move, he practically frolicked by her side.

24

PREPARING FOR THE FUTURE

THE FOLLOWING Sunday seemed years away, as Pauline went to work and came home without any way of progressing her investigation and with the tantalizing prospect of real evidence to suggest the Boothroyds may have had means and opportunity as well as motive just outside her grasp.

Finally, she couldn't stand the wait any longer and called Inspector Ramsay, whose amusement at her call was evident the moment he answered the phone.

"Good evening, Pauline," he said. "I hope this is a purely social call and nothing to do with suicides in Mitford."

"Of course, it isn't social," Pauline said. "I wouldn't waste your time that way. I'm sure you know Inspector Pringle interviewed the Boothroyds and, that being the case, I thought you may know more about what they were doing the night when Mrs. Elliott died." More than Pringle told me, anyway, Pauline thought grimly.

"The Boothroyds were the daughter and son-in-law, is that right?"

"Who else?"

"You'll have to forgive me," Ramsay said laughing. "This

isn't my case, I'm busy with my own work, and I talked this over with Inspector Pringle one afternoon for an hour almost a month ago. I can't remember everyone in your small mystery."

Pauline blushed and was pleased he wasn't there to see it. "I'm sorry," she said. "I tend to forget. I'm so wrapped up in this I assume everyone else is. Yes, the daughter and son-in-law."

"They were at home, listening to the radio. They live quiet retired lives, it seems."

"They did then," Pauline said sharply. "Now they have money, I hear they're becoming more sociable."

"Jealousy is a sin, Miss Riddell. I thought you knew that," Ramsay said. "Why shouldn't people go out more when their circumstances change for the better?"

Pauline ignored his teasing, though it did hit its mark. She realized that because she believed them guilty, she hated the thought they were benefitting from their ill-gotten gains. When she'd recovered her thoughts, she said, "So, they didn't go out at all?"

"They say not."

"That's all I need to know," Pauline said. "I'll let you get back to all that work you have on your plate. Bye."

After she hung up, she whispered, "Please let it be that night. Please."

It was only Wednesday evening so she had four more days to wait before she would learn if Boothroyd was out of the house on the night of Mrs. Elliott's death and lied about it. She returned to the living room where the Bertrams were listening to a play on the BBC. It clearly wasn't a gripping drama for Mr. Bertram was dozing and Mrs. Bertram was reading the local evening newspaper.

"There's something here that might interest you,

Pauline," Mrs. Bertram said, as Pauline was preparing to sit down. She held out the paper, pointing to an advertisement at the bottom of the page.

For a moment, Pauline couldn't imagine why any of the items would interest her until she saw it. It was posted by the YWCA, Young Woman's Christian Association, offering a self-defense course for women.

"You said you would need this if you continued investigating murders," Mrs. Bertram reminded her.

"I did. I'd forgotten," Pauline said, "and it does interest me. I'll drop in there tomorrow night and sign up for the spring session. Thank you."

"I wish you would make it unnecessary," Mrs. Bertram said, "by taking no further interest in such an unpleasant side of life."

"Doesn't the psalm say, 'not forever in green pastures, would we ask our way to be, but for strength to face the dangers and live our lives courageously,'" Pauline asked mischievously.

"It does, dear, but it doesn't say go out looking for danger, as you well know."

Pauline smiled her agreement, scratched the top of Jem's head and returned to her new book, recommended to her by Dr. Enderby, *Casino Royale*. He said as she liked catching spies, she might like this because apparently the author had been in the Secret Service during the last war and knew what he was talking about. Pauline hadn't read far and was already of the opinion it confirmed her own and her friend Inspector Ramsay's jaundiced view of Secret Service people. They weren't nice and the book's hero, James Bond, seemed like one of the least pleasant of them all. She was willing to acknowledge he was at least fighting for our side, unlike Murdock who'd been selling them out.

The following days, driving to and from work, her car slid in slush or slipped on ice so often, she felt by the end of February, she could participate in an Alpine winter car rally – and win. Somehow, she avoided hitting the other vehicles on the road, and the pedestrians, telegraph poles, lamp standards, and every other impediment her fellow citizens placed along her route.

By Saturday's drive home from work, she was tempted to point out to Mrs. Bertram that dangers weren't limited to just murderers. Winter roads were much worse. She didn't for she knew that good woman would suggest she give up driving if she wasn't confident enough to do it safely and that would lead to an argument.

"You won't be going to Mitford tomorrow, I hope, dear," Mrs. Bertram said, when Pauline entered the house. "The roads are awful, Mr. Bertram says, and they'll be worse in the country."

"Does he?" Pauline said, with cool surprise. "I didn't find them so." She went straight upstairs after saying this because she wasn't certain she could maintain a straight face.

25

FINALLY GETTING SOMEWHERE?

Pauline drove slowly and carefully out of town and straight to the old smithy, parking outside. The snow was deeper out in the country, the slush on the roadsides frozen. Mrs. Bertram had been right about that. She hammered on the door, and called, "Len," as loudly as she could.

As she waited for Len to appear she looked across the field behind the smithy where the old, ruined castle on its mound was a Christmas card picture. It only needed a robin and a holly bush to complete the scene.

The door opened and Len appraised her with jaundiced eyes. "Come in," he said, after what seemed like an eternity to Pauline who was frozen just waiting.

Inside was a mess. There was no getting around it. And it smelled stuffy, musty. Her nose wrinkled in disgust.

"Have you got the money?" Len demanded.

"Have you the information?"

"Aye but you'll get nought until I see your brass," he said.

Pauline had expected this and, opening her purse, she drew out a ten-shilling note. "Half now," she said, "and the rest when you've told me what you've learned." She held it out to him, and he grabbed it greedily.

"It were the night before Mrs. Elliott's body was found," he said. "My buyers remembered because they wondered later if I had anything to do with it, as I'd come to them late on Friday night. I wanted to punch him in the face when he said that," Len added, "but I reckoned he hadn't told the police so it were all right."

"I'll need you to tell the police this," Pauline said, "and I need their names. You don't have to say you were selling them poached birds, just that you met and talked the night you saw Boothroyd outdoors and it was the night Mrs. Elliott died."

Len considered and then nodded. The lure of how much drink the second ten-shillings would buy him was overwhelming. "The Farquarsons," he said. "They live in number four."

"Thank you, Len," Pauline said. "One more thing," she added, "where exactly did you see Boothroyd?"

"Where this lane meets the road," Len said.

"And was this before or after you'd delivered the pheasants to the Farquarsons?"

"It were after. Around nine o'clock, I reckon," Len said, holding out his hand for the note that Pauline was not yet offering.

Judging it best to leave the rest to the police, Pauline handed over the note and turned to go.

"Hey, miss," Len said, as she was about to open the door, "if you can't keep Jem, I'll be happy to. He's a great dog, that one."

"He is," Pauline said. "I may have to take you up on that offer one day. Though I'll be sorry to do so."

At Betty's cottage, Jem and Ranter renewed acquaintances by running around the snow-covered garden and following the tracks of rabbits to their exit points through the tumbled down walls.

"Is Ted around?" Pauline asked, after she and Betty had exchanged greetings.

"He's collecting wood. He'll be back soon," Betty replied.

"I'll wait before my walk then," Pauline said. "I have a question for him about the night Mrs. Elliott died."

"The kettle's boiled and the dogs can run off their energy while we enjoy some shortbread," Betty said.

"Do you always have baked goods or are you making them especially for me?" Pauline asked, uncomfortably aware her visits may be driving the old lady to spend money she didn't have on entertaining her.

"I bake for myself," Betty said, leading the way into the house, "but I do a little more now I have company. There's no pleasure in baking for myself."

This was what Pauline had feared. "I'll bring the snacks next Sunday," she said. "Do you like currant slice? I make a good one, though I say so myself. I even make a slice using sweet mincemeat if you prefer. Now that sugar rationing is ended, we can eat everything we like again."

They were still comfortably discussing baking when Ted opened the outer door and called, "I'm off, Mrs. Johnstone. See you tomorrow."

"Wait," Pauline cried, leaping up and almost spilling her tea. She ran to the door where Ted was waiting.

"I wanted to ask you about the night Mrs. Elliott died, the Friday before I found her," Pauline said.

"What about it?" Ted asked, puzzled.

"Were you out that evening, running errands maybe, and did you see Eustace Boothroyd out as well?"

Ted grinned. "He's out quite a lot after dark," he said. "He was likely out that night too."

Pauline was puzzled. "He goes out after dark most nights. Why?"

Ted laughed. "You'd best ask Mrs. Lavery that question. Her husband works nights, you see."

"I see," Pauline said. "Where do the Laverys live?"

"Their house is the one next to Mrs. Elliott's house," Ted said. "He has even less distance to walk now," he added, his grin growing wider.

"But can you remember seeing him that night, Ted?"

Ted shook his head. "It was a long time ago and one night is much like another in winter. Summer, now, there's always something to see."

Pauline frowned. "Think, Ted, please. It's important. Why are you out on a Friday night? Is it the same errand every week? That might help you to remember."

Ted gazed at her in what Pauline hoped was a sign of abstraction caused by deep thought. Finally, he said, "It's usually the same job, yes, but not always."

"Does it take you near Mrs. Elliott's house?"

"Of course," Ted said. "I have to pass it to get to the pub and come home."

Pauline understood his reticence. He was too young to buy alcohol but clearly someone the pub landlord knew was housebound and wanted a Friday night drink or two and Ted was their go-between. Ted would never be persuaded to go to the police about this for it would involve others in police charges and the landlord in likely ruin. How was she going to provide the police with proof of the Boothroyds' false alibis when no one who saw anything would come forward? Len had said he would testify to get the ten shillings, but she had no doubt that now he had the money, and it was drunk away, he'd deny all knowledge of their conversation.

She smiled. "Well, if you do remember that night, and you did see Mr. Boothroyd out and about, you will let me know, won't you?" she said.

"You think he did it," Ted said. He nodded. "He certainly had a big motive, I said that to my mam, and she said I was not to repeat it to others."

"I'm just trying to find the truth," Pauline said, "and I agree with your mam, don't tell anyone else what you thought or what I might be asking. There's no proof."

Ted nodded. "But," he said, "they had the key to the house and he has a motive, and his missus pretends he's home every night when half the village knows he's not, so he has the perfect cover."

"Still," Pauline said, "the police must have learned this and confirmed he was home that night so, I repeat, don't tell anyone what you think."

"I know how to keep my gob shut, don't you worry," Ted said, grinning. He turned and made his way back down the lane.

"I wish I'd asked Ted right from the start," Pauline said to herself. "It's taken me weeks to reach the conclusion he'd reached on the first day."

"What's that, dear?" Betty asked.

Pauline started, in surprise. She hadn't realized Betty had followed her out to the door.

"Nothing," Pauline said, "I was just remarking on what a clever young man Ted is."

"He is," Betty said, "and so kind. He'd do anything to make anyone's life better."

Pauline nodded her agreement, before saying, "It's time

Then There Were ... Two Murders? 129

for my walk and the dogs' run. Will you be joining us today?"

"Oh no, dear," Betty replied. "I'd slip and fall in that snow and that would be the end of me."

Pauline wrapped herself warmly, gathered the dog's leads and called them to heel, which they happily did.

"They do your bidding wonderfully well," Betty said.

Pauline laughed. "They know they're going out now, so they obey. The moment it's time to come home, they have selective hearing and can't quite catch what I say."

She set off with the dogs running ahead and her mind brooding on the information she'd been given. She now had a plausible suspect that the police should have already known about but had dismissed. Why? What was she missing? Could she get the Farquarsons to confirm Len's story? She'd call in on them before she left for home.

When she knocked on the door of the Farquarson house, it was answered by a thin, bespectacled man who asked politely, "Yes?"

Pauline was about to introduce herself when the man said brusquely, "Oh! I know who you are. You're that police stooge who's been hanging around the village."

"I'm not a police anything," Pauline said quickly, before he could get fully into a rant. "Mrs. Elliott asked for my help and I agreed. She is dead but I still want to do right by her."

He seemed mollified by this and said, "You want me to say I saw Len Turnbull on the Friday night she died. Well, I won't."

"You don't have to say why you saw and spoke to Len that night, only that you did," Pauline said.

"And when they ask how I can remember the momentous event of speaking to Len, how do I answer?"

"Surely, you can find a plausible answer," Pauline said.

"You can't speak to someone like Len so often that it isn't somewhat memorable."

"No, I can't find something plausible," he said. "PC Jarvis will know exactly why I was talking to Len and they'll charge me for receiving poached birds. Now go away."

He started to close the door when Pauline said, "If I tell them what I've learned they'll come to interview you anyway. Wouldn't it be better to be on the side of right when that happens?"

"I will deny speaking to Len if that happens. Do your worst," he said, and slammed the door, dislodging snow from the sill above it.

As Pauline was equally sure Len would also deny he spoke to Farquarson, and Ted would deny being out and seeing Boothroyd that night, Pauline realized none of what she learned was ever going to come out. Unless she took steps to bring it into the open.

26

SURVEILLANCE

Pauline found a telephone box near the village Post Office and called the Bertrams. She told them she was staying with Betty a little longer today and would be home late tonight, which started Mrs. Bertram into a spasm of concern about the weather and the roads. Pauline soothed her as best she could and once again vowed to find herself an apartment to rent as soon as she could.

Len had told her Boothroyd was out around nine o'clock at night. She tried to guess if this was after or before Boothroyd's tryst with Mrs. Lavery that Ted had told her about. Also, she thought about how could she get Mr. Lavery's night shift schedule, which would make her evenings watching the Lavery house more efficient. For tonight, she would trust to luck and watch until nine.

Where to watch from was also a problem she would have to solve on this first night. She couldn't stand on the street; it was too public and Boothroyd may use the back door now he and his mistress were neighbors. Nor could she watch from the lane at the back of the houses. Her car parked in that narrow lane would be much too visible. She returned to her car, keeping her eyes open, looking around the village, until her eyes alighted on the very spot. She'd driven that way on her first visit to the village.

Driving along the already empty street in the failing light, she saw how easy it was for people to be unseen here at night. There was only one streetlight, and it was at the junction where the road that ran past the castle ruin joined to the main street. Everywhere else was in darkness except for light from house windows and the pub's entrance. The car climbed the hill out of town toward the manor house that looked down over the village and valley. At the top, she used the manor's entranceway to turn and drive back to the brow of the hill, looking down on the village. She parked the car. Unfortunately, she couldn't see the village when she was sitting in the car, which meant nights of cold vigils standing on the hillside.

She stepped out into the wet snow and the cold, blustery wind that was swaying the trees. Wrapping her collar tighter, and holding her hat, she walked the short distance to where she could see into the village. The view was ideal. In summer, she wouldn't have been able to see the village at all but now, with bare trees on the hillside, the village was laid out before her like a map. She soon identified the houses she wanted to watch, checked the time, groaned at how long she would be stuck here, and returned to the car. She couldn't afford to run the engine to keep warm, she could barely afford petrol enough to last the week of driving to and from work, but at least in the car she was out of the wind.

As she waited, she ran through different ideas on how Boothroyd might explain his evening absences such that his wife could live with it. Perhaps he told her that as an artist he needed the solitude and evening light to revive his muse, or maybe he was going to the pub for a drink, or perhaps he had a studio outside the house he would retire to and work.

One of those, the pub, she could discount tonight. The pub would be shut on a Sunday. The outside studio she should be able to see if it existed. She left the comparative comfort of the car and went to look. There was a shed in the back garden that could be made into a studio, but as she remembered from her visit to the house, it wasn't one yet.

She returned to the car in deep thought. Maybe he no longer even pretended. Maybe he knew his wife knew and he just went out. Maybe she was happy he had intercourse with another woman and not with her. Pauline recalled the couple the few times she'd seen them. Did Mrs. Boothroyd look the sort of woman who didn't like intercourse or didn't mind sharing her husband?

Pauline decided she had no idea what that sort of woman might look like and speculation was useless. Useless. She smiled. That's what Len had called Boothroyd, and it struck her as amusing that a man like Len, who did no work and lived off petty thieving, would consider an artist as useless. The pot and the kettle came to mind. She sighed and checked her watch. Still much too early and her feet were like ice.

People were creatures of habit, she decided after only a few further minutes had passed, and Boothroyd would spend a specific amount of time with his mistress. If he was returning at nine on the night Mrs. Elliott died, then he'd leave his house at seven or eight. Just before seven, Pauline left the car, and returned to the edge of the hilltop. By 7:15, she couldn't stand the cold any longer, ran back to the car and started the engine. Slowly the air inside the car warmed and her fingers and toes began to ache as feeling returned to them. Tomorrow night, she vowed, she'd have thicker gloves, socks, and boots.

At eight o'clock she repeated the surveillance and was glad she did for after only a few minutes, she saw a man leave the back door of the Elliott house and hurry around to the Lavery house. She returned to the car in a dream. The elation she felt wiped the cold from her mind and stayed with her throughout the drive home. She was a detective, a real detective. And now she was sure she knew who had killed Mrs. Elliott and why. It wasn't just the money; it was also the convenience of being closer to his lover. Now she just had to provide the police with her evidence of his nocturnal movements, his motives, and his clear opportunity and it was in the bag. Another spectacular success for 'Detective Pauline Riddell.'

Her excitement, however, faded when she realized that providing the police with enough evidence was going to be tricky. She could, and would, watch the houses for the next few nights but that only meant Boothroyd had the opportunity to murder Mrs. Elliott, not that he did, and the police would need more than her word to convince them to use precious resources on nightly watches. Still, she needed to start somewhere.

"Is everything all right, Pauline?" Mrs. Bertram asked, as she stepped through the door.

Pauline was ready with her answer, she considered it carefully all the way home. "Yes," she said. "Betty isn't well, but it isn't really serious, not hospital serious anyway. I'm going to sit with her in the evenings for the next few days to give her daughter a break."

"I'm sorry to hear that," Mrs. Bertram said. "Is there anything you think might help her we could give you to take to her?"

"That's kind," Pauline said, and then added, "Some warm blankets would be good. Her own are getting rather thin, I feel." She could always give these to Betty after she'd finished using them herself, Pauline thought, pleased with her quick thinking.

"I'm sure we have some we keep for when we have visitors," Mrs. Bertram said. "We can always buy more if anyone should come to stay in the next few days."

With her story established, Pauline set out to prepare for gathering physical evidence. A camera would be useful and some training on how to take photos in the dark. There was very little light at the back of those houses at eight or nine o'clock on a January night.

27

SURVEILLANCE WITH CAMERA

SHE CALLED Poppy at work the following day. "Could your photographer get photos at that time of night?" she asked.

"You're in luck," Poppy said. "He's in the office today. I'll ask." She heard Poppy call to the photographer and then him say, "Hello, Pauline. You have a new story for us, I hear."

"I think so," Pauline said, "but I need something to show the police."

"I could get shadowy pictures on a clear, moonlit night," he said, "but if you want to see faces, I'd have to rig up some lights and catch him that way."

"I'd prefer not to alert him that I know what he's up to," Pauline said. "At least not at first."

"There's not a lot else I can do," the photographer said.

"In movies, it's often dark," Pauline asked. "How do they do it?"

"They shoot during the day and darken it, and for close ups they have the action take place near a light source," he replied. "Cameras need light to set the film."

"Then we pick a moonlit night to get some photos," Pauline said, "and when we have those, setting the scene if you like, we'll take one using the flash to show who the shadowy figure is."

"Then you take them to the police?"

"Exactly."

"If you take that last photo," the photographer said, "it's likely he won't visit his lady friend and the police will end up watching for days, see nothing, and think you made it all up."

"Then we just do the shadowy photos but with enough scene setting to show the house he leaves and the house he enters. That should be enough to convince the police to watch the next week and confront him with their evidence."

"And you think his wife will change her story and say he wasn't at home on the night of Mrs. Elliott's death?" Poppy asked, suddenly bursting into the conversation.

"Yes, and if the other woman says he wasn't with her, or he was but for a length of time that is shorter than his wife says he was out, we've got him," Pauline said.

"When do you want me there?" the photographer asked.

"Tonight, and every night the weather forecast calls for a clear night."

"This is England," the photographer said. "How many clear nights are we likely to have?"

"I don't know," Pauline said. "As many as it takes."

Armed with all her warmest winter clothes and the extra blankets from Mrs. Bertram, Pauline ate at a small café in Morpeth with Poppy and the photographer before heading out to begin their watch. She parked in the same spot as before and she showed Poppy and the photographer the houses and the route Boothroyd would take.

"This is a long distance for a photo with a recognizable face," the photographer said, shaking his head, "even with my biggest lens." He set up a tripod and fiddled with the camera to get the best settings. Above them, the night sky was lit by a half moon and bright stars, making the houses and their gardens visible whenever the clouds parted enough for moonlight to be cast upon them.

The photographer took a photo, the lens staying open for a long time. So long, Pauline thought it was never going to shut but eventually it did. The man nodded. "We won't know for sure until I can develop the film tomorrow," he said, "but if he comes out when the moon's out, we should get him."

The night air was icy. Still, there was no wind so standing waiting was better than on her previous watch. Even so, after thirty minutes when there was no sign of Boothroyd they retreated to the car to wait for eight o'clock.

"You know her husband may not be at work tonight," Poppy said, wrapping herself as tightly as she could in the plaid blanket Pauline had given her.

Pauline nodded. "I know that," she said. "But I have no sure way of finding his work schedule, so we have to take our chances."

With companions to talk with, Pauline found the wait for eight o'clock took no time at all and they were all back at the camera and tripod in good time.

The back door to the Elliott house opened and Pauline whispered, "Got him."

The camera clicked. A silhouetted man appeared in the light from the door and the camera clicked again. The figure moved quickly once the door was shut, and the camera struggled to capture the figure until it stopped at the door of the Lavery house. The camera clicked. The door opened and two figures were highlighted by the indoor light. The camera clicked. The door closed and Pauline and Poppy danced a jig in celebration.

"Thank God," Poppy said. "The thought of standing here every night this week wasn't appealing."

The photographer packing away his equipment, said, "I hate to burst your balloon, but we don't know what we've got until I see the film tomorrow. We might be back here yet."

Poppy groaned. "Do you know how much pub time we're already missing?" she asked plaintively.

"It will be worth it, you'll see," Pauline assured her.

28

EVIDENCE OF SOMETHING, AT LAST

Poppy phoned her at lunch time the following day. "The photos are great," she said. "We even got her face on one photo when she opened the door."

"I'll come by your office right after work and get them," Pauline said.

"If you're meeting Pringle right after, I'm going with you," Poppy said, "this is my story."

"I'm showing them to Inspector Ramsay first," Pauline said. "When I have his thoughts, his advice, we can take them to Pringle together."

Poppy was inclined to take exception, but Pauline was adamant. "We need an ally before we go to the local police," she said. "If they feel we've shown them as being negligent, they won't take kindly to our evidence and they may cause difficulties."

"Haven't they been negligent?" Poppy asked.

"They won't see it that way," Pauline said. "They did their jobs following the procedures they use. Boothroyd and his wife had good alibis and there was no evidence to suggest they'd done anything wrong, or that anyone has, to be honest. We have to tread carefully here."

"I suppose you're right," Poppy said seriously. "We haven't proved that he did murder his mother-in-law. Only that he could have done."

"It all depends on how the two women react when presented with this evidence," Poppy said. "Fortunately, there's little chance of them colluding so their statements may contradict each other causing the whole scheme to unravel."

"Till tonight then," Poppy said. "You know our photographer will want to be paid if we don't get a story out of this?"

"I know but I'm sure as I can be you'll have a story," Pauline said.

Pauline left her office the moment she put the phone down and practically ran to the telephone box outside the factory gates where she phoned Inspector Ramsay.

"I'll have some photos to show you later tonight," she said, getting straight to the point.

"Hello, Pauline," Ramsay said. "Nice to hear from you."

"Never mind all that," Pauline said. "Can we meet tonight?"

"We can. Shall we say in the Barley Mow at nine? They have a decent selection of malt whiskies in there."

"I'll be there as close to time as I can be," Pauline said. "I have to collect them from Morpeth first."

The afternoon dragged slowly, as she'd known it would when she had something important to do after work. After an hour, she put her watch in the desk drawer to stop herself looking at it.

"You seem on edge today, Pauline," Enderby said, puzzled.

"I'm expecting some good news this evening," Pauline replied. "That's all." She smiled in what she hoped was a reassuring way. It seemed to work for her boss shook his head and returned to his own office.

At five o'clock, Pauline ran out of the office, jumped in her car, and practically shot out of the parking area onto the road, which was crawling with rush hour traffic. The drive north seemed even worse than usual, though she knew it wasn't for she was passing the turn into the street where she lived at the usual time.

Eventually, she arrived at the offices of the Morpeth Herald, parked, and ran inside.

The photos were all that she could have wished for. Even as a silhouette, the man was recognizable as Eustace Boothroyd to anyone who knew him. She didn't know Mrs. Lavery but was sure when they met, she would recognize her as the woman in the photo. Now Pauline wished she'd arranged an earlier time to meet Ramsay; nine o'clock seemed a lifetime away.

"Can I use your phone to call Inspector Ramsay?" she asked Poppy.

Poppy dialed the number and when Ramsay answered, handed the phone to Pauline.

"I have the photos, Inspector," she said. "Can we meet at eight?" It was arranged and Pauline sighed with relief.

"What if Ramsay's advice is that these photos mean nothing, and he won't help?" Poppy asked.

"He won't," Pauline replied, "and nor will Pringle when we show them to him, though I'm sure he'll be angry."

"Then let's celebrate," Poppy said, "with a pie and a pint at the pub."

"A sherry and a sausage roll, maybe," Pauline said. "If their sausage rolls aren't too greasy."

Poppy shook her head. "Greasy is what makes food great, Pauline," she said. "Didn't they teach you anything at school?"

Clutching the envelope with the precious photos inside tightly to her chest, Pauline followed Poppy to the pub.

Inspector Ramsay was already enjoying his scotch with a pint of best bitter when Pauline arrived. Once she was seated, he went to the bar to get her a drink, which only served to frustrate Pauline's anticipation of his surprise when he saw and understood the photos.

When he was settled, she explained what she'd learned from Len and Ted and how she couldn't get either of them, or the Farquarsons, to tell the police what they'd seen. Then she explained about her observation.

"So," he said, smiling, "you finally got to do that surveillance you were longing for."

Pauline nodded. "And when I saw what Len and Ted had told me they'd seen, I had Poppy and the Herald's photographer help me with these." She handed over the envelope and watched as Ramsay leafed through the photos.

"It doesn't prove he murdered Mrs. Elliott," Ramsay said, "but it does give Pringle a real avenue to explore. Will the two women's stories match? That's the question."

"They are unlikely to be able to make them do so," Pauline said. "I think you should be able to pick them apart and arrive at the truth."

"Not me," Ramsay said. "Inspector Pringle. These should go straight to him."

"And they will," Pauline said. "I wanted your thoughts first."

"Take them to him tomorrow and get him started is my advice and don't tell him I saw them first, unless it becomes truly necessary."

"But you agree this is evidence of a possible suspect and needs to be investigated?"

He nodded. "Absolutely," he said. "You've done well."

29

HOPING A CORNER HAS BEEN TURNED

Lifted by Ramsay's praise, Pauline phoned Inspector Pringle at lunch time the following day and arranged to meet him at his office after work. She was there promptly, despite the miserable weather and the road. Even her journey lifted her spirits for it demonstrated how much better she was becoming at handling a car.

After explaining what she'd learned, she handed him the photos, which he viewed with pursed lips and a solemn expression.

"You make a compelling case, Miss Riddell," he said, at last, "and if you're right, and the two women's stories can be shown to be false, we have a credible suspect. However, there's a lot of ifs in there."

"I realize there's still work to be done, Inspector," Pauline said. "But I really do think this is the answer."

"It's better than your previous theory of the young Mrs. Churchill being the killer," he said.

Pauline didn't respond. Personally, she still felt there was a good chance that was possible, but an argument at this stage would jeopardize the police going forward with this investigation.

"Thank you, Miss Riddell," Pringle said, when it became clear Pauline wasn't about to argue about the earlier theory, "we'll take this from here."

"When might I hear from you regarding the outcome?"

"If it goes the way you wish it to, you'll hear that we've arrested Mr. Boothroyd," Pringle said. "If it doesn't go as you wish, you'll hear from me in due course."

With that, Pauline had to be satisfied. She left the office very uneasy, but glad she'd shown the photos to Ramsay. She could follow up herself if nothing developed soon.

Driving home, she found her temper rising at the curt way she'd been treated. It was as if she was making work for the police, work they didn't want to do. She'd given them two perfectly good possible murder suspects, along with plausible ways in which the murder could have been carried out and they dismissed her with little thanks. Arriving home, she went straight to her room. She felt she couldn't face Mrs. Bertram's well-meaning but overwhelming concern just at this moment, or at all, until she heard the outcome of the police interviews.

30

THIS TIME IT'S SERIOUS

Mrs. Bertram handed Pauline the phone. "It's that Inspector Pringle for you, dear," she said.

Pauline's heart skipped a beat. At last, they'd found something. She was sure of it.

"Miss Riddell," Pringle said, after she'd greeted him. "I'd like you to come to my office here at headquarters as soon as possible."

It was true. They had found something. Pauline could hardly hide the elation she felt as she replied, "I can be there in half an hour, Inspector."

Still filled with excited hope, Pauline parked at the Morpeth police headquarters and raced inside. The desk sergeant was clearly expecting her and had her escorted to Inspector Pringle's immediately.

As the office door closed behind her, Pauline said, "Well, Inspector, have you confirmed my evidence?" His grim expression, however, suggested he hadn't.

"No, Miss Riddell, we haven't," Inspector Pringle said. "While your theory had merit, we have *again* interviewed the people involved and *again* we can find no evidence they were doing anything other than what they say they were doing."

"But they would say that, wouldn't they, Inspector," Pauline said, exasperated.

"I haven't finished," he said coldly. "Furthermore, Mrs. Lavery was able to provide evidence her husband was at home that night," he held up his hand to prevent the increasingly agitated Pauline interjecting again, "and we have confirmed with his place of employment that he was not, in fact, at work that night."

Pauline slumped down into the chair. This was devastating. She couldn't deny it. If Mrs. Lavery's husband was at home that night, Boothroyd wouldn't have been going there.

"But, Inspector," Pauline began, realizing if Boothroyd was out and not going to his lover, where was he going? It was Pringle's turn to interject.

"You're going to say the witnesses who saw him out prove he was going to Mrs. Elliott's house and likely murdered her," he said. "But he has provided a good explanation of what he was doing, and your witnesses won't come forward, as you've already said. Also, I should remind you, there was no evidence of anyone in the house that night."

"But he had visited the house with his wife many times," Pauline objected. "It's just that his fingerprints can't be placed to that night."

"You're clutching at straws, Miss Riddell," Pringle said. "Let me remind you this is the second time you've created whimsical scenarios accusing innocent people of murder without any serious evidence. Hearsay and gossip are what you have and, quite possibly, malice on the part of your witnesses. Can you be sure your witnesses simply don't like Eustace Boothroyd?"

"I don't think many people like him, Inspector, but I

know no reason why the two people who say they saw him outside in the vicinity of Mrs. Elliott's house should wish him this much harm. They would know that if he proved his innocence, they'd be the ones suspected."

"Which is why they conveniently won't come forward. You are very young and naïve, Miss Riddell. I suggest you leave this kind of work until you have learned more about human nature," Pringle said firmly. He added, "Now, good day to you. I have real work to attend to."

Pauline left his office stunned. She'd been sure she had hit upon the truth and now she was being told she hadn't. Worse, she was being told she was harassing innocent people for no good reason, for that's what his lecture amounted to. But the rebuttal to the evidence wasn't enough, in her mind, to stop seeking. Surely, he didn't think so. She could imagine at least one plausible theory that met his evidence and still made Boothroyd a murderer.

She jumped into her car, slammed the door, and pushed the starter button so vigorously the engine seemed to screech in pain. That cooled her passion. The car was her ticket to freedom, and nothing must harm it. Not even her righteous anger. She patted the steering wheel consolingly and was relieved to hear the engine running with its normal purring sound.

"Sorry, Millie," she said. She'd named her car Millie from the story book, *Millie Molly Mandy*, she'd enjoyed as a child. Future cars, and she was already dreaming of such things, would be Molly and Mandy. As it was inconceivable she'd ever need, or afford, more than three in her lifetime, this seemed like a safe strategy.

By the time she'd reached home, however, her anger had evaporated, and she was calm enough to see that Inspector Pringle was right and she was wrong. It was a crushing blow.

"You look dejected, dear," Mrs. Bertram said, when Pauline entered the house. "Your meeting with Inspector Pringle didn't go well?"

Pauline laughed derisively. "It depends on what you mean by 'well'," she said.

"I think I mean what everyone means by well, Pauline," Mrs. Bertram said. "What other meaning do you want to put on the word?"

"I do apologize," Pauline said, contritely. "It went badly because he told me that Eustace Boothroyd didn't murder Mrs. Elliott, as I'd imagined, though he didn't say what Boothroyd *was* doing that night. However, it went well in the sense that I'm at last free of the whole wretched business."

"I'm glad to hear that," Mrs. Bertram said, as she followed Pauline upstairs. "I never liked the idea of you being mixed up with criminals, particularly murderers."

"You don't think women should be detectives?"

"My dear," Mrs. Bertram said. "I'm sure there are some few women who can physically hold their own against a man but they're very few. And you aren't one of them. You'd be dead in seconds if a murderer chose to kill you, as you should have learned last time you did this."

Pauline stopped at her room door and said, "You're right. And that's why I'm going to get trained, whether I continue doing this or not, but just now, I think it isn't my physical strength that's lacking. It's my brain."

She entered her room and very purposefully closed the door behind her. She didn't need Mrs. Bertram's well-meaning arguments to make her feel worse than she did. The elation she'd felt leaving the house this morning, expecting Inspector Pringle to praise her on the brilliance of her deductions and investigating, was now forgotten in a sea of misery.

31

DESPAIR DEEPENS

Her low spirits continued, even when she was at work the following day, causing her to be absentminded enough to earn her a rare rebuke from her boss, Dr. Enderby.

"Sorry," Pauline said, "I've had a setback that's left me floundering. I'm awake now," she added with a smile.

"Glad to hear it," Enderby said. "I need you on top of your game in the meeting we're going to."

He was taking Pauline to more meetings, ostensibly for notetaking but she found he often asked her opinion when the meeting was over, and she did not want to lose that support for her future. She gave herself a mental shake and re-focused her mind. She had an ally in him. He was already steering her into night school for accounting, something outside the purview of most secretaries, and she had to grab this opportunity while it was offered.

"I will be," she said. "You can count on me."

He nodded. "I believe I can," Enderby said, "but I think you've taken on more investigating work outside and I need your focus on our work here."

"It's true," Pauline said. "I did try to help an elderly

woman with a problem but that's all done with now. She's dead and her friend is too. There's no evidence of wrongdoing in either case, though I was sure there was so that's it over with."

"But you find it hard to let go?"

Pauline nodded. "I have to admit I still think something is wrong even though I have to accept the evidence."

"Most of life is like that, I think," Enderby said. "I listen to the news and ask myself if that's really what happened."

"Many of us are beginning to feel that way, I think," Pauline said, remembering how Inspector Ramsay spoke whenever the subject of politics came up.

"My meeting today is at Jobson Engineering and it's one where I will need your notes afterward for evidence, so get your mind off crime for an hour or so."

Jobson Engineering was a small, local supplier on the eastern end of the city. While it meant a longer drive home for Pauline, it would be a change from her usual crawl with the traffic heading north out of town.

"What time will we be leaving?"

"In an hour," Enderby said. "Be ready or I'll find another note taker."

The drive through the city along the banks of the Tyne river was the usual drab, industrial scene that Pauline had come to like, though her first impressions more than three years before had been exactly the opposite. 'Where there's muck, there's brass' went the saying and the 'brass' she got from her work had made her a car owner and an independent woman. For which she was grateful and, consequently, she defended its grime whenever it was derided by family or friends.

The noise of kittiwakes swooping around the Baltic Flour Mill where they nested in the spring, the scream of metal being shaved and cut, rivets being hammered into metal sheets, together with the smells carried on the wind from the brewery, the glue factory and fish quay at North Shields, could be heard and smelled even inside the car as she followed Dr. Enderby slowly through the busy streets where everyone was in a hurry. The city was alive with industry and over all of it you knew what made it so, coal. Coal was king here and the smell of coal soot and smoke rose from every factory and hearth in the houses on either side of the river.

At Jobson Engineering there was a different but also common smell. This was steam from boilers that powered steam engines, great pistons and cranks turning axles running dozens of machines by way of a complicated series of wheels and pulleys that drove tight, rubberized bands, which in turn, spun lathes or lifted and lowered forging stamps. A hellish, whirling mass of machines from which men fashioned pieces of equipment to be sent out to the world, and many of them just across town to the factory where Pauline worked.

They were met and escorted to the offices that lay above the factory floor, passing through drawing offices and a typing pool. The meeting went swiftly and, considering the message Enderby was delivering, reasonably amicably. He wrapped up like so, "We have done business with Jobson for almost a century, and we want to continue doing so for another century," he paused, "but you must find ways to bring down your costs. We can now buy the same parts with the same quality for much less – parts from America and Germany that have traveled much farther to get to us than yours do. You need to invest in new equipment and streamlined processes or we will be buying all we need elsewhere in the future."

Mr. Jobson, the grandson of the founder, replied, "Where do we get the money for these new machines? And your streamlined processes would lose half our workforce, men who have been with us all their lives and who produced equipment through two world wars. Don't we owe them some measure of security for their loyalty and commitment?"

"I'm sorry," Enderby said. "We're in a commercial war now and that requires sacrifices too. If you can find a way to meet our needs and maintain your staff, we'll continue to buy from you. That's all I can say. Good day, gentlemen."

Pauline and Enderby left the meeting room in silence. They didn't speak until they'd reached their cars and Enderby said, "I need your shorthand typed up and on my desk by nine tomorrow morning. I have to report on the meeting to our board at ten."

Pauline nodded. "They'll be ready," she said. "I do feel sorry for them though. It's a family firm in so many ways."

Enderby nodded. "I know," he said. "Family can be a burden as well as a help."

"Do you think they'll make the changes they need to make?"

"Sadly, I don't," Enderby said. "They're good people and choosing who in their family will 'live' and who will not, will be too hard for them. They'll all go down together rather than save some. It's how it is for some people."

"My family has a farm," Pauline said. "I wonder if I could make those decisions if the farm could no longer support us all and we had to choose who to save and who to let go."

"And could you?"

"I honestly don't know," Pauline replied. "Maybe I'd choose to attack instead of accept defeat."

"Going down in a blaze of glory shows spirit," Enderby said, laughing. "Here's hoping it never comes to that."

Pauline hoped so too but the day, and the dismal future it portended for so many good, honest people, simply added to her despair. The post-war world wasn't playing out as anyone had hoped. She started her car and prepared to drive away when her words, said more in despair than brash courage, came back to her. She paused as she decided if her words were true. She decided they were. If she was ever faced with such a decision, she would attack rather than wait for a miserable end. Anyone with spirit would. She shook herself to clear her head, slipped the car into gear and edged out of the parking area.

32

POPPY DROPS OUT

IN THE DAYS THAT FOLLOWED, Pauline continued hoping some new and different idea would revitalize her investigation. Something was nagging at her in the back of her mind, but nothing emerged. To raise her spirits, she phoned Poppy at work and arranged a meeting. Poppy, she was sure, with her infectious enthusiasm for life, would cheer her and may even have some ideas for what more they could do now all their investigative avenues were closed off.

When they did meet, in the inevitable public house, Pauline found they had little to say. Poppy wasn't even depressed by the ending of Pauline's investigation; she had her other stories to pursue. She was only mildly disappointed with the failure of this story and said, "It's often that way in journalism. Stories that seem so promising, just don't work out."

Pauline nodded glumly.

"Cheer up," Poppy said, when a silence had grown too much to bear, "it may never happen."

"That's what I'm afraid of," Pauline said. "How could I be so wrong?"

"You're working too hard," Poppy said. "All day at the office and then investigating in the evenings and weekends. You need a break."

"I do need a break," Pauline agreed, "just not the sort you're thinking of. What is it our Victorian forebears used to say? When you feel tired, vary your employment?"

"There's a reason no one likes them anymore," Poppy said. "And that kind of grinding morality has a lot to do with it."

"On the Marjorie case—"

"The only case," Poppy interjected.

"On my previous case," Pauline continued doggedly, "I could watch the houses and people because they were constantly doing things and it seemed reasonable that sooner or later, I'd see or hear something important. And I did."

"And it almost worked on this one too," Poppy pointed out.

"But not now because whether it is June Churchill or Eustace Boothroyd, their only sane strategy is to let time pass without them doing anything at all," Pauline said. "To confide in anyone or to make any further steps to improve their lot would risk losing everything they've gained."

Poppy nodded, sympathetically. "I can see how that must be frustrating," she said, then added with a grin, "But not having to stand out in all winter weathers hoping to catch someone out in a significant mistake has got to be good."

"If you can't say something helpful, say nothing at all," Pauline said.

"All right, here's what I think. We can rule out June Churchill," Poppy said. "You say the police have provided a pretty convincing case of her innocence, which only leaves Boothroyd in my mind. No one else is vaguely credible."

"We don't know of others," Pauline said, "but I agree we should concentrate on Boothroyd. His story, which the police find convincing, is still weak. He and his wife were at home listening to the radio, and he can describe what they listened to."

"Why don't you like that?"

"I listened to the radio last night," Pauline said, "and I can't tell you what was on. Nor could 99% of the population, if you asked them." She paused and then added, "I'll prove my point. What song is playing on the pub's radio right now?"

Poppy listened. "It's *Answer Me*," she said, "by Frankie Laine. The fellow you liked last year with his *I Believe* hit."

"And what was being played before this one?" Pauline asked.

"How should I know," Poppy said. "I wasn't listening."

"Exactly," Pauline said, "Nobody does, but he could remember what he heard days after. I don't believe it."

"Then how can you explain it?"

"Easy," Pauline said. "While he was drugging and poisoning Mrs. Elliott, his wife was at home making notes about the radio shows that were on."

"That means she was in on it," Poppy objected.

"She wouldn't be the first daughter who would happily murder her mother," Pauline said grimly.

Poppy laughed. "But none of us do murder our mothers," she said. "Why should Evelyn Boothroyd?"

"Because she wasn't the one doing it," Pauline said. "All she had to do was sit at home, knit, and listen to the radio."

"Pauline, seriously," Poppy said, "you have to let this go. You pressured the police into further investigating June

Churchill. There was nothing there. You did it again with Eustace Boothroyd, with the same result. Face it, you're wrong on this one. Give it up."

Pauline shook her head. "I can't let Mrs. Elliott down," she said.

"This has nothing to do with Mrs. Elliott now," Poppy said. "You just want to save face in front of Inspector Ramsay." She paused and added, "He's old enough to be your father, Pauline."

"I do not want to save face," Pauline almost yelled, disturbing the few others in the Snug. "And it isn't like that," she added.

"You don't know yourself," Poppy said. "That's your trouble."

Pauline stood up so quickly, she almost turned over the table with the drinks on. "Everything is about sex with you," she said, and marched away without looking back.

Outside, the cold air sobered her a little and she considered returning to apologize but then, with a shrug, continued to her car. Poppy could stew in her own juice for a day or two. She drove away, fuming at her friend, the police, and the world. One way or another, she would prove them all wrong.

Her desire to do that, however, took a knock when she sat through the vicar's sermon the next morning in church. His theme was, unusually for him, taken from one of the recent popular movies, *The Robe*, starring Britain's own Richard Burton. The vicar seemed uplifted by the fact two recent popular artistic presentations had a faith-based theme. First, Frankie Laine singing *I Believe* and now Richard Burton starring in *The Robe*. Perhaps, he said, the world had finally come to realize war with its inevitable aftermath wasn't the answer and people were returning to their faith.

For Pauline, it sounded like he was suggesting a more compliant, more traditional posture by everyone in our world, when there was danger surrounding us all. She was certainly in favor of being less aggressive but found the idea of simply accepting your fate as being God's will wasn't to her taste. She couldn't help feeling the old dissenter's motto 'God helps those who help themselves' more suited her mood.

As they drove home after the service, Mrs. Bertram said, "I think the vicar made a good point about us all carrying our faith out into the world, didn't you, Pauline?"

"Yes, but I'm always uncomfortable when people are using faith, any faith, to make money," Pauline said, "and his examples were just that. People making money without much thought to how that looks."

"I thought you liked *I Believe*," Mrs. Bertram said. "I remember you saying so."

"I liked the song," Pauline agreed. "It's the money-making from it that bothers me." And that, she suddenly realized, was what had hit her hardest. In the back of her mind, the depths of her soul, she too was looking to make money from something that should be pure.

She had pursued justice for Marjorie without any thought of making money from it. But when she answered Mrs. Elliott's cry for help, she did so with every intention of charging for her services and, if successful, charging anyone else who came to her in the future as well. The purity of her first murder investigation had been immediately subsumed into a cash grab by the time her second arrived.

She disliked it when she saw entertainers doing it to something she believed in, but until now had failed to see her own motives when it was something she had no strong belief in. She now saw why the police viewed people like her with such suspicion, and even dislike. At this moment, she saw herself as they did.

After Sunday dinner, she would visit Betty with no other motive than taking Ranter for a walk and passing the time with a lonely old lady.

33

MISS RIDDELL CARRIES ON

PAULINE PARKED her car on the street and began walking toward Betty's cottage with Jem straining at the leash, eager to see Ranter again. As she turned a corner in the lane, she saw Ted Watson approaching her.

"Hello, Ted," Pauline said. "Have you been delivering firewood?"

He nodded. "That I have," he said. He held out his hand, opened his fingers to show Pauline the half-crown piece he held. "Betty paid me," he said. "I didn't ask her to," he added, as if concerned Pauline would think he'd been begging.

"She's very grateful for the help you've given her these past weeks," Pauline said. "And I'm sure it has been good for her. She looks altogether better than she did when I first met her."

Ted nodded. "The cold is hard on old uns," he said. "It's what did it for my dad."

Pauline didn't know how to respond to that, so she changed the subject. "Betty says you hope to get an apprenticeship when you leave school. In engineering, I think."

Then There Were ... Two Murders? 163

Ted's expression darkened. He replied, "I did but I don't see how it's going to be possible."

"Betty said you'd worked out the buses and everything," Pauline said, "and it did seem quite difficult. Leaving home at five o'clock in the morning and getting home after six in the evening would be hard on anyone."

Ted nodded. "And one night at Technical College in Newcastle so not getting home until after ten o'clock that night," he replied. "But that isn't what's making it nigh on impossible," he added.

"What is?" Pauline asked.

"The bus fares will eat up all my wages for the first year of the apprenticeship," Ted said, "and the hours I'm away mean I couldn't do any of the jobs around here that put grub on our table. I don't see any way around that."

"I see," Pauline said, and she did see. A year without money coming in wasn't an option for people like Ted and his mother. "Well," she said, "you have two years to think about it and do some more planning. Who knows, apprentice wages might be raised in that time."

He nodded glumly. Clearly, Ted felt this wasn't likely. In truth, Pauline thought, any increase would be unlikely to make the difference he would need to make it work for him.

"Are there no firms closer than Newcastle?" Pauline asked, unhappy at this bleak future laid out for such a hard-working, intelligent young man.

'There's only garages and the like," he said. "I'll probably get in there, but they don't have any progression beyond mending cars."

"You want to become an engineer?"

"I do," he said. "I want to design and build space rockets or jet airliners or atomic power stations. Things like that. Not fix old Morris Minors."

Pauline laughed. "I aspire to a *new* Morris Minor so be careful what you say," she said.

Ted grinned. "There's nought wrong with them," he said. "I just want to do something more. Cars are all sorted out now. I want to be building new things."

"I hope you get to do that, Ted," Pauline said. "You deserve to have your dreams come true. Now, I must get on. Jem is growing frantic, and the tea Betty always has waiting will be stewed. She'll never forgive me."

Ted nodded. "I don't expect we'll see so much of you now the police have given up on Mrs. Elliott's death," he said.

"The police may have given up, Ted," Pauline said, as she walked away. "I haven't. I don't intend to give up until she has justice. Someone killed her and they must pay for that crime." The moment she said it, she knew it was true. All her shame yesterday about the money was a sham. She didn't know herself at all, she thought bitterly. I'm as venal as everyone is when it's something I desire. For a moment, she paused, staring into eternity. Jem stopped and glared at her for wasting time thinking when she should have been walking.

"I will only take expenses," she said to him. "No more. No less. Now, hurry up, Jem, it's cold out here." Hearing her tone and understanding her wish, he immediately trotted off towards the cottage, leaving Pauline to walk on alone.

At the cottage, she told Betty of her conversation with Ted and his despair over his future career.

"Don't give him too much hope, Pauline," Betty said. "It's cruel. You know it can never happen. Not from here and not for someone in his situation."

"There's always hope," Pauline said, but Betty just frowned and shook her head.

"Well," Pauline added somberly, "a lot can happen before then." And she meant it because she'd suddenly realized what had been bubbling away in the back of her mind these past days. She also realized she'd set the timer running on a time bomb. A bomb she was strapped to.

34

PREPARING

THE FRIDAY DRIVE HOME from work was a nightmare. Heavy snow blew sideways in a lashing wind that shook streetlights and trees alike. Many streetlights were out, and branches lay everywhere on paths and roads, ready to trip the unwary walking head down in the dark or puncture the radiator of any driver too slow to avoid them. Pauline inched her way home in a long line of cars and buses making their way out of the city.

"What a storm," Mrs. Bertram said, as Pauline practically ran into the house and slammed the door behind her. "We thought you'd broken down or were stuck somewhere," she added.

Pauline unwrapped her scarf from around her face and hung it on a coat hanger. "No," she said, "we just crawled all the way from Jesmond. The road hasn't been cleared and there were some abandoned cars blocking the way."

"Mr. Bertram said the same," Mrs. Bertram replied. "He only got home a few minutes ago as well."

"I hope it blows itself out before the morning," Pauline said, following Mrs. Bertram into the living room where

Mr. Bertram was warming himself in front of the blazing fire.

"You push Mr. Bertram aside, my dear," Mrs. Bertram said. "He must be warm enough by now."

"Indeed, I am, my dear," her husband agreed, grinning. "Get yourself over here Pauline and warm up." He left the fireplace and retreated to his regular armchair.

Pauline gratefully warmed her fingers at the fire. Despite her driving gloves, they were numb with cold.

"Dinner will be just a few minutes," Mrs. Bertram said, "so you rest there while I get it ready." She hurried off to the kitchen leaving Pauline and Mr. Bertram to discuss their respective journeys.

"I'm sure it will blow itself out," Mr. Bertram said, "and the road men will have everything shipshape for work in the morning."

Pauline nodded. "I hope so. We have a big order going out and Dr. Enderby has documents that have to be done," Pauline said. "He won't like it if the order is held up by his department, and by him particularly."

"Dinner's ready," Mrs. Bertram said, re-entering the room, "and there should be no talk of going to work tomorrow. It's madness."

"Well," her husband said, "we'll see what the morning brings before we decide what's best."

Morning was as Mr. Bertram had suggested it would be. The storm abated before midnight and the plows had cleared the major roads. Once she'd driven out of the short lane that led to the Great North Road, it was plain sailing all the way to work.

Few people were at work, so there were fewer than usual interruptions and Dr. Enderby was pleased to have his part of the paperwork finished well before quitting time.

"They say in the shipbuilding world that the weight of the paperwork equals the weight of the ship by the time it is done," he said happily when Pauline returned with the signed acknowledgements, "and I swear we're getting as bad."

"The government does like everything recorded," Pauline agreed. "They're frightened we taxpayers will one day rise and demand a full reckoning, I think."

"And we should keep them frightened," Enderby said. "The way they waste our money is enough to turn us all into revolutionaries."

Pauline smiled. "Still, it's satisfying when a project is completed and shipped out, don't you think?"

He nodded. "True," he said, "and I think we should celebrate by leaving early today. The roads will still be awful going home so let's get an early start."

Pauline accepted that gratefully. She had some shopping she wanted to do, and it might take some time.

In the middle of town, she parked her car and headed into Binns, which had been recently taken over by the more prestigious House of Fraser stores, so she was hoping for even greater things from the most popular department store in town.

A riding hat was her first target. She found the sporting goods department and asked for assistance. The saleswoman seemed glad to have a customer; the floor was empty of people.

"It's been very slow today," she said, leading Pauline to a corner where riding clothes and equipment were displayed. "Not like a regular Saturday at all."

"Yesterday's storm has everyone huddled around their hearths, I expect," Pauline said. "Or rushing straight home in case we get some more snow."

"We have a limited selection of riding wear," the saleswoman said. "If you're a serious rider you probably need to go to a shop that specializes." She laid out three different caps on the counter.

"I haven't ridden since I was a girl on our farm," Pauline said. "I've just taken a fancy to going out riding once or twice when the spring comes."

"You would follow the hunt, I expect, if you're from farming folk," the woman said.

Pauline laughed. "My pony trotted along after the hunt," she said. "We never kept up, but I loved it. Mother, me and my sister trotting out across the fields, dreaming of the day when we too would ride a great hunter and jump hedges and gates."

"Will you want a hunting jacket too?"

Pauline shook her head. "No," she said, trying on each helmet. "These days I don't find the idea of killing appealing, even though we keep hens on the farm, and I know what foxes can do if they get in a henhouse."

"That cap fits you perfect and the color suits you, too," the saleswoman said.

"Then I'll take it," Pauline said. "Where would I find collars for dogs?"

"In the basement," the woman said, wrapping the riding cap and handing it over. "You have a dog?"

"I've inherited one and the collar is too narrow," Pauline said. "Jem's a big dog and pulls hard. I worry the collar he has is biting into his neck so I'm looking for a broader one."

"You'll find what you need down there," the woman said. "We may not be horsey people here in the city, but we do like our dogs."

The saleswoman was right. It didn't take Pauline long to find a collar that was made of broad, thick leather with a little give in it. After some guessing at the size, she left the store with her purchases and headed home.

"Right on time," Mrs. Bertram said, when Pauline entered the house.

"Dr. Enderby decided we could leave early because we'd finished," Pauline said. "He thought the roads may be slow."

"That was good of him," Mrs. Bertram said. "I hope you will do the sensible thing and stay indoors for the rest of the weekend."

"Certainly, I will today," Pauline said, as she took off her coat. "Tomorrow, I'll visit Betty Johnstone if the weather is good."

"Lunch will be ready soon, dear," Mrs. Bertram said, "so don't be long freshening up." She headed for the kitchen, leaving Pauline to make her way upstairs to her room, Jem following closely behind.

In her room, Pauline removed her purchases from her bag and set them on the bed. "Will they do the trick do you think, Jem?" she asked.

Jem nuzzled her hand, clearly feeling some action on his part was called for.

"I hope so too," Pauline said. "I really hope so and I need you to play your part as well. You might be my savior."

35

A TRUE FRIEND

AFTER LUNCH, Pauline settled down to sewing. She'd told Mrs. Bertram she was writing her weekly letter to her mother, but the letter would have to wait. By late afternoon, she had made an awkward, ungainly hat that wouldn't win any fashion shows but might keep her safe. She altered her old leather coat into a jacket by sewing the hem up inside below the armpits. It too was strange but, underneath her usual winter coat would be unseen. The dog collar was new and uncomfortable but serviceable. Under a scarf, it too would be unseen. Tomorrow would decide whether she was a sleuth or a failure, one way or another.

She phoned Inspector Ramsay at his office and found him as unhappy at her plans, when she outlined them, as he'd been on the previous occasion.

"You can't keep putting yourself in harm's way, Pauline," he said angrily.

"But Inspector, as you and Inspector Pringle have proved to me beyond any shadow of a doubt, there can be no harm in what I'm doing," Pauline said, "because there are no murderers in Mitford."

"You know very well we said there was no *evidence*, not that there was no possibility of *murderers*," Ramsay said.

"And I agree with you, there was no evidence," Pauline said, "so once again, I intend to collect the evidence. I'm just asking you to be there to witness the evidence." She could practically hear his brain seething with the wish to tell her no, fighting with the knowledge he could never let her go alone into danger.

"Where and when shall we meet," he said, at last.

"Tomorrow after lunch," Pauline began, and described the place.

PAULINE PULLED her car onto the verge behind Ramsay's black Riley. She waved to him through the window as she collected her gloves and hats.

"What are you wearing?" Ramsay asked, smiling broadly, as she stepped out of the car.

"Don't you like it?" Pauline asked. "I'm disappointed because I dressed with such care."

Ramsay shook his head. "You look like the fat woman at the circus," he said.

"Charming," Pauline replied, grinning. "However, I didn't ask you here to comment on the latest fashions for women. I asked you here to show you my route and the places to watch out for."

She drew him to the edge of the hill looking down on Mitford. "Can you see that path running from right below us, where Betty's house is, though we can't see the house for the bushes, to the far end of the village over there," she said, pointing with her hand.

"I see it," Ramsay said.

"It runs behind that row of houses, the nearest of which is where the Churchill's live."

"That's the one where the extension has the smoking chimney?" Ramsay asked.

"That's it," Pauline said. "She's probably in there right now melting down the old key she made, the one that fitted Mrs. Elliott's side door, which your brother officers couldn't find."

Ramsay didn't reply to this obvious provocation. He just said, "And then?"

"The path exits the wooded area just past Mrs. Elliott's house, you know that one, I think?"

"I do," Ramsay agreed. "Then where will you go?"

"The dogs and I turn left into a narrow path the other side of that drystone field wall," Pauline said. "It runs up to that clump of trees there," she pointed to a bare copse to the north. "The dogs like it because there's a stream they can play in."

"A bit cold for that today," Ramsay said, shivering. "My concern, however, is how do I shadow you along that stretch between the fields. There's no cover at all."

"If nothing has happened by then, I imagine I'm safe today."

"I can't agree," Ramsay said. "Those walls are tall enough to conceal someone, and the copse and stream are good places for an ambush."

"Then I leave it to you to work out how to cover the ground, Inspector," Pauline said. "You're the expert, after all."

"Hmm," Ramsay said. "One day, Miss Riddell, you'll go too far. I only hope today isn't it."

"I have my guardian angels with me," Pauline said, "You, Jem, and Ranter."

"It's good to know I have top billing," Ramsay said. "Now, if only I could persuade you not to do this at all."

"Ranter would be devastated and so would Jem," Pauline said.

"And we can't have that, can we," Ramsay said, shaking his head in disbelief.

"Come, Watson," Pauline said, turning back to the car. "The game is afoot, and we must be in on it."

"I'm sure Sherlock Holmes didn't say it quite that way."

"This is 1954, Inspector," Pauline said. "Everything is modern now."

"Everything is always modern, to the people of the time," Ramsay said. "Even when progress is sliding backwards, it's always modern to the people in it."

Pauline had reached her car and was opening the door. "This is no time for philosophy, Inspector. This is a time for action." She swung herself into the driver seat, closed the door, and started the engine. With a final wave, she set off down the hill into the village as the Riley followed at a distance.

"No Ted today?" Pauline asked, when she arrived at Betty's cottage.

"He's around; he'll be back soon," Betty said. "He's just out collecting wood,"

"After Friday's storm, there'll be plenty of that," Pauline said, grinning.

"That's what he said," Betty replied. "And he wants to get as much firewood gathered before everyone else realizes what a goldmine is out there."

Ranter and Jem were clearly itching to move, and Pauline was ready to start out when Betty said, "You look like that advertising cartoon – Michelin Man – today."

Pauline nodded. "The storm and the cold we've had since have made me wary," she said. "I have thick winter stockings and woolen socks under my rubber boots. I've two petticoats under my thickest winter woolen skirt, a leather jacket under my winter coat, a huge scarf wrapped twice around my neck, and two hats on. If another storm rolls in while I'm walking, they'll find me safe and warm under a snowdrift come spring."

"If you aren't back in an hour, I'll set up a search party," Betty said. "There'll be no waiting till spring."

Pauline laughed. "It really isn't that cold today, so I feel like a total fraud in all this," she said. "I won't want tea when I return, I'll be begging for a cold drink."

The dogs had already run on ahead when Pauline entered the long, wooded stretch that bordered the path as it ran behind the cottages. Being winter, there were no leaves on the trees to shut out the light and hide the pale sun and ice-blue sky, which made the narrow tunnel through the trees look surprisingly safe. Wondering where the dogs were, she strode on into the narrow tunnel. After a few minutes, she knew something was wrong. The dogs were never away from her this long.

"Jem, Ranter," she called but there was no answering bark or rustling in the undergrowth to signal their return. She walked on, calling every few paces, until she reached the small clearing where another path joined. She looked about her. So much for Jem the guardian angel, she thought with a grim smile.

"Jem, Ranter, where are you?" she called as a shadow rose and fell. She had no time to avoid the sickening blow that rattled her teeth. Her head snapped forward under the impact, but the riding cap had done its job. She was still conscious and had strength enough to twist her body and lash out at the balaclava-clad face before a second blow struck her head and she lost her balance.

Ramsay hit the figure from behind in a rugby-style tackle that sent the log flying from her attacker's hand. In a moment, Ramsay had the figure handcuffed.

He sat up. "Are you all right, Pauline?" he asked.

"Never better," Pauline said, struggling to rise, "though I think my neck may ache for a day or two."

Ramsay removed the balaclava. "Edward Watson," he said, "I'm arresting you on suspicion of the murders of June Churchill and Dorothy Elliott and the attempted murder of Pauline Riddell. You do not have to..." He continued reciting the well-worn phrases to the end.

"What have you done with Jem and Ranter?" Pauline asked.

"Nothing. I've done nothing to them," Ted gasped. "Why would I hurt them? They never did me harm."

"Then where are they?"

"They're off chasing rabbits," Ted said. "They'll be back soon enough."

"They never chase rabbits," Pauline said.

"In their dreams, all dogs chase rabbits," Ted said.

"Where are they?"

"Over yonder," Ted said, gesturing with his head to a thick evergreen bush.

Pauline ran. Both dogs were lying behind the bush, moving fitfully, no doubt, as Ted had said, chasing rabbits in their minds. She shook them both, until, one-by-one, they struggled to raise their heads. She frowned. They had to walk. They were too big for her to carry and she couldn't leave them here for passing foxes or other dogs to maul.

"Help," she called. "Inspector. You have to help."

Ramsay arrived, dragging the unwilling prisoner with him.

"Can you carry Jem?" Pauline asked. "I'm sure I can carry Ranter."

"Pauline," Ramsay said. "I hate to disappoint you, but I have my hands full here. I'll take my prisoner to the police house and come back. I won't be more than fifteen minutes. Keep the dogs warm and awake. Everything will be fine."

"He's right," Ted said. "It's just a sleeping draught. It will soon wear off."

"I wish I'd landed just one punch on you," Pauline said, fury at his cool unconcern overcoming her usual calm.

"Fifteen minutes, Pauline," Ramsay said, pushing Ted ahead of him back along the trail.

Pauline took off her outer coat and the inner, leather one. She ripped open the stitches she'd sewn on the leather coat only yesterday, letting the coat's hem fall to its natural length and wrapped the two dogs in it. Jem took exception at first but was soon soothed into compliance. After putting her woolen coat back on, Pauline sat on a nearby fallen trunk and talked to the recovering dogs who were inclined to drift back off to sleep if she stopped.

It was twenty minutes before Ramsay and PC Jarvis returned to gather up the evidence, the two dogs, and Pauline, who promptly took exception to Ramsay treating her like an invalid.

"Miss Riddell," he said, sternly, "you have been violently assaulted with blows to the head. I insist you walk slowly and near me until we can have you checked by a doctor."

Pauline grinned sheepishly. "I'm behaving like Jem behaved toward me," she said. "Maybe I am a bit groggy. All right, Inspector, I'll come quietly," she added, joining him at his side where she could stroke Jem's sleepy head.

36

AFTERMATH

ONCE BACK AT POLICE HEADQUARTERS, they were all interviewed, Pauline, Inspector Ramsay and Ted. At times during the grilling by a detective she'd never met and who seemed to regard her as the criminal, Pauline wondered if she would be charged and Ted allowed to walk free.

As the interview wound down, however, Inspector Pringle entered the room and said, "I've had a police doctor called. He'll be here soon."

Pauline replied shortly, "I'm fine. I was shaken up, but my preparations were perfect. I don't need a doctor."

Inspector Pringle, his expression showing clearly what he thought of young women who prepared to be attacked by murderers, said, "Then I hope you can tell me why you fastened on Ted Watson as the murderer and about the attack that was made upon you today."

Pauline explained again how she'd seen yet another possible motive and who had it. How she'd inadvertently sown the seed that incited the attack in the days leading up to the event. How she'd created armor to cover all types of attack, and how she'd set out to allow it to happen.

"But, Miss Riddell," Pringle said, "how did he gain access to these houses so readily? The women can't have given him keys, can they?"

"Ted ran errands and did jobs for everyone," Pauline said, "and I fear old ladies have a soft spot for young boys who offer them help. I don't imagine they gave Ted a key in the normal way of things but I'm sure he would have access to the keys long enough to make copies. I think you'll find he had a copy of Mrs. Churchill's Yale key made at Moffat's garage and Mrs. Elliott's key at June Churchill's workshop. He will have planted that back at her workshop for you to find."

"But we didn't find it when we searched the premises," Pringle said.

"I think Mrs. Churchill found it and recognized it," Pauline said. "It was long gone by the time you got there."

"Then she destroyed evidence," Pringle said grimly, "that she should have brought to us."

"Her nature is such that she couldn't do that," Pauline said. "The world has not treated her kindly, in her mind. I imagine she felt you wouldn't either."

"What nonsense," Pringle said. "We have to be seen to do our jobs efficiently but if she had brought it to us, it would have prejudiced us in her favor if anything. Surely she would see that?"

Pauline, remembering how she'd felt only thirty minutes earlier while being interviewed, decided not to disabuse him of his quaint notions about how people felt when confronted with the police's efficiently incisive questions.

"I don't think she understood that Inspector," she said.

"Would that collar," Pringle pointing at the dog collar Pauline had removed to show him her defense against strangulation, "really have saved you, do you think?"

"Oh, yes," she replied. "Here, feel how stiff it is and by fastening it with the ends butted against each other, like this," she showed him. "There's no way a boy, even a strong boy like Ted, could collapse it."

"And your leather coat, would it stop a knife?"

"That's what most soldiers used in the past, those who couldn't afford armor," Pauline said, "and I'd doubled it to be sure."

"Your helmet looks suspicious," Pringle said. "I'm surprised he didn't spot that."

"It doesn't look good, I agree," Pauline said, "but many clothes woman wear often look odd to men and Ted was only a young man."

Pringle nodded. "It's true," he said. "Mrs. Pringle has two hats I'd happily throw in the sea if I could. They look so strange. Well, I'm not sure you and I should continue further today, Miss Riddell. I need to speak more with our suspect. If you won't let the police doctor see you, I hope you'll go straight from here to a hospital."

"They say hope springs eternal in the human breast, Inspector. I'd like to wait to hear what Ted has told you before I leave. I *hope* you won't say no to that."

Pringle laughed. "Wait with Inspector Ramsay and don't get out of his sight," he said.

"I won't," Pauline agreed, "you have my word. I'll be as good as gold – until I hear what Ted has to say. After that, I can't promise."

She was released from the interview room and joined Inspector Ramsay who was sitting in a small waiting area in front of the desk sergeant's counter.

An hour, and two cups of sweet tea later, Ramsay and Pauline were asked to join Inspector Pringle in his office.

"Does he understand what he's done?" Ramsay asked, the moment they'd taken their seats.

Pringle nodded. "He understands all right," he said. "He doesn't think he did very much wrong."

"How can he think that?" Pauline cried, astounded at such an admission.

"In his mind," Pringle said, "he helped two people who were ready to go and just needed his assistance to do what they couldn't. He didn't hurt them. They both died peacefully and showed no sign of wanting to live, which he feels proved he was right."

"Did he really think he was helping," Ramsay asked, "or did he wish it because it let him do what he wanted to do?"

"He says," Pringle replied, "both had told him more than once they were tired and longed to be re-united with their beloved husbands. He was sure they were signaling to him they wanted him to help them, which he did."

Ramsay frowned. "I don't see killing people as helping," he said.

"He sat with Mrs. Churchill before he gently held a pillow over her face," Pringle said. "He says she didn't struggle at all. With Mrs. Elliott, he made her cocoa and added her sleeping draught, which she drank without a murmur. He helped her drink the second cup with the aspirin and she didn't try to prevent him. That was *his* proof they were both ready to go."

"But Mrs. Elliott was drugged," Pauline said. "How could he imagine she was agreeing to what he was doing?"

"I repeat," Pringle said, "he says she'd told him, more than once, she was ready to go."

"But—" Pauline began, but Ramsay interjected.

"I'm sure he'll be sent to a mental institution for violent offenders," Ramsay said. "He won't hurt anyone else."

"In his mind, he didn't hurt these two victims either," Pauline said sarcastically. 'How does he explain his attack on me? I didn't tell him I wanted to go to heaven right now."

"He is unhappy, and feels bad, about that," Pringle said. "But your investigating was going to spoil everything. There was nothing else he could do."

"How did he think this would be shrugged off as an accident?" Pauline asked.

"It was cleverly done," Pringle said. "He really is a clever young man. It's such a shame he won't get to use it in good ways."

Pauline snorted sarcastically. "Your admiration will mean a lot to him, I'm sure," she said.

Pringle smiled. "Let me give you an example of the thoroughness of his thinking. He hit you with part of a trunk of a dead tree. It was a tree that had two narrow trunks growing from an earlier injury. Sometime recently it died, and the storm brought it down, but it had only fallen against another tree back along the path, leaving it leaning over the path. He snapped off this one trunk and fashioned it into a makeshift club, which he would use to kill you. Then he intended to carry your body to the path below the tree, push the tree on top of you and arrange the pieces of the broken trunk around your head. See? Admirably thought out and I'm sure it would have been equally coolly carried out. He really is a loss to our armed forces."

"It is good planning for a thirteen-year-old," Ramsay said. "I have to agree."

"What about my brilliant planning to foil this lunatic?" Pauline cried indignantly.

"True," Ramsay said, "but you hear too much praise. Any more wouldn't be good for you."

"And," Pringle said, "you're probably knocking years off

Then There Were ... Two Murders?

your own mother's life with your behavior, while young Ted was trying to do right by his mother. I feel we have to consider motives, don't you, Inspector?"

Pauline, realizing she was being teased, glowered at them both. "You're right about one thing," she said. "All this has been about his mother. Trying to get her a better life. With the Churchill house and money, she could have the life she deserved and didn't get. If two people hadn't died..."

"And a third nearly died," Ramsay added.

"Quite so," Pauline said, "If it wasn't for that, it would be truly admirable. Do you think he even knows that killing people is wrong?"

Inspector Pringle shook his head. "No," he said. "He really is that mad. When I put that question to him, do you know what he said?"

Pauline shook her head.

"He said that when it was time for him to leave school, the government would conscript him into the forces and send him abroad to kill people," Pringle said. "He asked me why it was good that he killed people for the government but not for his mother's health." He shook his head in disbelief, and then asked, "Now, are you sure you don't want to see a doctor, Miss Riddell. You may have injuries you're not yet aware of."

Pauline smiled. "I think Dr. Turner would murder me if I turned up in his surgery," she said, "but no, I'm fine. I don't need anything but some time to get over the shock."

"We can get you more tea with sugar if that will help."

Pauline shook her head. "I'm fine, really," she said. "I must be going or Mrs. Bertram, my landlady and stand-in mother, will think I *have* been murdered. She doesn't like me investigating murders any more than my real mother does."

"I'm sure I don't either, Miss Riddell," Pringle said, "but in this case all seems to have turned out well."

"I have to be going too," Ramsay said, preparing to leave. "I've got a pile of paperwork back at the office that I want done before work tomorrow."

"Just one last question, Miss Riddell," Pringle said, as they were heading to the door, "can I assume you now understand your whole reason for doing this was wrong? That the bridge really did break in the floodwaters and the noises were just branches scraping the walls and windows?"

Pauline frowned. She'd hoped neither of the men would be so ungentlemanly as to ask this question.

"The bridge, I do accept, Inspector," she said, at last, "the noises and the items being moved not so much. I think Ted was feeling his way, confirming an old woman couldn't hear or see him in the house in the dark. Maybe, testing his control over Jem. I still think that part of Mrs. Elliott's story was true."

Pringle smiled and shook his head. "Clutching at straws, Miss Riddell," he said. "Clutching at straws." He followed them to the castle-like doors of the police station and warned them to drive carefully for sleet was beginning to spot the ground.

Pauline and Ramsay left the building together, saying nothing until they were outside in the parking area and the two dogs, still groggy but able to walk, had been returned to her.

"Do you think Ted is mad?" Pauline asked, stroking both Jem and Ranter in equal measure.

Ramsay nodded. "I've seen the type before. Psychopaths have no empathy for others; they just do what seems sensible to them, even though it's horrific to the rest of us."

"His point about the government asking him to kill people, though, resonated with me," Pauline said.

"And with me," Ramsay said. "The difference between him and me, and I hope you, is I think both are wrong, personal *and* political murder. Neither sit well with me. Self-defense yes, protecting our interests, no."

Pauline nodded. "I came to that realization the hard way," she said, wiping the tears that were brimming on her eyelids.

"As did I," Ramsay said, quietly.

Pauline looked at him and saw, for the first time, intense pain behind his impassive features. Too much pain to be talked about on this darkening afternoon on a windy corner.

"I hope I see you again before the trial, Inspector," she said.

'We should have tea in your favorite teashop," he said, smiling. "To celebrate your continued existence. I'll pay for their best afternoon tea. What do you say?"

"I'd like that," Pauline said. "Shall we make a date for next Saturday at three?"

"We shall. I look forward to it. Goodnight, Pauline. Drive safely. It's settling in to be a stormy evening."

It was too late to stay long but Pauline had to go to Betty's cottage to return Ranter and reassure her friend she was alive and well. At Pauline's insistence, the police had already been to her house with the news of the attack.

37

EXPLANATIONS GIVEN

RANTER WAS OVERJOYED to be home and fussed at Betty's feet as if he knew that his life had been almost de-railed.

"I'm right glad to see you alive and well, Pauline," Betty said, ushering Pauline inside.

'I can't stay too long," Pauline objected, when Betty wanted to take her hat and coat.

"Well, at least tell me what made you suspect poor Ted," Betty asked.

"Poor Ted, indeed," Pauline said indignantly. "He killed two elderly women."

"Mebbe," Betty said, "but my question remains."

"It was something you said that set me thinking," Pauline said.

"I didn't say a word against the young man," Betty cried.

"No, you didn't. What you said was that he would be rich someday because he had the drive, the ambition, to get there. And you listed the jobs he did just to get ahead."

"And you thought that made him a madman?"

"No," Pauline said. "I thought it was admirable, but then later it made me wonder if someone who had a grudge against someone might see the opportunity to kill two old birds with one stone, if you'll pardon the expression."

Betty shivered. "I'm glad I wasn't on the list," she said.

"Only those who stood between him and old Mrs. Churchill's house and money were on the list."

"I don't see how poor Mrs. Elliott was in the way," Betty said.

"She told people, in strictest confidence of course, but you know what villagers are like, that she thought Mrs. Churchill's death was suspicious. Ted couldn't let her go on repeating that," Pauline said. "It would have made people question the death of Mrs. *Frank* Churchill."

"But she isn't dead," Betty said, puzzled.

"She soon would have been once the excitement of Mrs. Elliott's suicide was over," Pauline said, "and Frank Churchill would have been hanged for his wife's death."

"Why would he be suspected?" Betty asked.

"Because everyone knows he and his wife aren't getting along," Pauline said, "and you can be sure there would be evidence too."

Betty nodded. "It's true they aren't getting on," she said thoughtfully. "And they've only just married."

"How do you know they aren't getting along?" Pauline asked.

"Well, I heard... oh," she said.

Pauline nodded. "You know because Ted told you. He said he'd heard it, but can you be sure?"

"I heard Mrs. Cooper talking about it too."

"And Ted ran errands for her," Pauline said. "He was already building the evidence against Frank Churchill, ready for when the time came to strike."

"I can't believe it," Betty said, shaking her head. "People don't plan the deaths of four people just to get their hands on a house and some savings. Anyway, I remember Mrs. Elliott sharing her concerns about Mrs. Churchill's death and it was months ago. He can't have been planning her death since then, surely. Why not just let it slip out of people's minds?"

"You're probably right about Mrs. Elliott," Pauline said. "Once the inquest had pronounced a natural death, she'd let her idea go. I suspect what happened is someone remembered her saying it and repeated it in Ted's presence. Maybe at the time the person learned Mrs. Elliott had written to me voicing her concerns."

"But killing her then would have suggested she was right, surely?"

"If she'd been murdered, yes. If she committed suicide, it would just be grief over the death of her friend or simple despair at life. I'm not sure a boy of Ted's age would understand that adults can manage grief and despair without feelings of suicide."

Betty laughed. "That's true," she said. "I remember when I was that age I often thought to myself, 'they'll be sorry when I'm gone and they see what they made me do.' They being my parents, of course."

"It's a difficult age," Pauline agreed. "Suicide seems the sensible reaction to even the smallest setback."

"But none of us ever seriously did anything," Betty protested.

"*We* didn't but many do, every year," Pauline said, "and I suspect Ted thought that would be understood to be a sensible course of action for Mrs. Elliott. After all, what had she to live for? In his mind, her age, her widowhood, her difficult relations with her son-in-law must all have seemed the perfect cover for him."

"He missed the things that made it convincing, though," Betty said. "Like a note."

"There was no way for him to forge a note," Pauline agreed. "Not leaving a badly forged note was, I think, sensible on his part. He might have looked through her correspondence for something he could make into a note but in the end decided against."

"Yes, I see," Betty said. "I suppose this means we won't be seeing you and Jem again?"

"Spring is almost upon us," Pauline said. "We should give Ranter and Jem the chance to catch us both a rabbit for a pie, don't you think?"

"I do," Betty said. "Though I think meat rationing might have ended before they catch anything edible, even if the rabbits do have mixama-whatever-you-said, and I don't think meat rationing is ever going to end."

Pauline smiled and rose from her chair. "Till next Sunday, then," she said, pulling on her gloves before tying her headscarf under her chin.

"You'll be lost without a mystery to solve," Betty said. "This is two in a year."

"Oh, once Poppy has written this up in the local newspaper, and it gets picked up and maybe goes nationwide, there will be others looking for my help, you'll see," Pauline said, laughing.

"I hope it doesn't go nationwide," Betty said, alarmed. "We don't want reporters from London tramping all over our village."

"Poppy will be heartbroken if it doesn't," Pauline said. "She's always hoping her next story is the story to launch her to reporting fame."

"Then I'm sorry for her," Betty said. "I know little of these things, of course, but fame isn't a good thing. Whenever I hear someone famous talking on the radio, I hear the desperation in their voices. I always feel sorry for them."

"I don't imagine famous people share your opinion," Pauline said, smiling. "They wouldn't understand your sorrow."

"People rarely know what's good for them until it's too late," Betty said.

Pauline opened the car door and let Jem jump in. She waved as she settled herself in the driving seat and started the engine. Were Betty's words meant for her? Was she warning her not to let this life of excitement detour her from a more fulfilling life? Pauline waved again as she pulled away. Betty and Ranter waved back, Betty with her hand, Ranter with his ever-wagging tail.

It was too soon for such important thoughts, Pauline decided as she turned onto the main road and her homeward journey. In her life right now, she wanted excitement. Like Ted, she wanted to be part of something bigger than life had mapped out for her. Now she had the chance; she had to take it.

Driving through Morpeth on her way home, she chose not to stop at Poppy's flat. She hadn't quite forgiven Poppy for abandoning her when she needed help, for losing faith in her when the tide of events was running against her. Poppy could come to her for a story, and she'd make her work to get it.

She turned to Jem. "Poppy shall drink sherry, or I take my story elsewhere," she said, grinning. "That'll teach her."

Jem grinned too. He really was an intelligent dog, though a little too inclined to take treats from untrustworthy people.

38

POPPY MAKES AMENDS

Next morning at work, Pauline was sitting at her desk when her phone rang. It was Poppy.

"You can't call me here," Pauline said, before Poppy could speak.

"Then you phone me at lunch time," Poppy said. "I'll be waiting by the phone."

"I'm not sure I should," Pauline said. "When I was solving the case, you were nowhere to be found."

"I know, I'm sorry," Poppy said. "I'll eat as much humble pie as you want me to, but I must have the story."

"We'll meet tonight at the Black Bull and you will buy us both a large glass of sherry – and you'll drink it," Pauline said.

Poppy laughed. "That's asking a lot... all right, all right," she said quickly, hearing Pauline whisper 'Bye.'

"A large glass and all of it drunk," Pauline said, "before I say one word about the case and its ending."

"You are a monster, Pauline," Poppy said, "but it's a deal. One glass of sherry for your story."

"One *large* glass," Pauline reiterated.

"Seven o'clock, Black Bull, one large glass of nasty foreign grape juice," Poppy said. "Don't be late. I can make the morning edition if I have it in by nine o'clock."

Their meeting began slowly. Pauline was still unwilling to let her friend off the hook too easily and Poppy was, as always, too pushy.

"Why did you think it was two murders, though?" Poppy asked. "They never have one there, let alone two."

"I remember you telling me that," Pauline said. "You said it hadn't happened in centuries as though that was a guarantee it couldn't happen, but probabilities aren't like that. Once in a million years doesn't mean it will happen in a million years' time or even that it can't happen today and again tomorrow. It just means the chances are small."

"But still, you admit the bridge was nature doing what nature does and you only think the noises were Ted practicing for his final stroke," Poppy said. "Your senses weren't really solid there so, I ask again, why?"

"I don't know," Pauline said flatly. "All I can say is I felt it. Like my great-uncle Thomas feels a change in the weather."

Poppy snorted. "Every old codger in the country claims to feel a change in the weather," she said.

"And they're usually right," Pauline said. "Our senses are a lot better than we give them credit for and we should listen to them when they alert us."

"If we did that, we'd be in a constant state of alarm," Poppy said. "Practically everyone has some hobby horse they believe to be right. I can't write *Pauline's knee tells her when a murder has been committed*. I'd never get it published."

"I didn't say my knee told me," Pauline said, smiling at the absurdity of her friend's suggestion. "I just said I feel it. My senses tell me something is wrong; they warn me. I think I spot little things, inconsequential things, things I don't even realize I've seen or heard at first, and then my mind tells me. That's the best I can do to explain."

"Well, it's better that great-uncle Thomas's bones," Poppy said, finishing the last mouthful of sherry with a grimace. "There," she added, "I've done it. Now, tell me everything."

From then on, the meeting was a success. At its end, they were on friendly terms again. Poppy even agreed sherry wasn't so very bad if drunk with a Newcastle Brown Ale chaser. By eight o'clock, she'd left Pauline and run to the Herald's offices where the story was set on the front page of the next day's edition.

* * *

Pauline received calls from the Newcastle papers all that Tuesday and Wednesday, but she refused to speak to them. Poppy deserved a head start, at least.

On Friday, Poppy phoned Pauline again at work.

"You have to stop doing this," Pauline said, growing concerned she really would get into trouble for misusing company phones.

"Meet me tonight," Poppy said, excitedly. "I've things to show you." She hung up immediately, leaving Pauline shaking her head at such un-ladylike exuberance.

That evening, after work, Pauline rang the bell to Poppy's flat and Poppy came out carrying a heavy satchel, which she slung on her back as they walked to the pub.

"What is it?" Pauline asked.

"You'll see," Poppy said. She positively buzzed with joy. Pauline had never seen her so happy.

They entered the Snug, sat in a quiet area in the corner where Poppy unbuckled the satchel and dropped a pile of newspapers on the small table. They landed with a thud that echoed around the room.

"What's this?" Pauline asked, picking up a Manchester Guardian and reading the headline.

"It's our ticket to fame and fortune, Pauline," Poppy said.

"The headline is about a possible rail worker's strike," Pauline said, glancing at the front page.

"We aren't on the front page. Yet." Poppy agreed. "But look." She took the paper from Pauline and opened it to a headline that read:

Super-sleuth does it again, by our northern correspondent, Poppy Kennedy.

"I didn't know you were their northern correspondent," Pauline said, puzzled.

"Nor did they till this story broke," Poppy said, grinning. "Now I'm a northern correspondent for four of the country's biggest dailies."

"You can't be a northern correspondent and also be down south in Fleet Street, London," Pauline said.

"One or two more good stories and they'll pay my fare to the Big Smoke – and not as their northern correspondent, you'll see," Poppy replied. "I'll invite you to the nicer parties," she added.

"I don't believe they have nice parties in London," Pauline said.

"That's Inspector Ramsay speaking," Poppy said. "You're too young to be such a cynic. Where is he, by the way? I thought you would have invited him."

"I did," Pauline said. "He's probably just been held back in the office. He'll arrive soon. Now show me all our mentions. I won't be satisfied until I've read every one of your entirely truthful words of praise for me."

"I may have made a mistake bringing these here," Poppy

said. "You'll grow too conceited and stop hobnobbing with lowly people like me."

Pauline became alarmed. "Poppy, you haven't been silly about this, have you?"

Poppy sighed. "Pauline," she said, "you have to promote yourself in this world if you're ever going to reach the top. You can't be the wallflower all your life."

With a sinking feeling growing in the pit of her stomach, Pauline sipped her sherry and began to read. It was worse than she thought. Nothing Poppy wrote was untrue, but it was much too sensational to be describing Pauline Riddell, secretary and country girl. The only thing that kept her from boxing Poppy's ears was the knowledge no one she knew read the London or Manchester papers.

"What do you think?" Poppy said, before taking a great draught of her beer, and then adding, "I've put you on the map, don't you think? Scotland Yard will be consulting you from now on."

Pauline didn't know what to say. She didn't want to hurt Poppy's feelings, but this was too much, too soon. If Scotland Yard did consult, she'd fall flat on her face and be laughed out of town.

"It's wonderful, Poppy," she said, at last. "I just don't think I deserve it and it makes me uncomfortable."

Poppy shook her head. "When will you deserve it, Pauline? Fifty years after you're dead?"

"I just mean what has happened could just be luck."

"Here he is," Poppy said, seeing Ramsay making his way into the Snug. "You're late, Inspector. We're a drink ahead of you. You'll have to buy us a second when you buy yours."

Ramsay smiled. "What are you having?" he asked.

He returned a few minutes later with the drinks on a tray.

"It's ungentlemanly to keep a lady waiting," Poppy said. "Keeping two waiting is unforgivable."

"Unfortunately, something came up at work and I had to stay and set the team in motion," he said. "Cheers!" He lifted his glass and they responded.

"Anything in my line, Inspector?" Poppy asked eagerly.

Ramsay shook his head. "Not yet," he said, "but there maybe something for Miss Riddell to ponder."

CLICK HERE to learn what it is Inspector Ramsay is talking about.

***

THANK you for reading my book. If you love this book, please, please, please don't forget to leave a review! Every review matters and it matters a lot!

Head over to Amazon (or wherever you purchased this book) to leave a review for me. Here's the link on Amazon:

Then There Were ... Two Murders?

I THANK you now and forever :-)

SNEAK PEEK BONUS CONTENT

Miss Riddell and the Pet Thefts
by
P.C. James

Chapter 1: North Riding of Yorkshire, Summer, 1958

Pauline loved the farmhouse garden, which her parents tended to so earnestly to provide fruit and vegetables for their family. Sitting in the sunshine, with the scent of herbs and the song of birds for company was the perfect antidote to her days spent in smoke-filled offices. She didn't mind the smell of tobacco, she just wished they'd go outside to smoke. Every evening when she got home, she had to hang her clothes to air and wash her hair to get rid of the smell.

"Pauline," Mrs. Riddell said, arriving with a basket to pick raspberries, and interrupting Pauline's reverie. "Will you speak to Jane? Your father and I have tried but she just won't listen."

Jane was the youngest of the Riddell children and Pauline's sister. Though there were only eight years between them, somehow it felt like they were from two different times. Jane's life revolved around popular songs, films, and the latest fashions in hair and clothes. Pauline couldn't share her interest in any of them.

"Jane and I never have a word to say to each other, Mum," Pauline said. "She won't listen to me. I'm too old, in her eyes."

"She might this time," Mrs. Riddell said. "She's got her 'A' levels and can go to university. You're doing well in your career, maybe she will respond to that and take your advice."

Her parents wanted Jane to follow an academic path to success. Mrs. Riddell, in particular, but even Pauline's father was anxious for his daughters to do well and not just become a farmer's wife. The world was opening up and the Riddells were clever; they could do things beyond the circles of work in the Dales.

"I'll try, Mum," Pauline said, "but she's headstrong and stubborn and pushing her may well send her in the opposite direction from the one we want." Pauline was nervous about this request. She knew better than her mother, the friction between herself and Jane. Pauline had 'an old head on her shoulders' people would say even when she was a child. Jane seemed like she'd never grow up.

"Just make it a conversation," her mother advised. "You must have to deal with awkward so-and-sos where you work."

Pauline laughed. "They're easier to persuade than our Jane has ever been."

Over the weekend, Pauline discovered Jane had applied to universities, as her parents wanted, but was working in a 'pet shop and grooming' business to earn some money. The shop belonged to Jane's best friend's parents and Jane loved it there. It was all she would talk about, becoming a pet groomer.

"Why not do veterinary studies at university?" Pauline asked, hoping to steer the conversation to where she knew her mother wanted.

"Vets stick their fingers and arms up animals' bums," Jane laughed. "How is that anything like clipping their coats?"

"It isn't, of course," Pauline said, "but you would be working with animals and using your brain as well. You'll soon tire of clipping coats and claws; you know you will."

"Last week," Jane said, "we went to Skelsdale Hall and clipped Lady Cecilia's Russian Samoyed. We made more money that afternoon than Dad makes in a week."

"But rich people's dogs aren't groomed every week," Pauline protested, "and there are lots of other people who groom them. Dog groomers aren't among the country's wealthiest citizens, Jane."

"I bet they are in London," Jane replied. "That place is crawling with rich people and their dogs. I bet down there pet groomers are richer than vets."

Pauline realized the conversation was developing that nervous edge all her conversations with Jane had. "Well, think about it. You know how disappointed Mum and Dad will be if you don't go to university."

"More years of sitting behind a desk might suit you, Pauline," Jane mocked her, "but I want to live now. Everywhere except here, people are partying. We're still up to our bums in mud and I want no part of it." She was almost yelling now.

Pauline, already in her thirties and long out of college, felt ancient in the face of such passion. Passion she'd never felt.

Even as a young woman, the dances and parties Pauline had attended weren't the kind Jane longed for. Her engagement to Stephen, cut short when he was killed in Korea, had been wonderfully peaceful. A feeling they were meant for each other without the wild histrionics novels or movies portrayed.

"There'll be parties at university, Jane, you'll see. Mum and dad only want what's best for you."

"It's my life, not theirs – or yours," Jane said, gesturing to Pauline to go before flouncing off into the yard to fuss over the dogs.

Pauline watched her go with regret. Jane was clever and attractive, her honey-blonde hair was always styled after whatever film star was in fashion. This week it was Leslie Caron in Gigi, her clothes too were the very latest thing, though where she got the money for them Pauline didn't want to guess. For dances in the village hall, Jane usually wore dresses, home-made like everyone else's in their village, but today she was in her favored denim jeans. Her clear skin, with just a sprinkling of freckles across her nose, and ice blue eyes were true Yorkshire; a legacy from all those Vikings of centuries gone by.

Sadly, the teenage rebellion that Pauline was reading so much about in the news was raging in Jane and her choices in almost everything were growing more expensive, which was difficult for her parents to afford from a small family farm income. Half the arguments she had with her parents came down to her friends having more than she had. Deflated, Pauline made her way back to the house knowing she'd once again widened the yawning gap between herself and her youngest sister. It had been so easy when Jane was a toddler, she'd followed her older sisters everywhere wanting to be part of everything they did. Now, Jane had no time for any of them nor her parents. Jane would soon storm out of the home Pauline was sure of it; she hoped today's 'conversation' wasn't what pushed her over the edge. As she'd warned her mother, her meetings with Jane had always been a series of sharp stabbing sentences that didn't flow or fit together to make a conversation.

If this excerpt has piqued your interest, you can pre-order the book here: Miss Riddell and the Pet Thefts.

BOOKS BY P.C. JAMES

On Amazon, my books can be found at the
Miss Riddell Cozy Mysteries series page.

And for someone who likes listening to books, *In the Beginning, There Was a Murder* is now available as an audiobook on Amazon and here on Audible and many others, including:

Kobo
Chirp
Audiobooks
Scribd
Bingebooks
Apple
StoryTel

You can find more books here:

P.C. James Author Page: https://www.amazon.com/P.-C.-James/e/B08VTN7Z8Y

P.C. James & Kathryn Mykel: Duchess Series

Paul James Author Page: https://www.amazon.com/-/e/B01DFGG2U2

GoodReads: https://www.amazon.com/P.-C.-James/e/B08VTN7Z8Y

And for something completely different, my books by Paul James at: https://www.amazon.com/-/e/B01DFGG2U2

Copyright © 2021 by P.C. James All rights reserved.

No part of this book may be reproduced in any form or by any electronic or mechanical means, including information storage and retrieval systems, without written permission from the author, except for the use of brief quotations in a book review.

Then There Were...Two Murders?© Copyright <> Paul James writing as PC James Copyright notice: All rights reserved under the International and Pan-American Copyright Conventions. No part of this book may be reproduced or transmitted in any form or by any means, electronic or mechanical, including photocopying and recording, or by any information storage and retrieval system, without permission in writing from publisher. This is a work of fiction. Names, places, characters, and incidents are either the product of the author's imagination or are used fictitiously, and any resemblance to any actual persons, living or dead, organizations, events, or locales is entirely coincidental. Warning: the unauthorized reproduction or distribution of this copyrighted work is illegal. Criminal copyright infringement, including infringement without monetary gain, is investigated by the FBI and is punishable by up to 5 years in prison and a fine of $250,000.

For more information: email: pcjames@pcjamesauthor.com

Facebook: https://www.facebook.com/pauljamesauthor

Facebook: https://www.facebook.com/PCJamesAuthor

DEDICATION

For my family. The inspiration they provide and the time they allow me for imagining and typing makes everything possible.

ACKNOWLEDGMENTS

I'd also like to thank my editors, illustrator and the many others who have helped with this book. You know who you are.

ABOUT THE AUTHOR

I've always loved mysteries, especially those involving Agatha Christie's Miss Marple. Perhaps because Miss Marple reminds me of my aunts when I was growing up. But Agatha never told us much about Miss Marple's earlier life. While writing my own elderly super-sleuth series, I'm tracing her career from the start. As you'll see, if you follow the Miss Riddell Cozy Mysteries series.

However, this is my Bio, not Miss Riddell's, so here goes with all you need to know about me: After retiring, I became a writer and when I'm not feverishly typing on my laptop, you'll find me running, cycling, walking, and taking wildlife photos wherever and whenever I can.

My cozy mystery series begins in northern England because that was my home growing up and that's also the home of so many great cozy mysteries. Stay with me though because Miss Riddell loves to travel as much as I do and the stories will take us to the many different places around the world I've lived in or visited.